BLACK EAGLE
FORCE
Eye of the Storm
(REVISED)

THE AUTHORS

Ken Farmer – After proudly serving his country as a US Marine, Ken attended Stephen F. Austin State University on a full football scholarship, receiving his Bachelors Degree in Business and Speech & Drama. Ken quickly discovered his love for acting when he starred as a cowboy in a Dairy Queen commercial when he was raising registered Beefmaster cattle and Quarter Horses at his ranch in East Texas. Ken has over 41 years as a professional actor, with memorable roles *Silverado, Friday Night Lights, The Newton Boys* and *Uncommon Valor*. He was the spokesman for Wolf Brand Chili for eight years. Ken was a professional and celebrity Team Penner for over twenty years—twice penning at the National Finals—and participated in the Ben Johnson Pro-Celebrity Rodeos until Ben's death in '96. Ken now lives near Gainesville, TX, where he continues to write novels.

Ken wrote a screenplay back in the '80s, *The Tumbleweed Wagon*. He and his writing partner, Buck Stienke adapted it to a historical fiction western, *THE NATIONS*—a Finalist for the Elmer Kelton Award. They released the sequel, *HAUNTED FALLS*—winner of the Laramie Award for Best Action Western, 2013—in June of 2013. *HELL HOLE* was the third in the Bass Reeves saga written by Ken alone.

Buck and Ken have completed twelve novels to date together including the westerns.

 **Buck Stienke** – Captain – Fighter Pilot - United States Air Force, has an extensive background in military aviation and weaponry. A graduate of the Air Force Academy, Buck (call sign 'Shoehorn') was a member of the undefeated Rugby team and was on the Dean's List. After leaving the Air Force, Buck was a pilot for Delta Airlines for over twenty-five years. He has vast knowledge of weapons, tactics and survival techniques. Buck is the owner of Lone Star Shooting Supply, Gainesville, TX. As a successful actor, writer and businessman, Buck lives in Gainesville with his wife, Carolyn. Buck was Executive Producer for the award winning film, *Rockabilly Baby*.

Cover by:
Ken Farmer

BLACK EAGLE FORCE
EYE of the
STORM
(REVISED)

SEMPER PARO BELLUM

BY

BUCK STIENKE & KEN FARMER

M600 BLACK EAGLE

ISBN: (13) 978-0-615-42889-5
ISBN: (10) 0615428894

Printed in the United States of America
Published by:
Timber Creek Press
312 N. Commerce St.
Gainesville, Texas 76240

WINNER - BEST ADULT FICTION -
North Texas Book Festival - 2012

EXCERPT FROM THE MILITARY OATH

---I will support and defend the Constitution of the United States against all enemies, foreign and domestic---

An oath is forever!

Buck Stienke & Ken Farmer

DEDICATION

BLACK EAGLE FORCE is dedicated to all United States military service personnel, past and present, who have gone in harm's way to protect and preserve this country. Many are now our Wounded Warriors and many gave the ultimate sacrifice.
May God bless and keep them.
Semper Fi.

ACKNOWLEDGMENT

The authors gratefully acknowledge the help from Pierre O'Rourke, Stephanie Dunnam, John Eastman Major USMC (ret.) and Robert Ahola in proofing and suggestions. A special salute to Colonel John G. "Bug" Worman USMC for suggestions, advice and correcting our occasional technical military errors and keeping us on the straight and narrow.

Semper Fi, Bug.

BEF ENDORSEMENTS

Grab the take-up straps on your five point hook up and hold on because you're in for an exciting ride. Black Eagle Force is an invisiable group of incredible warriors all with a unique skill set that when called upon to stop or bring down major threats around the world they are ready at a moments notice. The last thing you will never hear is Black Eagle if they lock on to you and get tone. You will not be able to stop reading once you start. Rivoting.
Marshall Teague
Actor/ US Navy retired - Star of *Last Ounce of Courage*
****

The techno-thriller genre is littered with all manner of wannabes who think data is story. Buck Stienke and Ken Farmer are two writers who understand the distinction. What they've written here in BLACK EAGLE FORCE is one helluva great tale. When I cracked open this book I found myself grabbed by the collar and thrust into a gut-wrenching tale full of surprises and action. All the characters were well rounded, the dialogue reflected their experience in the movie and television industry so that everything flowed the way it should. Given my background as a writer and and editor, I did see a few things that I thought were weak. That said, those points did not detract from my enjoyment of their story. Stienke and Farmer wrote a wonderful and entertaining tale--and anyone looking to have a good read with a book will be well served to buy this book. It's a keeper.

Dwight Jon Zimmerman - Co-author of *Lincoln's Last Days*
****

Buck Stienke and Ken Farmer take an intriguing premise and run hard with it in their new novel, Eye of the Storm. From the rattle of 50s to the smooth whine of the engines on their near-future aircraft, the book sings with authenticity and action. Readers will lose sleep with this one - I know I did. - Jim DeFelice - Co-author of the Dreamland series, *Omar Bradley: General at War* and *American Sniper*
****

Black Eagle Force is a contemporary action packed thriller with its roots firmly planted in Texas history and folklore. There are a lot of good guys, bad guys and dead guys. If you like fast paced military action this is the series for you.

Phil Ward - Author of the *Rading Forces* series.
****

This well written and exciting adventure story is **reminiscent of the Tom Clancy novels at their best,** but this book has more action. The authors describe the battles and other exploits of a unique battle force in fascinating detail that draw readers into the clashes. Readers will react as they read and as they finish this action-packed drama: "Wow! When will the next book come out?" Dr. Israel Drazin - Amazon Top 1000 Reviewer
****

I liked *Black Eagle Force* very, very much, and I'm not an easy sell. I found it a quick, page-turning read. I recommend it to anyone who likes story, adventure, hard-hitting and constant action and many distinct, likable and appealing characters. Your devotion to detail, clarity and authenticity was admirable; as was the subject matter's relevance and topicality. - Cliff Osmond (actor/writer/director, wrote and directed *THE PENITENT* starring Raul Julia and Amand Asante)

****

Absolutely loved *Black Eagle Force*....HONESTLY...I could not put it down. Great fast-paced read. Love the beginning with its historical setting. Not just a book for guys or military junkies! And the end was a surprise! Can't wait for sequel....and movie!!! - Jocelyn K. White, "Designing DFW" TV Show Host

****

OTHER NOVELS FROM
TIMBER CREEK PRESS
www.timbercreekpress.net

MILITARY ACTION/TECHNO

BLACK EAGLE FORCE: Sacred Mountain (Book #2)
by Buck Stienke and Ken Farmer
www.tinyurl.com/SacMtn2

RETURN of the STARFIGHTER (Book #3)
by Buck Stienke and Ken Farmer
www.tinyurl.com/StarF01

BLACK EAGLE FORCE: BLOOD IVORY (Book #4)
by Buck Stienke and Ken Farmer with Doran Ingrham
www.tinyurl.com/befivory

BLACK EAGLE FORCE: FOURTH REICH (Book #5)
By Buck Stienke and Ken Farmer
www.tinyurl.com/befreich

BLOOD BROTHERS - Doran Ingrham, Buck Stienke and Ken Farmer
Www.tinyurl.com/bloodbrothers1

DARK SECRET - Doran Ingrham
Http://tinyurl.com/darksecret-2

BLACK STAR BAY by T.C. Miller
Http://amzn.to/1oYSFO6

HISTORICAL FICTION WESTERN
THE NATIONS by Ken Farmer and Buck Stienke
Www.tinyurl.com/the-nations-Bass
Audio version: www.tinyurl.com/NationsAudio
HAUNTED FALLS by Ken Farmer and Buck Stienke
Www.tinyurl.com/haunted-falls-Bass
Audio version: www.tinyurl.com/HauntedFallsAudio
HELL HOLE by Ken Farmer
Www.tinyurl.com/hell-hole-Bass3

Audio version: www.tinyurl.com/HellHoleAudio
ACROSS the RED by Ken Farmer & Buck Stienke
Www.tinyurl.com/AcrossRed

Audio version: www.tinyurl.com/AcrossRedAudio
DEVIL'S CANYON by Buck Stienke
Http://tinyurl.com/devils-canyon-B
SYFY
LEGEND OF AURORA by Ken Farmer & Buck
Stienke
www.tinyurl.com/LegendAurora-E
AURORA: INVASION by Ken Farmer & Buck Stienke
www.tinyurl.com/AuroraInvasion
Coming Soon
MILITARY ACTION/TECHNO
BLACK STAR BAY by T.C. Miller
HISTORICAL FICTION WESTERN
BASS and the LADY by Ken Farmer & Buck Stienke
Book five of the Bass Reeves Saga

TIMBER CREEK PRESS

BLACK EAGLE FORCE

Prologue

February 11, 1836

SANTA ANNA'S ENCAMPMENT

A stinging rain blew through the camp as unseasonably cold weather continued to plague the expedition. Rivulets of water ran off the white canvas command tent and pooled around the muddy black boots of the guards. A brief flash of lightning reflected off the yellow oilskin ponchos that covered the guards from neck to knees. A dozen brass torchieres on finely-turned white oak staffs lit up the gray sky as dawn approached.

Inside the command tent, General Antonio Lopez De Santa Anna Perez De Lebron sat up on the side of his bed. He glanced beside him as Emily West de Zavala—know as the *Yellow Rose*—stirred from her slumber. The raven-haired mulatto beauty with striking aquamarine eyes lay naked beneath the light blue silk sheets. *Being President of Mexico has its perks,* Santa Anna mused as he playfully swatted her shapely hips. "Time to get up, my sweet," he softly spoke into her ear.

Emily smiled as she reached for her nightshirt lying on the woven silk rug. It was an army tent, but it was furnished more richly than even the better Mexican homes. The gilded Louis XIV style chairs had been copied from expensive European ones imported for the Palace in Mexico City.

She slipped on the nightshirt, donned her silken slippers, and then wrapped herself in a warm forest green woolen robe before she blew a kiss to her General and departed. The general's young valet seated in the next chamber quickly glanced at the gorgeous mistress as she walked toward her nearby tent.

Emilio put together the garish uniform preferred by the General and walked to the flap in the tent separating him from the sleeping quarters. "Your Excellency, your uniform awaits, as requested."

"Enter," came the reply.

Emilio nodded his head toward the barber and manicurist. The three entered the room as Santa Anna took his usual seat facing a tall pier mirror against the wall of the command tent.

He watched as the barber skillfully shaved him with a straight razor. The general cast a dispassionate look down at the manicurist as she trimmed, cleaned and polished his nails. His gaze returned to the mirror as he searched for signs of gray in his hair. None were visible and a slight smile came across his thin lips.

His forty-second birthday was two weeks away. He had hoped to defeat the ragtag band of Texians at their pitiful fort located in the Alamo Mission near San Antonio de Béxar as a birthday present to himself. The rain and cold weather was now putting that plan in jeopardy. He knew they were only a half-day ride to the Río Bravo del Norte and would be in hostile territory once they crossed.

As the barber finished, he wiped the general's face with a warm towel, bowed and left. Moments later, the manicurist finished her morning task. Emilio held the freshly cleaned shirt for Santa Anna; slipped it over his head and fastened the small metal hooks for the upraised collar. Following the shirt was the heavy crimson tunic with gold epaulets. A matching fabric sash completed the uniform as befitting the self-styled *Napoleon of the West*. The general took one last look in the mirror, turned and exited the tent. Emilio silently followed behind carrying Santa Anna's sword and hat.

EAGLE NEST RANCH

Some twenty miles to the north in what is present-day Webb County, Texas, a wiry young cowboy was awakened by the incessant repertoire of a mockingbird. Dawn was creeping through the leaden skies to the south and east, but patches of blue could be seen overhead as the last of the stars winked out in silent recognition of the sun's imminent arrival. To the west, the gray skies were clearing as the last major cold front of the winter pushed through to the Gulf of Mexico.

Twenty-five years earlier, Dieter Hermann purchased a three thousand acre parcel from Don Julio de la Garza's Spanish land grant for two hundred dollars in gold. Dieter, a successful mill owner, moved his wife, Hilda, two daughters, Ingrid and Mary Catherine and a son, Friedrich, from Pennsylvania to the property located along the north bank of the Rio Bravo. Hilda, bore Dieter another son shortly after arriving at their new home—they named him Jonathan.

Hilda was the first of the family to spot the bald eagle nests in the towering cypress trees just south of the chosen home site. Dieter enthusiastically agreed to her suggestion that they call their new ranch *Eagle Nest*.

Dieter and Friedrich built a two story German-style house of native stone near Bacerro Creek. Close to the house, they constructed a stone barn, smoke house and adjoining corrals. On the creek itself, they erected a grist mill similar to the one they had back in Pennsylvania.

The previous week, Jonathan's brother Friedrich had left the Hermann Ranch for the springtime supply run to the small village of Edinburgh. The round trip took six days, but was a necessary journey for those supplies the growing family could not raise or make themselves.

Eight miles from the house, Jonathan Hermann shivered as he tossed the thin wool blanket off, sat up under the lean-to, slipped on his boots and pulled his broad-brimmed hat over his long blond hair. Slowly he buttoned up his handmade sheepskin coat and reached for his batwing chaps. The canvas had kept the wind and most of the rain off, but the small fire had all but died as he slept.

A yawn overtook Jonathan as he moved the flat rocks he had placed to cover the coals. He knelt down, poked the remaining embers together and added some dry grass, a few oak sticks and some mesquite bark he had placed under the lean-to to keep dry. The grass began to smoke and then burst into a tiny flame that quickly ignited the rest of the tender.

His red and white painted cow pony looked on with interest as he stood and stepped away from the lean-to. The hungry filly knew that Jonathan would soon fill the homespun cloth feed bag with precious grain and slip it over her ears. The winter had been a long one and the lush spring grasses were late in coming.

He walked a few feet from the campsite and removed his heavy fur-lined gloves so he could find the buttons to his fly. A few seconds later, he felt the relief of the first morning pee as he watered a clump of prickly pear. "Susie," he said when he was finished, "let us get some victuals."

Jonathan walked back to the lean-to, grabbed his poke sack, removed a battered skillet, coffee pot, a slab of bacon and a seal-tight of beans. He poured some water into the pot from his canteen, threw a handful of ground-up, roasted mesquite beans and post oak acorns in lieu of coffee and set it on one of the flat rocks next to the growing fire.

The Deiter family had run out of real coffee several weeks before. Roasting and grinding mesquite beans and acorns made a passable substitute. Jonathan cut a few thick slices of bacon, laid them in the skillet and balanced it on three rocks set around the small fire. He opened the can of beans with his knife and dumped them on top of the sizzling bacon.

The young cowboy went back to a separate sack and removed the feed bag—threw a few handfuls of dried mesquite beans and wild oats in and slipped it over the pony's ears. "Here you go girl…eat up. We got a long day ahead of us."

Walking back to the lean-to, Jonathan retrieved the oilskin poncho he had slept on and laid it closer to the campfire. He picked up the skillet with his glove, scraped the beans and bacon into a tin plate—grabbed the coffee pot and poured some of the strong dark aromatic brew into a tin cup.

He sat down cross-legged on the poncho and began to eat with his hunting knife. Looking up to the east, he saw the morning sun breaking through the receding gray clouds. "Yessir, gonna be a good day." His thoughts turned to the longhorn cattle that were just beginning to drop their spring calves. "Wonder how many new ones we will find today?…No, that is all right, girl, do not talk with your mouth full."

SANTA ANNA'S CAMP

The general's staff rose when Santa Anna entered. As he motioned them to be seated, his aide-de-camp, Lieutenant Goez, pulled the chair out and slipped it back beneath him as he sat.

A procession of waiters carried trays of scrambled eggs, chorizo sausages and corn tortillas to serve the finest of Santa Anna's invasion force. As the waiters left, the Catholic priest appointed to accompany the command group gave a blessing for the food and thanked God for the men assembled to do his will.

Padre Hernandez also prayed for the souls lost in the journey to date and asked for the safety and success of the mission.

Santa Anna claimed to be a devout Catholic, but only obeyed the teachings of the church when it was politically expeditious to do so. He crossed himself as did all the other officers as Hernandez finished his prayers and left the tent. No one dared make a move until Santa Anna took his first bite. The President General had absolute power of life and death over everyone in Mexico and the men knew it.

As they ate with gusto, Santa Anna cast an eye toward Colonel Gutierrez, head of artillery. His aide had mentioned the problems the lack of an adequate number of mules and burros was causing in the rear of the supply train. The heavy caissons were constantly being stuck in the muddy conditions the army had encountered.

"How are your artillery companies doing in this weather?"

Colonel Gutierrez knew better than to lie. "We have experienced some difficulties, your Excellency. My men have to double up some of the mule teams to clear the mud, but my scouts have indicated there is higher ground north of the river crossing. The terrain is firmer with limestone at the surface in many places."

"So you will be able to get the cannons across the river today?"

Gutierrez thought for a moment, and then replied, "Yes, your Excellency, it is my plan to cross today with the rest of the army. I do not relish the idea of being unable to supply artillery support to the infantry when entering rebel territory any more than you, my General."

Several of the senior officers glanced at each other. Such brash talk to the Commander was bordering on insubordination in their eyes. For reasons known only to Santa Anna, he acted as if he did not notice.

He even smiled a little as he remarked, "I'm glad you recognize the importance of a coordinated attack, Colonel. Perhaps you would like to sit in on my planning meeting before our assault on the Texians."

Colonel Gutierrez broke in to a broad smile. "My General, you flatter me with such a gracious offer. I look forward to learning at the side of the Eagle!"

Santa Anna nodded with a slight smile at the compliment. He suddenly noticed something different in the morning air. "The rain! It has stopped!"

He started to send his aide outside to check when the first beams of sunshine broke through the cloud deck to the southeast. The sun's rays offered little warmth, but as they made the white canvas radiate—the mood inside the tent brightened considerably.

The General raised his glass of juice. "Tonight, gentlemen, we shall sleep in Texas!"

"Viva Mexico! Viva Santa Anna!" came the enthusiastic reply.

Colonel Victorio De Sanchez, head of the Infantry, smiled and thought as the cheers died down. *Today, I do not have to be the bearer of bad news*. He knew that sixty more of the conscripts from the state of Yucatan had died overnight from dysentery and the brutal cold would not be welcome news.

There was no need to spoil the mood—not today. The deaths of more than four hundred soldiers and dozens of horses and mules since the force left Mexico City could not be denied.

The Army still numbered over six thousand men and included almost five hundred well-trained cavalry. *That should be more than enough to crush the rebels and drive the remaining Anglos out of Texas.* Colonel Sanchez was an educated man. He had read the history books about Napoleon's bitter defeat by the Russian winter—how he had lost almost ninety percent of his forces after finding Moscow abandoned.

As Sanchez exited the officer's mess tent, he tried to push the visions of French soldiers freezing to death in the Russian snow out of his mind. The bitter cold wind blowing off the barren grounds of northern Mexico did not make it an easy thing to do.

EAGLE NEST RANCH

Susie alerted Jonathan as she spotted a newborn calf lying near a patch of bee brush. He noted the filly's ears perk up and rewarded her with a gentle pat on the neck. "Good girl! That makes eighteen so far today. Pappa is gonna be real happy with this year's crop."

Dieter had brought an outstanding Angus bull all the way from Pennsylvania, along with some Guernsey milk cows. The cross between the native Longhorn and the European Angus had made for a meatier animal that could still put up with the Texas heat.

Come fall, Dieter, Friedrich and Jonathan planned to drive fifty head upriver to the small town of Laredo. The locals always looked forward to the Hermann's arrival with their wagon loaded down with German style cheeses and sausages. Their beef brought top dollar as well.

"Yep. This year is really gonna be something!" Jonathan said to Susie.

EAGLE NEST RANCH HOUSE

As the first company of lancers crossed the Rio Grande, Mary Catherine Hermann Richter watched with wonder from the wrap-around porch surrounding the ranch house. *Who are these mounted men dressed in flashy red coats with gleaming helmets of polished steel?* They reminded her of the brightly painted wooden nutcrackers they used at Christmas time. *Is this some sort of parade?* She looked south across the river and as far as she could see, were rank upon rank of uniformed soldiers.

She didn't understand. Her father would know. As she turned to enter the house, she felt a kick deep inside her. The baby was getting close.

The previous spring, she had married Hans Michael Richter from New Braunsfels, the only son of a Lutheran minister in that small central Texas town. He had heard of the beautiful Mary Catherine from an older cousin who had immigrated to Texas at the same time as the Hermanns. The young suitor had ridden for a week just to meet her and never returned to New Braunsfels.

"Pappa! Pappa! Come quick!"

10

Dieter was busy at the grindstone sharpening the butchering and kitchen knives. "What is that you say, girl?" He looked up.

The look of fear on her face changed his happy continence to one of concern. "What? What is it?" He left the grindstone spinning as he picked up the knives and quickly strode to the porch. "Is it time?…I'll get Momma."

Mary Catherine grabbed his elbow and tugged him toward the corner of the porch. "Who are they?" Her voice shook.

"They?…What they?" he stammered as he turned the corner.

In the distance, the third company of lancers crossed the river—three more followed behind. The drum and bugle corps led a column of dragoons that numbered over twenty-five hundred. The steady cadence of the drums was no longer borne completely away by the cold north wind—the sound was not unlike distant thunder. One of the kitchen knives slipped from Dieter's hand, stuck vertically and quivered in the hand-hewn plank deck of the porch as his jaw dropped open.

"Mein Gott."

RIO GRANDE CROSSING

Santa Anna noticed the water-driven mill on Becerro Creek, just a half mile upstream from the confluence with the Rio Bravo. He wanted to follow the waterway northward to assure fresh water for his troops and livestock.

He looked through a polished brass telescope he had removed from a saddle bag on his white Andalusian charger. As he followed the path up the hill from the mill, a large stone house with several outbuildings came into view.

On the porch stood two figures, one male, one female with flowing blonde hair that danced with the wind. He watched as they hurriedly left the porch and disappeared around the east side of the house. "Anglos," he said to his aide. "Lieutenant Goez, have Colonel Ramirez send one of his companies of lancers to liberate provisions from that ranch house...No surrender. No prisoners."

"Yes, my General." Goez started to wheel his horse about, and then looked back at Santa Anna. "Sir? Did you mean to say..."

Santa Anna cut him off with fire in his eyes. His right hand went to the bejeweled hilt of his sword and drew it out four inches. "You heard my orders, Lieutenant!"

The color drained from his face as Goez wheeled and spurred his horse up the column. As he drew up alongside the commander of cavalry, Goez's heart was racing. He saluted and excitedly passed the orders to Ramirez.

The colonel showed no emotion. He briefly glanced back at Santa Anna astride his sixteen hand steed. The small man always needed a stool to boost up into the stirrups. He reminded Ramirez of a painting he had seen of Napoleon.

He spurred his horse forward to the fifth company and passed the order to the commander. Major Jorge Salas repeated them back incredulously, "No surrender? No prisoners?"

Colonel Ramirez nodded in the affirmative.

Major Salas saluted and continued to the river crossing.

Colonel Ramirez backed his black gelding fifteen feet to give way to the last company of lancers and the first of the infantry that rapidly approached. He remembered the Gutierrez-MaGee Expedition in Texas led by General Joaquin De Arrendondo years before.

Santa Anna had also served under Arrendondo and had rapidly risen in rank as he gladly embraced the wholesale murder of men, women and children as well as the slaughter of men who had surrendered.

It turned Ramirez's stomach then and did so again today. He was aware of a letter Santa Anna had sent to the United States President Andrew Jackson decrying the perceived American interference with Mexico over Texas. Santa Anna had announced his proposed lethal treatment of Anglo settlers as pirates and would grant them no quarter. The unfortunate settlers downstream were not aware of any of these events that had transpired thousands of miles away.

EAGLE NEST RANCH HOUSE

Dieter Hermann had never been a soldier. His grandfather, Otto Paul Hermann, had been an infantry officer and served in several wars. He had assisted the Prussian General Friedrich Wilhelm Augustin Ludolf Gerhard who helped train George Washington's troops at Valley Forge.

After the American Revolution, Otto returned to Germany and helped defeat Napoleon Bonaparte at Waterloo in what is now Belgium. Otto would discuss warfare and tactics and loved history lessons with his grandchildren, but never glamorized the brutality. "War is hell on earth," he would say in his deep German accent.

He sadly told of the misery forced upon those noncombatants who, by accidents of geography, found themselves on the battlefield. Dieter had heard the stories firsthand after his grandfather moved to Pennsylvania to live with his son and family. Otto Paul had died in his sleep at the ripe old age of eighty-three the year Dieter and his family moved to Texas.

Mary Catherine, Ingrid and Dieter watched as a company of lancers crossed the Rio Grande, the water splashing in the midday sun.

Bright yellow gold pendants fluttered as they flew near the end of the fourteen foot long lances—which gave the formation its name. At the very end of the lance was a twelve-inch sharpened blade. Each man carried a slightly curved saber in a leather covered metal scabbard on his offside. A functional pommel featuring a hand-guard with a sharkskin and wire-wrapped grip completed the weapon. These were not for show.

Every razor-sharp saber could cut off an arm or a head with a swift blow from the battle-hardened rider. Individual cavalrymen had two single-shot muzzle-loading pistols stored in leather holsters sewn to the pommel of their saddle. Their polished metal helmets offered some protection from other saber blows as did their leather-lined metal chin straps.

The red horsehair crest on Major Salas's helmet waved in the breeze as he ordered the company to change formation. "To the right flank!" he shouted so that all seventy-five of his mounted troops could hear.

In unison, they turned their horses to the right and faced southeast toward the house.

"Forward at the trot!" rang out Salas's command as they started the half-mile ride to the mill.

They rode line abreast with the wind at their backs. There was no need to sound a charge as there was no armed presence visible. The soldiers would simply take what they wanted and kill all who were there.

"Stack the rifles, powder and shot where I showed you!" shouted Dieter as the lancers turned toward the ranch house.

"Who are they?" cried Mary Catherine.

"Calm down, daughter. They are Mexican Regulars," scolded Dieter. "Go to the smokehouse and bar the door. Do not come out unless I tell you."

"But, Pappa," she pleaded.

The front door burst open as Ingrid and Hans ran in from the barn.

"No buts!...Ingrid, take your sister and lock yourselves in the smokehouse."

She looked at her pregnant sister and started to cry. Dieter scooped up both girls in his arms as Hilda reached out for them.

"I love you girls...Now do as I say. It is going to be all right," Dieter tried to reassure them though there was fear in his own eyes.

Hans moved to help the women toward the door.

"I am going to need you here, son. You can not fight from the smokehouse."

The two sisters ran the thirty yards to the smokehouse. Once inside, they picked a candle from the shelf and struck a nearby phosphorus match to give some illumination.

Dieter stared toward the mill where a number of Mexican dragoons were beating the door open with the butts of their rifles. Two wagons had pulled up to the building and other soldiers began loading bags of grain and flour from the storeroom to the wagons. He could see a squad of cavalry leading two more wagons toward the house, followed by a company of dragoons.

"Close all the shutters," he yelled to Hilda and Hans.

EAGLE NEST RANCH

Jonathan squatted by a clear spring-fed creek at a bend that had formed a pool. He looked down into the crystal clear limestone creek as he filled his canteen and watched a large black bass chase a small perch across the pool. The perch ducked under exposed roots from a willow tree on the opposite bank. The bass swam around the roots for a moment and then moved off in search of easier prey.

Jonathan corked his canteen, pulled a piece of jerky from his coat pocket and tore off a chunk of the tough peppered dry beef. Susie turned her head sharply downstream, ears alert. "What is it girl?"

She snorted nervously and stomped a front hoof. He cocked his head. "I do not hear anything. Are you getting spooky on me?"

He rubbed the side of her neck, she relaxed and nuzzled his shoulder. Jonathan popped the last of the jerky into his mouth, stuck his foot into the rawhide *tapaderas*-covered stirrup and swung easily into the saddle. He squeezed his knees slightly—Susie climbed the sloping bank of the creek and he reined her south, in the direction of the ranch house. The filly shied to the left as a white-tailed doe with two fawns broke out of some dense brush in front of them. The startled animals cut across their path, ran down the creek bank and across the creek.

"See, just a deer and her babies…That is all it was. Nothing to worry about."

Susie blew, shook her head and continued southward.

EAGLE NEST RANCH HOUSE

Hilda was upstairs closing the last of the heavy wooden shutters and saw flames rising from the mill in the distance. The dark smoke boiled upward and then curved southeastward toward the river. She turned and ran to the stairway. "Dieter, Dieter!…They are burning the mill!" she yelled as she hurried down the stairs.

Dieter turned from loading the double-barreled flintlock shotgun. "Quickly, woman, help me load these weapons," he snapped at her. There were firing slots built into the stone walls with hinged iron covers that could be rotated down to provide a firing rest. "Hans, take the left side port, I will take the right. Do not let them get closer than fifty yards!"

His son-in-law opened the slot and extended his rifle through. Dieter did the same.

"Mama, be ready to load."

The look on Dieter's face was resolute. Hilda knew they were fighting for their lives.

Major Salas split his force of lancers into two columns that circled the house at a distance of one hundred yards. Seeing the layout of the barn, corrals, haystacks and cattle pens, he ordered Sergeant Lua to take possession of the corralled horses and milk cows. Lua directed four lancers to dismount and help him with the gates.

Salas led twelve lancers cautiously toward the house. "Come out and you will not be harmed," he yelled perfidiously toward the heavy front door. At a distance of slightly less than sixty yards, he raised his hand, halting the advance.

Hilda asked pleadingly, "Poppa, what should we do? They say…"

Her question was answered by the loud report of Dieter's long gun.

Major Salas saw the smoke from the firing port to his left—it was the last thing he would ever see. Dieter's rifle ball struck him square in the forehead and he tumbled backward out of the saddle. His horse shied sideways as the body hit the ground. The first casualty of the Battle of the Alamo was a minor Mexican officer arrogantly following orders—it would not be the last.

Captain Enriquez, the mounted officer leading the company of dragoons saw Salas fall from the saddle. He quickly spurred forward to take command—pointing at one man. "Return to the column and have artillery bring up a four-pounder."

The soldier spun his mount and raced back toward the column still down at the river.

Two more puffs of white smoke from the house—and two more lancers fell from their saddles.

"Fall back! Fall back!" Captain Enriquez shouted.

The lancers retreated out of range of the deadly rifles sticking out of the firing slots at the house.

Sergeant Lua and his squad of four rode toward the other lancers driving six horses and four milk cows, staying well out of range of the house.

The barn and haystacks were burning in the background. The sergeant had seen the milling horses in front of the house and spotted the red-crested helmet of Major Salas. He sent the four lancers driving the stolen horses and cows back to the column of men steadily crossing the river.

He believed the President General would be pleased with the acquisition of the much needed supplies. Perhaps he would be decorated. But for now, the tactical problems of the ranch house and smokehouse were still to be solved. Lua took five lancers and swung east to make an approach from the north. Hidden by dense brush, the six men approached the rear of the smokehouse and dismounted.

The building was built for two purposes. It primarily provided the family with a source of preserved meat when it was not feasible to butcher in the heat of the Texas summer. Secondly, it provided shelter from Comanche raids, something Lua recognized as he studied the structure. It had no windows and the door was reinforced beyond belief.

Thick wrought-iron bands crossed the cypress slabs used to construct the door. The steeply pitched roof was covered in cedar shakes, but even the lowest point of the eves was ten feet above ground.

Small wonder the Comanches had little success breaching it in past raids. Lua had not seen the rifle fire from the north side of the ranch house. He reasoned there were only a couple of riflemen inside. *What was lying in wait in the smokehouse?* He could only imagine. It was good for him to choose two privates to try to breach the door. They took positions against the reinforced door and proceeded to try their luck.

Hilda took turns looking out different firing positions on the west and north side of the house. Hans and Dieter had their eyes on lancers and dragoons just out of range to the east and south.

She looked apprehensively out the north side port just in time to see two Mexican lancers trying to breach the door of the smokehouse. Without thinking, she pointed the muzzle of the double-barreled shotgun at the hapless soldiers and pulled both triggers. The recoil knocked her back and down to the floor.

Dieter wheeled and rushed to her aid. She cried softly and spoke with a shaky voice, "I never killed anyone before."

He picked her up and brushed the tears from her eyes. "I know. Now reload."

The sixty-year old rancher handed his wife the shotgun that she quickly loaded with buck and ball. The different sized shot packed tightly in the twelve gauge bore was very effective out to seventy yards and beyond.

Dieter looked out the north side of the house toward the nearby smokehouse and was relieved the door was still intact. A corporal made the mistake of trying to see what happened to his young privates—his head was exposed too long. Dieter snapped the long Pennsylvania rifle into the firing slot and lifted the top of the corporal's skull several feet into the air.

The sulfurous smell of black powder quickly dissipated as the north wind blew the smoke away.

Lua watched helplessly as the corporal's helmet hit the ground and bounced several feet away. One of the younger members of the lancers vomited involuntarily as bits of the corporal's brain drifted down behind the smokehouse and landed in his gaping mouth.

The sergeant grabbed the fallen corporal's boots, pulled him behind the rear wall and studied the macabre results. The entrance hole above the left eye was smaller than the seventy caliber that his dragoons carried. He estimated it at forty-five or fifty caliber and marveled at the force with which the ball had struck his young man.

The skin was torn beneath his neck where the sturdy helmet leather strap had ripped in two. Lua made the quick decision to wait until the dragoons had reinforcement from their artillery. He and his remaining lancers made their way back to their horses and rode down the hill away from the house.

Ingrid and Mary Catherine crouched in terror behind the pockmarked, bloodstained door to the smokehouse. The sounds of the gun battle and cries of the wounded and dying soldiers and cavalry pulled at their very souls. Without a single window in the smokehouse, they could only imagine the carnage happening outside.

Mary Catherine, always the more beautiful and delicate of the pair, was sobbing into her apron trying to mask the sounds of her fear. She started to hyperventilate and was getting more and more agitated with each passing moment.

Ingrid looked on and removed the cream-colored ceramic top from a large glazed terra-cotta jug that contained spring water for use in emergencies. She dipped the tin cup in and drew out some to try to help her sister calm herself. Mary nervously drank and her breathing slowed.

The girls had stayed here during numerous Indian raids as they grew up, but in recent years, the Comanches had given a wide berth to the Hermann Ranch. Word of the powerful medicine these whites possessed and how many raiding parties came home mourning losses instead of celebrating was related far and wide. Mary Catherine handed the empty cup back to Ingrid and tried to smile.

"Thank you."

The smile dissolved as she felt a cramp and watched in horror as a pink-tinged clear liquid ran over the stone floor and seeped into the cracks. Her eyes met Ingrid's as the stark realization hit with the power of a runaway wagon.

Colonel Gutierrez wheeled his black stallion impatiently and cursed his men. As the teams of mules strained to pull the cannons from the mire, some of the soldiers he had ordered to help the effort, slipped and fell into the brown custard.

The rain had stopped early in the day, but thousands of troops marching along with hundreds of horses and mules had left the trail a quagmire of mud, animal urine, feces and blood.

The constant cold did not help. The colonel had ordered his men to forgo the noon meal to get the artillery closer to the river, but that decision had come back to haunt him.

One look at the sun told him it was near three o'clock and that gave him only three more hours of daylight to cross and set up camp.

A mile might as well have been ten at that rate. To make matters worse, Colonel De Sanchez, head of the infantry, had sent Captain Mata to inquire in the strongest of terms where the four-pounder was he had ordered just after noon.

At the time, eleven of his dragoons and nine lancers had been lost in the battle near the crossing. Captain Mata had been gone for over an hour. As Gutierrez looked northward toward the crossing—there were no infantry in sight. They had all crossed the river and a single rider loped toward him. When he realized who it was, his heart sank.

Colonel Lebron, second in command to Colonel De Sanchez, was furious as he rode south to see the debacle unfolding. He developed a solution to the impasse as he looked at the thinning brush beside the muddy road. He would pass on the suggestion to the young commander of the artillery.

EAGLE NEST RANCH

Susie acted more and more agitated as the youngest of the Hermann family worked his way toward home. The cold air seemed to cut him to the bone as the sun sank lower in the western sky. Jonathan pulled the fleece collar of the sheepskin coat up tight against his neck.

As he looked over his left shoulder, he saw a sight he did not like—gray clouds at low and middle altitudes were scudding in from the east. At the surface, the winds still blew from the north northwest—snow was coming.

He was still almost six miles from the ranch house and had high hopes of making it home before dark. Jonathan detected the sound of distant thunder, *That is most unusual.*

Susie alerted once more. He heard the sound of thunder once again. Over the top of the ever-present bee brush, he spotted two yellow gold pendants on long staffs with gleaming blades attached at the tip. The two small pointed flags snapped and popped in unison like sheets drying on a clothesline in a summer wind. They were coming straight at him.

EAGLE NEST RANCH HOUSE

The first position chosen by Colonel Gutierrez's cannoneers was unfortunate. The radius in the rise of the terrain obscured the ranch house as the sergeant placed his brass sighting pin in the slot at the rear of the four-pounder cannon. He could see the rocky ground covered the first floor as he knelt behind the tube.

Quickly, he ordered the crew to pull the gun forward another thirty yards and make ready. The men, filthy, hungry and exhausted from the unpleasant task of cutting a new road in the sea of briars and cactus, were near the breaking point.

Colonel Gutierrez had had suffered enough embarrassment to last a lifetime in the past few hours. As the men slowly pushed and pulled the heavy cannon uphill into place, he berated and cursed their slowness.

He rode up to the last man in line on the heavy rope and gave him a blow across the upper back with the flat side of his saber. "Faster! Put your back into it you son-of-a-whore!"

The private turned to see the Colonel on his magnificent black charger with his perfectly clean uniform and spotless white riding gloves. The sneer on Gutierrez's face as he looked down in contempt at the wretched private was an image burned into his memory until his dying day. So was the sight of two simultaneous puffs of smoke from the upper windows of the ranch house one hundred yards away.

From their firing ports on the second floor, Dieter and Hans had a perfect view of the gun crew. The brash young Colonel riding into the range of their long rifles was a bonus they had not expected. As they fired, the officer dropped his shiny saber at the feet of the filthy private he was cursing and looked down to see blood oozing from a ragged hole in his tunic, two inches above his heart. The ball shattered his spine and the last thought though his brain was a simple one. *It doesn't hurt.*

The sergeant of the gun crew was hit in the liver and right kidney and collapsed like a wet sack. He reached for help from his crew, but they had other ideas.

The filthy conscripts from a coastal village in the south of the Yucatan never even slowed down. The sergeant saw them disappear over the crest of the limestone ridge, running south for their lives. One of the men carried the saber—he never looked back

Dieter handed his long rifle to Hilda to reload. They shared a quick moment as their eyes met. He had no expectation whatsoever of living through the day. His thoughts of his family were just under the surface.

Dieter never had been overly demonstrative in his affection. *It was not the German way*, he supposed. What he wanted most of all was to hold all his children once again and share a meal at the round oak table he and Friedrich had built. He never saw the ambitious grenadiers who had crept up on the north side of the house and planted charges at the base of the front door and the one to the smokehouse. He never knew he had a new grandson Mary Catherine had named Dieter Michael Richter.

EAGLE NEST RANCH

Jonathan rode for his life. Brush tore at his face, arms and coat. The first two lancers he encountered attempted to run him through with their namesake lances. Quick footwork by Susie spoiled their first attack, bee brush spoiled their second.

Frustrated by their lack of success, they decided their pistols would be a better weapon of choice. It didn't take long to discover the inability to maneuver with a pistol in one hand and a lance in the other. It left no hand to control the reins and leg commands didn't work well on the exhausted, underfed horses. They had lost the young Anglo in the brush.

Jonathan cautiously worked his way through the brush he knew like the back of his hand. He couldn't believe those soldiers had tried to kill him without provocation. *What the hell is going on?* He could still hear the cadence of the drums behind him, although the sound was fainter now. He deduced that they were from a marching Mexican Army patrol. He could skirt the patrol and still get home before dark. The sound of a series of explosions just seconds apart shook him to his core. They came from the ranch house!

Soldiers of the last two companies of Mexican infantry looked back over their shoulders at the sound of the blasts. They knew someone or something had defeated the gringo force at the mill. A cheer went up in celebration of the great victory.

Jonathan had heard the noise also and spurred his beloved Susie homeward. Too late, he heard the cheers of the infantry companies a mile behind the drum and bugle corps. His faithful

27

mount slid to a stop as Jonathan reined her in panic. He was directly between two fully-armed Mexican companies. He spurred her on toward home as one of the troopers excitedly yelled, "Fire!"

His sudden appearance had startled the green soldiers. Some fired in the air before their seventy caliber Enfield muskets were even pointed at him. Others fired at point blank range where the horse had been.

In their excitement, at least a dozen men had fired without thought of where their muzzles were actually pointing. As the smoke cleared, twelve of Santa Anna's Invincible Ones lay dead or dying in the trail. Most could not believe they had missed the blonde Anglo.

Two corporals who had seen combat before, were certain they had not missed—they were correct. Sixty yards away in the dense vegetation, Jonathan Otto Hermann slipped off his beloved paint pony for the last time—Susie continued racing homeward.

EAGLE NEST RANCH HOUSE

Friedrich Hermann arrived home just before dark, cold and wet, as the rain had started to fall. The scene of almost complete devastation shocked him beyond words. The bodies of his family had been mutilated, bayoneted and desecrated after they were tied to the two long hitching posts in front of the house.

Dead Mexican soldiers and horses littered the hilltop. The house had been stripped of anything of value. The smokehouse was empty save fresh blood on the floor mixed with splintered wood from the explosive charges.

At the hitching post, Friedrich held his mother's hand and said a prayer. He cut his father's bonds and laid his body down gently. As he stood to walk to the other rail where his two sisters had died, Susie galloped into view and stood stamping her feet. Blood from a minor bullet graze under her left ear and splatters on the saddle told him all he ever needed to know about his younger brother's fate. The loss of all his family in one violent day was almost too much to bear.

It was then he saw him through the dull ache in his chest, a small perfect little boy lying in Mary Catherine's lap—his baby blue eyes stared unseeing at the uncle he never knew. A Mexican silver crucifix had been laid across his tiny body as a hollow act of atonement by an unknown Mexican soldier. Friedrich sobbed loudly as he flung the offending talisman far away into the encroaching darkness. As he rocked and cradled the cold body of his only nephew, the rain turned into snow.

***

CHAPTER ONE

WEBB COUNTY, TEXAS
Present Day
28 June

The early morning Texas sun cast long finger-like shadows through the tall cottonwoods and out onto the sluggish, shallow Rio Grande River as it flowed past the Hermann ranch.

The wheels of a two-ton refrigerated Dodge box truck rolled through the muddy water up to the hubs. The truck climbed out of the river and up the bank on the Texas side, preceded by a black Humvee. The two vehicles approached a five strand barb-wire fence and stopped. Sergeant Roberto Garza got out of the one in the front with a fencing tool, walked up and proceeded to cut all five wires. He peeled them back and returned to the truck. The two vehicles passed through the gap and drove half a mile into Texas.

The Hummer turned off the trail and parked under a large live oak. The Dodge stopped in the middle of the path, a short, slightly built man wearing the dark olive-drab uniform and balaclava of the Mexican Federal Army got out. He walked to the back and unlocked the double doors.

Twelve frightened Hispanic men and women exited the truck at gun point. He forced them to strip naked, and then gunned them down with his suppressed AK-47. Two of the victims tried to run and were shot in the back. The soldier slapped another thirty-round magazine into the weapon and emptied half of it into the still-twitching bodies on the trail.

EAGLE NEST RANCH

A ten yard wide strip of mesquite, prickly pear and bee brush ran between the river and a cultivated three-hundred-acre field of mature hay grazer. The lush forgage—a sorghum crossed with sudan hybrid—was at baling height. A well-maintained dirt road inside a barb-wire fence encircled the field. A mama javelina and her eight piglets trotted lazily across the road toward the field.

A rangy, broad-shouldered, blond-headed rancher was driving a green John Deere six-wheel Gator. He wore a faded jean jacket, Wranglers, an old yellow Caterpillar gimme cap and carried his two hundred twenty-five pounds on his six foot-four frame like a panther.

Mike Hermann drove the utility vehicle through the opening, walked back to the red bow-gate and latched it closed. His worn cowboy boots left distinctive tracks in the dry dust of the ranch road. A herd of Beefmaster cattle grazed along the fence showing a marked interest in getting into the lush hay grazer.

It had been a decision of his father, Gunter, to start a herd of registered Beefmasters over twenty-five years earlier. He had reasoned that the Brahma-Hereford-Shorthorn cross was ideally suited for that rugged country. The Beefmaster cross had been developed in Falfurrias County by Tom Lasater in the 1930s, especially to deal with the south Texas climate and available native forage. They produced exceptionally fine, lean beef.

Thirty-year-old Michael Otto Hermann was the fifth generation of Hermanns to occupy the three thousand acre parcel of land bordering the Rio Grande. The expansive spread was forty miles south of the county seat, Laredo, and forty miles north of Falcon Reservoir. His progenitor, Dieter Hermann, had purchased the tract of an original Spanish land grant from Don Julio de la Garza in 1811.

Mike had been born and raised on the property and knew every rock and bush on it as well as his family's tragic history. His only absence from the ranch were his two tours of duty with the Marine Corps in Iraq and one tour in Afghanistan after graduating from Texas A & M-Kingsville. He had been awarded two Silver Stars for valor and a Purple Heart. Mike was an inactive Marine—there being no such thing as an ex-Marine.

Mike loved the corps and regarded his fellow jarheads as true brothers. He lived the Marine Corps motto, *Semper Fi*.

The one thing he could not stomach was the gutless, politically correct, ROE—rules of engagement—forced down the troops collective throats by the liberal members of the past two administrations.

The thought of good Marines dying for lack of air cover, adequate artillery fire support and a confusing myriad of ever-changing restrictions on engaging the enemy, ran against his conscience like a chain saw. Repeated heated discussions with higher ranking Marine officers eventually lead Captain Hermann to be labeled a malcontent.

He still remembered, word for word, when he lost his temper with a Colonel Clarence Ogilsvey, Director of Logistics in Afghanistan. His requisition for additional night vision goggles had been denied for a second time. The forty-year-old staff puke had threatened to call the Marine MPs if Mike didn't lower his voice. Ogilsvey had never so much as fired one shot in anger.

He had looked him square in the eye and snapped, "Do what ever you're man enough to do."

He wheeled around and exited the room without so much as a "By-your-leave." Mike resigned his commission and three days later he was back in Texas at his beloved Eagle Nest.

The summer sun reached its zenith as he pulled under the shade of a large spreading cottonwood next to a bend that had formed a deep clear pool on the spring-fed Bacerro Creek. He reached into a cooler in the small rear bed of the Gator and retrieved a bottle of water and a sandwich his sister had made for him from the ranch's own mesquite smoked ham.

Mike took a bite and noticed a small frog swimming across the spring-fed pool. The water suddenly exploded as a large black bass hit the surface, taking the frog as his own lunch. He smiled as he savored the flavor of the ham and contemplated the eternal life-and-death struggle in nature.

In the months since he'd left active duty, Mike had fallen easily back into the daily rhythm of a working rancher. His father still owned the ranch, but had not yet fully recovered from injuries sustained in a horse fall. Luckily, his shattered right hip was on the mend and a cane allowed him decent mobility—stairs were still a bitch, though.

Mike's twenty-seven-year-old younger sister, Carla, known to friends and family as Blaze, a five-foot-ten-inch-tall, shapely beauty with flaming Maureen O'Hara red hair and emerald green eyes, had moved her father's personal belonging downstairs to a guest bedroom in the one-story wing added by their grandfather fifty years before. She had always been a big help around the ranch, but had become indispensable since their dad's tumble.

Mike was still away serving in the Marines, but Carla acted quickly when Gunter's horse limped back home alone. She walked the buckskin gelding to the barn and turned the care of injured animal to the staff veterinarian, Ron.

Dirt had flown from the tires of her four-wheel-drive Ford diesel pickup as she raced to the 10,000 ft. ranch airstrip. Mike had bulldozed the runway out of the brush on a long plateau some four years earlier and paved it when he was last home on leave.

They needed a strip for all the private jets that were bringing buyers from all over the world for the ranch's high-priced Beefmaster breeding stock and their registered Quarter horses.

Eagle Nest registered Quarter horse bloodline was unbroken back to Traveler, one of the foundation stallions of the breed. The runway was a short three miles from the ranch house—but that day seemed like a hundred miles to Blaze.

After a quick preflight, she soon had the Cessna 180 rolling down the paved strip. Leveling off at 500 feet above the rugged terrain, Blaze accelerated to 145 knots until she reached the general vicinity she felt sure her dad had been riding.

Gunter had mentioned checking the fence lines northwest along the river up to the confluence of Aguadulce Creek. They had experienced recent trouble with fence cutting along the river.

Illegal aliens and, he suspected, drug smugglers had shown complete disregard for international law and landowners property rights. It wasn't unusual to find fences down, bits of tattered clothing, shoes and plastic water bottles strewn with abandon.

It was forty miles to Laredo as the crow flies and the county sheriff department didn't have the manpower to cover the miles and miles of river frontage along Webb County. Most of all, Gunter was concerned about his prized breeding stock being caught in the quicksand often found along the banks of the slow-moving Rio Grande.

Turning northward to scan the fence line, she descended to 200 feet above the ground and 150 feet east of the fence. Four minutes later, a flash of red and white from Gunter's shirt drew her attention. She could see her father lying on a rocky outcrop—her heart stopped for a moment until she had seen him rise up on one elbow and wave his straw hat. She had given a sigh of relief and set up for a 180-degree turn, added power, rolled into a 30-degree left bank and descended to 100 feet as she came out of the turn. She waggled her wings and smiled when he responded with a thumbs-up.

Blaze briefly considered landing on the nearby sandbar in the middle of the shallow river. The Horner STOL or Short Take Off and Landing kit gave the *Skywagon* great performance. Landing with full flaps and the fat Tundra tires, she could get it stopped in under 300 feet in a no-wind condition.

She had decided discretion was the better part of valor as she would have had to carry her 210-pound father down the limestone cliff, through the water and onto the sandbar. It was obvious he could not walk. "Eagle Nest, this is Songbird. Come in Nacho."

Ingnacio "Nacho" Cantu, the small, wiry Hispanic ranch manager, answered the office radio. "*Si*, Miss Blaze, this is Nacho. Go ahead."

"Get the big Gator with the flat bed, one of the other hands and follow the river fence north four miles. Dad is hurt. I'll circle overhead until you get here."

Nacho nodded and replied, "*Si*, Miss Blaze. Should I bring the first aid kit?"

"Yes...I'll call Care Flight out of Laredo to meet us at the strip."

She had been a take-charge—if not a little headstrong—girl all of her life. They lost their mother five years earlier in an automobile accident. Blaze became the woman of the house and ran it as such. She, like Mike, had only been away from Eagle Nest when necessary.

She was a certified genius and earned her undergraduate and Ph.D. degrees in electrical engineering and physics at Rice University in a little more than five years. Most of the three dozen technology firms who tried to recruit her after graduation had long since given up in frustration. They could not conceive that a bright young graduate like her would politely decline their six-figure offers.

Eagle Nest was her home and she wanted to continue her research there. Many suitors likewise had their romantic plans shot out of the saddle. She wasn't ready to settle down, and besides, she had her father and Eagle Nest to care for.

After the broken-hip incident, Gunter had made a ranch policy that nobody would leave the ranch house for any distance without a two-way radio and GPS. There were just too many places on the property where a person could get themselves in a tight and not be found quickly enough. He'd dodged the bullet that time, but someone else just might not be so lucky.

He would often quote, "There's an old saying in the Texas brush country: What won't stick you or grab you, will bite you." It was always meant as a little bit of humor about the cactus, thorny brush, and snakes.

These days, perhaps it needed to be modified a bit. With the rise in drug cartels in Mexico that are as powerful and lethal as those in Columbia in times past, the words, or shoot you, should be added. Gunter was well aware of the ranchers in Arizona who had been murdered on their own property and the man who had been shot while jet skiing on nearby Falcon Reservoir.

A swallow of cold water washed down the last of Mike's ham sandwich. He screwed the cap back on the bottle and tossed it in the cooler. At the house, it would be refilled with the same cool artesian water which fed the springs and creeks which ran full time on the Eagle Nest. Water there was life and one of the many things that made this remote piece of Texas so special. One last look at the fish cruising the clear pool and Mike hopped back into the Gator.

As he slowly drove the game and cattle trail back up the ridge, he spotted a group of black turkey vultures—buzzards as the locals call them. *Nature's own glider pilots. Yeah, that's what they are*, thought Mike.

Then he noticed they were circling a given location and had formed a vertical stack, like a vortex, of six—no, seven birds in one area. That always meant one thing—something big was already or just about to become dead. "Damn," he muttered, as he sat in the six-wheeler on the north end of the ranch. "Looks like it's near the bull pasture."

The breeding-age bulls were kept in a separate trap located between Mike's present location and the ranch house when it wasn't breeding season.

He skillfully drove the ATV through the gaps in the brush and across the cattle guards toward the circling buzzards. A quick count showed an even ten in the queue. *Definitely a dead bull, dammit*. Mike thought. *No doubt about it*. He was wrong.

One of the things he appreciated about the Gator was not only can you go almost anywhere a horse can, but it was quiet. It wasn't like most of those sport four-wheelers that sound like chain saws with wheels that you could hear coming for miles on a still day.

He made the turn onto the *Trail of Misery*—the name given by his family to the route Santa Anna took across Eagle Nest when he was headed to the Alamo. He came upon a scene that caused instant flashbacks to Iraq in 2003. A dozen naked men and women lay sprawled across the rutted trail—a single dark figure was tugging at the hand of one of the bodies.

"What the hell?" Mike stepped out onto the trail.

The dark figure that he had assumed to be a very large buzzard stood up and turned to face him. The man's eyes narrowed when he realized there was a witness to his butchery. His hand brought up an AK-47 equipped with a sound suppressor.

He instantly recognized the weapon as it was shouldered and instinctively dove for cover. The figure fired a burst that almost missed Mike completely. One of the sixteen subsonic rounds burned a path across the back of his left calf.

Eight rounds tore into the radiator of the utility vehicle—lucent-green antifreeze dribbled on to the dusty soil and disappeared. One shot hit the front transaxle and sent it to junk part heaven.

Mike was shocked at how little sound came out of the fully automatic AK, but then again, the Marine Corps never had been big on being quiet once the battle was on.

The man in olive drab cursed himself for not reloading after he had fired the first half of the second magazine. The first mag he emptied had killed or knocked down all twelve of the unfortunates who had paid up to $2,000 to be smuggled into the US. The second half had taken care of the wounded.

If it weren't for the limitless greed of the cartel thugs, he wouldn't be looking at the very pissed-off inactive Marine. He should have let them go. He should have let them keep their rings and watches. He should have let them keep their cheaply made clothes, boots and shoes. But most of all, he should have practiced reloading under pressure—but he didn't.

Years of Marine training and combat experience didn't go to waste. As Mike dove for cover, his hands went for the Sig Sauer .45 pistol he carried in a cross-draw DeSantis holster.

As he rolled over, he assumed a prone position facing the gunman. The two white lines on the front and rear sights stood out in stark contrast to the dark green utilities worn by the soldier.

Three shots rang out across the ranch almost as one—two to the chest, one to the head—just in case he was wearing body armor.

Arterial blood sprayed from the chest wounds and the balaclava assumed an odd shape as the slightly built man was knocked off his feet and lay still—he was dead.

Driving all night and half the day from the interior Mexico town of Torreón had left the rogue Mexican soldier in the Humvee passenger seat exhausted. Both he and the driver had stayed awake all night during their trip to the border with the twelve smuggled aliens and were trying to catch some much-needed sleep. The shots woke him and he screamed, "Go! Go! Go!"

The driver didn't need any further prompting, he started the big diesel engine in the black Hummer and pulled out from under the shade of the ancient oak west of the trail.

Mike heard the familiar sound of the engine and eased to the edge of the trail. As the vehicle came into view, the one driving tried a quick shot at Mike with his left hand. The MAC-11 machine pistol missed wildly as the panicked driver turned the wheel with his right hand.

The Humvee plowed into the thick brush on the east side of the narrow trail and was slowed down enough for Mike to get a shot at the darkly tinted rear glass—it shattered completely. Mike took aim at the driver's head, but the lumbering SUV bounced over a rock ledge and the bullet struck the tailgate with little effect. His next two shots broke the windshield and destroyed the rear view mirror.

The vehicle was sixty yards away and starting to pick up speed. Another hundred yards and they would be over the ridge and heading back downhill to the Rio Grande and Mexico.

The passenger picked up a Mexican issued M-16 and fired a three shot burst out the broken back window at Mike as the SUV rocked along the limestone trail.

Bullets bounced off the rocky trail mere inches from his feet and screamed as they ricocheted skyward. His Sig barked once, the slide locked open, but the 185 grain hollow-point flew true—it impacted the back of the driver's head.

He jerked the wheel involuntarily to the right as he died and crashed into a majestic live oak that had been just a sapling back when the Napoleon of the West passed through Eagle Nest.

The passenger opened the door, grabbed the M-16 and attempted to run. Mike sprinted toward the truck, bent low and scooped the AK from the shooter's dead hands.

The third mag, partially inserted in the well was full—Mike glanced at it and slammed it home. He didn't take his eyes off the truck as he pulled back on the bloody cocking handle and let the bolt fly forward.

The soldier was shocked at how quickly the Texan had covered the eighty yards between them. He had barely reached the rear bumper of the vehicle when he heard the booming command. "Halt!"

The order echoed across the pasture. Roberto knew better than to run. He turned to face the blond Rambo and smiled as he dropped the rifle. "I surrender, gringo."

Roberto had friends in the highest places. He would never spend much time in an American jail. He was, of course, right.

Michael Otto Hermann had had it. He had fucking well had it with all the bullshit rules of engagement in the war on terror. He had had it with all the illegal aliens, sleazy, liberal, corrupt politicians and pontificators, violent drug cartels and rogue soldiers of the Mexican Army.

Blood dripped down his left calf and stained the white sock in his worn Lucchese boot. These useless bastards had defiled his Eagle Nest and placed a member of the Hermann family at risk for the last God damn time. He had the Mexican sergeant in his sights, his finger was on the trigger—he squeezed...

***

CHAPTER TWO

EAGLE NEST RANCH
28 June

The soldier's body toppled back and lay still. Smoke from the hot suppressor curled up in a thin gray column. Mike's senses were on an adrenaline-boosted high alert as he scanned the surrounding brush for additional threats. Seeing none, he cautiously turned and headed back to the crippled Gator.

A radio transmission caught him in mid-stride. "Big Eagle, Silver Eagle…Come in Mike."

The call caught him off-guard. It didn't come from the shattered radio mounted in the Gator. This call was coming over the radio in the Humvee still idling against the massive oak.

"Son of a bitch! The bastards have been monitoring us on the ranch frequency."

He cautiously moved behind the vehicle with the AK-47 at the ready position. The driver lay slumped against the steering wheel with what remained of his skull exposed to the dry summer heat. Several green flies already noisily circled the pink and gray mass in anticipation of a feast.

He opened the door and the still warm MAC-11 fell to the ground at his feet. Mike grabbed the back of the man's collar and yanked the body from the seat in one powerful motion. He tossed the gun inside, slid into the familiar driver's seat and slipped the transmission into reverse.

The military Humvee rolled back, exposing a twelve-inch scar on the oak where the bark was ripped away. *So far so good.* Mike looked at the bullet-crazed and blood-splattered windshield. "Can't see out of that piece of shit," he muttered as he slid the seat back slightly.

Like he had done a couple of times in Iraq, he cocked his right leg and gave the windshield a size twelve mule kick. It exploded outward, taking the black rubber seal as it slid off the hood. He picked up the mic, visually cleared all around and calmly spoke, "Silver Eagle, go big Winchester."

At the ranch house, Gunter sat wondering what the hell was going on. He had heard several rapid pistol shots, followed by the unmistakable sounds of two full automatic weapons as he hobbled into house from the porch. Mike was giving him the code words to change to the VHF channel 303.0 on the upper side band—he did so without question.

"Big Eagle, Silver Eagle. Come back." Gunter sat in silence for ten seconds. "Big Eagle, Silver Eagle. Say again, come back…Please respond."

Mike watched the radio intently to see if it performed an auto scan. Thankfully it had not. He quickly switched to 303.0 upper side band just in time to hear, "…respond." He pressed the mic key. "Lock and load, Dad. We have bad actors on the place again…Pass the word."

Gunter sat stoically as the information sank in. He had hoped to avoid the growing threat of violence that was occurring all along the border. He knew from the first, however, that staying out of the fray was a lost cause.

Eagle Nest's location had historically been one of the best Rio Grande River crossing points for many miles. "Message received and acknowledged." He pressed the button on the base of the mic stand. "All stations, Silver Eagle…Code red, repeat, code red. This is not a drill. Silver Eagle out."

WARBIRD RESTORATION, INC.
NORTH TEXAS REGIONAL AIRPORT
DENISON, TEXAS

The large weathered sign above the massive hangar doors could definitely use a fresh coat of paint. The company CEO was Archimedes "Dare" Phillips, Colonel, USMC (Ret.) and graduate of the United States Naval Academy ('81). His last duty station before retirement had been CO of HMLA-205 light attack helicopter squadron at Marine Corps Air Ground Combat Center Twentynine Palms, California. Dare Phillips—no one dared call him Archimedes—liked the sign the way it was.

Warbird Restoration, Inc. was, in fact, a legitimate business cover for BEF, LLC.

BEF was an acronym for Black Eagle Force, a paramilitary quick strike interdiction unit composed of former military Special Ops members or pilots from all branches, Army, Navy, Marine Corps, Air Force and even CIA agents.

BEF was under contract with the DoD, the Department of Defense, and was created for missions that are not—and cannot be—officially approved. BEF's unique intelligence gathering and operational capabilities filled a niche left gaping by the Posse Comitatus Act of 1878 prohibiting the US military from enforcing civil law.

The middle large gray hangar once housed two squadrons of one of the top fighter/interceptors of its day, the Convair F-102 *Delta Dagger*. Back then, the field had been known as Perrin Air Force Base in the Air Defense Command.

Budget cuts and programmed airspace requirement for the Dallas/Fort Worth International Airport led to Perrin's closure on May 13, 1971. BEF purchased the three unused hangars on the west side of the field from Grayson County and began renovations in 1986.

Civilian pilots taxiing by the large hangars would see a handful of mechanics slowly proceeding with detailed restorations of expensive World War II, Korean and Vietnam era fighters, bombers and occasionally transports. What they could not see was the underground eight and one-half acres of aircraft parking, storage, command center, offices, sleeping quarters and training facilities of the clandestine group.

Seventy-five feet below the hangar floor, some of the very latest state-of-the-art military equipment and all the electronics currently available were operationally connected to the vast telecommunications network of the US government.

Even a trained observer would probably not pick up the purpose of the large metal rectangle in the hangar floor. It did not serve as a seam between big concrete sections—it was, in fact, the edge of a huge naval aircraft carrier elevator connecting the upper hangar to the secret lower deck.

In front of the large central hangar, one of the mechanics casually walked over to the tug attached to a B-25. He started it up and effortlessly towed the *Mitchell* out onto the apron and over to the north hangar where a silver North American P-51 *Mustang* and a sleek black Vought F-4U *Corsair* were being restored.

A klaxon sounded downstairs as circuits closed, energizing huge hydraulic pumps. They whined and the massive platform descended into position flush with the lower hangar deck. No sooner had the elevator stopped its motion when the crew chief in black and gray digital camo directed a tug driver over to one of three black futuristic looking aircraft parked in a side area.

Another crewman hooked the yoke from the towbar to the nose wheel of the craft and the driver moved it onto the elevator. He repeated the procedure once more and the three craft were lined nose to tail—total time elapsed, two minutes and thirty-three seconds.

The klaxon sounded again and the pumps lifted the elevator to the hangar above.

A specially modified Lockheed Martin C-5M *Super Galaxy* was backed into the center hangar—its aft ramp at the edge of the elevator.

Loadmasters maneuvered the three unique craft up into the massive cargo hold. They rolled the last flat-black M600/A into position and secured it to the tie-down rings hinged into depressions along the deck. Red *DO NOT FLY* streamers hung from safetied weapons mounted on the engine nacelle struts fore and aft and gave the futuristic craft a menacing, lethal look.

The M600/A, a four nacelle VTOL or Vertical Take-Off and Landing aircraft manufactured by Moller International had been modified extensively starting with ultra-high-tech avionics and a stealth coating of multiple layers of a radar absorptive Teflon-like material similar to that used on the F-117 *Nighthawk*.

Lightweight Dragonskin armor, composed of silicon carbide ceramic matrices and titanium laminates, was installed inside the aircraft's skin under critical cockpit, avionics and engine nacelle areas. The Skycar was re-designated as the M600/A *Black Eagle* by the BEF.

The craft was twenty-six feet long, fourteen feet wide with the rear nacelles folded up and twenty-two feet wide with the rear nacelles extended. It had a gross weight of 3,800 pounds with eight 1500cc rotary engines for the four nacelles, developing 170 hp each.

A GAU 17/A 7.62 cal Gatling gun was mounted in center of the aerodynamic nose. Two *Hellfire* AGM-114K and two Precision Attack Air-to-Surface Missiles or *PAASMs* were pylon mounted on top of the rear wing nacelle struts and four AIM 92 *Stinger* heat seeking air-to-air missiles were mounted under the front wing nacelle supports.

The *Black Eagle* had a top dash speed over 400 knots with a ceiling of 36,000 feet and four passenger configuration plus weapons. The fuel cells were self-sealing inert foam-filled-type bags under the passenger compartment.

"Mister Phillips to the Command Center," a pleasant female voice said over the intercom system.

The trim, silver-haired CEO smiled as he patted the loadmaster on the shoulder. "Good job, Max." He turned to make his way back to the Command Center.

After twenty-seven years in the Corps and eleven months in the BEF, he still wasn't used to being called Mister Phillips. Old habits die hard. *What's up today?* He didn't remember any planning meeting he had possibly overlooked. It didn't really matter as it only took forty seconds to walk to the Command Center elevator and slide his ID across the access panel.

The computer controlled security camera had already scanned his facial characteristics and crossed-checked them against the chip embedded in the card. Twenty milliseconds later, the panel light turned green and the door slid open with an audible hiss.

Chief Operations Officer and former Army Special Forces Major Kevin "Kit" Kitaen, was engaged in a phone conversation with Herbert Richards regarding a farm-out of their contract from the DoD. Richards was one of the GS-11 civilian supervisors from Immigration and Customs Enforcement Special Operations and Intelligence units in Bethesda Maryland. ICE was the largest division inside the Department of Homeland Security with almost 20,000 employees.

A long series of flat seventy-two inch monitors covered the east wall of the Command Center. Kit was coordinating the displays with three of the highly-trained duty technicians.

Satellite aerial photographs of large sections of rolling hills covered with brush, bisected with a river, were visible. The image changed and reappeared as a photo of approximately eight hundred acres. Details such as roads and buildings were discernible.

"What's up, Kit?" inquired Dare as he walked up.

A serious Kit concentrated on the phone conversation, held up his index finger signaling—hold on a sec—to Dare, and then pointed at an unused handset on the console and mouthed, "Line four."

He picked up in mid-conversation as Herbert Richards continued, "...target of interest identified by our contact in Mexico will be the small Dodge box truck with the refrigeration unit. It will be the second vehicle crossing the river and is following a black Humvee."

The fourth photo from the series emerged and the vehicle in question was clearly visible. A third hung back and remained across the river.

"Eyes on target," confirmed Kit.

Dare nodded agreement.

As the fifth photo was displayed, the two vehicles were stopped an estimated eight hundred yards from the river.

"We confirmed the location to be Webb County, Texas. We're running a check of tax records to determine ownership and cross-referencing tax returns to determine identity of all known residents," explained the GS-11.

Damn, these guys are thorough, Dare thought.

"How are you coming with the isolation and compression on the target activities?" Kit asked.

Good question, mused Dare. *These are interesting shots of people crossing the border illegally, but it happens every day. Over 200,000 illegals come over each month. It seems like a little overkill to call the BEF in on one truck and Humvee.*

"Sorry, back with you now. We have a sped-up version of the event, magnified to point five meters. It takes a while, even with our Crays."

Dare comprehended the capacity of the powerful Cray super computers. *What the hell is this all about?*

As they watched the six foot monitor, the Hummer turned off the intermittent path and vanished beneath a tree. The refrigerated Dodge box truck turned around in a wide spot and pointed back toward the river. One man from the Humvee proceeded to the back of the truck. A group of people disembarked from the back and took off their clothes as the truck started moving slowly back down the trail toward the river. The man then raised what appeared to be a rifle and the group of naked people fell to the ground.

"Freeze Frame," ordered the CEO of the Black Eagle Force.

The jerky Keystone Cops antics on the speeded up clip froze as ordered.

"Herbert, this is Dare Phillips on the line. What the hell are we watching?"

Herbert Richards quickly responded, "I'm sorry, Mister Phillips, I didn't realize that you had picked up...As I told Mister Kitaen, elements believed to belong to the *Veintiuno de Abril Negro* are growing increasingly dangerous and our citizens on the border are at risk."

"What the hell kind of terrorist group is that? Were those Americans that we just saw gunned down? What do you want us to do about it?" For the first time, Dare felt the responsibilities of leading the Black Eagle Force were going to tax him to the limit.

The GS-11 recognized frustration in his voice. "Mister Phillips, again I am sorry. The name of the group in English is Black April 21st. It refers to the perceived massacre of Mexican troops under General Santa Anna back in April, 1836. The Mexican rout and the Battle of San Jacinto is still a matter of lost pride in some ultra nationalists' minds."

Dare couldn't believe what he was hearing. "1836! You are joking, right?"

The line was silent for a moment. Herbert spoke again, "No, sir, we never joke at ICE...By the way, those people murdered from the truck are believed to be Mexican and Guatemalan nationals...We don't know who killed the shooters."

Dare was more confused than ever, but he tried his Marine best to conceal it. "Someone killed the shooters?" he asked in a controlled voice.

"Oh, sure. Roll the rest of the footage."

Dare and Kit watched in awe as the fast-forward version of the gun battle between Mike Hermann and the evil minions of the Black April group unfolded.

The recording stopped just before Mike and the Humvee reached the Rio Grande. Kit turned to Dare and pointed at the picture of the man in the yellow Caterpillar gimme hat. "And who the hell is that?"

"Damn," said Dare to the ICE man. "Bad Karma day at Black Rock for the visiting team."

"No, sir," came the reply from the fed. "The location name is not Black Rock. They just handed me information on the location of the incident. It's called Eagle Nest Ranch."

Not only do they not joke at ICE, they wouldn't know one if it bit them on the butt, thought Dare.

"Got any info on the residents of said ranch?" asked a slightly amused Kit.

Richards nodded to his technician. "Certainly. I'm sending all the related driver's license and passport photos over now. We have twelve positive hits for that address."

The government IDs filled the screen. Dare and Kit continued to scan the faces until they both stopped on a blond-haired, ice blue-eyed Captain in an official US Marine Corps photo. Kit started to raise a finger to point at the one he thought could have led the counterattack against the murderous Mexican operatives.

Kit was surprised as Dare recognized the man in the photo. "I'll be damned."

EAGLE NEST RANCH
BLAZE'S ELECTRONICS LAB

"Dammit to hell!" cursed Blaze as the *Code Red* message from her father came over the secure intercom.

She turned off the power to the three gigawatt laser on the test bed as she secured the lab. She hated being interrupted in her private research, even more so when it had to do with ranch security. Her flaming red hair was pulled back in a pony tail which swayed from side to side as she removed her protective goggles, dropped them on the desk near her laptop computer and walked quickly to the gun vault.

Her dad always believed in the old Boy Scout motto, *Be Prepared*. However, it had been her brother Michael's idea to install a secure inter-phone system to all fifteen of the outlying ranch buildings. He had become an expert in planning for contingencies while in the Corps and wisely pre-positioned secure weapon storage lockers and comm gear in all of them.

Opening the keyed vault, she stepped in and slipped on the lightweight A-500 body armor and pulled the Velcro tabs tightly. As Mike had demonstrated dozens of times, she snapped two mag carriers and her ranch VHF radio to the Molle vest, and then wrapped the heavily loaded combat belt around her tiny waist. The sturdy nylon clasp at the front clicked when it closed—she picked up her scoped AR-15, pulled the charging handle back and released it. The bolt slammed home with a solid *thunk*, and then she flipped the fire control selector and safed the weapon.

Lastly, she picked up the Steiner 7x50 Marine binoculars and a Leica laser range finder. Almost ready to rock and roll, she tuned the ranch radio to 303.0 as instructed and adjusted the squelch so that the volume was correct in her earpiece. "Songbird ops ready."

Mike heard the message over the radio as he crested the last ridge leading down to the Rio Grande. Overhead, the bright Texas sun was heating the ground enough to cause a shimmering mirage to blur the sight of the small truck as it slowly rocked back and forth over the uneven terrain.

"Tango truck nearing the river," Mike transmitted. "Anybody else have eyes on it?"

Tall cottonwood trees near the creek where the family mill had been rebuilt obscured the view to the west from the ranch house.

"Negative," came the report from Silver Eagle.

Dammit! Mike thought. *I'm the sole contact with the target. Don't know their strength, don't know their disposition or if they have reinforcements.* He could be running into an armed retreat with ambushes set up on either side. Discretion would be to lay back and follow at a safe distance.

Mike grabbed the seat belt and clicked it home. He took a deep breath and stomped the accelerator to the floor. The turbo charger took two seconds to spin up to its max operating range. The big diesel roared to life, causing all four tundra tires to spin on the soft caliche rocks.

Slowly at first, then rapidly picking up speed, he careened down the rugged trail bouncing and kicking up small rooster tails of debris and dust behind each tire as they made intermittent contact. Mike clutched the AK with his right hand and tried to focus on the truck getting larger and larger in the hole where the windshield had been.

Enrique Morales and his cousin Jose sat in relative comfort in the air-conditioned cab as they crawled down the last limestone ridge. They had their stereo on one of the popular Nuevo Laredo stations and were singing along with Luis Miguel. Life was good. In two minutes they would be back in Mexico and pick up their $500 fee for delivering the merchandise to Texas.

Jose jumped a foot to his left when the screaming SUV flashed by less than six inches away from his right arm. He cursed in Spanish as it slid broadside in their path and stopped. "*Jaime tu puto!*"

Enrique slammed on the brakes, throwing his cousin violently into the windshield—resulting in a major concussion. Jose slumped to the floor like a blowup doll with a burst seam as Enrique tried to find reverse on the column stick-shift.

The sight of the Anglo kicking the door open and aiming the suppressed weapon at his head caused him to miss Reverse and land in Park. He stomped the gas pedal to the floor.

Oily gray smoke billowed out of the single exhaust as the valve stem seals leaked dirty 30 weight oil from the heads into the hot exhaust ports.

Mike quickly stepped around the open door and moved out of the crush zone if the truck were to lurch forward. The muzzle never moved from Enrique's forehead. *No use trying to yell over that engine noise.* He signaled to Enrique to kill the engine by drawing his hand across his throat.

The signal worked well with most people used to military signals. Unfortunately, Enrique took it literally, like most of the other men in the gang of thieves and murderers would. The sign to terminate or kill put his fear factor into overdrive as he panicked and looked at the transmission selector.

He immediately saw his previous error and yanked the shifter back down into Reverse. With his foot still on the accelerator, the amount of engine torque available was three times what the old worn transmission could take. Seals blew out and the torque converter split at the rolled seam between the two half-shells. Hot transmission fluid sprayed out from under the truck like rain from a thunderstorm. This truck was never going anywhere.

He slowly realized there was no way out and turned off the tortured engine. Enrique raised both hands and tried to look innocent as he faced Big Eagle.

Mike gave him a come here signal with his left hand.

Enrique pushed the door open, swung his legs out carefully and slowly slipped out of the seat and into the dusty roadway.

Damn, he thought, *if I only had gotten another sixty yards, I'd be home free.* He felt the Colt 1911 in .38 Super stuck in the back of his dirty jeans. *This stupid gringo somehow got Jesus' gun and killed Jaime and Roberto. I'm gonna make him fuckin' pay for that.*

"*Déme su pistola con cuidado, puto*," came the order from the tall Yankee.

Enrique showed no emotion, but inside, he was smiling, *I'll give you my pistola, you gringo piece of dog shit!* Like a mongoose striking at a King cobra, he leaped to his left. His right hand snaked behind him, pulling the Colt from its hiding place. In one fluid, lightning fast move, the nickel-plated gun was pointing at the spot where Mike stood.

Flame erupted from the barrel as the sound of the shot echoed off the cottonwood trees lining the river.

If Mike Hermann were a cobra, Enrique Morales would still be breathing. But he matched the Mexican driver's movement. By the time the bullet reached where Mike had been, six rounds from the Kalashnikov had already struck home. They were followed by two more before he could release his finger.

His last shot took out both gold-plated front teeth as he permanently wiped the smile off the face of the overconfident gangster. Mike landed heavily on his right side, face to face with his adversary. From eight feet away he could see the surprise frozen in the dead Mexican's brown eyes.

He got up, scanned the nearby brush, stepped over to the body and pulled the shiny Colt out of his still warm hand. Mike checked the chamber to confirm it was loaded. A press of the

Stienke & Farmer

release behind the trigger guard dropped the nearly full mag into his left hand. He glanced at it, smacked it smartly back home and stuck it inside his waist band of his jeans.

He looked into the open driver's side door and saw the collapsed figure of the man in the passenger side floorboard. The blood on his forehead gave him an indication of what had happened. "Don't you guys believe in seat belts?"

Mike moved around the front and carefully opened the door. There, on the unconscious man's hip, was the matching mate to the other 1911. *Nice.* Both Colts had *"El Jefe"* laser etched into the slides and a pair of real ivory grips embellished with the seal of Mexico carved into them.

He picked up the unfired Colt and stuck it in the other side of his Wranglers—which were beginning to get a little uncomfortable. Like most Texas cowboys, his jeans were cut as a second skin and did not offer much room for an two additional weapons. Mike reached to drag the injured Mexican coyote out of the truck.

Bullets tore into the windshield and shattered the glass of the door window. Small rectangular shards of tempered glass showered Mike like a blizzard of diamonds.

They didn't cut him, but the effect on his nerves was electric. He pushed away from the truck and rolled backward in a tight ball. He rose to a crouched position as the familiar sound of an AK on full auto came from across the river.

The front of the Dodge was taking multiple rounds from a shooter standing near another black Humvee. It had not been there thirty seconds earlier when he cleared the area. The sound

60

of the pistol must have alerted them that something was amiss on the Texas side.

Mike eased to his right where he knew he wouldn't be visible through the brush. He picked a small opening where he could take aim at the lone gunman.

He didn't give a hoot in hell for international law or protocol. Lining up the shooter in his sights, he moved the selector up to semi-auto and squeezed the trigger.

Across the Rio Grande, one of the Mexican gangbangers was trying to see the gringo in the yellow cap. He never saw the flash of the AK because it didn't flash and the sound was captured by the American made suppressor—he truly never knew what hit him. His knees buckled and he fell backwards onto the hot sand bank of the Rio Bravo Del Norte with a neat round hole in his forehead. The Mexican sun shone down directly into his dark brown eyes—but he never blinked.

Mike sprinted back to the still open driver's door and hit the ignition switch as a second black Hummer pulled into sight. The engine turned over and immediately roared to life. He threw it into drive. Two, then three black-clad shooters piled out of the two vehicles and fired in his direction.

The rounds from the two M-16s and the one Uzi tore the Dodge truck grill to shreds as Mike's Hummer, without most of its glass, lurched forward. As the gunmen shot at the fleeing vehicle, their view was interrupted by a small stand of mature cottonwood trees.

Their bullets tore into the trunks, leaving tiny unremarkable holes where they struck the rough white bark and disappeared. Only where they grazed a path nearly tangent to the tree did they penetrate fully and send chips of the soft wood flying.

The small stand offered cover for only twenty yards or so. If he could see the river, the shooters could see him. He hit the brakes and slid to a stop with the front bumper just even with the trees.

Mike used a trick he had used when hunting one winter—he left the engine running and exited silently, leaving the door open. He grabbed the AK once more and ran crouching to the north end of the stand of trees. Hiding behind a four foot wide cottonwood trunk, he leveled the iron sights on one of the gunmen and squeezed the trigger—one black figure fell.

He heard yelling on the far side of the river as the other two looked for him. Mike picked out another target—he fell. Bullets sprayed the trees nearby and kicked small bits of bark onto him as he took cover directly behind the trunk. The thought finally occurred to him that he was not wearing digital camo in this firefight. "Dumbass!" he muttered.

He couldn't believe he had made a rookie mistake that almost cost him his life. The yellow Caterpillar hat was screaming *shoot me* for one of the more dangerous gunfights of his life. He tossed it in the brush and slipped the selector to auto—moved ten feet left and found a small opening.

Mike took aim at the head of the last shooter visible over the hood of his Humvee. He fired a short burst and the head dropped out of sight. No clear hit. He took a short burst at the engine block of the Hummer on the left. Sliding back to his right, he had a shot at the front tire and fender of the second. He squeezed the trigger gently and nothing happened. Mike looked at the open bolt. "Fuck!"

EAGLE NEST RANCH
BLAZE'S ELECTRONICS LAB

Blaze could hear the automatic rifle fire coming from one mile west of her lab. No updates had come for several minutes. She picked up the mic. "Silver Eagle, Songbird, SITREP please."

Gunter Hermann cradled a Springfield M1A as he sat in a chair facing the river and wished he could be more specific. *Situation Report? Hell, I don't know any more than you.* "Songbird, Silver Eagle. Unsure of Big Eagle location. Sounds like automatic weapon fire from the old river crossing. Say your twenty."

"Leaving the lab for control. ETA in two."

"Roger that," Gunter acknowledged and went back to his binoculars. "I should have cut those damned trees twenty years ago."

At that moment, Mike was glad they were still standing. He made a break for the Hummer, tossed the empty rifle on the passenger floor and reached for the M-16. Two full mags were on the seat as he dropped the vehicle in gear. He floored it to take advantage of any confusion on the other side of the river and picked up the mic. "Silver Eagle, Big Eagle, over." He glanced back through the shattered rear window as he was passing the restored Hermann Mill. The two Humvees entering the river were followed thirty yards back by two long black 4WD Ford Excursions. *Damn! They called for reinforcements.* His heart sank a notch.

"Go ahead Big Eagle," said Gunter with heartfelt thanks in his voice.

"Break out the Barrett 50's, Dad...They're coming."

***

CHAPTER THREE

WARBIRD RESTORATION, INC.
NORTH TEXAS REGIONAL AIRPORT
DENISON, TEXAS
28 June

Dare Phillips could clearly recall the face of the Marine captain displayed on the large monitor in the BEF Command Center. He had really wanted to court martial the young captain for insubordination in Iraq. Dare had been in command of a squadron of *Super Cobra* attack helicopters involved in a firefight in Najaf when the brash young captain had called him a stupid son of a bitch on the tactical radio. Dare smiled as he remembered how mad he was back then.

Mujahideen Shiite fighters had taken up positions inside a supposedly sacred mosque. Two dozen of them had pinned down the two squads under Captain Hermann's direct command. Several Marines were wounded and two were dead. Dare had refused to fire missiles at the mosque as very clear ROEs had recently been issued to prohibit such actions.

Nobody—particularly a young Marine—was going to call Dare a stupid son of a bitch.

Dare hovered 200 feet above the dust-colored town after he had responded *Unable* to the request made by the unseen officer somewhere beneath him. Suddenly, one of the hundreds of former Iraqi military men, now a mujahideen, stepped out of the low mud-colored building connected to the west side of the gilded mosque and lined him up in the sights of his Russian made RPG-7.

He had fired and in less than a second, the tail rotor assembly of Dare's *Super Cobra* was history. Lift rotor torque forced his crippled bird to spin rapidly without the counter acting force of the tail rotor. The mortally wounded chopper had landed hard and flipped over on impact, slightly injuring both Dare and his copilot/gunner.

The rangy, broad shouldered Marine from Texas reacted quickly and dropped the insurgent who fired the rocket propelled grenade that took down Dare's craft. His three shot burst had bracketed the Iraqi's heart.

He was also the one who dragged Dare and his copilot out of the wreckage, even while under fire from the mosque. That action is where Mike was awarded his first Silver Star and his Purple Heart—yes, Dare Phillips knew the man in the picture well.

"Cowboy, what the hell have you gotten yourself into?"

"You know this guy?" Kit asked Dare.

"Oh, yeah…we go way back." Dare continued into the phone, "Mister Richards, Dare Phillips again. How old is this satellite feed we've been watching?"

He checked his watch. "Twenty minutes, give or take. I can get you some additional footage in thirty-five minutes when the next NERA satellite comes within range."

Dare thought for a second. The Near Earth Reconnaissance Asset, was not necessary. BEF had a Remote Piloted Vehicle drone setup in Laredo—it could be launched remotely and in place in under 15 minutes.

Kit watched the transformation come over Dare as his mind raced with the adrenaline one always gets before combat. He had seen it before in many other men, but this was the first time he had witnessed it in him.

Dare spoke quickly to Richards, "That won't be necessary. We'll deploy our own nearby resources. With your concurrence, BEF will take over operational responsibility of this incident, Standard Protocol on my mark. The time is now…1705 Zulu…Mark."

Back at the ICE intelligence facility, GS-11 Herbert Richards had noticed a change in Dare's voice. He had not personally met him, but knew he was thoroughly vetted all the way to Top Secret NOFORN clearance by the entire US federal security hierarchy.

Richards could not put his finger on the subtle change he heard, but it sounded something like steel was being forged on the other end of the phone. "Homeland Security concurs the transfer of operational responsibility, Standard Protocol, at 1705 Zulu…Standing by if you require further assistance."

Richards knew all the conversations were encrypted, time stamped, recorded and transcribed. As the phone connection terminated, he felt a slight tinge of pity for the people who would face the Black Eagle Force.

"Launch Manta, out of Laredo. Use these coordinates." Dare punched a button on the intercom and moved a cursor over the last satellite picture.

"Manta hangar doors already open as we speak," replied the Comm Center supervisor, Tom Tallman.

Tom had been an Army fixed-wing and helo pilot, but had been recruited by the BEF for his computer skills. He had a Masters degree in Computer Science from Stanford he had picked up while on active duty.

Like his name implied, Tom was, in fact, a tall man, and at six feet eight, too tall for US Air Force pilot training. The Air Force's loss was the Army's gain as he had been instrumental in the development of many of the Army's current remotely piloted vehicles.

"I want the Galaxy wheels up in one-five mikes. Full tactical teams, brief in the air." Dare turned to make way to his office to change into his combat gear.

"On it," came Kit's reply as he reached for the intercom button. "Eagles one, two, three and Raptor Team Four, saddle up. Galaxy departure in one-five mikes."

Red lights in all rooms began to revolve as the various members of the first four teams rushed preparations to launch.

Members of teams five and six aided where necessary to gear up the men and women of the first four.

Inside the two locker rooms, pilots and Raptors were rapidly making ready for the unknown mission. Kit had only given the barest of information—south Texas, going in hot and heavy.

Jill McElheney was the pilot in *Black Eagle* Two with Glenn "Bug" Haug as her WSO. Her six foot frame was long for a fighter pilot's, but she had bested many a man in her F-22 and had been involved in the development testing of the F-35 at the Tonopah Test Range. It took a lot of persuading from the BEF to pry her away from the test group.

Glenn was the elder statesman aviator of the group with over twelve years service with the BEF. A graduate of the United States Naval Academy, class of '78—his last duty before retiring as a Lt. Colonel from the Marine Corps was test flying the AH-1Z *Viper* variant of the *Super Cobra*.

Jill zipped up her flying boots, pulled down the legs of her black Nomex flight suit and closed the bottom zippers over the tops. She stood up and grabbed the lightweight Dragonskin body armor all BEF operatives were required to wear. One last look at the small mirror in the locker door and satisfied that her blonde pony tail was straight, she patted the letters on the top shelf for luck.

All the BEF members kept personal information letters in their lockers per company policy. They all knew well that they were the pointed end of a clandestine spear protecting American interests. Sometimes one or more of the members didn't make it home. BEF had not lost a operative in the last five missions. They were on a roll—for now.

She picked up her helmet bag and headed toward the crew elevator that would take her upstairs. "See you onboard," she said cheerfully to the only other female in the woman's locker room.

Karen "Hammer" Gibbs nodded. "Last one off is a rotten egg!"

Jill chuckled as she walked through the door. She knew Karen would be first out of the *Galaxy* in *Black Eagle* Three. She and the former USMC *Super Cobra* pilot had a friendly rivalry going.

Karen's shoulder length strawberry blonde hair would do without a pony tail. She simply swept it back with her hands and pulled her helmet on when it was time to saddle up.

Ben "Killer" Kilgore was Hammer's WSO. He had served with the Green Berets in Iraq, Afghanistan and Iran. His missions in Iran were so secret, even his BEF cohorts did not know the particulars. They did not have the *need to know*. The mission details which could compromise the other team members still active in the Army were locked inside him.

Frank Formby was already sitting the left seat of the C-5M *Super Galaxy*. He had external power connected to the aircraft and had begun programming the route of flight in the Flight Management System. Called "Gears" by all the BEF members, Formby had been Chief Design Engineer for Lockheed-Martin and was instrumental in the design of the F-35 at Skunk Works.

He still missed the thrill of operations as an AC-130 H *Spectre* gunship pilot, so when the man stopped by to discuss the Black Eagle Force, he listened.

A generous separation bonus from Lockheed-Martin was appreciated, but it wasn't about money anyway—in fact, both companies paid well. The BEF allowed him the chance to build a stealthy *Super Galaxy* and convert the M600/A—A for Attack—to stealth with all sorts of capabilities the active military services could not conceive of or only had in the planning stages.

Copilot and Mission Commander Kit Kitaen was a jack-of-all-trades, rated pilot, former Army Special Forces major and master parachutist and did them all equally well. He exercised responsibility for the overall planning and briefing of the entire team and provide eye-in-the-sky command responsibility of the teams.

CEO Dare Phillips would lead the aerial assault in *Black Eagle* One. Kit took his place in the right seat. "AC, ready to begin the Before Engine Start Checklist?"

Gears nodded and the two began. Nine minutes had elapsed since the mission launch notification was given.

EAGLE NEST RANCH

Blaze Hermann slammed on the brakes of her F-250 pickup. She mulled what she had heard. *Break out the Barrett 50s? Dammit, we only have two and Dad is not up to deploying one of them.* Her mind raced through a myriad of solutions when she concluded the best one was still on the test bed in the back of the lab.

Blaze put the truck in reverse and spun around. She hammered down on the accelerator as she flew back to her lab.

Nickola Tesla had always been her idea of a real scientist and inventor. His outlandish ideas about the very nature of electricity and magnetism brought him scorn from many of the so-called "leading minds" of his time.

The closed-minded individuals who scoffed at him were merely showing their own ignorance. Thomas Edison had viewed Tesla as a crackpot showman, but it was Tesla's AC ideas which ultimately eclipsed Edison's DC and was eventually used through out the entire world.

Even Guglielmo Marconi had to concede that his wireless radio was stolen from Tesla's earlier patents. Studying some of his theories about electromagnetism helped Blaze with her work on her revolutionary coil gun.

Ronald Reagan's ambitious Star Wars defense program had generated hundreds of millions of dollars for defense related ideas. The Navy's Rail Gun was initially conceived as a satellite killer or perhaps an antimissile defense system. It certainly was simple enough in theory. A ferromagnetic object, bullet or sabot, was subjected to powerful electromagnetic force fields surrounding a long set of parallel rails and a series of electric pulses flowing from one end to the other would accelerate the bullet to ultrahigh velocities.

Baseball great, Yogi Berra, once said, "In theory, there is no difference between theory and practice. In practice, there is."

Huge power supplies needed to propel large projectiles over long distances at targets moving five to fifteen hundred miles an hour made these Rail Guns immense and cumbersome, however, test models were already deployed on specialized Navy ships of the line. Accuracy was a problem as was electromagnet switching and heat—targeting radars and computers added to the misery.

The switching, Blaze discovered, could be handled via solid state powered-metal/oxide/semiconductor field-effect transistors or *MOSFET*, which could easily be switched off mid-pulse and semi-conductor-controlled rectifiers, *SCRs,* that released all stored energy before turning off.

She addressed the heat problem by using a superconducting nano-tube wire of her own invention.

The Soviet threat passed away with the USSR and funding dried up. Raytheon and GE were not interested in funding a white elephant by themselves, but work had continued through the DoD and functional units proved out in testing.

Blaze wasn't interested in knocking down satellites. She only wanted to kill coyotes endangering her family's Beefmasters at calving time without all the noise a rifle makes.

She studied some of Tesla's theories, read industry papers about the failures in the *Star Wars* program and built herself a miniature rifle version she called a *Coil Gun* that used a nonconductive metallic tube instead of rails.

She had clocked sixteen penny headless nails at just under 12,000 feet per second in the lab chronograph with three freshly charged nine volt lithium ion batteries. Her first attempt had burned through the steel bullet trap, the exterior concrete block wall and a two foot thick bois d'arc tree outside—she never recovered the nail.

Blaze mounted an EoTech holographic sight on it and put it aside until the next spring's calf crop.

The three batteries were still on the charger when she got to the lab. She scooped them up along with the coil gun and a box of modified sixteen penny framing nails.

WARBIRD RESTORATION, INC.
BEF CONTROL CENTER

Twelve minutes had passed since Dare Phillips gave the order to launch. The other members of the Black Eagle team, were in place.

"Roll call!" he shouted to the assembled force.

"Eagle One Ready!"

"Eagle Two Ready!"

"Eagle Three Ready!"

"Raptor Team Four Ready!"

Dare picked up the interphone to the cockpit and relayed the status to the MC. "All teams present and accounted for."

Kit replied, "Thank you, Dare."

The lead ground crewman, Bobby Don Stevenson, looked up at the cockpit. He raised his right arm straight up, his index finger extended from his closed fist and pointed at the ceiling of the hangar. He quickly rotated his forearm and finger in a counter clockwise rotation.

Gears nodded and turned to Kit. "APU start."

"Roger." Kit reached up and toggled the switch. He watched it rapidly spin up until the RPM was in the green band and exhaust temp stable. He flipped the electric power transfer switch and watched the cockpit lights flicker as they accepted the different source of power. "Cleared to disconnect external power."

Gears looked down to the crew chief and gave him the signal.

A lanky redheaded mechanic, dressed in his sky blue Warbird Restoration, Inc. coveralls standing fire guard near the roll-around fire extinguisher, acknowledged. He rushed to the side of the fuselage and tugged the heavy power cord from the receptacle and closed the access door.

The eight huge overlapping hangar doors slid back to their full open position. A large low-slung electric tug attached to the nose gear, slowly towed the massive bird clear of the cavernous building.

It was already starting to get hot back in the cargo compartment. Tiny beads of sweat had formed on the faces of some of the team members—it had nothing to do with the heat.

The lead mechanic disconnected the tug. He scanned the surrounding area and made circles in the air with his right index finger.

Gears nodded. "Starting Engine Checklist."

ICE OFFICES
US DEPARTMENT OF HOMELAND SECURITY
BETHESDA, MD

Herbert Richards was on the secure phone line with the Deputy Director, Ronald Diggers. "Yes, sir…No, sir…Yes, sir."

Richards dreaded these mandatory notification calls when the Black Eagle Force was called in. The deputy director hated the whole idea of civilian contractors eating into the budget he loved to squander like a drunken sailor on leave. Never mind the fact that the drunken sailor was spending his own money and Diggers spent the taxpayer's.

He alone spent over a half million dollars renovating his new office shortly after the 9-11 attack. In response, the previous administration turned the spigots on, making Homeland Security the biggest department in the federal government after the military. It was even bigger than the Marines and Diggers liked it that way.

Richards assured him that this clandestine operation would be a mopping up, after-the-fact procedure. There was no way they could get to south Texas in time to aid the locals.

He indeed would call back with all the information as soon as the BEF got boots on the ground. This would let the deputy director spin up the twin massacres of innocent civilians to epic proportions for the press, and more importantly, the House Appropriations Committee.

"Yes, sir, have a great day." Herbert hung up. He thought he was going to be sick.

Ronald Diggers knew just what to do. He was required to notify the office of the President of the United States when the Black Eagle Force was activated. His friend and like-minded liberal was serving as the Assistant National Security Advisor for the President. He picked up his receiver again and buzzed his secretary. "Get me Clarence Ogilsvey at the White House...I'll hold."

EAGLE NEST RANCH

Mike Hermann was eighty-five yards south of the main house lying prone on a rocky ledge with little vegetation. He had a great view from the ridge all the way to the river—he could even see the mill. The only areas he couldn't see well were north and east of the house.

Gunter covered the north side, Buddy, the horse trainer and Ron, the vet tech, were covering the road leading to the house. Neither had served in the military, but they were good shots and loyal to a fault.

The first Humvee he had seen crossing the river behind him, now lay dead and smoking sixty yards east of the mill. Mike had made it back to the ranch. He figured he won the Hummer fair and square in a gun battle and screw 'em if they wanted it back.

Nacho had carried the Barrett .50 cal out on the porch from its home under the elder Hermann's bed to Mike.

Big Eagle had taken no time in lighting up the bouncing vehicle with Armor Piercing Incendiary rounds. Two of the big

.50 cal bullets aimed at the hood and one to each side of the windshield had stopped the aggressors cold.

Actually, it was not exactly cold. The first round stuck the fuel pump and sprayed diesel under high pressure across the side of the block, as well as all over the dry land willow brush.

The second hit the steel cylinder head and the aluminum sheath between the copper jacket and the hardened steel core did what aluminum does under extreme pressure—it flashed. The diesel torched off, quickly spread and immolated the corpses of the four hired mercenaries—they never felt the flames.

Two more rounds punched through the windshield and kept on trucking, as they say. One passed through the driver, the left rear seat passenger and the rear fuel tank and buried in the relatively soft limestone of the road. The other flashed as it hit the windshield, blinding the shooter holding the Uzi across his chest.

The massive bullet hit the open bolt of the machine gun. The shattered steel sent shards into his neck as the .50 caliber bullet deflected down and tumbled. The big slug tore through him, taking out four inches of his spine before shredding through the seat and emasculating the man in the back seat. The bullet only had strength remaining to penetrate the right rear tire and circle inside four times before the tire deflated.

From the second Humvee driver's viewpoint, the first vehicle appeared to just halt and start smoldering. They assumed that it had lost its radiator, maybe the transmission, and therefore elected go around it.

The second vehicle was a crossing target for Mike. He didn't lead quite far enough as the driver saw what had happened to the other driver's head when it exploded and stomped the pedal to the floor. All four wheels grabbed and the black beast leapt forward like a cougar chasing a marmot.

Mike's first shot struck the pillar between the doors before it hit the man in the right rear seat and tore his right arm off at the elbow. He screamed like a woman and scared the man in the right front seat so badly that he bailed out at 20 miles per hour.

That choice was probably what saved his life as he sprinted toward the brush and dove over the five strand barb wire fence that ran along the river.

Mike made his corrections and pumped four more rounds into the passenger compartment insuring no more tangos were going to exit. The SUV slowed to a crawl and ended up lodged against a mesquite tree.

He kept an eye on the brush where the mercenary had hidden. He couldn't see him, but he knew he couldn't have gone far—the tall grass would give away any quick movement. Mike calmly released the empty ten round magazine and tossed it over his shoulder to Nacho. "Reload."

The diminutive Mexican took the empty and started pressing the long lethal rounds in one-by-one. His hands shook as he recited the Rosary again and again.

Mike picked up the spare magazine he had placed by the left leg of the bipod. He slapped it into place without looking and stared at the brush. Sweat dripped from his brow as the sun beat down. He missed his hat, but could live without it. The only thing shiny about him now were the two Colts laid out to his right side.

The earplugs he had always tied to the scope were snug in each ear—the multi-chambered muzzle brake was more than noisy. It was not unlike a 105mm howitzer next to your head.

Mike made sure everyone was well aware of its damaging effect on their hearing. The biggest disadvantage to earplugs was you don't hear everything around you. He didn't notice when Blaze jogged up and knelt down ten feet behind him.

"Here goes nothin." Mike touched off a round at the suspected gunman's hiding space.

His sister screamed at the horrendous report. "Ow!" She duck-walked up to him and kicked his leg. "You could have warned me, you big oaf!"

Mike was momentarily distracted from the river, but a flash of movement caught his eye.

The round had struck six inches left of the prone man. *Enough of this shit…ain't worth it.* He leapt up and dived head first off the fifteen foot high bluff into the muddy water of the river. The cool water was only thirteen inches deep, a very unlucky number for the late cartel hired gun.

Mike rolled over on his left shoulder and scowled. "Get your bubble butt down! Now!"

The urgency in his voice startled her into action as she lay down prone to his left.

"You can't stay here without ear protection," he said in a more normal tone.

"What?" She looked confused.

"I said…" He stopped and pointed at the yellow foam plugs in his ears.

Mike looked back at Nacho and pointed at his earplugs and then at the green metal ammo can lying between them. He reached inside and picked up another sealed plastic bag with yellow plugs, tossed them to Blaze.

"Bubble butt! Who you callin' bubble butt? Numbnuts."

Mike pulled his right earplug and picked up the handheld radio Nacho had brought him. "Silver Eagle, Big Eagle, do you have eyes on the black Excursions?"

"Negative, Big Eagle, they split up after the Hummers were hit. One is on the far side of Bacerro Creek, the other on this side. Both heading east, lost them in the brush. I think they're trying to flank us."

"Copy that. Keep me posted. Out."

Two clicks came in rapid succession indicating Gunter had received Mike's transmission.

Mike turned to Nacho. "Get Ron over at the horse barn and go check out that one down there against the tree. If it's still operational, bring it back. Don't forget to call to identify yourself before you drive toward the house. Leave the bodies for the buzzards...Be careful. I don't want my big brother gettin' killed."

He swallowed hard and then smiled, trying not to show his fear. Nacho was ten years old when the Hermann's took him in the big house after his mother had died of cancer. He helped raise the young Mike who was only three at the time.

He still smiled when the six feet-four inch tall Mike called him his big brother. He grabbed the AR-15 lying beside him and drew himself to his full five feet-five inches. "See you in a few minutes and you be careful little brother."

Nacho looked around and ran a zigzag path to the horse barn.

Mike picked up the radio and called to Ron, "Equine, Big Eagle."

"Go ahead Mike. This is Equine. Come back."

Mike shook his head. Obviously the lessons of radio discipline had not been taken to heart by all the ranch staff. No matter. ComSec was the least of their problems.

Two black Ford Excursions full of armed drug gang muscle were roaming the ranch and hell-bent on revenge. Nobody knew where the big SUV's were and that was a problem—so was shooting at the first thing that moved. Friendly fire was just as lethal as enemy fire.

"Be advised Little Cheese moving to your location," Mike continued.

"Uh, roger that, Mike...I mean Big Eagle."

Ron covered the door with his AR-15 and swung the muzzle clear when he saw Nacho enter. He waved at Buddy at the far end of the barn. The young horse trainer jogged over to the other two men. "What's up, boss?"

Nacho explained Mike's orders and Buddy's forehead wrinkled in concern. "Ya'll are gonna leave me here by myself?" The twenty-six year old animal lover had never liked the idea of shooting anything live. The idea someone would try to shoot and kill him sent an involuntary shiver up his spine

"Buddy, we'll be back in five minutes. I promise," the young ranch manager reassured him.

"Make it four."

C-5M SUPER GALAXY
NORTH TEXAS REGIONAL AIRPORT

"November two-zero-zero-six Bravo, clear for takeoff on three four left," came the tower clearance as the matte black C-5M taxied southward toward the approach end on the parallel runways.

"Takeoff checklist," Gears called out as Kit acknowledged the clearance.

The latest version of the C-5M in US military usage required one flight engineer, but the BEF carried two. Crew chief and lead flight engineer, Barry "Partsman" Meadows, read the required items for power settings, flap position, stabilizer trim settings and transponder as the pilot, copilot and number two flight engineer, Mad Max Matthews, responded in sequence. Everything was checked and verified by another crew member.

Gears, turned the tiller on the left side of the cockpit to steer the generic looking bird into position as he gently pushed all four throttles up to takeoff power. The four General Electric turbofan engines spooled up.

Behind the craft, winds equal in speed to that of a tornado tossed small gray and black pebbles crazily across the weather-worn asphalt overrun. The huge black *Galaxy* rolled forward, slowly at first, then with faster and faster acceleration as the centerline stripes passed directly beneath the nose wheels.

Formby took his hand off the steering tiller and his feet took over the directional control. His left hand held the yoke in its neutral position while his right hand remained on the throttles in the case of an aborted takeoff.

Partsman placed his hands under the plastic throttle knobs—he could tell just by the vibration if an engine was even a hair out of sync.

Kit scanned the instruments while cross-checking the runway environment for safety. Mad Max monitored all the hydraulic, pressurization and electrical systems.

"Engines in the green," Partsman announced.

"All systems go," Mad Max added.

As the speed increased, the 525,000 pound craft slipped the surly bonds of earth once again. Total takeoff roll had been 6,200 feet.

"Gear up," said Gears.

Kit leaned forward, pulled the tire-shaped handle out and then up to its *gear up* position. Amber lights came on the three gear position indicators as the retraction progressed. The gear locked into the up position and the doors closed.

Back in the rear, Dare looked at his watch. Sixteen minutes to wheels up from launch command. He just hoped it was fast enough.

Jill McElheney breathed a little easier now that cooler conditioned air was flowing in the upper deck crew area. Years of training and simulated combat in the skies over Nevada had shown that she was a topnotch fighter pilot. She was one of the best there was. However, she had never flown a single sortie in actual combat. She was not afraid. Jill had confidence in herself—but still…

"November two-zero-zero-six Bravo, turn left two-two-zero and contact departure control on 129.2." The tower controller took a sip of his diet Coke.

The black bird rolled left to pick up the new heading as the flaps retracted fully up.

"Zero-six Bravo, good day," came the response from Kit.

The controller pulled the paper flight-following strip out of its plastic holder and dropped it in the small gray government issued waste basket. *That C-5 could sure use some paint*, he thought as he picked up a Hot Rod magazine and settled in for a boring shift.

On the tail of the *Galaxy*, a thin very high-tech polymer panel turned a flat black as all evidence of the required FAA registration numbers disappeared and the scarlet-and-gold BEF logo took its place.

***

CHAPTER FOUR

ICE OFFICES
US DEPARTMENT OF HOMELAND SECURITY
BETHESDA, MD

Ronald Diggers was on the phone with Clarence Ogilsvey at the National Security Advisor's office in DC.

"I know, Clarence. Wasn't high on my list either," Ronald Diggers replied.

"Who is the property owner where this little fracas is taking place?"

"Let me check…It's at the Eagle Nest Ranch in Webb county…Owned by the Hermann family since 1811."

"Don't tell me that a former Marine by the name of Michael Otto Hermann is the head of the clan," stated the Deputy Advisor.

"No, the registered owner is Gunter Hermann…but he is Michael Hermann's father."

"Son of a bitch!"

"Excuse me?"

"He was that arrogant bastard I told you about a while back. He smart-mouthed me when we were serving in Afghanistan…Me, a colonel and him just a damned captain. That, my friend, is a no-no. I tried to get the asshole canned, but he beat me to it and resigned his commission the very next day…Maybe it's time for some payback."

Diggers signaled to his secretary that he needed a fresh cup of coffee. The attractive blonde sitting across from his desk picked up his cup and walked to the door.

After she left, he continued, "What did you have in mind, Clarence?"

EAGLE NEST RANCH

Nacho and Ron cautiously approached the Humvee as Mike had directed. The glass was missing from all front and back side windows and it was obvious that none of the occupants would ever be a threat again. Mike's last five rounds had found their marks and left them suitable only for a closed casket funeral.

The two viewed the macabre scene momentarily then Nacho remarked, "Let's drag them the hell out and get back up to the house before their friends come looking for them." He pointed at the large hole left on the door frame from Mike's one miss, and then put his finger in it up to the second knuckle. "Big gun, no?"

Ron nodded as he pointed his rifle at the dead men inside. He was taking no chances. Nacho pulled the handle on the driver's door, reached across the body and released the seat belt latch. When he withdrew his hand, the right eyeball of the driver stuck to it and appeared to look at him. Nacho yelled and leaped back in surprise.

"What, what?"

Nacho could not answer—he turned to vomit forcefully. Ron grabbed the heavyset driver and tugged the man to the ground. He opened the rear door and pulled the blood-soaked AK off the dead man's lap and dragged the second body out. "Are you gonna help me or what?" He glanced at the recovering Nacho.

"I be okay in a minute." He wiped the edges of his mouth, crossed himself twice for the recently departed unredeemed souls and walked to the back.

They policed the hardware left by the would-be shooters. Ron elected to drive. Nacho was upset that he had forgotten to call the ranch house to let them know who was driving the black beast. Luckily for him, his big little brother was watching through his binoculars as they recovered the vehicle.

"Back it in directly in front of the south hitching post," Big Eagle called on the ranch radio frequency.

Nacho was embarrassed, but Mike didn't made a big deal about it. He was too busy trying to figure out how to keep from dying with two Ford Excursions full of gangbangers and contract killers roaming Eagle Nest.

HUGHES 500 HELICOPTER
OVER MEXICO

Three miles west of the river crossing, a Hughes 500 jet helicopter circled at 1,500 feet above the brushy terrain. The pilot was a former Mexican Army Captain who found a much better paying job as the personal pilot for the *Tres Locos* drug gang. The cartel was into all manner of organized crime and black market dealings—murder, kidnapping, drugs, smuggling illegal immigrants, prostitution, human trafficking and armed robbery.

The *Tres Locos* had started out as three crazy friends, but once the money started pouring in from smuggling pot and cocaine across into Laredo and San Antonio, the friendship had gone away.

Infighting over how to split the profits ended up with a knife fight between Raoul and Marco. Raoul won the fight. Luis killed him a week later when the opportunity presented itself.

Luis Torrejon could easily be recognized by his two tattoos. One was the black teardrop under his left eye. He had it done the day after Marco died. Luis loved him like a brother—for good reason. Unbeknownst to either, they were both the sons of Jorge Montelban, a whore-mongering drunkard with a bad temper and an eye for the ladies.

Jorge had sired his two sons three weeks apart one summer, just before a jealous husband caught him in the act and put a bullet in the big man's brain. The young boys became best friends on the mean streets of Nuevo Laredo.

Raoul moved to the wild border town at age fourteen and fell in with the petty thieves. They were like the three musketeers of crime. One of them came up with the name *Tres Locos* while on a tequila power drunk. Each claimed it was his idea, but it didn't really matter. They had stopped into a tattoo parlor and all three got LLL inked forever into the left side of their necks.

90

After Luis killed Raoul, the LLL tattoo started to piss him off. After all, he had to look at it every day. Since one of the most famous bull fighting venues in all of Mexico was held in Torrejon, Luis decided to cover the LLL tattoo with a large bull head. The menacing head led to a new nickname—*El Toro*. It fit quite well and fed Luis' enormous ego. He stood six foot-one, tall for his race, and weighed in at 225 pounds. With angry black, soulless eyes, a low flat forehead and a unibrow above his eyes, all he needed was a pair of horns to complete the picture.

Eventually Nuevo Laredo was run by the large gang *El Toro* headed. If the Chief of Police didn't play nice, he was killed in front of his family. If the gang couldn't hit the Chief fast enough, they killed one of his kids and dropped the body off at the station at night.

Mexican Federal Police and the military knew about the gang, but due to the endemic corruption in both organizations, they were unable to move against him effectively. Informants always told Torrejon about planned raids, with the result that he often created elaborate ambushes that resulted in massive casualties.

The quick $25,000 job to drop off a dozen illegals who had paid passage to San Antonio, turned into a nightmare for *El Toro*. He had agreed to take the stupid job as a subcontractor for Javier Cojone.

This massive goat rope had already cost him $200,000 in vehicles, weapons and fifteen trusted thugs. Hell, he could always get more. Mexico had millions of men who would do dirty work for money. But the gringo sons-of-bitches had embarrassed him by killing three of his men on Mexican soil.

Luis owned that part of Mexico and would pay any price to have the head of that blonde-haired bastard. Every stinkin' person on that piss-ant cattle ranch would pay.

Luis was on his cell talking to his boy back in Nuevo Laredo.

"Yes *Patron*, I'll see to it personally. Six heavy trucks...Yes, sir, I got it. You want the Russian rocket propelled grenades?...Yes sir," Martine Aguilar said.

Luis was steaming. "And forty men! With rifles. Not *pistolas*! You got that Martine? Call Colonel Garcia on his personal number. See if you can borrow an armored personnel carrier."

"*Si Señor*!"

"Do not fail me Martine!" He slammed his cell phone shut and looked out the acrylic bubble. "Where the hell are my men in the Fords?"

EAGLE NEST RANCH

Gunter Hermann looked as if he had aged ten years in the last hour. He hobbled across the broad cypress floor beams laid down by his ancestors almost two centuries before and the thought of his family once again being in a war on their own ranch hung heavy on his heart.

He had only fired four shots, two at one Humvee and two at the other. The Excursion had been too far out and partially covered by the natural curve of the sloping terrain between the ranch house and the mill.

The Springfield .308 suddenly didn't seem like enough to protect his family under rapidly deteriorating conditions. He

92

understood how his forebearer had felt facing Santa Anna's onslaught.

Mike came back downstairs when Nacho and Ron entered the house. Blaze remained upstairs in the northwest corner bedroom and kept a watchful eye out for the two SUVs. Nacho cradled the four bloody weapons recovered from the Humvee.

Mike looked at them. "Drop the mags, take 'em outside and hose 'em down. There's a can of WD-40 under the sink...leave 'em on the kitchen table.

"Ron, get back over to the horse barn. You and Buddy cover the main road. Call if you see anything...Nacho you're with us on the south wall." Mike could see a little fear in both men's eyes. "We can do this, guys...trust me."

They glanced at each other and headed for the door.

"We won't let you down," Ron said as he stopped and turned to look at Mike and Gunter.

Gunter looked at his strapping son with a growing sense of pride. Both shared Marine backgrounds—Gunter had served multiple tours in 'Nam as the conflict was winding down, but this was the first time he had ever seen his son under fire.

Three combat tours tended to forge a man who did not fold when the going got tough.

"Son, who the hell are these guys and what's your plan?"

Mike shook his head. "Pop, all I know is these guys are ruthless killers. Don't know their overall operation, but I suspect they're cartel coyotes who murder their cargo once they get 'em across the river...They shot at me when I stumbled onto them on the Trail of Misery...Then all hell broke loose.

"Why they had so God damned much firepower is beyond me."

"Doesn't make much sense. Does it? Were they all on this side of the river?"

"Uh uh, they had several vehicles hanging back on the other side. They could have been from La Espaeranza down on Highway 2 between Nuevo Laredo and Reynosa…not sure. Maybe they were backup bodyguards for some higher gangbanger…Got here pretty damn quick…Their methodology reminds me of al-Qaeda…the way they butchered the folks they brought across in the truck."

Gunter frowned. *Organized criminal gangs with al-Qaeda methodology. Narco terrorists…Outfuckingstanding.*

Both men had the same thought simultaneously. *These guys have to coordinate actions somehow. Must be radios—cell phones are too spotty along the river.*

"The scanner!" they blurted out together.

C-5M SUPER GALAXY
OVER LAKE BUCHANAN, TEXAS

The BEF C-5M, nicknamed *Mama Bird,* was cruising at 20,000 feet and passing over Lake Buchanan, north of San Antonio. Dare got up from his gray leather recliner in the upper deck of the craft and walked forward to the comm station.

The team radio operator, Beth "Sparky" O'Neil, former Petty Officer, USN, was almost as good with radio and satellite communications and handling the RPVs as Tallman—she had to be. Sparky was responsible for keeping the field teams communications with Tom back at the Control Center open and active. She was a petite, curly-haired black girl with a body that would stop a train. Standing only five-one to Tom's six-eight, the team sometimes referred to them as Mutt and Jeff.

"Sparky, check *Manta* status with Tom. Should be able to transfer control to your console by now," Dare said.

"Aye-aye, sir."

Even though she was no longer on active duty in the Navy, habits were hard to break. She punched in the code for BEF's secure band and adjusted her mic. "Eagle base, Mama Bird, how copy?"

"Five by five, Mama Bird," replied Tom. "Be advised Manta is on station and should be in your control range. Eyeballs on two black Hummers parked in front of a large stone house near several other outbuildings. Assume that is the ranch house, it corresponds to previous satellite telemetry. We have one large SUV at 800 meters east-northeast of main building and a second, four miles north-northeast. Target identifiers are locked on both."

Dare stood silent. The worst case scenario had happened. The bad guys had apparently taken the ranch house. "Show me what you've got."

Sparky tapped a few keys on the keyboard and the sixty inch screen over her station picked up the satellite repeater feed from *Manta's* position in a racetrack pattern orbit over the ranch. "Control, Mama Bird has good feed from Manta. Request transfer control this station."

"Copy request, Mama Bird, you have her."

Tom keyed three alpha numeric characters and hit *Enter*. A pop-up screen appeared and confirmed the transfer.

"Transfer received," Sparky replied.

As much as Dare hated to witness what he feared was happening 120 miles south of his location, he requested a zoom-in to the ranch house proper—a figure was seen through the upstairs window on the northwest side of the house, but the two vehicles were partially blocked by the two-story structure, "Fly wider south and give me a view on the east side."

Sparky, sat at the RPV pilot station next to sensor and weapons operator, Lanie Hayes. She rolled the small joystick right and picked up a heading of 180 degrees. Lanie had a similar joystick that controlled the sensitive visual, infrared and laser designator units on the black RPV. Orbiting overhead at 35,000 feet, the *Manta* was all but invisible to anyone on the ground.

Thirty seconds went by—Sparky rolled the drone left and turned the autopilot on to establish another racetrack with the ranch house in the center.

"Can you get me tighter?" asked Dare.

"Sure, let me know when it's close enough," Lanie confirmed.

The camera zoomed in on the two Humvees and it was clear they both had been shot up. *He gave it to them good. Made the bastards pay before they got him.*

As he mourned the loss of the man who had saved his life, a lanky figure wearing a faded red Marine T-shirt and jeans walked out of the house and opened the door to one of the Hummers.

"Closer."

Lanie zoomed on in until the figure almost filled the giant frame. His closely cropped blonde hair was obvious.

"Kiss my ass!…Shoulda known."

"Should have known what, sir?" Lanie asked.

"Some Marines are just too tough to die…and he's one."

EAGLE NEST RANCH

In the one-hundred-ninety-one-year-old German style ranch house, the VHF scanner was constantly switching frequencies from airline traffic inbound and outbound from Corpus Christi, to San Antonio Center and to military traffic in Randolph Air Force Base.

Occasionally it would stop at a broadcast in Spanish, but most of that could be attributed to Mexican pilots in the vicinity of Nuevo Laredo and the Mexican army base some 20 miles southwest of the ranch.

The one-hundred-foot-tall tower the Hermann's had set up on the ridge north of the house was great for ranch communications on a dedicated frequency, but it was working against them in scanning mode. Great ideas don't always bear fruit quickly.

Mike had the idea of checking on the last captured Humvee to see if it was also operating on the old ranch radio frequency.

Once back inside, he approached Gunter with his plan. "These guys are transmitting and receiving on 126.6."

"So, what are we going to do, son?"

"We set up a ranch handheld radio by the base station here. Leave the it on 303.0 upper side band and set the handheld to

126.6…If they transmit, we'll be able to monitor 'em…the same in the Humvee."

"You're planning to go mobile after them?"

"Can't stay here and do nothing, Dad. You know this house is not really defensible from a concerted attack with modern firepower…Hell, it was built to defend against arrows.

"Don't know what we're up against yet. Could be as many as twelve or fourteen men in those Excursions…could have RPGs…What do you think?"

It had been quite a while since anyone asked him for his military input. Gunter thought for a few seconds to put his words into a coherent pattern. "You say two of the dead guys had LLL tattoos on their necks and one was wearing a current Mexican uniform?…My money would be on a heavyweight drug cartel running the show with rogue soldiers workin' part time as mercs."

Mike nodded, and then Gunter continued, "One Excursion was headed east on the far side of Bercerro Creek. He can't cross it above the lake because of the limestone cliffs…until he works back west onto the Trail of Misery. That's six miles and the trail doesn't cross a ranch road this way for another four…It's at least eight miles back around until they could get to the commercial smoke house and processing plant."

"Got all that, Dad. Ralph and the crew in the plant will call us if they see anything…They're all well armed…What's your point?"

"All right…We don't know where the other vehicle is. This place is too damned big and has too much cover for you to drive around looking to get your ass shot off. That'd leave us with only three to cover all four directions and the house will fall for sure."

He paused. "Like you said, it was built to defend against Indians…For all we know the tangos could be closing in on us right now with encrypted tactical radios in their helmets."

The planning session was cut short by a series of three shot bursts of M-16 fire from the south side of the horse barn. The assault had begun…

***

CHAPTER FIVE

C-5M SUPER GALAXY
SOUTH OF SAN ANTONIO

Kit left the copilot's seat and was replaced by Partsman. He headed aft to the cargo bay. It was his responsibility to plan and brief the operation. Using the latest RPV intelligence photos, he could pinpoint the location of the only black vehicles on the ranch.

The Eagle Nest Ranch vehicles were white with a *Flying Eagle* painted on the door. The same logo was familiar to hundreds of thousands of shoppers who purchased their organic beef, German sausages, smoked turkeys and hams.

Tom had tagged the tango vehicles electronically and any time one was in view of the optical camera of *Manta*, an icon would appear on the monitor screen. As the camera panned away, the laser identifier would lock on to it until the visual camera came back around.

Kit addressed the BEF teams, "Dare, we'll deploy the 600s at five thousand feet, standard V formation, Eagle Two on the right, Eagle Three on the left and your Eagle One in the center. Make your approach from the west to take advantage of the setting sun.

"Formation breaks at 3,000 feet...Eagle Two takes the northernmost target at four miles. Three has the one 800 meters east-northeast. Do not, I repeat, do not engage any Humvee unless authorized by Eagle One.

"Dare, your job is to proceed to the ranch house and make contact with its defenders...Any questions so far?"

"What about Raptor Four?" asked Leroy Poole.

"I was just getting to you," Kit continued. "Your team will HALO from 12,000 feet after Eagle One makes contact. We don't want you mistaken for tangos."

"Mister Kitaen. There's something you need to see," came the call over the intercom.

Kit knew Lanie would not interrupt him in a briefing unless absolutely mission essential. "Hold that thought. I'll be right back," he said to the assembled crew gathered on either side of *Eagle* One.

Space was at a premium in the crowded cargo bay. Kit moved upstairs to the monitor above Lanie's position as she zoomed in to a tighter picture of the south side of the horse barn. *Manta* was circling at the southernmost position of its oval racetrack shaped orbit.

He watched as four figures, clad in olive drab BDUs, hugged the south wall of the one hundred and sixty foot long building. The lead shooter stepped into the fifteen foot wide opening at the end of the breezeway extending through the entire structure.

He appeared to fire a short burst then moved quickly to his left, clearing the door. The man fired another burst from the left side of the doorway and motioned to one of the other three to join him.

Kit spoke into his interphone, "AC, range to target?"

Gears glanced at his FMC. "Sixty miles."

Kit's mind raced as he weighed his options. Ten minutes is a lifetime in a firefight. The only thing he could do to cut the time down was launch the *Eagles* early.

Everyone felt the C-5M slowly enter a descent. They knew they were getting closer to combat with each passing second.

Kit called back again to the cockpit, "Best forward speed, Gears. Keep it at the barber pole. We're gonna launch as soon as the Eagles are hot." He switched to PA. "Change one, people. Load up and make the birds hot. We launch ASAP. Team Three do not wait to form up. Attack when in range. Same for Two and One. Ranch house is engaged...Let's saddle up."

EAGLE NEST RANCH

Buddy Williams was tired of standing near the south end of the horse barn and had started to walk back to the mid-point where a green injection molded chair would allow him to sit for a while.

He stopped to pet the head of Smoky, the bay mare in the third stall from the end. She snuffled nervously and he instinctively wanted to calm her. Buddy had a gentle way with animals and loved his work as much as any person could.

As he stroked her neck and whispered softly, six rounds from the Mexican Lieutenant Rudy Cardonez's M-16 tore through his body and ended his twenty-six years on earth.

Ron spun rapidly from his post in the east window of the office. He couldn't believe it when he peered around the corner and saw Buddy lying still in the concrete breeze way. A crimson stain grew on the gray concrete floor around him. They had just spoken five minutes before.

From the left side of the south end doorway, the Mexican lieutenant aimed his M-16 at the young Texan's head.

Ron reacted to the movement and snapped his AR-15 to his shoulder. Both men fired simultaneously and jerked back from the rounds splintering the wood near their heads.

The lieutenant blasted another quick burst down the alleyway and motioned a private to cross. As he did, Ron barely caught the last half-second of the man's crossing.

"Damn," he said in a low disgusted manner.

Two of the Mexicans had passed the end of the barn and were about to make a run for the house. Ron pulled the rifle to his shoulder and made ready.

A corporal got the cross signal—fast as he could, he covered the sixteen-foot gap toward the stone walls comprising the bulk of the horse barn. Ron blasted four rounds in rapid succession as the soldier crossed, striking him once in the right femur with a second round through both kidneys.

He went down hard and screamed in pain as his life's blood spurted from his torn femoral artery. The corporal tried to stem the blood flow with one hand as his other tightened firmly on the grip of his M-16—he swung the muzzle toward the terrified Ron.

"Ahhhhh!" he screamed as he fired the complete twenty-round mag in retaliation.

The muzzle climbed and many rounds impacted the rustic looking 2x12 rafters. A shower of splinters and dust fell from the north end of the barn.

Somewhere Ron found the courage to look out past the tattered wooden door frame of the office as the last of the rounds cycled through the rifle. He centered the soldier's head above the front sight and squeezed the trigger.

The Mexican corporal had made big plans for the $500 dollars he would earn. The $10,000 reward for the head of the big blond gringo would have bought him and his wife a new house. His pregnant young widow would never see either...

Blaze left her post in Mike's bedroom on the northwest corner of the house and headed across the hall to hers. It had a much better view to the east where sounds of the rifle fire were coming from.

She could still see to the north through the tall narrow windows. The renovations done back in the nineteen nineties included replacement of the original old float glass window panes with modern custom-made double-pane units. The Hermanns could raise the bottom windows and slide them up to a locked position and let fresh air in the house whenever the temperature allowed.

Blaze had missed the ambiance and history associated with the old float glass, but today she was thankful that the windows could be opened. She pulled a chair over from her desk, opened and locked the window facing the horse barn in the up position. She sat down, placed the forend of her *Coyote Gun* on the broad painted oak sill and waited.

NUEVO LAREDO, MEXICO

Martine Aguilar was nervous about the phone call as he punched in the number. His sociopathic boss was not going to be happy. Not by a long shot. Colonel Hernando Garcia was trying to shake him down for use of the Mexican Army Armored Personnel Carriers and wanted even more money than usual to have an additional squad of active duty troops man them in a daylight raid across the border. The risks were too high, Garcia had said. There was no element of surprise.

"$50,000 each? For a two hour rental? And five hundred dollars for each man in the squads? Who the hell does that slimy bastard think he is dealing with? *Pendejo*! I made him what he is! He thinks he is gonna screw me? Well, to hell with him!"

Martine shuddered until Luis continued in his normal voice, "Okay, Okay, call him back and tell him I will pay what he wants. I want the APCs here in forty minutes or the deal's off…You tell him. And tell him to meet Manny at the cut off from highway 2 north of La Esperanza…He will lead them across."

"Si, El Toro, I will tell him," Martine said weakly.

"Oh, and Martine," Luis said with no emotion at all.

"Yes sir?"

After Garcia's men deliver the APC's…I want you to kill him…Personally…Hang his body on the flag pole outside the base tonight."

It took all of his strength to force out the two words. "Yes, Sir." Martine's mouth was so dry, he could not swallow.

EAGLE NEST RANCH

"Equine come in." The radio crackled to life.

Ron reached for the handheld unit and as he brought it to his head, a soldier stepped around the left door frame and another stepped around the right side and fired. Bullets tore through the radio, Ron's right forearm, shoulder and leg. He fell hard into the concrete breezeway and didn't move.

"Two gringos down," the PFC announced over his headset.

A sergeant's team was in a flanking position some distance from the house in the brush. He smiled at the report on his radio as he led his three men silently toward the back of the old smokehouse.

One of the three men at the horse barn dropped an empty mag from his M-4 on the cream-colored caliche parking lot. The empty aluminum mag resonated with a tinny sound as it bounced twice and came to rest. They moved cautiously to the corner and the lieutenant took a quick peek around to study the layout. The only sound was the *ching* as another soldier slapped the bolt release on his carbine and the bolt carrier and plunger assembly flew forward.

Sweat from combat in ninety-six degree Texas heat ran down the three men's backs and turned their olive drab uniforms to near black.

The lieutenant had a plan. "There are two Humvees parked outside the house. If we stay low they can't see to shoot at us from the first floor. Lay down suppressive fire at the four upper windows. Once we get to the Humvees, we will use grenades to blow the door."

"Equine, Equine, Big Eagle, come in."

The silence was disheartening. *Two good men dead.* Mike looked at the horse barn with a deepening sadness. His planning had gotten men killed. Worst yet, his idea to park the Humvees near the house wasn't the best thing he had ever thought of.

As he looked out the window nearest the door, he could now see blind spots in his field of fire. *How can I forget every damn thing I learned in the Corps?* "Dad, stay away from the door. They'll probably use grenades or RPGs to breach it."

"Where you going?" Gunter called as Mike turned and ran toward the stairs.

"Blaze's room!" he said as he turned the corner at the stairs leading to the upper story.

Gunter kept a close watch on the front yard and suddenly realized why Mike left in such a hurry. "Oh, shit."

"Nacho! Your room…east side!" Mike barked as he topped the stairs and sprinted left down the long narrow hall.

The small ranch manager wanted to ask him what rifle to take. The big Barrett .50 was set up in a west window covering long open terrain down to the mill. There was an AR-15 against the wall. He had heard shooting from the other side of the house and no response from Ron's radio. Nacho hesitated, then chose the AR and headed across the hall to his room.

The sound of two M-16s and one M-4 carbine firing simultaneously broke the tomb-like silence. Glass shattered in all the upper east side windows as the three Mexican mercenaries raked the Hermann ranch house with automatic fire. Mike was still in the hall almost at the door to Blaze's room when he heard an unfamiliar sound, then another.

Ponk! Blap!

Came from outside. The rifle fire slowed from three full auto rifles firing—to one.

Mike turned the corner and continued running on into Blaze's room. He slipped slightly on the lavender embroidered throw rug at the foot of her bed as he tried to stop. She was seated in her oak desk chair in front of the window facing east, pointing a Remington bolt action rifle out the window at a target Mike could not yet see.

Ponk! Blap!

Mike moved directly behind her—he could see one large red blotch on the caliche drive at seventy yards and another blotch forming from a ten foot raggedly shaped red spray at fifty-five yards. In the closer mist, he could identify an M-16 on the crushed stone drive and shredded remains of what once was a Mexican Army Corporal.

He saw parts of boots, what could possibly be a hand and pieces of blood-soaked uniform. He watched as a human head in a green Kevlar helmet dropped from a height of thirty feet and bounced a few feet before coming to rest.

The lieutenant ran for his life through the open door on the west side of the horse barn. Mike and Blaze heard six shots in rapid succession, followed by four more evenly spaced, measured shots—then it was quiet.

"What the hell kind of gun is that?" asked Mike.

"It's my coyote rifle," she said softly.

Mike brushed back the flaming red hair and could see small cuts from the shattered glass which had fallen down during the attack. He saw tears filling her eyes.

"You're hurt."

"No, I was just thinking about Ron and Buddy."

"I know," Mike said as his eyes welled up too—a Marine could cry over lost friends.

"I never killed anyone before," she whispered.

Mike took his sister in his arms and held her for a second.

"I know…You didn't have a choice. You didn't start this." Mike looked directly in her eyes. "You're a good decent person, Sissy…And you probably just saved our lives."

With that said, Mike reverted back into the combat Marine mode. He spun around and headed for the door. "Cover me."

C-5M SUPER GALAXY
NORTH OF LAREDO

The C-5M passed through 15,000 feet and slowed to 350 knots. The flight engineer started to slowly reduce pressure in the cabin in anticipation of the launch.

In the back of the *Galaxy*, the loadmaster supervised Team Four as the three *Eagles* were readied for a launch that was going to be much more dangerous than normal. Speed was a problem.

Normal operations called for slowing the C-5M to 145 knots. With lives at stake Kit asked the flight crew for 250 and would just be slowing to that as the small high-tech attack craft were pushed out onto the ramp.

The most dangerous part, not involving flying, was the arming process. The pilot and weapons systems officer placed their hands in view inside the canopy as the crew pulled the red *Do Not Fly* streamers and their related *safe pins* which prevented the missiles and nose gun from firing while inside the mother ship.

All the crew noticed the pressure changes as their ears popped—it was getting close. One by one the *Black Eagles* were ready and the loadmaster notified the aircraft commander.

"AC , launch when ready. All birds are go."

"Roger load, slowing to two-fifty. Go on green."

Gears spoke as if he did this every day. If he was nervous, you couldn't tell.

Nonessential members of Team Four took their seats and buckled in. BEF members on launch duty harnessed themselves to heavy nylon braided straps to prevent an accidental fall off the open ramp.

A round green light illuminated on the centerline roof of the huge cargo hold and the ramp started to open. The bay became colder as the fifty-six degree turbulent air made its way inside.

Loadmaster, David "Gunnz" Garner, gave *Eagle* Three the power-up signal and Karen smoothly brought all eight engines up to fifty percent. A chain system in the floor activated and a drive paddle raised, engaging the nose wheel of the craft. The small VTOL began to move aft toward the open rear cargo ramp. In seconds, it was in launch position.

Karen took her left hand from the throttle and flipped the small lever marked *Rear Nacelles* down to the *Extend* position. Hydraulic lines from the rear engine driven pumps pressurized twin actuators in each rear nacelle strut. In stowed position, each had been folded upward ninety degrees at the midpoint hinge like planes on an aircraft carrier—the carbon fiber composite structures extended horizontally to flight position.

As they reached their full down position, thick titanium rods were driven out into their respective locking lugs, making the strut assembly rigid. Karen gently increased power until the *weight on wheels* light extinguished and the small black craft floated up from the ramp and backward into the slip stream.

She toggled a small switch on the throttle marked, *Auto Level*. Seven different flight control computers were engaged, in a *fly-by-wire* system similar to the F-22.

Hammer pulled back on the side-mounted control stick beside her right knee and the four nacelles maintained their forty-five degree upward angle. The stainless steel deflection vanes in the rear of the nacelles pivoted downward. The lethal black bird inched backward away from the slowly descending mother ship.

When safely clear, Gunnz gave a thumbs-up.

"Gear up," she said to her WSO.

Killer pulled up on the lever and the landing gear folded smoothly into the fuselage. Hammer disengaged the *Auto Level* mode and pushed forward on the stick. *Black Eagle* Three dove as she advanced the throttle, quickly accelerated and disappeared under *Mama Bird*. Total time for the launch was fifteen seconds.

***

CHAPTER SIX

ICE OFFICES
US DEPARTMENT OF HOMELAND SECURITY
BETHESDA, MD

"Mister Richards, Ronald Diggers on line two," his secretary said over the intercom.

"Oh, damn," muttered Richards as he picked up his phone and punched the flashing red button. "Mister Diggers, how can I help you?"

"You need to contact BEF and cancel the operations order for the Texas situation."

"Excuse me? Did you say cancel?"

"I don't recall stuttering, Mister Richards. Cancel the operation immediately."

"On whose authority, sir?"

"The office of the National Security Advisor. Deputy Advisor, Clarence Ogilsvey. That good enough for you?"

Richards shook his head in confusion. "Yes, sir, I'll get right on it."

He hung up his phone. "Connie, get me BEF operations center."

"Yes, sir."

She punched the secure code.

"Tallman here."

"Sir, Herbert Richards needs to speak with Mister Phillips, ASAP."

"I'm sorry, Connie, Dare is already wheels up, en route to target."

"Hold one moment, Mister Tallman." She punched the intercom.

"Did you get Dare, Connie?"

"Tom Tallman stated that Mister Phillips is already wheels up."

"God dammit!…See if he can patch me through on the radio…urgent."

"Right away, sir." She released the hold. "Mister Tallman, can you patch through to Mister Phillips on your radio?"

"I can try." He keyed his radio mic. "Mama Bird, Black Eagle base, you copy?"

"Black Eagle base, Mama Bird has you loud and clear," replied Sparky O'Neil.

"Mama Bird, need to speak with Dare."

"Base, Mama Bird, Eagle One launched five minutes ago."

"Roger, patch me through."

"Aye-aye, sir." She simultaneously pressed two buttons on her panel. "Go ahead Eagle base, Eagle One is on."

"Eagle One, Eagle base, patching you through to Herbert Richards at ICE."

Dare rolled his eyes under his helmet. "Fuck me runnin'…now what?" He keyed his mike button on the throttle. "Eagle One, go ahead Herbert and make it quick. We're fixing to get kinda busy."

"Dare, got an order to terminate the operation immediately."

"Say again? Whose order?"

"This comes from the National Security Advisors office."

"Okay…just who at the National Security Advisors office?"

"Uh, Deputy National Security Advisor Clarence Ogilsvey."

Dare clinched his jaw. "You tell that wormy little turd to read the contract and then go pound sand in his ass."

Richards cringed, *Oh shit*. "Uh…I don't think I can tell him that, sir."

"The contract says that once we assume responsibility via Standard Protocol, it is ours until completion. Tell him that and that Iron Horse says to go fuck himself…Eagle One out."

Richards gently hung up his phone, reached into his desk drawer and pulled out a bottle of twenty year old Dewars Scotch. He started to walk over the credenza and pick up a crystal glass, *Aw, hell…it's gonna be one of those days*. He removed the cap and knocked back a healthy swig.

115

EAGLE NEST RANCH HOUSE

Mike hurriedly exited Blaze's room. "Nacho! Take the west side!"

The diminutive Mexican took one last look out the window at the two red blotches on the driveway. He crossed himself twice before he turned and headed toward the hallway. "What did you do to them, my brother?"

"Didn't do anything. Baby sister did."

The confused look on Nacho's face was definitely a Kodak moment, but Mike had bigger fish to fry.

He jogged down stairs, grabbed two spare mags for his suppressed AK and two more for his Sig 220. He stuffed the pistol mags into his back pocket. "Dad, I'm going to move the Humvees south, out of our line of sight…Cover me."

"Be careful."

"I'm gonna clear the horse barn…One of 'em got away."

Mike assumed a tactical position by the main door, pulled it open with one hand and swept the parking area with the muzzle of the rifle. He stepped outside and closed the door behind him. With long powerful strides, he ran to the first Hummer, fired it up and drove forward eighty yards down the south slope—hopped out and repeated the procedure with the second.

Mike glanced back to the upstairs window in Blaze's room to see her give him a thumbs-up. He waved a brief acknowledgment as he jogged to the northwest corner of the horse barn.

He toe-heeled silently like an Indian, as he covered the distance to the open breezeway, knelt on one knee and took a quick peek down the length of the barn. He didn't see what he had expected. Mike stood and took another glance. He knew better than to give a shooter the same shot twice.

He saw the body of a Mexican lieutenant. Somebody had punched his ticket—but who?

His senses were at maximum alert as he silently entered the barn. He moved along the left side of the breezeway, taking small steps. The nervous horses at the far end stomped their feet and nickered. At each empty stall he passed, he quickly scanned for a waiting tango.

As he approached the office in the center of the building, Mike spotted a small pool of blood—drag marks led inside. He took a deep breath, grabbed an apple picker, pushed the door open with the handle and lunged in, sweeping the room with his rifle.

"Don't shoot…" Ron said weakly from the floor. "…what took you so long?" His eyes rolled up as he passed out.

Mike quickly closed the door and propped his rifle against the wall. He saw the open first-aid kit. *Tried to dress his own wounds…good man.*

Mike grabbed what he needed from the medicine cabinet—wiped Ron's arm with an alcohol-soaked cotton ball, inserted the needle and started a Ringers Lactate IV.

He hung the bag on a drawer pull, took a roll of bright green Vetwrap and turned one layer around Ron's arm, securing the tube. He reached for the surgical scissors in the first-aid kit, cut the jeans and located the pass-through wound on his thigh.

Mike reached into his back pocket and took out a loose-leaf pack of Red Man Chewing Tobacco and stuffed a wad deep into the entrance and exit wounds, covered them with gauze pads and wrapped it tightly with the elastic Vetwrap. Chewing tobacco is a mild cauterizing agent and stanched the flow of blood—he had saved more than one horses' life with the same treatment.

Mike continued the triage to Ron's arm and shoulder. He finished with a 10cc inter-muscular shot of Procaine G penicillin next to the thigh wound. *If it's good enough for a registered horse, it's good enough for me*. Mike smiled and grabbed his radio.

"Little Cheese, Big Eagle."

Nacho jumped as he heard his call sign. "Big Eagle, Little Cheese, go ahead, Mike."

"I need your help with Equine, in the barn office."

HUGHES 500 HELICOPTER
3,000 FEET ABOVE MEXICO

Luis was starting to get happy for the first time all day. The convoy of *Tres Locos* paid muscle was north of La Esperanza and would be at the river crossing in three minutes or so. *About fucking time, Martine.*

The smallish accountant had done exactly what he was ordered to do and was about to make *El Toro's* revenge a reality. *I may give that little chicken shit a raise.*

Pedro, driving in the lost Excursion, had finally gotten high enough for cell phone service. Luis chewed his ass out for three minutes straight and put the fear of God back into him.

Pedro would be at the mill in less than a minute and up to the house in two. The APC's had been unloaded from the flatbed trailers and were following the convoy in a cloud of dust. *I love it when a plan comes together.*

His pilot looked nervously at the fuel gage. Fourteen gallons remaining didn't give him much more loiter time—just under forty minutes to tanks dry at the current rate of 21 gallons per hour. He figured six more minutes on station and it would be time to call bingo fuel and head for Nuevo Laredo.

The idea that he would have to tell his volatile boss that he could not watch his personal army crush the pesky gringos made him want to puke. *I can always set down before we run out of fuel.*

The story about his predecessor was what actually had him on edge. That guy had saved Torrejon's bacon when the oil line ruptured. The auto-rotation had scared Luis until he wet his pants. No, *El Toro* didn't give the guy a raise—he pistol whipped the pilot and the unfortunate aviator lost an eye.

Former Captain Humberto Castillo wished he was somewhere else as he watched the digital fuel gage drop to thirteen.

EAGLE NEST BARN

Across the river, Nacho and Mike had gotten Ron to his feet. The IV helped and he regained consciousness, but was so weak that the two men had to hold him erect.

The longtime friends were very mismatched in size, causing Mike to walk crouched over as they slowly made their way down the breezeway. Nacho carried Buddy's bloody AR-15 over his left shoulder. His right arm was wrapped around Ron's waist, forcing him to carry his own rifle in his hand. Mike was adamant about not leaving functioning arms where the attackers could use them.

The M-16 from Cardenez and Ron's AR-15 rattled together on Mike's right shoulder. He carried his suppressed AK as if it were a pistol.

Twenty feet from the north door, the radios on their belts came to life. "All stations, all stations, Silver Eagle, multiple vehicles inbound near the mill…Get in here, Big Eagle."

Nacho had a plaintive look on his face. Mike sorted through multiple options—leaving Ron on the horse barn floor was not acceptable.

"Go!" he shouted to Nacho. With a low grunt, he tossed the 170 pound trainer over his shoulder in a fireman's carry and jogged toward the door. "Move it!"

The tone of Mike's voice overcame Nacho's fear and he sprinted out ahead.

EAGLE NEST RANCH

Boom!...Boom!...Boom! Boom! Silver Eagle engaged the black Excursion with the Barrett .50 and it rattled to a halt with pieces of the diesel engine trailing behind it. Smoke poured out from under the hood as six surviving Mexican mercenaries tried to exit and head for cover.

At seven hundred yards they did not make a large target, but Gunter punched two rounds through the open doors on the passenger side and dropped a pair of uniformed soldiers with the second bullet.

The noise of the big gun firing spurred Nacho faster. He was almost twenty yards in front of Mike when a string of bullets kicked up caliche rock dust in the parking lot behind him.

Seventy yards away, the sergeant had reinitiated the attack on the ranch house with his three men. When the lieutenant's team had been taken out, he decided to hunker down until reinforcements arrived. The line of trucks, pickups and SUV's streaming across the Rio Bravo would surely keep the Anglos in the house tied up.

He had some pint-sized Chicano hotfooting across the parking lot—he adjusted his aim as the stream of bullets inched closer.

The twenty-fourth round caught Nacho's right boot heel. The impact tore the heel off snapping his ankle to the left—he went down hard.

Mike had already passed the north end of the horse barn at a rapid pace, considering the human cargo he carried. His right hand had a vice-like hold on the pistol grip of the suppressed AK-47 as it instinctively rose toward the Mexican Sergeant.

One steady pull on the trigger and bullets poured out of the suppressor like water from Hell's own hose. The only sound Mike could hear was the *clack, clack, clack* of the bolt cycling until the returning *splat* of bullets as they ripped into the man's chest.

He dropped the empty AK as he approached the unconscious Nacho. He grabbed the short-sleeved denim shirt by the collar, and with an adrenaline boosted yell, he sprinted toward the house, carrying one man and dragging the other.

Ten yards before he passed the smokehouse, he snapped a quick glance back toward the body with eleven weeping gunshot wounds. *Target fixation, he never saw me coming…They never do.*

Mike caught a glimpse of two—now three—more men with rifles as they rose from the knee-high brush less than eighty yards away—he could feel the sights lining up on him.

He didn't know how that happened. It's something a warrior just seems to feel in combat. Perhaps it was a holdover from prehistoric DNA—from a time long past when men were not the top of the food chain. Whatever the reason, Mike could sense the three shooter's intentions as their fingers moved to their triggers and took up slack. For the first time ever, Mike had a really, really bad thought…*Damn, I'm not gonna make it.*

Blaze moved to the west side bedroom after she heard the radio transmission from her Dad. She saw the disabled Excursion a hundred yards out past the burnt-out Humvee. *Why the hell did I put the EoTech on the coyote gun? It had no magnification, just a red dot inside a red ring. These guys are almost a half-mile away.*

She picked up her Steiners and located one of the attackers as he ran from the Excursion. He stopped and fired his rifle at the house. She couldn't hear the sound yet, but a gray cloud at the muzzle of his M-16 was a dead giveaway.

Instinctively, she popped her head to the left behind the safety of the stone walls. The short burst impacted eight feet below her and twenty feet left. *The moron was shooting at the house, not me.*

Blaze picked up her Remington and lined up the shooter in the reticle. The tiny one mil dot covered half the shooter's body width at that range. *That's about right. He should be about fourteen inches wide at the waist, with the dot at seven inches in diameter.* She started to raise the rifle slightly higher when the electronic trigger fired.

Ponk!

The modified sixteen penny nail was levitated into the chamber and out the bore in thirty micro seconds. It departed the muzzle at 12,000 feet per second, leaving a light blue plasma trail in its wake.

A high pitched sonic crack, similar to that of a bull whip, followed the projectile as it flew the seven hundred yards to its intended target.

The private in the Mexican Army was wondering where the hell his older brother was when the nail struck him directly in the navel. The tiny spot on his body marking the connection he had to his mother before birth was ironically the same spot which would prophetically connect him with his missing big brother. The sergeant had punched his little brother in the left arm and made a joke just two hours earlier, before they split up and walked toward their separate vehicles.

"See you in Hell."

DEPARTMENT OF DEFENSE
THE PENTAGON

Secretary of Defense Harold Baker picked up his secure line phone on the second ring. "Baker. What's on your mind, Herbert?"

"Mister Secretary, we have a possible situation, as we speak, in south Texas involving some Mexican nationals…and according to our satellite views, apparently some Mexican Federal troops on our side of the Rio Grande. We dispatched BEF on Standard Protocol to take over operational responsibility of this incident at 1705 Zulu. BEF is currently on station,"

"Well, with the BEF on station, sounds like the situation is in good hands. What's the problem?"

"Mister Diggers of Homeland Security issued a cancellation and recall of the BEF per Deputy National Security Advisor Clarence Ogilsvey. The order is, according to the DoD contract with BEF, invalid on its face. As I'm sure you're aware, sir, once Standard Protocol operational responsibility is invoked, it is irrevocable. But I'm catching all sorts of hell from Diggers."

Baker got to his feet. "What in the Sam Hill is a hack like Ogilsvey getting involved for? He has absolutely no authority! He's a God damned advisor, for Christ's sake!"

"Uh, yes, sir, I know. But I felt that some intervention from a higher source than my GS-11 status might be in order before he stirs up a real shit storm."

"Agreed...Glad you informed me. Ogilsvey doesn't want to tangle with Iron Horse Phillips. He served under me in Iraq...and Grenada before that...He's one bad ass. Hell, I wouldn't tangle with him on a bet...All right, Richards, I'll keep Homeland Security off your ass. I'm not gonna have a bunch of political appointees fucking with one of the best assets this country has. Keep me informed of all developments...clear?"

"Yes, sir...and thank you, sir."

"No. Thank you, Richards. This is good to know...Oh, one more thing. You said that apparently there were Mexican Federal troops on our side of the border...that right?"

"That's correct, sir. Some of the men in the satellite photos are wearing Mexican Federal Army uniforms."

"Send me the link to the satellite imagery. If that is indeed the case...it qualifies as an incursion. However, if the troops on the ground are Mexican Federales, they could be rogue.

"It would take twenty-four to forty-eight hours to mobilize the National Guard and up to seventy-two to get a MEU activated. Our nearest Special Ops unit is at Ft. Bragg…In any case, I'm damned comfortable with Dare Phillips and his BEF already on station."

"Agree, sir."

Baker hung up his phone and took out a yellow legal pad.

EAGLE NEST RANCH

Mike looked apprehensively at the shooters—he expected the worst. The scene changed completely when hundreds of bullets pounded the area and a cloud of dust rose from the dry terrain surrounding the mercenaries.

All three fell under the steel rain from Heaven. From the west came the familiar sound of a GAU 17/A Mini-Gun. All Mike knew was some avenging angel had just saved his ass and the lives of two close friends. He looked up where the sound emanated and saw nothing but the hot Texas sun.

Setting Nacho down, he shaded his eyes. Off to the side, Mike could see a small black object diving through 1,000 feet. There was no sound that he could detect whatsoever. "What the hell?"

Karen "Hammer" Gibbs pulled back hard on the stick as she smoothly added power to *Eagle* Three. Earlier, she had retarded the power to idle as she approached red line at 410 MPH in the thirty degree dive.

WSO Kilgore, in charge of the Hellfire, PAASM and Stinger missiles on the craft, monitored the bird's altitude and ground obstacles.

"Two thousand," Killer said as he made the mandatory altitude call out.

Hammer had arced the craft downward as the 600 continued to hurtle toward the target. She had placed the pipper of the Heads Up Display directly on the tango closest to the three Texans and squeezed the red trigger on the military style grip atop her stick. She walked the rudder slightly to cover the other two targets with her two second burst, plastering them with over 200 rounds of 7.62mm bullets.

The eight Freedom Rotapower engines responded in unison as the nacelles rotated upward and the vanes inside the rear of each nacelle pivoted downward to vector the increasing thrust.

All four occupants experienced four times the earth's natural pull as the *G* forces pulled them down in their carbon fiber, leather lined seats. The *Black Eagle* pulled out of its dive at 500 feet and zoomed quickly back up to 3,000 feet.

Karen announced her position. "Three off."

"Target neutralized," came confirmation from Lanie on *Mama Bird*.

"Two is in hot," announced Jill McElheney in *Eagle* Two.

She targeted the first two vehicles that had driven around the crippled Excursion and were now within 300 yards of the house. Following the BEF TAP, the threats deemed highest priority were hit first. The policy had earlier determined the stationary Excursion was a low threat and the mission was reallocated en route.

Jill approached the convoy from the west over Mexican airspace and, like Hammer, selected the mini-gun to kill the light trucks. Every tenth round was loaded with a red tracer.

With the cyclic rate of 6,000 rounds per minute, the hail of bullets looked like a bright red laser pointing at the target. The first one, a blue Chevy pickup with six men in the back, closed to two hundred yards of the house.

Just before Jill pulled the trigger, one of the shooters, firing a Ruger Mini 14 over the cab of the truck, slumped as his head exploded in a red cloud. She could not see the action from the distance, but someone else had scored.

The Gatling Gun roared to life in the nose of the stealthy black bird with the sound of a giant blender mating with a chain saw.

Jill watched intently as she maintained the pipper on the first truck for a one second burst, dispensing over 100 rounds. Releasing the trigger briefly, she pushed the nose over and tracked the other truck for a moment before she pulled the trigger a second time.

Each had burst into flames in sequence as the tracers ignited the unleaded gasoline from the ruptured fuel tanks. "Eagle Two off," came the call as the blonde-haired fighter pilot scored her first two real kills.

She was breathing quickly and her pulse was racing, but then again, so were those of her crew mates.

Automatic rifle fire from the following trucks was now focused upward at *Eagle* Three as it pulled up and out of the gun pass. Most of the rounds passed dozens of yards behind the Skycar, but three punched through the carbon fiber shell on the belly before the Dragonskin inner lining stopped their penetration. The crew members heard three quick light thumps, but carried on as briefed when no master caution lights illuminated.

"Targets neutralized," came the radio confirmation from Lanie, as *Manta* kept a close watch overhead.

Mike saw the second strange black craft high over the ranch house as he stood with the injured Ron still draped over his left shoulder.

At his feet, Nacho awoke from his brief period of unconsciousness and moaned from his injuries. In addition to his badly sprained right ankle, he had hit hard and gotten a nasty cut on his chin.

Noting the little man was not bleeding anywhere else, Mike took Ron over to the south side of the old smokehouse and leaned him against the rock wall.

He slipped off the M-16 slung over his right shoulder and checked the chamber. He found it empty with the bolt locked back by the mag catch. Apparently, the Mexican Lieutenant which Ron had killed had run dry during the assault on the ranch house. *Wonderful.*

Mike looked over at Nacho and saw three rifles lying on the ground just past him. Drawing his Sig, he sprinted to them. He crouched and tactically cleared the area back where the four dead soldiers lay. He detected no motion—holstered his Sig and grabbed the rifles by their slings.

Nacho was up on his feet, holding his chin wound closed. He could not walk on the painful right ankle, but was trying to hop toward the ranch house as best he could. Mike turned to see Nacho making his way to the back door, and as he carried all three AR's, he ran over, picked up Ron again and moved as quickly as he could to the house.

Ponk! *Blang*! Blaze was still at work with her coil gun. She computed a battery life of sixty to seventy rounds.

The flexible carbon fiber nanotubes she created to house the silver liquid mercury were one of her proudest accomplishments. She had patented the technology while working on her Doctorates at Rice University.

The switching microprocessor to activate successive series of coils was tricky, but a former suitor had personally made up the requisite silicone chip at an HP lab in California. All it cost her was a plane ticket to San Jose and a dinner date with the enamored computer design geek. It worked great. She had epoxied the switching chip onto the side of the existing electronic trigger of the Remington 700 Stainless Fluted Varmint rifle.

The effect on a running truck engine was not as spectacular as on a human body. The hypersonic nails worked similarly to the plasma jet created by a shaped charge in a antitank explosive warhead. Those weapons used an explosion to create an ultra high-speed jet of superheated plasma or copper to burn through the dense layer of steel armor.

In this case the nail *was* the high-speed jet and it took a lot to stop it. High velocity is a quantum force of its own.

Tres Locos gang members driving the trucks could not tell what hit the engine. The hood bulged upward and they could hear the grating sound of metal on metal. Smoke and steam boiled out and the idiot lights illuminated as oil pressure dropped and the alternator ceased to function. What was not visible was the plasma jet from Mach-ten steel igniting vapors in the oil pan and valve covers.

Dare Phillips was late to the party—actually, only forty seconds later than *Eagle* Three. He felt bad that he was not the one to save Mike's life directly.

He set up for a gun pass on the final two deuce-and-half trucks filled with soldiers as *Eagles* Two and Three turned back inbound for runs from both the north and south. He had briefed the maneuvers en route—Jill and Hammer complied as expected. Now Dare was coming in hot at the speed of heat with two major tangos on the top of the TAP list.

As weapons officer Bull Gaspar called out the altitudes, Lanie broke in with disturbing news, "APCs crossing the river. Heavy machine guns."

Dare looked down to the left and sure enough, there they were. There was no stinkin' way *Eagle* One could make the Hellfire shot from this speed and angle and its nose gun was too light to penetrate the vehicle's armor. He was committed to the big trucks on this pass.

As his laser range finder showed the range to target was fast approaching optimum, Dare took one last quick look back at the

APC. What he saw made his heart skip a beat. "Heavy machine guns, my ass…these bastards have Stingers!"

"No shit?"

The second personnel carrier was stopped on the road some eighty yards north of the Hermann grist mill. The ramp was down and several soldiers had deployed. One was facing *Eagle* One directly with a long tubular object on his right shoulder. Discriminating software scanned the area within the rectangular target area of the view finder and locked on to the multiple engine exhaust signature of the *Eagle*.

The staff sergeant noted the green *lock* icon in the viewfinder, pulled the red trigger on the pistol grip and launched the missile skyward at the turning target.

The six-foot long weapon made a *poomp* sound as the low pressure motor punched the missile clear of the tube. Eight folded guidance fins snapped out into position as the main two-stage rocket motor kicked in. A dense trail of white smoke lingered behind as the missile accelerated to Mach 2.2 and closed in on *Black Eagle* One.

***

CHAPTER SEVEN

EAGLE NEST RANCH

At six hundred and fifty yards, the APC was in range of the Barrett. Mike finished stuffing the spare ten round magazine with red and silver-tipped, APIT rounds. He had taken control of the big gun as Gunter tended to the injured Nacho and Ron.

Taking the partially loaded mag from underneath the thirty-five pound rifle, he sat it down on the ammo can. Keeping his eyes on the approaching APC, Mike slid the full mag into the cavernous magazine well.

He touched the earplugs in each ear to confirm their installation and raised the rifle to his shoulder. The rifle bipod was solidly supported by the broad painted sill in the narrow window. As Mike maneuvered the rifle to line up on the APC driver's assumed position, the sharp metal edges of the bipod feet peeled small white curls of oil-based paint from the wood.

Ron jumped at the blast from the big gun when it resonated across the ranch. All the others in the house, including Blaze upstairs, still had on their ear protection. The fact that the big muzzle brake was outside the house helped tremendously as most of its powerful force was blocked by the stone walls.

Ron now felt more alive than dead as he drank the sucrose solution Mike suggested that his dad make. He quickly downed the mixture as prescribed. The clear liquid tasted like the sweetest Kool-Aid one could ever imagine—minus the coloring and artificial strawberry flavor—but served the same purpose as a glucose IV.

The thirty-six inch barrel of the big Barrett recoiled four inches as thirteen thousand foot pounds of kinetic energy were released downrange. The Armor Piercing Incendiary Tracer round flashed on the steel armor—the sharp, hardened core penetrated easily inside, breaking the right arm of the driver and killing one of the other soldiers. The APC was not driving directly at the house and Mike had misjudged the location of the driver.

The driver naturally let go of the right steering arm of the combat vehicle and the corresponding track stopped instantly—causing it to lurch to that side violently.

Troops inside were slammed around as it came to rest. One of the men got up to pull the wounded driver out of the seat, but was killed by the next round which penetrated the side of the hull and ricocheted around inside. Like a hornet from hell, the red phosphorus in the projectile tracer element glowed brightly as the hot steel created its mayhem—six more tracers followed.

Mike watched through his scope and could see the impact of each round as he followed the projectiles all the way to the target.

On top of the cupola, a shaken and badly frightened gunner climbed back into position. He had nearly been thrown off when it slewed to the right. Had it not been for the Vietnam era flack jacket he wore, he would have suffered broken ribs when he hit the left side.

Corporal Henri Domingez knew what to do now. He had seen where the shooter was firing by backtracking the tracers to the first floor of the rock house. He cranked back the charging handle on the M2 Browning machine gun, let the bolt fly home, swung the seventy pound gun at the house and pressed the butterfly trigger. Ma Deuce roared to life with its distinctive marked cadence as he walked a line of .50 BMG rounds right back at Mike…

AIRSPACE OVER EAGLE NEST RANCH

Dare instantly reacted upon first sight of the missile threat by aborting the truck attack even before the launch and pulled the stick back hard. The craft arced upward into an ever-increasing steep climb—the airspeed bled back quickly from four hundred knots to two hundred fifty. He initiated a right turn toward the incoming missile to keep it in sight.

"Missile alert," warned the tracking system on board *Mama Bird.* The signal was automatically relayed to all *Eagle* aircraft in the area.

As the missile closed in, Dare cut power abruptly and slammed the stick forward while clicking the *flare* button on the left side of the throttle. Atop the fuselage of the sleek black craft, a specially designed infrared-only flare was blasted upward from its launch tube just in front of the vertical stabilizer on the swept back tail.

The chemical mixture inside burned at 900 degrees Fahrenheit and heated the foot-long pointed stainless steel tube to just short of cherry red, but there was no bright UV signature as one would expect from a magnesium flare.

Eight Rotapower engines spooled down as the composite blades continued to blow relatively cool air over the exhaust ducts inside the nacelles. The four nacelles aligned with the fuselage as the M600/A reached a level position. *Eagle* One became weightless as it started to float downward from its 4,500 feet apogee.

Inside the Raytheon Stinger IR and UV heat seeking tracker, the loss of a viable heat signature from the rapidly cooling engine exhausts caused the missile to maintain the last computed intercept heading—then picking up a valid heat signature from the IR flare rising three hundred feet above the craft, its eight guidance fins pivoted sharply to intercept.

Dare and Bull watched silently as the Stinger flashed by only seventy yards away and exploded into the flare well above them with a huge yellow fireball—both felt and heard the concussion.

Eagle One was falling unpowered though 4,000 feet when Dare smoothly pushed the throttle forward and said calmly, "Bull, get me a Hellfire on the lead APC."

"Damn, that was close," Bull muttered when he could speak again.

"Roger that."

Mike observed the close call *Eagle* One just had with the Stinger. *Who the hell is flying that Jetsonmobile on steroids?* The damned things looked like alien craft and flew unlike any thing he ever seen before—Mike owed them big time.

That gunner on the Ma Deuce had Mike's number and was about to punch his ticket when Bull's Hellfire missile sent him there. He knew better than to trade shot for shot with a guy in an armored cupola when all he had was a stone wall in front of him. He had slid down below the narrow window when he saw the .50 cal machine gun sweep his direction and open fire.

The discussion with Gunter about the inevitable failure of a defensive battle without reinforcements raced through his mind. It was apparent that something had changed—air power. Someone was up there kicking some major butt. Mike just wished he had a clue who they were.

Blaze could see the strange black craft which had just jinked and dodged a heat-seeking missile. It had come to a stop, then fell vertically hundreds of feet and finally just hovered in midair. *What kind of ship does that?*

As a pilot, she could not put a name to it, but whatever and whoever it was, she was glad for the help. She watched as the Hellfire missile had been fired, but to her naked eyes, the missile came from above the craft.

Her engineer's mind was full of questions, but there were targets out there with rifles and what appeared to be rocket propelled grenades. *Time to get busy...*

The two other M600/As were rolling in for separate attacks from opposite directions. Hammer Gibbs in *Eagle* Three initiated first from her perch north of the battle zone. She had briefed her WSO to stand by the flare control now that Stingers had been brought to the fray.

Jill in *Eagle* Two was five thousand feet above the Rio Grande when she heard Karen's call, "Three is in hot."

Hammer had been assigned the only truck still moving, a deuce and a half full of uniformed Mexican Army soldiers.

They didn't know who they were fighting, only that their officers had taken a call from a higher up and told them to get in the trucks. They didn't know that they had broken international law. They didn't know that they were at the center of a HUD and the small pipper was tracking them from 2,500 feet. There is a old country saying, 'What you don't know can't hurt you'. Many old sayings have a grain of truth in them—not this one.

Gibbs fired a two-second burst that killed or wounded every man in the big army truck. The hot olive drab canvas which had provided shade from the searing Texas summer sun provided no protection from the rain of death from the mini-gun.

The fire quickly spread from the fuel ignited by the tracers. No one escaped from the funeral pyre on wheels. Black smoke roiled upwards as the tires became engulfed in the spreading inferno. There was no breeze to take the stench of burning flesh and hair away.

After the sound of the Hellfire missile ripping apart the APC, it was quiet for a couple of seconds. Mike took a combat peek out the window and slid back down under the cover of the stone. He processed the view and realized he couldn't see the shooter because the tracked vehicle had simply vanished.

Parts had been scattered in a 200 foot radius and none of them was readily recognizable—scratch one APC. He picked up the Barrett and set up for more action.

Nacho crawled over from the kitchen—his chin wound painted with iodine and pulled back together with Steri-Strips. Gunter had done a good job. Two tours in 'Nam had made him much more proficient in first-aid than he ever wanted to be. Nacho couldn't walk, but he was willing to help. "What can I do?"

Mike looked over his shoulder. "Here you go sunshine, fill 'er up." He tossed him the empty mag.

"Regular or Premium?" He attempted to smile, but it hurt too much.

"Just the API. We don't need to let them know exactly where we are." Mike scanned the battlefield north of the house.

Nacho quickly had ten rounds loaded and passed them back. "Here you are, Captain."

Mike spotted four guys running east between a disabled truck and the brush two hundred yards away—he took down two.

The Barrett was empty. A quick mag change and he was able to take the other two down with four follow-up shots.

He tossed the empty back to Nacho, then a funny thought

struck him. *Captain? He never called me that before. It was always Mike, brother, baby brother, Big Mike...Dumb shit.* He rightly guessed that during all the time he had spent in the sand box and in the cold hard mountains of Afghanistan as a Marine officer, Nacho could not really get his head around what he had done for a living. Today, all that changed in the time some people took to eat lunch.

Mike had seen several soldiers bail out of the back of the troop truck and suspected that a few were still hiding behind it. He placed the crosshairs of the Leupold Tactical scope just below the bumper—started to take up slack. Before the rifle fired, the deuce and a half disappeared in another volley of mini-gun rounds.

This time it was from Jill in *Eagle* Two. She bracketed the stationary truck like it was on a weapons range and scored 94% hits with the modern Gatling gun.

The sight caused Mike to release pressure on the trigger. He watched as the truck began to burn and then heard the sound of the GAU. He knew the bullets flew almost three times the speed of sound and always arrived at the target before the sound of the shot. The sound came from his left and as he looked up, *Eagle* Two was pulling out of its dive and was only 1,000 feet above the ground.

Mike grabbed his Steiners and watched the craft roll right as it climbed to the north and east. This time, he could actually see two people in the cockpit—picked out four distinct engine nacelles and, although he was not certain, would swear he saw a black and gold eagle emblem on the tail. *What in God's green earth?*

In *Eagle* One, Dare had swung the nose away from the southernmost APC that Bull had turned into scrap metal. The explosion had been so severe that even the fuel was destroyed in the blast and there was almost no residual fire. He placed the pipper on the originating point of the white smoke trail left by the Stinger.

The smoke obscured the ground as he pulled the red trigger on his stick. Like a painter covering a wall, he walked the stream of tracers from left to right through the upper portion of the slowly thinning cloud. He released the trigger, bunted the stick ever so slightly forward, and as the nose of the Skycar responded, he eased a touch of left rudder and repeated the process from right to left. A final pass back right and all the area had been covered—seven soldiers lay dead behind the APC.

Staff Sergeant Pedro LaVaca had walked out from under the massive white cloud to view his marksmanship with the gringo surface-to-air missile. He had never missed during training in El Paso, but they had been shooting at radio-controlled drones. He wanted to see if he was as good as he thought. *Must have been a defective missile.*

He had not seen the tiny silver thermal flare deploy from the slant range distance of almost 2,000 yards. Nor had he seen the Hellfire launched at the lead APC, although he definitely heard the horrendous blast when the soldiers in that coffin-on-tracks were turned to buzzard bait. Pedro had started back toward the

APC when the storm of bullets tore into his platoon. He spun and ran fast as he could, still carrying the empty Stinger launch tube. *My lieutenant would kill me if I lost it,* he thought as he beat feet to the north.

There is an old saying among warriors, 'Run and you'll just die tired'. As *Eagle* One dove toward the smoke trail, Dare could see a lone soldier running north toward the river crossing.

For a second, he thought, *aw hell, let the poor bastard go. He's out of the fight anyway*. Then, as he was passing 800 feet, Dare saw the Stinger launch tube in the soldier's sweating hands.

Running in Texas heat in utilities and combat boots, carrying the cumbersome launcher, had left the out-of-shape desk jockey winded. He huffed and puffed as a stitch in his side became painful.

Pedro slowed to a walk and bent over to relieve the pain. He glanced back south as the T-tailed black craft came in silently—only 100 feet above the smoke-covered ranch road. He could see two helmeted figures looking his way through the tinted canopy as the GAU 17/A sang its mournful dirge of death.

HUGHES 500 HELICOPTER
AIRSPACE ABOVE MEXICO

Hughes 500 pilot Castillo was really scared. The discussion with Torrejon about the fuel status went about as badly as he had anticipated. He had not foreseen the big man's absolute fury at the interference created by the unknown black flying machines.

Humberto felt the cold steel of a engraved Colt 1911 pressed hard against the side of his head. It was a beautiful pistol, with a gold inlaid *El Toro* on the nickel plated slide and a hand-carved Bull's head on each elephant ivory grip panel.

The beauty paled in comparison to the fear that gripped the pilot as he wiped blood from his lips. He cautiously tongued a loose tooth on the left side. Luis had nearly broken his jaw when he mentioned the bingo fuel level. All the psychopathic man was concerned about now was revenge and screw the fuel. He wanted him to engage the black birds with the mini-gun mounted on the right skid.

The Hughes 500 screamed down from its cooler air heights into the bumpy convective air currents near the surface. Airspeed increased to 155 miles per hour as the nimble egg-shaped craft closed the distance to the bloody battlefield across the river.

This time, it was the small chopper's turn to have the advantage of the sun at its back. Humberto added left rudder to the craft to compensate for the asymmetric parasitic drag of the GAU 17/A on one skid. There was no tail rotor on this model, just a complex vane system to divert turbine engine exhaust to counteract main rotor torque.

High above the battlefield in an orbit of 12,000 feet, Lanie in *Mama Bird*, issued a warning to all the *Eagle* craft, "Bogey bearing two seven zero, angels two and descending. Manta confirms it is hostile."

Dare and Bull, in the front seats of *Eagle* One, were concentrating on the tall cottonwood trees lining the river as the bird streaked by at four hundred and sixty feet per second.

Although he had flown *Super Cobra* attack helicopters in the Marine Corps, the 600 was almost three times as fast. The adrenaline rush was palpable. One mistake in heading or pitch could result in a Controlled Flight Into Terrain fatality.

Rocks and trees could leave you just as dead as missiles and guns. The bogey call had his attention as he once again pulled back hard on the stick. The sun was directly in his eyes as he and Bull scanned for the incoming threat.

Lacking its own onboard radar due to weight considerations and the location of the internal gun, the *Eagle* could not directly identify an incoming unknown rider. Data feed from *Mama Bird* and *Manta* could be displayed on one of the flat screens on the instrument panel. Bull selected *Radar* on his WSO menu.

"Say bogey type," Dare called on the BEF frequency, as he snap-rolled left and pulled just above the tree tops.

The small agile craft streaked across the Rio Grande at only one hundred and fifty feet before he put it in a steep climb.

"Hughes 500 helo with skid mounted mini-gun," came Lanie's terse reply.

"Roger."

South of the developing air battle, the APC which had carried the lone Stinger operator, was raising its rear ramp and clanking forward toward the ranch. The vortex from Dare's attack dive had finally dissipated the Stinger smoke enough to where the gunner on the cupola of that APC could see.

The gunner slid his Ma Deuce around to get a shot at the departing craft. He was not fast enough, though, and the fifty round burst sent branches crashing down from the cottonwoods. Dozens of the broad cottonwood leaves helicoptered down from the tree tops and littered the surface of the muddy waters of the Rio Grande.

Dare planned to jink back right after the initial offset maneuver to the left. He still could not see the incoming helo, but the .50 caliber tracers from the Mexican Ma Deuce passed well to his right and below as he started the roll.

He pulled right for just a second, passing through 500 feet, then reversed hard left and slightly released back pressure. He didn't want to lose the kinetic energy and speed advantage over a nimble Hughes 500. *Never fight the enemy's fight*, he reminded himself as the *Eagle* climbed like a homesick angel.

Humberto had followed the black machine as it flew north along the river. He had the sucker right under the black "*X*" marked on his canopy. The thing was crossing the river and climbing fast—very fast. *What the hell is that?* The pilot slammed the stick hard to the right and pushed the left rudder in to center the black "*X*."

Luis screamed at him, "Shoot. Shoot, damn you!" He slapped him in the back of the head with the Colt.

Humberto pressed the silver electric switch attached to the stick with a metal hose clamp. The mini-gun sent a stream of bullets a hundred feet behind and well below the climbing 600.

The chopper started to shudder badly as it buffeted from excessive sideslip at the high rate of speed. The bird was aerodynamic like an egg, but the added gun was not.

Humberto eased off the rudder, pulled back on the cyclic and raised the collective to pull out of the steep dive and slowed to turn and re-engage.

Bull called out the visual acquisition, "Tally ho the helo, two-thirty high."

Dare refocused his visual scan and picked up the bandit. "Contact there."

The little chopper rapidly sunk below the streaking *Eagle* as the two maneuvered in a lethal three dimensional game of chess.

"You missed! I don't pay you five thousand dollars a month to miss!" exploded the drug gang leader as he cracked the Colt over Humberto's head and split his scalp.

Blood ran down the collar of his white starched shirt as he winced. He tried to concentrate on the helicopter's airspeed and rate of descent. When he was slowed down to thirty miles per hour, he stood on the right rudder and spun the craft around.

Luis almost came unglued again at the weird sensations of flying backward, but the little bird's rotors clawed at the air and soon it was flying forward once again. *All right. Where the hell is that black bastard?*

Both men looked around, but neither could see it. *Eagle* One had vanished…

EAGLE NEST RANCH HOUSE

"Songbird, Big Eagle. Whatchu got up there?"

Blaze had almost forgotten they had radios. Everyone in the house had been so engaged, there had been no time to talk. She searched though her field glasses—nothing was moving nearby. The last thing she could see was a line of tracer fire over the top of some trees near the mill. "Big Eagle, Songbird. Negative activity."

"Roger that. Same here. Keep us advised. Big Eagle Out."

"Sausageman, Big Eagle."

In the commercial smoke house, Ralph Steinmetz picked up the radio to speak for the first time. He was a fifty year old, forth generation Texan and meat master. Ralph had helped make the Hermann Eagle Nest Brand of sausage, ham and beef become a household name. He was given responsibility for the safety and security of eleven other people in the plant. "Big Eagle, Sausageman, go."

All the other younger men and women cutters, smokers and packers looked on with concern.

"Any thing to report? Come, back."

"Negative, Big Eagle. All quiet over this way. We'll keep our eyes open."

"Copy, Big Eagle out."

"Uh, Big Eagle, Sausageman."

"Go ahead," Mike answered as he wondered what the transmission would be.

"What's the word on Ron and Buddy?...Over."

Hearts fell across the big Texas spread when Mike keyed the portable. "Ron's gonna be okay...We...we lost Buddy."

Tears fell from the strong man's eyes. "Copy that...I'll tell his mom."

Ralph did not have to say a word. Buddy's mom, Laverne was standing just ten feet away. She sobbed loudly and covered her face as she heard the confirmation of what she had prayed would not be. Three of the other women on the close-knit ranch closed in to comfort her in her unfathomable despair.

Mike returned the radio to his belt and looked out at the devastation spread across the ranch he loved, *What the hell is all this death and destruction about?*

The lone APC made its way past the mill. Blaze studied the distant movement. The sun was still quite high and mirage was a problem at over seven hundred yards. "Armored Personnel Carrier passing the mill!"

The announcement snapped Mike out of his momentary reverie. His view was blocked by the hulk of a burned-out deuce and a half. "Can't see from here. Try to hold 'em 'til I can get up there!" He jerked the Barrett up by the fold-down handle like a briefcase, tucked a mag under one arm, grabbed the full ammo can and charged up the stairs. "Nacho, there's an M-16 on the kitchen table...Cover me from down there!"

"Got it, Big Eagle."

Jill sighted the moving APC and initiated a missile attack. She rolled off her perch high to the north and east. "Bug, give me a PAASM."

"You got it, little lady."

HUGHES 500 HELICOPTER
AIRSPACE ABOVE MEXICO

Across the river, Humberto and Luis argued about where the black craft had gone when they saw it diving.

"There it is!" the pilot said, still trying to figure how the hell it got back over the river without them seeing it.

"Get it! Shoot! Shoot!"

Humberto knew they were out of range as he twisted the throttle to the stop and pulled up on the collective. As he picked up some airspeed, he eased back on the stick and placed the black "X" in front of the rapidly accelerating *Eagle* Two.

A steady stream of tracers emanated from the six revolving barrels of his mini-gun. The 1,500 yard distance was too much for the little 7.62 rounds and they dropped below the black craft, although his lead was improving considerably.

Luis yelled as he punched him in the arm, "Closer! Get closer, dammit! Do I have to tell you everything?"

Humberto took his finger off the silver button and pushed forward on the stick until the little whirly bird was again moving at one hundred fifty miles per hour. As he watched the black bird hurtle steeply down at the APC, a missile screamed

149

off the rear nacelle wing support at 2,500 feet, trailing a short bright white flame.

EAGLE NEST RANCH

On the top of the APC, the gunner's attention was attracted by *God's Chain Saw*—what some people call the sound of the chopper's GAU. Even over the noise of the APC, he could hear it and looked up to catch a line of tracers pointing at the diving craft.

I got him this time, he thought, as he swung the muzzle upward. He held tightly on the twin wood-covered grips. Lining up the black craft in the hooded front sight, he pressed firmly down on the butterfly trigger. The Ma Deuce rattled away as smoke-covered empties clattered at his feet.

Blaze reacted quickly when the heavy machine gun roared to life on top of the approaching APC. She set the binoculars down and picked up her rifle, placed the red one mil dot above the gunner's head—and pressed the trigger.

Ponk. A miss.

Ponk.

The Ma Deuce fell silent. The sixteen penny nail had contacted the gunner's neck and his bodiless head fell down into crew compartment under the cupola. The APC disappeared in a flash of white light as a tremendous roar echoed up and down the Rio Grande valley.

She looked at her coyote rifle in disbelief. *What the*…

AIRSPACE ABOVE EAGLE NEST RANCH

Jill rolled right and started to pull up from the attack when two strong hits from the world's oldest heavy machine gun still in use struck the attack craft in the right forward nacelle and fuselage.

The gunner had just picked his tracer stream up to compensate for the long slant range to the attacking *Eagle* when he was hammered by the carpenter 16 penny nail.

Jill looked down at the *Number Three Engine Master Caution Light* flashing red. "Damn!"

Glenn Haug broke into her momentary fog as he calmly announced, "I'm hit."

Smoke poured from the right nacelle as the oil from the damaged forward rotary engine hit the hot exhaust manifold. The flight computers had already automatically shut off fuel and oil to the damaged engine and the rear engine was fully capable of driving the hydraulic pumps, rotor fan blades and generator. Jill canceled the roll right and turned back left toward the long paved strip she had seen on the ranch. "Eagle Two is hit with an injury to my WSO. I'm setting it down on the airstrip."

"Mama Bird copies. Medic on the way in one," resonded Kit before he switched to the onboard PA. "Team Four Medic HALO in one."

Gears had already turned the C-5M toward the airstrip and leveled off at 12,000 feet. He noted the winds and made a rapid computation of the direction and distance for the HALO.

In the back, the med-tech and former Navy SEAL, Andy Long, grabbed the sixty pound medical go-kit and snapped the twenty foot lanyard to his parawing harness. He walked to the left rear door of the mostly empty cargo bay as another member of Team Four checked his gear one last time.

The aircraft approached the drop zone, depressurised again and the jump door opened. Andy adjusted his goggles tighter and gave the thumbs-up signal.

Ten seconds passed until the craft hit the predetermined coordinates, and as the green light illuminated over the door, loadmaster Mad Max patted him on the shoulder. Andy and all his combat and medical gear were out the door in a flash. He wouldn't pull the ripcord for another ten thousand feet.

HUGHES 500 HELICOPTER

Luis was happy. He saw the smoke trailing from the damaged black craft and had assumed it would crash. After all, it made a descending turn away and disappeared behind a ridge to the east. He set the Colt down on his right leg and patted the pilot on the back. The *Fuel Low Master Caution* light had been on for several minutes and they were out of options.

"You got him. You got him!"

Humberto knew that he did not shoot the mystery craft down. He had clearly seen that they were out of range. *If this stinking animal wanted to think he shot it down, let him.*

"No hard feelings, my friend," Luis said with a crooked smile. He extended a hand to congratulate the pilot on his magnificent kill.

Humberto had no plans to get the crap beat out of himself when he had to land in the brushy country or make an unavoidable auto rotation. He took Luis' hand and held on for dear life. Holding the stick neutral between his knees, he slipped his left hand off the throttle and collective and picked up the nickel-plated Colt 1911.

Luis' gold front tooth was shining in the Texas sun. The Colt barked five times into his right side and *El Toro* was dead. He slumped, his body leaning sloppily against the left door.

"Fuck you! No hard feelings, Luis!" Humberto looked back west to find a suitable place on the Mexican side of the river to set down.

Bull Gaspar's AIM 92 Stinger missile flew right up the Hughes exhaust. A huge blast scattered small pieces of debris widely across the river where they rapidly sank.

"Splash one bogey," said Bull as Dare turned back toward US territory.

MAMA BIRD ABOVE EAGLE NEST RANCH

"Mama Bird, Eagle One."

"Eagle One, Mama Bird, go ahead."

"Splash one bogey. Requesting area-wide target damage assessment." Dare was cautiously holding at five thousand feet north of the main area of destruction

"Roger, Eagle One, stand by." Lanie toggled the *Manta* sensors at different locations. She pressed several keystrokes on the laptop causing the computer to begin a rapid correlation of picture frames separated by seconds in the area.

The only movement the computer could detect was the smoke columns from the burning truck tires on the heavy trucks. "Eagle One, all targets confirmed destroyed. No movement detected. Mike Charlie recommends deploy Team Four to confirm."

"Mama Bird, Eagle One copies, have Mike Charlie hold Team Four until I make contact on the ground."

Dare didn't want to put Team Four at risk until he had a chance to do a face-to-face with survivors in the ranch house. *Those poor bastards have had hell today and might be a little trigger happy.*

Mission Commander Kit Kitaen agreed with Dare's request and made the call. "Eagle One, cleared for contact. Mike Charlie out."

Dare eased the throttle back as *Eagle* One entered the dive. He studied the battlefield as it slowly passed under the nose. *Damn, that's worse than the initial push into Baghdad.*

Bull came to the same conclusion, although neither man had said a word. War was not a beautiful thing and the afternoon's engagement had certainly been a war.

EAGLE NEST RANCH HOUSE

Mike watched as the strange craft hovered and descended south of the house. "Hold your fire. All stations...I say again, hold your fire."

He kept the Barrett at port arms as the gear extended as it hovered lower and began to kick up dust. Mike watched it set down gently and the engines were shut down.

A wide gull-wing door opened on the left side of the craft behind the cockpit. Two well-equipped armed men in gray and black digital camo ducked under the door. Mike threw the Barrett to his shoulder, dropped the bipod on the window sill and lined up one in his sights.

The first man from the craft assumed a standing position, but set his rifle at the order arms position beside his right leg. The other did the same.

Mike relaxed only a bit. *Who are these guys?* A tall man in a black flight suit with a lightweight survival vest, stepped out from under the door and removed his black helmet. Mike got a good look at him through the scope. "Ho…ly shit."

He propped the Barrett up against the inside of the window sill, sped down the stairs three steps at a time and headed for the door.

"What is it, son?" Gunter asked as he stormed by.

"The cavalry."

Mike ran across the parking lot and slowed as he got to the strange looking vehicle. He walked the final few feet up to the black-clad aviator and extended his big hand to the silver-haired flyer. "Iron Horse, you old son of a bitch…nice of you to drop by."

"Dammit, Cowboy, what did I tell you about calling me a son of a bitch?" Dare grinned.

"Well, at least I didn't say stupid."

They gave each other backslapping bear hugs.

"Looks like we're even." Mike smiled.

Dare looked around at the carnage. "I don't know, I'd say you were doin' pretty good."

"Yeah, but I think we'd just run out of rope when you showed up...and what the hell is that?" Mike pointed to *Eagle* One.

"That little thing? That's the Moller M600/A fast attack VTOL. Got a squadron of 10 of these little babies...We launch out of the back of a C-5M."

"No shit?...Out of the back...in flight?"

"Oh, yeah, it's a trip...Oh, just a minute, gotta make a call."

Dare stepped to *Eagle* One and stuck his head inside. "Bull, call Mike Charlie and tell him to launch Raptor Four."

"Can do, Boss."

Dare turned around and pointed skyward. "Watch this."

Mike looked up, shaded his eyes and saw the *Galaxy* at around 12,000 feet as five tiny specs exited out the side and go into free fall.

The stack of dots plummeted at terminal velocity of 120 miles per hour as they fell. In sixty-six seconds, the first had reached 2,000 feet and deployed his parawing. The other four followed in sequence.

The five parachutists spiraled down toward the ranch house. At one hundred feet, each dropped his gear bag on a twenty-five foot lanyard. The bags hit the ground first, followed quickly by each Raptor.

They all landed standing, quickly collapsed one side of their chute to prevent being dragged and pulled the shroud lines in. Each unbuckled his harness and expertly rolled up the canopies. They all grabbed their gear bags, extracted their M-4 carbines and donned their rucksacks.

Leroy Poole led the team at double-time to Dare and Mike. "Raptor Four reporting as ordered, Boss."

"Glad you could join us, Bad. Have your team sweep the area for intel, live ordinance, functional weapons and wounded…Although I don't think you'll find any of the latter."

Mike stuck out his hand to Leroy. "Bad, I'm Mike Hermann. We're damned happy to see ya'll…Listen, there are two Gators in the equipment barn and those two Humvees over there are a little worse for wear, but still run if you want some wheels…This is a big place."

"Thank you, sir. Heard a lot about you…Appreciate the rides. Makes our job go a lot quicker."

"Keys are in 'em. Help yourselves."

"You heard the man, let's move out, ladies."

Bull stuck his head out of *Eagle* One. "Say, Boss, Hammer wants to know where you want her to set down."

"Tell her to come here. We need her GIBs."

"Roger that." Bull ducked back inside.

"Her? Hammer is a her?" asked Mike.

"Hell, she's the one that saved your bacon with those three tangos over by the barn…I'd be real nice to her…if I was you." Dare laughed.

"Ya think?…How many of these 600/As or what ever you call 'em do you have here?"

"We only have three on this mission. *Eagles* Two and Three are piloted by our lady flyers…They're both great sticks."

"Noticed."

Mike's radio on his hip crackled. "Big Eagle, Silver Eagle. I'm assuming from all the palaver going on out there that we can stand down."

"Damn…Affirmative, Silver Eagle. All units stand down and acknowledge. Come on down and meet the cavalry."

"Copy all. Silver Eagle out."

"Sausageman copies."

"Songbird copies all."

Something about the lilt of the feminine voice on the radio caught Dare's attention. "Mother?"

"Baby sister, Carla. She's a piece of work…I think you'll like her."

***

CHAPTER EIGHT

**DEPARTMENT OF DEFENSE
THE PENTAGON
28 July**

Secretary of Defense Harold Baker finished making notes on his yellow legal pad and called to Willamena Parker. "Bill"—as everyone referred to her—had served every Secretary of Defense since she was hired in 1970 during the Nixon administration—she was sixty-four years young.

Bill not only was Executive Assistant to the SecDef, but some people would say she *ran* the DoD. If asked who her favorite President was, she would say without hesitation, 'Reagan'.

"Bill, I need you for a moment."

She quickly entered. "Yes, sir, how may I help you?"

"I've made some notes on the BEF. I need you to pull their file to fill in some of the blanks."

"I could have saved you a lot of trouble, Mister Baker. You should have asked before making your notes...I drafted the original contract for the BEF during President Reagan's second term…The whole concept was his idea."

"Should have known…Is there anything about the DoD you don't know?"

"Not much, sir. I am in my forty-fourth year here…the Gipper was always concerned with the Posse Comitatus Act and felt we needed an ultra-rapid deployment black ops strike unit that is not—and cannot be—officially approved and is independent of the military for plausible deniability. He suggested to his SecDef, that he create a contract group made up of all former special ops personnel from all branches…The crème de la crème, as it were."

She laid out the history of the BEF… "The SecDef set up the group and since he had been a fan and collector of the old Black Hawk comic books when he was a teenager, he decided to call the group the Black Eagle Force.

"Reagan made it an Executive Order for the civilian group's existence via contract with the DoD under *TOP SECRET NOFORN* status. BEF was set up as a corporation in the state of Nevada and was to be funded from the discretionary black ops funds in the DoD."

"Why Nevada?"

"Nevada doesn't require the recordation of the corporate organizers."

"Of course."

She continued, "The Secretary had me select facilities and equipment the unit might need and sell it to the corporation for one dollar and other good and valuable consideration.

"We have continued upgrading their operational equipment with the very latest technology…much of it before it was deployed to the services."

"How do they get on station?"

"The first iteration of the BEF used armed dune buggies dropped by parachute from their original C-130. The team deployed in after the vehicles. They now have a C-5M Super Galaxy…They were so successful domestically, that their role has been expanded to global."

"Who was the first leader of the BEF?"

"A crusty Vietnam vet, Marine Brigadier General "Wild Bill" Edwards. Medal of Honor recipient and one hard-nosed son of a bitch…if you'll pardon my language, sir."

"Wild Bill! I'll be damned…never knew."

"Not many did. He was the first in a long line of gutsy BEF leaders. They have been SEALs, Rangers, Delta Force and Marine Force Recon. There have been a total of three MoH recipients with the team since its inception. The BEF has its own traditions…Their motto is, *Semper Paro Bellum*."

"Latin for Always Ready for War?"

"You got it. With the rapid escalation of technology and the development of the VTOL Skycar by Moller International, the BEF finally reached their full potential envisioned by President Reagan.

"They can be notified, contracted by Standard Protocol and be wheels-up in less than fifteen minutes to anywhere in this hemisphere. It takes a little longer if they have to go to Asia or Europe."

"What's a little longer?"

"Almost an hour...We have to coordinate refueling and sanctuary with our nearest base or carrier group," replied Bill.

"Carrier group?"

"On occasion, sir. Their M600/A Black Eagles have a range of over seven hundred miles and have had to land on one of our carriers for refueling, maintenance and rearming when their C-5M mother ship doesn't have a place to set down...Oh, they launch from the back of the Galaxy when they arrive on station, usually at ten thousand feet...They call the C-5, *Mama Bird*."

"My God, no wonder they're one of our most valuable assets...Prepare a complete operational file of the BEF...I'm sure Madam President hasn't seen it yet."

"Right away, sir."

EAGLE NEST RANCH

Mike saw Gunter step out on the porch with his cane. He turned to Dare. "Come on, I want to introduce you to my dad. He's an old jarhead too...'Nam."

"I'd be honored." Dare noticed the cane. "Old war wound?"

"Nah, horse wreck couple months back, broke his hip...On the mend though." Mike chuckled. "He's tougher than mule hide."

As the two walked toward the house, Dare noticed the large blood smears on the caliche drive. "Jesus, what did you use on those guys, a grenade launcher?"

"Nope...Carla's coyote gun."

"Coyote gun? What the hell caliber coyote gun can do that?"

"Hmm...I'd say sixteen penny."

"Excuse me? Did you say sixteen penny?"

"Yep, does a good job, huh?...Nailed those bastards."

"You're pullin' my leg."

"Get her to show you her little toy."

"Toy my ass."

They stepped up on the porch. Gunter held out his hand. "Gunter Hermann...welcome to Eagle Nest and I really mean that...Semper Fi."

Dare took his hand and shook it firmly with both of his. "Semper Fi, Mister Hermann. Dare Phillips...It's an honor to finally meet Mike's dad."

Blaze stepped out on the porch—Gunter turned. "Oh, Dare, I want you to meet my baby...Carla."

She extended her hand, Dare took it gently.

"Dad!...How do you do? My friends call me Blaze... Dare?...That's an interesting name. Is there a story that goes with it?"

He was captivated by the emerald green eyes of the willowy, five foot-ten, redheaded beauty. "You could say that...but we'll save it for another time...Blaze."

"I'll hold you to that." She winked.

Dare noticed the tiny cuts and dried blood on her face and neck. "You're hurt. I've got a med-tech on my team. He's currently treating one of the pilots up at your landing strip. As soon as he's done, I'll have him take a look at your wounds."

"These are nothing, but we've got one of our people inside with multiple gunshot wounds and another that needs stitches."

Dare took the encrypted CSEL survival radio from the upper left pouch on the vest and changed the frequency from 121.5 guard to the secure operational BEF frequency for this mission. "Doc, Eagle One."

"Eagle One, Doc. Just finished patching up Bug. Eagle Two took a couple hits from a 50 cal. He was lucky...stopped one of 'em with his butt before it did any real damage. It had already gone through two layers of Dragonskin, so was fairly well spent. He'll have a nice scar he won't be able to show in mixed company...What's up?"

"I've got two wounded here at the ranch house that need treatment. I'm sending Bull in Eagle One to pick you up."

"Roger that."

"You copy that, Bull?"

"Copied all. Starting engines now."

Dare turned back to Gunter. "Mister Hermann, do you mind if we set our C-5 down on your strip? We have some repairs to do on Eagle Two."

"Certainly, *mi casa, su casa*...and please call me Gunter."

Dare nodded and keyed his radio. "Mike Charlie, Eagle One."

"Eagle One, Mike Charlie, go ahead."

"You can set down on the ranch strip. I'm leaving Eagle Two's Raptors to help Partsman with the engine exchange."

"Partsman won't need much help. Those engines only weigh 80 pounds," MC replied.

"I know, just wanted to give them something to do. They can hold it while Partsman hooks it up."

"Roger that."

Eagle One lifted off in a cloud of dust. As it cleared the trees surrounding the house area and headed east toward the strip, Hammer, in *Eagle* Three, settled to the ground.

The side door opened after the eight engines spooled down. The first to exit were the Raptors followed by Killer Kilgore and then Karen. The five foot-six pilot stood back up after she cleared the door, removed her black flight helmet and shook her strawberry blonde hair loose.

Dare elbowed Mike. "There's your guardian angel."

"Jesus H. Christ and all his disciples."

The snug black flight suit did nothing to hide her hourglass figure as she walked toward the porch. Mike could not help but notice her ample bosom even underneath her survival vest. Her striking antique gold eyes seemed to sparkle when she glanced at him. He was sure he saw her smile widen, showing her even white teeth, when their eyes met. Or was it his imagination?

"Hammer, this is the guy whose butt you saved on the first pass. Meet Mike Hermann...Cowboy, Karen Gibbs, better known as Hammer."

"Normally I would shake hands...but I think this occasion calls for a hug." Mike grinned.

He stepped closer and gave her a real hug. Hammer responded with equal fervor. She finally broke and stepped back.

She looked up at the towering blonde Texan in the faded Marine Corps T shirt. "Please don't tell me you're a damn jarhead like him." She jerked her thumb at Dare.

"Guilty as charged."

165

"I told you not to tell me…Anybody got any cold water? It's been a long day."

Blaze piped up, "Excuse my block-headed brother for his lack of manners. I'm Blaze…ya'll come on inside where it's cooler and I'll make some iced tea. Or you can have just good old spring water…your choice."

"Blaze, Mike tells me you've invented an interesting new toy," Dare mentioned to her as they walked to the front door.

"Toy! Did you see what my toy can do?" She retorted.

"I saw the results and I'd love to see the weapon."

"Oh…well if you insist, it's inside."

EAGLE NEST RANCH
LANDING STRIP

The C-5M touched down on the asphalt strip. Smoke billowed from the big tires as Gears pulled the throttles momentarily to idle and then reversed the big jet engines. He pushed the reverse levers back to idle as he braked the big black bird to a halt 3,900 feet down the runway.

The *Galaxy* executed a 180 degree turn and taxied back toward the small hangar at the south end of the strip. *Eagles* One and Two were parked in front.

Eagle One powered up and lifted off with Bull and Doc, and then headed back to the ranch house as *Mama Bird* approached.

The powerful General Electric CF6-80C2 engines spooled down once Gears closed the throttles.

Partsman opened the rear ramp and wheeled a dolly down with the replacement 1500 cc Rotapower engine for *Eagle* Two.

On top of the engine crate were his gray metal tool box and resin repair kit for skin damage.

The two Raptors had already removed the cowling from the right side front nacelle. Partsman opened his tool kit and began unbolting the ruined engine from its mounts.

Jill stood by observing. "Be gentle, Partsman...this is my baby."

"I'm painless, I can guarantee you that. Looks like you took a golden BB through the nose cone right into the front engine...It's a good thing you were at max range of that Ma Deuce or the round would have gotten them both."

"Thank goodness for redundant engines...I should have known better and launched from 3,000 feet instead of 2,500, then Bug wouldn't have been hit."

Partsman looked at the anguished face of the young pilot—he'd seen this before. He stopped unbolting the aerodynamic nose cone. "Jill, I may be just an old wrench turner, but let me tell you something. What we do for our country is damned dangerous work. Anytime you go up, you're going in harm's way...You're not the first pilot to second guess themselves after a mission...and you won't be the last. Count your blessings and learn from your mistakes...Now go get me a bottle of water while you're resting...working in the sun is hot."

Jill smiled. "You got it, Partsman...and thank you."

She turned, trotted up the ramp and headed for the coolers.

EAGLE NEST RANCH HOUSE

Blaze came downstairs with her coyote gun cradled in her arms and walked into the spacious kitchen where everyone was sitting around the large rustic breakfast table drinking iced tea or ice water.

Dare got to his feet as she approached. "That little thing did all that damage?"

She opened the bolt. "It did. The electromagnetic pulse accelerator or coil gun propels a ferromagnetic projectile at ultrahigh velocity. The kinetic energy developed at 12,000 feet per second was shown to exhibit characteristics similar to KE weapons fired from an Abrams tank.

"Of course, the coyote gun velocity is over twice that of the latest M829A2 munition which is clocked at only 5,038 feet per second. The plasma field generated upon impact with metallic objects, showed complete burn-through on all vehicles targeted. I haven't had the chance to personally review the extent of damage to the truck drive trains."

"But what about those red spots out on the driveway?" Dare inquired.

"The human, or animal body for that matter, is composed almost entirely of water, which, as we all know, is not compressible…At the point of impact, the projectile sets up a hydrostatic shock wave with a force of such magnitude that it exceeds the fracture strength of the calcium skeletal matrix…as well as leading to instantaneous plastic deformation and tensile failure of the internal musculature, organs and epidermis."

"What did she say?" Killer had a deer in the headlight look.

"She said it kicks ass," answered Mike.

Dare looked at her in wonder. "You mean they…"

Blaze cupped her hands and clapped them together making a popping sound. "They just disintegrate…simple as that. Like popping a balloon."

Karen's jaw dropped. "Simple? Just who are you…a Stephen Hawking clone?"

"I understand the concept…I think," mused Dare.

"She got her Ph.Ds. in Electrical Engineering and Physics at Rice University when she was twenty-one," Mike chimed in.

"Who'd of ever thunk?" Karen commented.

Bull and Doc entered the kitchen. Andy was carrying his med-tech kit. Blaze laid the coil gun on the table and turned toward Bull and Doc. Dare instantly snatched up the weapon and started looking it over closely.

"Where are the wounded?" Doc looked around.

Blaze pointed at the hallway. "Ron is the most serious…he's back in Dad's bedroom. Nacho is in the den in the Lazy Boy icing his severely sprained ankle…Mike, would you get Bull something to drink, I'll show the Doc where dad's bedroom is."

Mike poured a big glass of iced tea.

"Thanks…I really needed this." Bull took three long gulps.

"Pick a chair and take a load off."

"Pass, I've been sitting for over five hours already…my ass's numb."

"Been there, done that." Mike returned to his chair at the table. "Iron Horse, flip the rifle over and press the release button on the floorplate."

169

Dare was still studying Blaze's coyote gun. He looked up and did as instructed and saw the column of headless sixteen penny nails in a spring-loaded custom aluminum magazine. His eyes got wide. "That's what this thing uses?"

"Well, they are ferromagnetic, right?"

"I'll be damned."

"You know something?…The one thing I can't figure out is how all these vehicles got over here in the first place." Mike sipped his ice tea.

Blaze came back into the kitchen and saw that Dare's glass was almost empty, picked up the tan crock pitcher.

"I'd say that was pretty obvious," Dare replied as she filled his glass. "Thank you, pretty lady…We need to talk later about your little invention."

"Be a pleasure." Blaze looked at him with a twinkle in her eye.

He watched as she walked back to the stove and started boiling some more water for tea. *Damn, she looks just as good from this side as the other,* he thought, and then turned to Mike. "They drove across at the low water crossing 800 yards north of here."

He looked Dare straight in the eye. "Look, Colonel. I've lived here most all my life, except when I was off to college or in the Corps deployed someplace…The river is a good six feet deep along this side.

"I tried to wade across back when I was home on leave two years ago…Can't see that Dodge box truck or those pickups crossing…Shoot, even the Humvees would have played hell gettin' across. I've been too busy dodging bullets all afternoon to think of it till now."

Dare set his glass down and pulled the radio out of his vest. "Mama Bird, Eagle One."

Lanie pressed the talk button on the console. "Eagle One, Mama Bird, go."

"You still got Manta on station?"

"Affirmative. Mike Charlie is monitoring the sweep crews. Looks like they've made it almost all the way north to the crossing, over."

"Can you get me a LADAR image of the river bottom at the crossing?"

"Can do easy, boss…It will take a couple minutes for the computer to build it. Stand by."

"LADAR?" asked Mike.

"New technology. Laser Detection And Ranging. It's a powerful laser in our Predator we call Manta. We can use the same laser for targeting our JDAMs, and PAASMs."

"Predators? Ya'll have Predators?…Do you have JDAMs on the 600s?" Mike asked excitedly.

"Yeah, we have a type of a Predator overhead…shaped more like a B-2 though…and no, we don't have JDAMs on the Black Eagles. We keep them on Mama Bird." Dare had a slight smile.

"You guys are loaded for bear!…Who the hell do you work for if you are not in the Marines any more?"

Dare held up one hand. "Hold on there, Cowboy. Some things are *TOP SECRET NOFORN* about our merry little band. I can't go around telling everything, even to old Marine buddies…Hope you understand."

Mike nodded. "Got it. Security clearances and all that crap." *Who are these guys?*

Dare grinned. "Now, 'course if you worked for me, you'd have the need-to-know…And I'd tell you in a New York minute."

"Right." Mike nodded again. *Wait a minute! Was that a job offer?* His head was swimming.

"Eagle One, Mama Bird."

"Mama Bird, Eagle One, what have you got?"

"Your suspicions were spot on, boss. There's a solid low-water crossing about eighteen inches below the surface. It's almost fifteen feet wide…I'll upload a view to Eagle One."

"Thank you, Lanie, Dare out." He looked at Mike with a big grin. "Sometimes a blind hog can find an acorn…You folks have a big backhoe?"

"Sure. Got a big Case 580 to clean out ditches and creeks," Mike replied.

"Well come on then, let's get into the excavation business."

Mike joined him as Dare led the way to the front. He stopped just before reaching the heavy plank door. "On second thought…don't think we'll need your backhoe after all. Lose the ice tea glass, Cowboy. We don't permit open containers on board…."

"But I thought…"

"I'm driving. You get to watch," said the silver-haired CEO. They walked across the drive out to the black craft.

Inside *Eagle* One, Mike's eyes were huge as Dare showed him the flat CRT screen displays. The LADAR clearly showed a massive river crossing had been secretly constructed using native fieldstone. As Mike strapped in the WSO seat, Dare closed the side entrance door electrically and started the engines. In two minutes they lifted off vertically and were airborne overlooking the former battlefield at an altitude of 200 feet.

"Team Four, Eagle One."

"Bad here, Dare, go ahead," Leroy Poole answered.

"Clear your team four hundred meters a mile south of the mill. We'll be going hot at the river."

"Roger that."

Dare accelerated the small bird to 300 knots and transferred the controls over to Mike. "You have the aircraft."

"I have the aircraft." He put his left hand on the side stick by his knee and his right on the center mount throttle.

"Take us up to four thousand and fly heading 360."

Mike pulled back on the stick, added power, turned smoothly to the north and rolled out.

"Keep it below ninety percent." Dare pointed at the engine RPM.

Mike marveled at the power of the engines. "Lots of thrust at ninety from these four engines."

"Eight engines actually...two per nacelle, 172 hp each," Dare corrected.

Mike leveled at four thousand feet. "This flies a lot easier than our Cessna 180."

Dare smiled once again. "Press the switch on the throttle marked Altitude Hold."

Mike complied and grinned when Dare told him to take his hand off the stick.

"Now pull the throttle back to forty percent and watch the nacelles."

As the airspeed dropped, the nacelles began to rotate vertically and as the speed slowed below sixty knots, the engine RPM climbed without input from either pilot. Airspeed fell to zero and the engines were spooled up to seventy-eight percent.

"That is friggin' awesome."

"All computer controlled," Dare added. "Move the stick to the left and roll out on the river crossing."

As if by magic, the craft slowly rotated left and stopped when Mike centered the controls.

Dare pointed at the instrument panel. "See that button on the right of the CRT screen marked Overlay?...Press it."

In seconds the image of the LADAR was ghosted over the visual image on the forward-looking camera displayed on the medium-sized flat display.

"Now press the blue button on the pistol grip atop the stick."

Mike complied and the *HUD* appeared before him.

"Use the round black trim button at the back of the stick to move the orange H on to the low water crossing."

Mike watched as the icon glided across the *HUD* and an identical one moved across the Center Targeting Display.

"Small movements, like this." Dare demonstrated.

"Got it." Mike quickly corrected to the center of the structure.

"Nice...Slightly lower...A little more. Stop. TLAR."

Mike smiled at the familiar That-Looks-About-Right. *Some things don't change.*

"Eagle One going hot," Dare announced on company ops frequency. "Flip the second covered switch to ARM."

Mike complied. "Are we really going to...."

"Hold there and squeeze the red trigger on the pistol grip."

Mike swallowed and pulled it. An AGM *Hellfire* missile on the top of the right rear nacelle wing strut, blasted off the pylon rail and roared off.

It accelerated to Mach 1.3 following a laser identifier transmitted from *Manta* circling high above. Five seconds after launch, the 106 pound missile traversed the one and one-half mile distance down to the Rio Grande River crossing.

When the twenty pound HE warhead detonated, tons of rocks, water and a handful of channel catfish and carp flew four hundred and fifty feet through the air. The secret causeway was no more. In minutes, the slow moving river looked exactly as it had before.

"Yee haa!" Mike blurted on the intercom. "I have *got* to get me one of these!"

Iron Horse had a big grin on his face, too. "When do you want to start?"

EAGLE NEST RANCH HOUSE

Gunter looked at his watch. *4:30, gosh, it seems like a lot later*. But he and the others in the house had lived a lifetime in less than two and a half hours.

The sun was getting lower, but outside, the heat still lingered on. *Eagle* One was returning from the north and settled down as another came in from the airstrip to the east.

Gunter watched from the house as Mike and Dare bent down to clear the gull wing crew door on the left side of the *Eagle*. The two men talked and laughed while making highly animated sweeping motions with their hands. Gunter recognized hand flying when he saw it. He had seen Huey and Cobra pilots do it in briefing rooms back when he served in Vietnam.

He hasn't laughed like that since he got back from Afghanistan, he thought. Mike worked hard to be a good rancher, but something was missing in his life and Gunter sensed what that something was.

Dare and Mike stopped as they reached the porch and Dare pointed at the way the gear extended on *Eagle* Two as Jill brought it to a hover fifteen feet above the ground and slowly let the bird kiss the earth. Two men in black flight suits stepped from the plane.

Dare turned to Mike. "Cowboy, I'd like you to meet our Galaxy AC, Gears Formby and our MC, Kit Kitaen…also Chief Operating Officer."

Gears extended his hand. "Good to meet you, Mike. Dare sure thinks highly of you."

"Nice to meet you, sir."

Kitaen's grip was firm, like that of the warrior he was. "Howdy...All my friends call me Kit."

"Pleasure is all mine...Kit. You guys did a helluva job today."

The MC smiled at the compliment. "And our gals weren't half shabby, either."

"Shabby?"

Mike looked over and almost forgot to breathe as he saw the most beautiful woman he had ever seen walking up.

The six foot blonde with dark blue, almost violet, eyes had left her survival vest, along with her flight helmet, in the seat of her bird. Her eyes, dramatically framed with expertly applied eyeliner and smoky gray shadow, brought Mike deeper into her captivating beauty.

The BEF black flight suit hugged her toned athletic body. The partially unzipped suit showed a tiny gold cross on a slender gold chain as it hung just above her tanned cleavage. Her smile radiated from perfectly white teeth that had never had a single cavity. Mike stared at her full lips covered in a glossy bright red lipstick. "Who you callin' shabby, Mike Charlie?"

Kit laughed. "Give 'em too many attaboys and they get the big head."

Dare noticed the *goddess affect* Jill had on the speechless Mike. He had seen it before when men met her for the first time.

"Jill, this is Mike Hermann. Also goes by Cowboy or Big Eagle...Take your pick."

She smiled coyly and her eyes sparkled. "I like them all."

"This little lady here is our resident fighter pilot and newest member of the BEF. She was flying Eagle Two that took out one of the big trucks as well as the last APC," Dare continued.

Mike stuck his hand out and stammered, "Pleased to mate your acquaintance." He was clearly smitten, big time.

Jill glanced down at the bare ring finger on his left hand. *Nice...*

Inside, the introductions continued with the rest of the Hermann family. Gunter approached Dare. "What do you folks have planned for dinner?"

Dare looked at Kit—he shrugged. "I'm afraid our plans for today didn't get as far as dinner."

Gunter looked at his watch—it was 4:45. If he hurried, he could catch Ralph before the main day crew left for home. "It would be our honor to feed you some of our own products...It's the least we can do...Not open to discussion," Silver Eagle declared.

Dare looked back at Kit, who nodded enthusiastically. *Time to feed the teams and still make it back to headquarters by 2100.* "Sounds like a plan to me...We certainly appreciate it."

Gunter looked at Blaze and Mike. "Let's get busy, children."

The portable tables and benches were set up quickly under the spreading branches of a large live oak tree near the house with the help of the BEF team.

What started out earlier as a combat mission was almost taking on the feeling of a picnic, except, the Hermann ranch had lost a good peaceful man and two others involved were injured in the fight.

DEPARTMENT OF DEFENSE
THE PENTAGON

Bill Parker entered the Secretary of Defense's private office with a small sixteen gig flash drive in her hand.

"I'm glad I finished downloading these BEF mission files before you left. Give you something to read at home," she said.

He looked at the flash drive. "Great guns, Bill...full? All of that BEF?

She nodded. "Yes, sir. It includes all of the government agencies that have contracted the BEF from DoD...CIA, DEA, Homeland Security...you name it."

"I'm assuming since you named the CIA, it includes world wide."

"It does. Starting with the USSR, then China, the Balkans, Libya, Colombia, Syria, Argentina, Cambodia, Malaysia, China again, Ukraine, Moldavia, Lithuania, Russian Federation, Bulgaria, Albania...."

"Ok, ok, king's X...That's quite a litany of missions," Baker interrupted.

"They include, in addition to quick strikes, hostage rescues, surveillance, infiltrations and extractions...None of their missions have ever lasted over three days," Bill added.

"Jesus, Mary and Joseph!"

"On the downside, eight BEF members have been KIA...All have been deniable."

The SecDef leaned back in his burgundy leather executive chair. "Such a pity that great Americans like that have to go unrecognized or even acknowledged for their patriotic heroism. No medals, no commendations...Just a lonely grave some-where."

"Yes, sir...however, the BEF has, by far, the lowest percentage mortality rate than any of our official Special Ops...They try to go in unseen and quietly leave the same way...except for the bodies they leave in their wake."

OFFICE OF MARTINE AGUILAR

It was 6:30PM in Nuevo Laredo. Martine nervously sat awaiting a return phone call from his boss, Luis Torrejon. He had called twice on his cell, something he really didn't like to do when his boss was in a bad mood.

Luis should have been back by 3:30PM at the latest, at least that's what Chico down at the Todo El Mundo Helicopter Rentals had said. He told Martine the Hughes 500 had only enough fuel for three hours and El Toro and his pilot had left just after lunch time. If they were going to be much longer, it was going to cost more.

Chico called again after five. "Where the hell is my helicopter?"

Luis was not able to receive calls on his cell phone—it had been shattered by the third shot from his own custom engraved Colt 1911. After passing through his right kidney, the Aguilla jacketed hollow point had continued its upward path and wrecked havoc on his ascending large intestine, stomach, heart and sternum before tearing a quarter-sized hole in his left breast and shirt pocket.

The phone had the misfortune to be in the unlucky pocket when the slug exited the big man's body—not that it mattered much. The bodies of Luis and his assailant were, shortly thereafter, both blasted to small pieces which were being consumed by some very happy fish and turtles.

Martine had no intention of personally carrying out Torrejon's order to kill Colonel Hernando Garcia. He was an accountant, not a butcher.

He had diversified the *Tres Locos* illicit cash and bought several profitable businesses as well as laundering millions through banks in Nicaragua and the Cayman Islands. Over twenty million US dollars in clean deposits lay in two Swiss numbered accounts and five more in the Cayman Caribbean Trust account. Martine kept the account information in his locked office safe.

Colonel Hernado Garcia was not a man who normally worried. His deep involvement in drug wars and smuggling was buried in a system of clandestine codes and protocols he had worked out with his intelligence chief.

When the lieutenant picked to help *El Toro* vanquish the Texans did not call back by 1630, Garcia was not worried, but he did send a coded text message to his intelligence chief, Major de Lopez to make inquiries.

At 1700 hours, a coded reply indicated negative contact. Garcia still was not concerned, but with a considerable sum of money due the colonel from the rental of two squads and two M113 APCs, he directed de Lopez to send out a maintenance flight in one of brigade's Hueys.

He shouted into the phone at his major. "Yes, dammit, overtime will be covered at a bonus rate!" *Damn. Won't anyone in this Army do his job as a duty anymore? Apparently not,* he concluded.

EAGLE NEST RANCH

Hammer and Killer gave Nacho and Ron a quick safety briefing that they made up on the spot. They had never carried passengers before, only trained Raptors—wounded civilians were a first.

Doc had given Ron a shot of morphine to help ease his considerable pain and the injured man was only slightly aware of his surroundings. In the morning, he would probably not remember how he had gotten to the hospital.

Nacho, on the other hand, had taken only an Aleve and was not in much pain, except when he bumped his inflatable boot on the back of Karen's seat. He was not in a great mood for his first ever plane ride.

Andy Long had insisted on cutting off his right boot to examine the ankle. There wasn't anything else he could do—it had swollen so quickly while Gunter tended Ron, and later to Nacho's chin injury, that he couldn't have gotten it off anyway. Still, the old Tony Lamas were his favorite and he had hoped to buy a new heel and be back in business.

The other thing affecting Nacho, was his morbid fear of flying. He would never get in the Cessna with Blaze or Mike—the thought terrified him to his core.

He was flying in some kind of UFO contraption without a window to look out. Nacho never said a word after takeoff until he could see the lights of Laredo come into view through the space in between Hammer and Killer's shoulders.

The cool air from the air conditioning ducts made the temperature pleasant as could be expected. Slowly, the fear in the ranch manager seemed to be a distant childish bogeyman and Nacho willed it away. "Is that what Laredo looks like?"

"That's it. First time to see it from up here?" asked Killer.

"First time to see anything from the air." Nacho's eyes were like saucers. "It so big, now...I remember when I was little, I could ride my bike all the way across town."

LAREDO MEMORIAL HOSPITAL ROOF

Hammer set the small black VTOL on the hospital rooftop helipad. She quickly ran through the shutdown sequence and opened the rear door. "Watch your feet," she admonished as she gingerly stepped between the two injured men.

Usually the Raptors exited first, but both of these special backseaters needed assistance. The 600 did not offer much room to spare in its width.

"Here goes nothing." Karen patted Killer on the shoulder as she ducked under the door and headed to the double doors leading to the ER downstairs.

LAREDO MEMORIAL HOSPITAL
EMERGENCY ROOM

Dare had concocted a wild story about the men's injuries and their strange craft. It was Hammer's job to keep it straight when she fed the line of bull to the nurse in charge of admissions.

She charged up to the nurses station. "I need some orderlies with a gurney and a wheelchair to the helipad, please."

"Helipad? How did you get to the helipad?"

"In a VTOL…A helicopter…sort of."

"You have injured on board?"

"Yes, ma'am, that's why I asked for a gurney and a wheelchair…They are stable."

The nurse keyed her intercom. "Orderlies to the helipad, one gurney…" She glanced up. "…one wheelchair." She then took out a form and handed it to Hammer. "Please fill this out, note the party responsible for the charges, injured parties' names and pertinent information…How were they injured?"

"We're…uh, a movie company filming a documentary. An air compressor on set ruptured and two of our stuntmen were close by…One of the men had a drain plug go completely through his thigh as well as some shrapnel wounds from the exploding tank in his arm and shoulder.

"The other stuntman needs stitches in his chin…and has a badly sprained ankle…could be broken. The production company will assume all charges…it'll be on the form."

On the roof, the orderlies were assisting Ron onto the gurney and Nacho into the wheelchair when Hammer came back out. "You men need any help?"

One of them turned to her. "No, ma'am, we're old hands at this...If you don't mind my asking, just what kind of helicopter is this?"

"Oh, it's just a movie prop," Karen replied as she entered *Eagle* Three and closed the side door.

The orderlies moved the injured men off the pad toward the door as Hammer spooled up and lifted off.

The orderly pushing the wheelchair stopped, turned around and watched the sleek black craft as it gained altitude and vanished into the darkness. "Movie prop?"

***

CHAPTER NINE

ISLA GUKUMATZ
COJONE COMPOUND
28 July

"Mister Aguilar, one of our customers in San Antonio, is very upset with your delivery service. It seems his twelve crates of Mahi-Mahi were not delivered today as promised. They should have been there by four o'clock, but the shipment never arrived. I tried calling that bull-headed friend of yours, but he doesn't answer his cell and the mail box is full."

Ronaldo DeSantis—the number one man in the Cojone organization—was speaking in coded phrases on the Motorola Iridium satellite phone as he knew the transmissions could be monitored by US law enforcement agencies.

His boss, Javier Cojone, was one of the richest arms dealers in the world. However, to call him just an arms dealer would be to render a grave injustice.

He could broker arms deals with legitimate countries, wannabe revolutionaries and coup planners as well as supply anything a narcoterrorist could put on an order.

The tall distinguished son of a former Mexican Ambassador to France didn't limit himself to arms. Additionally, blood diamonds out of Africa, cocaine and heroin were four of his top smuggled and brokered deals. The fifth was human trafficking. White slaves, sex slaves, people of all nationalities wanting undocumented entry into the Colossus of the North—as the USA was called—from Mexico and points south.

Javier Cojone was an equal opportunity exploiter of human greed and ambition. Providing what people want had been a good choice for him. With a net worth of $1.2 billion US dollars, he was clearly a major player on the world stage and had many friends in high places both at home and abroad.

Unfortunately, his choice of livelihood had also made him unpopular in certain law enforcement communities. Cojone was wanted by Interpol, the FBI, DEA, ICE and a couple of dozen countries who had nearly fallen to military uprisings powered by arms delivered by his extensive organization. The United Nations had an interest in his activities in human trafficking, but the resolution was dropped from Security Council action by the *No* votes from China, Russia, Mexico and Angola. Mexico had steadfastly refused extradition.

Lights on the Cojone compound lit up the one hundred and thirty-foot tall Mayan pyramid, like it was day. Palm trees lined the freshly trimmed lawn inside a ten foot stone wall surrounding the structure built to indulge one of Javier's obsessions.

He was fascinated by the Mayan culture native to this area of the Yucatan for hundreds of years and had bought the island because it actually was the site of a undiscovered pyramid found only in 2006 by satellite thermal imagery.

An archeologist friend in the Mexico University Department of Archeology had sent him the information, then altered the imagery to prevent its disclosure. His friend was $100,000 richer and Javier bought the entire remote island for virtually nothing.

Inside the stone pyramid, in a modern marble and glass office, DeSantis continued his conversation.

OFFICE OF MARTINE AGUILAR

"I'm just as concerned about the fish as you gentlemen are. Fresh seafood is our specialty here and I assure you that there must be a problem with the refrigerator truck. Perhaps there is also a technical problem with my friend's cell phone. I'll get on it as soon as the Telemex office opens in the morning. You can count on me," Martine lied.

"You had better clear the problem up tonight, Martine...Or we shall find it necessary to come to your office in Nuevo Laredo tomorrow and collect our deposit...you were paid in advance," DeSantis coldly stated.

The line went dead—Martine was sweating bullets. Major De Lopez had called Colonel Garcia with the bad news about his two APCs, the two troop trucks and his four squads of soldiers.

A Mexican Army Huey had flown down to La Esperanza where the pilot had personally seen the smoke across the river from the still burning truck tires. He had used binoculars and had seen, potentially, at least one destroyed APC.

In additions, small groups of black clad soldiers had been combing the area. He could not confirm what the debris was before it was spread across the Texas ranch.

The other APC was obscured behind some trees and he did not want to raise suspicions any further by flying any closer—he departed the area to the south and then returned to the base after flying west ten miles.

Colonel Garcia had called from the officer's club with a demand of $500,000 for the lost equipment and men. Luis Torrejon was presumed dead and things in Nuevo Laredo were chaotic.

Surviving members of the gang were contemplating power plays to replace their feared leader, *El Toro*. And now these guys from a big, really big time operation down south were wanting to talk to Luis.

Martine walked to the wall safe hidden behind the large portrait of Luis Torrejon and took down the gilded framed painting. He took out all the black ledger books, $40,000 in cash, a slightly used Nicaraguan passport with his picture and laid them on his desk.

He placed the items in his briefcase after removing all his other identification. Aguilar reached into his brown leather wallet, removed his Mexican driver's license and set it in the ashtray on his desk.

Finally, he reached back into the safe and opened an envelope with a Nicaraguan driver's license in the name of Ricardo Blanco. The picture on the license was quite good, very close to the one in his newly forged passport.

The newly christened Ricardo pulled a gold lighter from the desk drawer, set the Mexican driver's license ablaze on one corner and dropped the flaming document into the octagonal ashtray.

He watched it curl up and char before being almost completely consumed. Martine took one last look around the office in which he had worked for seven years and walked out the door, leaving it ajar.

Outside, he looked both ways to insure no one was watching. He crossed the dark and empty red brick street to the blue Ford Taurus rental car and carefully drove at the speed limit to the nearest international bridge to Laredo.

EAGLE NEST RANCH

Gears Formby and Blaze Hermann were engaged in a spirited, yet friendly conversation in the kitchen about the relative recharge rates of the new aluminum ion batteries versus other more generic lead acid and copper sulfate alloys.

The Alabama native had suggested a multiplexed inductive process to accelerate capacitor recharge speed even on her fascinating coil gun which had stimulated his and Dare's interest.

Dare was amused by the intellectual *tête-à-tête* between the two geniuses. They definitely spoke each other's language and it was a toss up as to who would win an IQ test in a head-to-head match up—so to speak.

Iron Horse had a chance to speak to Mike seriously about coming onboard after the impromptu dinner for the team.

Everyone had enjoyed the meal and had taken to heart the blessing Gunter had given. It was obvious to the team, that Buddy Williams, the young horse trainer killed early in the assault, was like a member of the family.

Tears flowed freely among the family and ranch employees. By the end of the evening, his death was turned into what could be called a wake, with most folks telling their favorite memory and jokes about him as a child. The talk was cathartic for everyone and helped put a softer edge to the loss they had jointly experienced.

Mike was sitting in the porch swing out on the south end of the wraparound porch, sipping on a Shiner Bock and gazing out across the property. He wanted to join the elite band of warriors more than anything he had experienced.

The facts kept staring him in the face. His father was still recuperating from a debilitating injury. The ranch foreman, Nacho, would be off his feet for days—if not weeks. Ron, the vet tech was out of commission for an unknown time and his trainer in residence was dead. There was no way he could leave Eagle Nest like this...

Gunter hobbled out onto the porch, his cane in one hand, a beer in the other and sat down. "How's it coming, son?"

"How's what coming?"

"The wrestling match."

"What are you talking about, Dad?"

"The one you're having with yourself."

"Oh, yeah…that." He looked out across the river for a moment. "Pop, I don't know what to do…The Black Eagle Force is the most exciting thing I've seen since I got out of the corps…and they want me. But…with Buddy gone, Nacho slowed down, Ron laid up for God knows how long and you not being up to full speed yet…I just can't leave Eagle Nest shorthanded."

"Oh, bullshit, boy. You think this ranch revolves around you? Hell, I can call Dean Carlisle at A&M and get a recent graduate vet to come and intern…Got a list of horse trainers long as my arm wanting to come to work here…We can handle this…It'll work out. Now…gotta go back inside. Dare wants to talk to me about something or other."

Gunter got up and negotiated his way back to the front door.

Duty to home and family was strong as Mike sat alone contemplating what his dad had said—he continued to nurse his longneck. He didn't hear Jill McElheney walk around the corner.

"Penny?"

Jill's question caught him off guard. "Penny?…Gonna take more than that." He started to rise.

"Got my checkbook…" She motioned for him to stay seated. "Mind if I join you?"

"Oh, no, please a have a seat."

Mind? Are you kidding? Mike watched her every move. Earlier at dinner he had to physically force himself to stop staring at her as she sat across the long table. This was the first chance he had to be alone with her.

She noticed that one of his pant legs was cut up from the bottom and there was dried blood soaked into the denim. "You're hurt."

"It's nothin'…Doc patched it up a while ago…Had to cut my favorite pair of Wranglers, though."

"Painful?"

"Well, yeah…just got these jeans broken in."

She giggled. "No, silly, your calf."

"Oh…Had worse."

Jill looked out toward the river for a few seconds. "Nice view."

The dry night air was crystal clear once the smoke from the burning tires stopped. A light breeze from the east helped as the temperature dropped into the low eighties after sunset.

Lights from distant Mexican villages and farms across the Rio Grande twinkled like stars in the deepening blackness. The moon was rising and the half-full golden orb brought a soft mellow glow to the limestone bluffs which frequently defined the river channel.

Looking at her sitting in his favorite spot on the ranch porch made Mike warm inside. Her classic beauty was highlighted in silhouette from the yellow light coming through the slender window behind her. "I do love the view here…helps keep me centered. It's the one thing about home I can always see in my mind whenever I'm away."

"That is so sweet…I moved around a lot when I was a kid…Air Force brat. I remember base housing, but never really got a feeling of permanence.

"My dad was, I mean is, a pilot…He retired from the Air Force last year." Something about him made her nervous. *I'm not like this*.

It was Mike's turn to smile. He could sense her nervousness. *Hell's bells…I was more calm in fire fights. What is it about her that makes me so damned jumpy?* He took in a deep breath. *Get a hold of yourself, dude.* "Where did you learn to fly?"

"Oh, I went to UPT at Willy…Of course my dad made sure I had a multiengine instrument rating before I went.

"Flew F-22s on active duty and was in the testing and development program on the F-35 at Tonopah when Dare made me an offer I couldn't refuse," she babbled on in rapid fire staccato, and then took a breath. *Why can't I talk normally? Why do I feel like a fourteen year old with my first crush?*

Jesus! Mike looked on with growing admiration. *Where the hell did Dare find this one? Are all the people in the BEF as overqualified as her?* "You flew the Raptor?…Nice. I thought getting a chance to fly the Black Eagle and shooting a Hellfire at that underwater causeway was the coolest thing I ever did.

"Although I got a few minutes in a Osprey when the copilot got shot up on a mission in Afghanistan. Now that would be a bear to try to land without some VTOL experience," Mike chattered—it was his turn to feel like a teenager. "Pardon my manners, would you like a beer?"

"Can't. Still on duty...Got to fly back to Mama Bird in a bit...Thanks for the offer, though."

"Can't believe I'm such a dumb ass. Of course you can't...What was I thinkin'?"

"Take a glass of ice tea."

"Comin' right up." Mike got up and headed to the door.

This guy is a fearsome warrior on the ground and Dare lets him fly Eagle One and operate weapons systems on his dollar ride? Where does he find these guys? Jill watched him walk away.

Gunter sat in the saddle brown Lazy Boy with his feet elevated. He had taken an Aleve to ease the dull ache in his hip.

Dare was nearby in an old stuffed leather chair. "I'm truly sorry we couldn't have gotten here sooner, Gunter. Our primary location is great for planned deployments, but we can't get to border taskings as rapidly as we would want...My gut tells me they're going to get more frequent...and a lot more violent."

"You can't be everywhere and you can't save everybody, Colonel. I learned that as a private on my first tour...You know it too...no need to apologize...It's a sign of weakness." Gunter's expression took on a serious demeanor. "I do, unfortunately, agree with your assessment of the border problems.

"Neither of our two gutless political parties have the cojones to do what's right…All they seem to give a damn about is getting reelected and playing their self-serving pork-barrel games in Washington…Leaves us folks down by the border to fend for ourselves…If it hadn't been for you guys…"

Dare looked on as Gunter turned silent in reflection. He was right. If it hadn't been for the BEF, it would have gotten ugly in the Hermann home for a second time in it's history.

There were still some folks who worked for the government who cared about the relentless onslaught of illegal immigrants as well as drug gangs, criminals and potential terrorists—Gunter was sitting next to one.

"Silver Eagle, I have a proposition that might make both of us sleep a little better at night…"

In the kitchen, Gears and Blaze were busy on a Mac laptop making the changes they had discussed on a CAD drawing of the coyote gun electrical engineering schematic.

Mike walked into the kitchen to get Jill's tea and another beer. He watched Blaze and Gears point at the screen, bickering.

"I am firmly convinced that the new aluminum ion batteries are far superior."

"Vanadium pentoxide are more readily available and are only slightly inferior."

"But the AI's recharge rate outweighs anything else."

Each had a strong preference. Finally, Gears broke the stalemate. "Shoot, little missy, let's build test rifles with one of each. Money is not an issue. Reliability and overall battery life are what's gonna make the difference. That's my story and I'm stickin' to it." He nodded sharply.

"Agreed." Blaze laughed as she saved the schematic.

She got up, walked to the far left kitchen drawer, pulled out a small black PNY Attaché eight gig flash drive, saved a copy of their work and gave the drive to Gears. "Here you go, Gears, let's have a little friendly competition. Twenty bucks for the highest velocity and another twenty for battery life."

"You're on." He slipped the tiny drive into his upper left chest pocket on his flight suit and zipped it closed.

Mike looked at Dare, Kit and Gunter huddled in a deep conversation at the far end of the room as he headed back to the front door. *Must be telling old war stories*.

Outside, he walked down the heavy weather-worn planks as the waxing moon continued to rise behind the trees lining the driveway. It was still low in the sky and had not lost its light yellow cast as the moonlight filtered obliquely through the atmosphere. He handed Jill the tea and didn't take his eyes off her.

"Thanks, Cowboy."

The golden moonlight filtered though her long blonde hair as she slid the rubber hair band off the end of the bouncy strands. She leaned back and slowly shook her head, allowing her flowing mane to cascade in a waterfall of corn silk in the moonlight.

She sat erect, as half of her hair fell over her left shoulder and took a sip of her ice tea. "Ah, that's better."

"Yes, it is." He never took his eyes from the beautiful creature beside him.

Jill felt the warmth of his stare, but was not intimidated, annoyed or afraid. She turned, smiled demurely and placed her hand in his. Together, they swung slowly in silence—the only sound was the gentle squeaking of the chains supporting the swing.

Back inside, Leroy Poole was in the den typing his sweep report on a BEF Mac laptop. To the best of their ability, the Raptors could identify sixty-eight casualties—not including the twelve civilians.

He had taken fingerprints of all unburned bodies and high resolution pictures of the dead as well as all the VIN or Identaplates on the vehicles.

DNA samples were taken and cross-referenced against the photos for future clarification. The new classified app for the iPhone Six had worked great for scanning the fingerprints—pressing the fingers in the blue rectangle on the screen, the internal touch screen digitized the print in two seconds.

The team had recovered thirty-one serviceable weapons and six still usable for parts. Most of the rest were too badly burned, melted or demolished from the Hellfire or PAASM missiles.

The Raptors had to count boots and divide by two to estimate the numbers killed in the APC's—not much was left there to bury. Over forty Mexican soldiers in uniform were identified—ID and rank were logged when available.

"Shit's gonna hit the fan," Bad predicted as he made the entries about the Mexican soldiers.

He knew the top brass in the DoD would ping when that little piece of info became available. He figured correctly that the Mexican government would deny any direct involvement and claim they were all AWOL rogues or some such bullshit. He'd seen that dog and pony show before.

The DNA samples and paper identification collected had been sealed in heavy plastic containers already on *Mama Bird*. The weapons were stockpiled in one of the Humvees and ready to go when the team headed back to the airstrip.

Leroy attached the iPhone to the Mac and downloaded all the information collected in the field. In a couple of minutes, he finished and walked out to the driveway where he had a clear view of the southern sky.

He unfolded a small metallic transmitter tripod from a black ballistic cloth case with its twelve-inch long high-tech sender. He opened the laptop and clicked an icon on the screen and sent the information.

The connection terminated automatically when complete. He stood up, stretched and yawned. It had been a long day. Bad packed his gear back up and walked into the living room. "Excuse me, sir, sweep report is on its way."

Kit nodded. "Great job."

"Thank you, sir...I'll round up the Raptors and get them back on Mama Bird."

Gunter grinned at Dare and Kit. "Well, boys...let's go tell them the news."

On board *Mama Bird*, Lanie and Sparky were kicked back with their feet up. Things had been quiet for an hour or so and Sparky had *Manta* on autopilot as it circled overhead at 12,000 feet. It was stealthy, so no one would see it on radar and it was too small to see from the ground—especially at night.

Sparky kept one eye on the Terminal Collision Avoidance System installed on the small black bird. Its transmitters were off, but the receivers were on alert for possible collisions with civil or military traffic. Not much was moving in a fifty mile radius.

It was the TCAS that first alerted Sparky of the Mexican Army Huey three hours earlier. She had Lanie tag it electronically and tracked its movement all the way back to the Army base outside of Nuevo Laredo. She also had Lanie record all radio and cellular traffic during the chopper's flight.

Her suspicions were well founded when the report came back through the Defense Intelligence Agency at Huntsville, Alabama. The DIA continuously monitored electronic transmissions worldwide and constantly made analysis of how these millions of conversations and data streams might affect our national security. Analysts were able to cross reference the Huey pilot's voice over the radio with his Army base tower and ground control and match it with the cell phone conversation he had with a Major DeSantis.

The transcript of the conversation was translated by a DIA native Spanish speaker and converted to text for the BEF.

Sparky read the transcript and hit the *print* button on the laptop and stored the information in the current operation file.

Follow up on the intel would be part of the BEF standard operational procedure, with Dare making the final decision to either maintain operational responsibility or turn the info over to the DoD for final resolution. In any event, confirmation of active duty Mexican Army troops engaged in illegal operations on US sovereign territory was big news.

Dare, Kit and Gunter walked around the wrap-around porch toward the swing.

"...Friedrich Hermann was the only survivor of Santa Anna's attack. He played a big part in the Texas victory at the battle of San Jacinto."

"That's fascinating that a man who had lost everything near and dear would pursue the Mexican Army and wage a one-man guerilla war against stragglers, foragers and scouts."

"Yeah, he had ridden countless hundreds of miles and helped warn other Texans about the invading force. In the final battle, nearly ninety of Sam Houston's nine hundred troops had been recruited personally by Friedrich...He married a lady from Brenham...my fifth great grandmother...that he met on the trip home to Eagle Nest.

"She helped him rebuild his shattered life and bore him five children. Friedrich wrote his memoirs, *Trail of Misery*, in 1853...fifteen years before his death."

"Do you have a copy?" asked Jill.

"Of course. It's in a place of honor in Dad's den, next to a shadow box case with a silver Spanish crucifix I discovered with a metal detector when I was in high school...We believe it was the one he found on his baby nephew when he returned...I'd be happy to show it to you before you leave tonight. I think..."

"That won't be necessary," Dare interrupted.

Mike turned to see the three men approaching. "But she said she..."

Dare interrupted again, "I've got a high priority mission for her to start on as soon as possible."

Jill got to her feet. "Yes, sir. What is it you need?"

"I need my best tactics and training pilot to get the newest Black Eagle pilot and weapons systems operator up to speed on the short short." There was not a hint of a smile on Dare's face.

"Yes, sir. I'll get right on..." She stopped in mid-sentence. *Wait a minute. We don't have any new pilots inbound. Who?* She was stumped. "Sir, and just who would I be training?"

Dare finally started to have a hint of a smile. Both Gunter and Kit were already grinning like a pair of jackasses eating prickly pear.

"Him." He pointed to the stunned Mike.

EAGLE NEST AIRSTRIP

Gunter, Blaze, Jill, Mike and Dare looked on as *Mama Bird* rotated and became airborne. The asphalt strip was not nearly wide enough to provide protection of the grass and crushed stone from the jet blast of the outboard engines. Each had created a cloud of dust behind the big craft, and as the *Galaxy* lifted off, wingtip vortices formed into compact horizontal mini-tornadoes in the dust—in seconds, she was gone.

Even in the pale moonlight, the dull radar-absorbing paint reflected so little light that *Mama Bird* transformed into a ghost ship in the sky. BEF procedures called for clandestine departures from all operations sites. Kit would call ATC for an IFR flight plan clearance at 17,000 feet climbing over San Antonio.

Mike watched the C-5 disappear into the night. "I never expected to have anything that big land and take off from this strip. Glad I put an extra thick layer of support base down before I paved it."

"Damn good thing you did, Cowboy. There will probably be a lot of heavy traffic here in the next twelve months," Dare added.

Blaze giggled. "Should we open a concession stand?"

"Burgers and fries. Can't go wrong," Dare replied.

The BEF crews had rearmed, refueled and done a maintenance diagnostic on *Eagle* One. The deadly backbone of the Black Eagle Force looked especially sleek and modern in the hangar next to the Cessna 180 the Hermanns used to get around the ranch and make trips to faraway Texas towns. It was the first of several M600/A and M200 birds planned to be remotely stationed at Eagle Nest.

The M200 was a small, very fast two-seater, five nacelle version designed for surveillance, reconnaissance and close air support with mini-gun only.

Dare was staying over to supervise the cleanup of the combat area over the next thirty-six hours. EOD teams from Dyess Air Force Base in Abilene, Texas, were on tap to clear any dangerous ordnance. Mortuary services teams from Corpus Christi Naval Air Station, Lackland Air Force Base and Fort Sam Houston in San Antonio, would recover the bodies.

A contingent of combat engineers from Fort Hood near Killeen would be airlifted in the next day to haul off the debris, scrape the burned spots, remove and replace any damaged vegetation. After three days, the ranch would look as if the fierce gun battles had never happened.

Jill held her BEF Mac computer under her left arm. It had both M600 textbooks, called a Pilots Reference Manual, and Procedures Operations Manual, loaded onto the hard drive.

It replaced the old Dash-1 manuals she had used when she started out in Undergraduate Pilot Training. A separate Flight Operations Procedures Manual was included to cover BEF team procedures, protocol and all guidance that were thought to be helpful.

"Well, guess that's that," Dare said as the sound of the distant C-5 faded.

"Take us home, son," directed Gunter with a big grin.

The five walked to the long white crew cab pickup parked under the glow of a single mercury vapor light next to the hangar.

Mike opened the rear door for the ladies on the driver's side. Gunter slowly made his way around the front and found Dare had already opened the passenger's door for him as well as his own.

"I'm not an invalid, Dare, just a little gimpy at the moment."

"You take shotgun…Age before beauty, Marine," Dare taunted.

He ducked the roundhouse cane swung playfully at his head as Gunter slipped into the front seat. Dare got into the back next to Blaze.

Mike hopped behind the wheel of the Ford F-250. He cranked up the big diesel engine and made a wide right turn back onto the ranch road leading to the main house three miles away.

Jill was a little upset that she had no change of clothes. "I'm gonna need to run into town and get some clothes…I'm wearing all I've got with me."

Blaze laughed. "It's eighty miles by road to the nearest shopping center…Tell you what. I've got tons of stuff you can wear. You're about a size four, right?

"Yeah, but I'm a long-legged four and sometimes it takes a six…What size shoes do you have?"

"I have boats for feet. I wear a nine."

"Me, too!" Jill squealed.

Both girls started to laugh. All the way back to the house, the two beauties carried on like a couple of school girls on a sleep-over.

Mike looked back at them in the dim light of the instrument's glow and thought, *Nice that they were getting along so well. It's nice to see her laugh after the day we had.*

Gunter took a quick glance over his left shoulder at Blaze and her new friend.

Dare mentally reviewed the events of the day—he added six more items to his already long *To Do* list. The touch of Blaze's thigh against his was warm and he could smell the freshness of the shower she had taken after dinner. He looked at the girls laughing and smiled. *What a day*. He turned and looked out the truck window.

***

CHAPTER TEN

EAGLE NEST RANCH
29 June

The golden early morning sun hadn't quite cleared the top of the horse barn. Dare was in the kitchen, making coffee when Blaze walked in, dressed in her jeans, boots and white polo shirt with the Eagle Nest logo on the front.

"Well, glad to see you know how to make coffee."

He chuckled. "Shoot, single guys can do a lot of things around the house…I make a mean lasagna and a killer peach cobbler…also do my own laundry…Like a cup?"

She nodded. "Black."

Dare filled a blue porcelain mug from the counter.

She blew on the surface of the coffee and then took a sip. "My, my, you are talented…Sleep well?"

"Like a dead man…you?"

"Well, actually, Jill and I talked till about 1:30…Haven't had another woman to talk to since my mom died."

"Oh, I'm sorry for your loss…When did she pass away?"

"She died in a car wreck between here and San Antonio when I was twenty-two."

"That's a tough age for a girl to lose her mom. But, I suppose any time is a tough age…lost both my folks while I was deployed in Saudi Arabia in the build up to Desert Storm."

"Oh, Dare…both of them? I'm so sorry."

He shrugged. "Time heals all wounds."

"I kinda became the woman of the house…Finished my post grad work at Rice and moved back home…Figured Dad needed a woman's touch around here to keep him in line." She smiled.

Dare grinned back and nodded. "That was about five years ago, according to my third grade math…Oh, I remember now…it was just after Mike pulled my butt out of my Cobra…Got himself shot in the leg in the process. Had to take emergency leave to come home for his mom's funeral."

"Yeah, Mike came to the service using a cane. I could tell he was still in quite a bit of pain…Is that how you guys met?"

"Well…we did have a little run in on the radio just prior…"

"Oh!" She laughed. "You're *that* stupid son of a bitch!"

"I see he told you the story."

"After I dragged it out of him…But he never mentioned anyone's name from over there…Actually, he doesn't talk much about it at all."

"Goes with the territory. Most people can't relate to combat and the stress it can put on a person."

Blaze nodded and took another sip of her coffee. "I know I didn't…till yesterday."

"You guys did a kick-ass job."

"Dad knew what to do and Mike was a hell of a leader…I've never seen him like that…"

"I have. That's why I want him on our Black Eagle team."

"I can tell that he's so excited…Think he kinda likes Jill… and between you, me and the fence post…she likes him too."

They heard the heavy front door open and then close. A sweaty Mike walked into the kitchen. He was wearing only gray shorts and running shoes. "Breakfast ready?"

"Got your run in, I see…What's that around your calf?" Dare noticed the neon-green wrap.

"Yep, three miles…Vetrap. Got clipped yesterday. We use it on our horses during training. It's non-adhesive, sticks to itself and won't slide down…Works great for people too. Gave Doc a case before they left last night."

"You lead a charmed life, Cowboy."

"I wouldn't say that damned charmed…He got a piece of me, didn't he?"

"You are going to shower before breakfast," Blaze quipped.

"Maybe not." Mike smelled his armpit. "Then again…maybe I will…Thought I'd get some water first…If that's all right with you, baby sister."

Jill walked in the kitchen, make-up in place, hair freshly brushed and tied back in her bouncy pony tail that waved good morning as she walked. She was wearing a pair of Blaze's Cruel Girl jeans that clung to her body like a second skin and one of her pink polo shirts that was slightly too-tight. She had already showered and was strikingly beautiful even in casual clothes. She saw his six-four ripped, glistening torso first.

Mike, slightly embarrassed, went to the fridge and grabbed a bottle of Eagle Nest Spring Water, twisted the cap off and took a big drink. "I apologize for being so undressed. Figured everybody would be sleeping in till after my run...Let me go up and hose off the big chunks."

"You look fine to me," Jill said coyly.

Blaze swatted him with a dishtowel. "Well, hustle on up, Tarzan, I'll start breakfast. Dad should be here any minute."

"I'll help...How do you like your eggs?" asked Jill.

"He normally likes them over easy, but everybody is getting scrambled today...with sausage, salsa and tortillas for taquitos...Now move it or you'll be getting cold eggs." Blaze pointed to the door.

"Yes, ma'am," Mike replied on the way out the kitchen door.

After he left, Jill commented, "Goodness, he looks like he could wrestle a bear...and win."

"He was All-American linebacker at Texas A & M, Kingsville. Got drafted by the Cowboys, but he had also been in Naval ROTC and took his commission in the Marine Corps when he graduated. His unit was deployed to Iraq after his six months IOC training at Quantico."

"Knowing Mike, he could probably still play," Dare offered.

Blaze stirred the eggs. "I think he would consider it a bit tame after Iraq and Afghanistan...He's constantly looking for new challenges. I bet he's going to fit in with the BEF just fine."

210

She went to the refrigerator and took out more breakfast fixings. She handed the packet of tortillas to Jill. "Nuke these for about a minute when the eggs and sausage are almost done…if you would."

"Can do."

Jill separated them into stacks of five and covered each stack with a damp paper towel.

Dare found a large cast iron skillet and set it on the stove. "Got any extra-virgin coconut oil?"

Blaze pointed to a cabinet next to the stove. Dare opened the door and took out the jar and spooned a small amount into the skillet as Blaze unwrapped the package of Eagle Nest Hot Breakfast Sausage and handed it to him.

He started to lay small chunks of the sausage in the skillet, took a spatula and began to chop it up. "You know, I've been thinking."

"Uh oh…smell trouble coming," Jill said.

"No, really…Blaze, how would you like to come to work for the BEF too?"

She stopped and turned to him. "You can't be serious. I'm not a soldier…What I did yesterday, I did because I had to."

"Not asking you to be a soldier…Although, I do think you'd make a good one…I want you to design new weapons for the BEF…Specifically, I'd like to see if you could convert our GAUs to coil gun operation."

She thought for a moment while Dare stirred the sausage. "Wow! What a concept. A six-barreled coil gun. Now that would be a challenge."

"You could work right here at Eagle Nest in your own lab...which I'd like to see, by the way."

"Could you get me the schematics on the GAU?"

"The schematics and we'll bring one of our spares from Denison...How's that?"

"Perfect. I'll get our D-6 and bulldoze a test firing range into the side of a hill."

"You can operate a bulldozer?" asked Jill.

"Of course...Can't everybody?"

ISLA GUKUMATZ
COJONE COMPOUND

Ronaldo DeSantis finished the last of his eggs benedict, blotted his mouth with his napkin and looked across the breakfast table at Javier. "Excellent suggestion, sir. I'll get four of our men and fly to Nuevo Laredo and get to the bottom of this fiasco with *El Toro*...The bastard is on the bubble with me anyway."

"If they can't show a legitimate reason why the drop of a dozen illegals did not occur..."

Ronaldo smiled. "Yes, sir. It will be time for a...permanent replacement."

It was Cojone's turn to smile. *This man is ruthless. Gets things done...Just like me.* "Report back when you find something concrete. I don't want to lose my customer in Mexico City."

Ronaldo nodded and excused himself from the table. He knew Javier was referring to a billionaire by the name of Juan Phillipe de la Cruz. His father had been the past president of the

Mexican state-run oil company, Pemex, and like all really high-level Mexican functionaries, had managed to skim over a billion dollars into a Swiss numbered account before he died of pancreatic cancer two years earlier.

De la Cruz disdained business, but he did covet the things that money could buy. He was an ultra-nationalist who hated the United States for all the humiliation that Mexico had suffered at the hands of the greedy gringos.

He was the founder of the shadowy group *Veintiuno de Abril Negro* and had plans known only to himself and a handful of others.

Hate and the arms needed to enact deep heartfelt revenge were just the tickets that made the world of Javier Cojone so profitable.

It was DeSantis' pleasure—and a well paid one at that—to keep the blue-eyed boss-man happy. He motioned to the four men seated near the first floor elevator as he stepped out. Renaldo carried a briefcase full of information about the *Tres Locos* gang and pictures of the top ten leaders—and their accountant, Martine Aguilar.

The four hired thugs were dressed in casual clothes, khaki pants and oversized Caribbean tropical print shirts. They followed their boss who wore a white loosely woven tropical shirt over flax-colored drawstring pants. His expensive shoes gave him the look of a well-heeled vacationer—but hid his real mission. If things didn't check out with the *Tres Locos*, there would be hell to pay.

Javier watched from the glass penthouse on top of the stone Mayan pyramid as the five men drove in an all-white open-sided jitney toward the east gate portal in the cut-coral wall surrounding the temple grounds.

The guards waved to Ronaldo as they opened the huge wrought-iron gates and the jitney drove through. The car continued down the crushed coral road toward the airfield and disappeared into the tall jungle foliage.

Vivian Montalban entered the room from a doorway to the pool and hot tub on the south side of the spacious upper deck of the pyramid. She wore a tiny fuchsia bikini top, a matching thong bottom and stood nearly six feet with four-inch leopard print pumps.

She carried a silver tray in her left hand with a pair of expensive Italian sunglasses, a cold Carta Blanca beer and a small china saucer with two small blue pills on it.

Her long black hair was swept over her left shoulder, came down and covered her perfectly shaped breasts. Vivian—a beauty queen contestant from Venezuela—had been at the compound since she mysteriously disappeared from a Caracas party two years earlier.

She had been a favorite to win the Miss World Competition, but the last thing she remembered was accepting a drink from one of the organizers. "The girls are all waiting for you, Javier," she purred as she tugged at the sleeve of his white Egyptian cotton robe.

Javier smiled broadly as he looked at her and then out at the other five beauties who awaited his presence. Two blondes, a brunette and two redheads, all naked, were sunning themselves on thick white towels that covered the alabaster pool furniture. The infinity pool was tiled in blue that matched the colors of the warm waters of the Gulf of Mexico.

He took the two Viagra and washed them down with a swallow of the beer. "Put the glasses on the table." He held Vivian by the nape of the neck with his left hand and kissed her passionately.

He slid his right hand down over the shaved mons veneris inside her tiny thong. She moaned slightly, exciting him even more. He felt a stirring in his manhood as he broke off the deep penetrating kiss.

He strode forward through the open glass door to the pool, dropped the robe to the limestone deck and stood naked for a moment so that the awaiting slaves could admire him.

Magnificently beautiful young women—taken from the beaches of the Cayman Islands, Aruba, St. Croix, Santa Monica and Miami—turned toward him and smiled as if their lives depended on it—and it did. The obviously stimulated Javier dove into the pool—the five sex slaves followed.

Vivian set the sunglasses and beer on the small inlaid tile table next to Javier's lounge chair. She reached back and tugged at the bow to the bikini top. It slid off her deeply tanned arms and dropped on her high heels as she stepped out of the thong.

She was a picture of fluid grace-in-motion as she dove into

the cool waters of the pool and surfaced near the hedonistic billionaire…

MANSION DE LA CRUZ
MEXICO CITY

High in the hills south of one of the most populous cities in the world, sat a massive 22,000 square foot mansion dedicated to Mexican culture with emphasis on the Aztec heritage. Built with money stolen from the excesses of the Mexican oil boom of the '90s, it was a testament to the vision and avarice of Juan Phillipe de la Cruz. Over three hundred fifty million dollars had been spent on the architecture and furnishings—he was still not satisfied.

The actual throne used by Montezuma sat in his great hall framed by solid jade Aztec calendars recovered from the Chimalpopoca palace.

His next acquisition was the famed Stone of Tizoc—the actual artifact used in Aztec human sacrifice during the late 1400s. Excavations continued daily in the city that sprawled below and although they were supposedly controlled by the Mexican Department of Antiquities, Juan had first choice of any discoveries through a far-reaching system of bribes.

His rigid belief that he was a direct descendant of Montezuma lay through one of the daughters born to the ill-fated ruler of Mexico. Teccuichpo Ixcaxochitzin was the oldest of Montezuma's legitimate heirs. The legendary ruler had two wives and many mistresses and produced eight daughters and eleven sons.

Teccuichpo was later renamed by the Spanish conquistadors as Dona Isabela Montezuma—after her father was murdered during Hernán Cortés' occupation of the Aztec capital in the year 1520.

Tenochtitlan—as Montezuma's ruling palace of his Aztec empire was called—was located on an island in the Lake Texcoco. The waters surrounding the palace complex had all but disappeared in the subsequent five hundred years. Over eighteen million people lived under the view of Juan de la Cruz.

He believed his plans would bring them to their feet in admiration and clamoring for his rightful selection as King of a new Aztlán—such were the dreams of a billionaire narcissist.

ISLA GUKUMATZ
COJONE COMPOUND

As Javier cavorted in the pool, a glistening white Gulfstream IV lifted off his private airstrip. It appeared to take off out of the very jungle itself.

One of the young naked blondes in the pool noticed the gear retract as it climbed its way north. Tears filled her eyes for a couple of moments. She slid beneath the surface of the crystal clear water, and with a rapid flip of her head, tossed her long wet golden hair back in place down the tanned middle of her back. She turned to face Javier and smiled—the tears were nowhere to be seen.

EAGLE NEST RANCH

The midday sun was high as the last of the unexploded ordnance was moved with robots by the EOD team to a depression near the Rio Grande.

One severely damaged Stinger, six RPG-7 rocket propelled grenades and twelve Mark 2 fragmentation grenades were in place. All would be covered with a tamping layer of earth once Master Sergeant Nolan inserted the blasting caps into the tan block of C-4. The bomb disposal suit was hot and cumbersome, but like the American Express commercial once said, he wouldn't leave home without it.

Less than a mile northeast, mortuary services teams in white coveralls and respirators were collecting the bodies along the Trail of Misery. The twelve victims and three perpetrators were bagged and tagged into heavy green vinyl bags numbered in accordance with information on sheets and photographs generated by the BEF sweep team. The gruesome work picking up scattered body parts of the battlefield would not initiate until the EOD team finished.

Jill and Mike were finishing the aircraft basic systems testing phase of the Pilot's Reference Manual for the M600/A in the study. Mike was a quick student and the systems themselves were straightforward—even if very advanced.

The BEF wanted its people to know how to use the systems, not build them. Therefore, needless information about limit switches, exact engine specifications and generator phase outputs were omitted. The redundant computer systems in the aircraft itself would indicate if something was wrong and the self-diagnostic software would advise the operator if the operational restrictions resulted from a malfunction.

"Whump."

Jill looked nervously at Mike as she heard the muted sound of the C-4 detonating under several yards of earth and rock.

"EOD," he calmly remarked. He had heard this dozens of times in the Corps. "Wanna take a break? It's almost…" He looked at his watch.

"Thirteen hundred." Jill beat him to the punch. She stood, stretched, and then twisted at the waist. "Yeah, let's knock off for a while. We've been at it for almost five hours. About my limit on the laptop. A little hard on the eyes…and the butt."

Mike got up, yawned and politely covered his mouth, looked around the room and then back at her. "You know, for two smart people, we should have thought to hook the laptop to the flat screen TV monitor…It's HD and 60 inches across."

Jill smiled and lightly tapped her head with the heel of her right hand. "Duh!"

"Come on…buy you lunch." Mike grinned.

Dare was sitting at the dinner table looking at his iPhone appointment page. Beside him was a long yellow legal pad with names of the contacts that were on the ranch for the cleanup.

Jill and Mike walked in. "Hey, boss, make you a sandwich?" asked Jill.

"Wow, yeah, thanks…Got any of that smoked turkey left?"

Mike headed toward the kitchen. "Sure…Mayo, lettuce and tomato?"

"That would be perfect."

"Have a seat…I got it." Jill cut him off at the door and pointed back to the table.

"Yessum." Mike grinned and took a seat.

"How's the system training coming?" inquired Dare.

"Piece of cake…Like the way it's laid out…No extraneous bullshit."

"You can thank Jill for that…had her rewrite it just for us after she finished her checkout."

"Really? She never mentioned that little fact…must be shy."

Dare chuckled. "Not exactly…she just didn't want to look like she was braggin'…Lots of talented folks on the team."

"I can believe that. The cleanup is gettin' done a lot quicker than I would have thought…You guys must have had a lot of practice."

Dare shook his head. "First time, actually."

Mike's face showed his confusion.

"Other than our domestic jobs, most of our contracts to date have been oversees except for Argentina and Columbia. Get in, get out, minimum time on target…We let the locals clean up. They never know who hit them. They never saw us. It never happened…We don't exist." He winked.

"Hadn't thought about it like that."

"In Iraq and Afghanistan, we were fighting a war and attempting to nation-build at the same time…Had to clean up there because we were gonna be there tomorrow."

"Got it."

There was a knock on the front door. Mike yelled out, "Come on in."

Master Sergeant Nolan entered and addressed Dare, "Mister Phillips, we're all clear here...unless you've got something else."

"I think we're good, Master Sergeant. Tell all your people how much we appreciate their work. I know that what ya'll do is highly dangerous." Dare stood and shook the veteran soldier's hand.

Nolan grinned. "That's why we get the big bucks."

"Yeah, right," Mike chimed in.

"We'll head up to the strip, load up our Herc and boogie back to beautiful Abilene...Oh, just wanted to say, that's a great strip you got there. Never expected something like that."

"We have a few biz jets come in from time to time. The pilots frowned on landing in the pastures." It was Mike's turn to grin.

"Copy that." Nolan turned toward the door and passed Jill as she came in with a tray of sandwiches. He nodded. "Ma'am." He promptly ran into a chair as he looked over his shoulder at her.

Jill giggled as he recovered and went out the front door blushing. She set the sandwich tray on the table, picked up her's and pointed at another. "Boss that one's yours."

Mike grabbed his, lifted the whole wheat bread and saw two slices of stacker bread-and-butter pickles. "How did you know?"

"I watched when you made your sandwich last night...I'm a very observant person."

"Wow, may have to take you home with me...oh wait, we are home."

They heard Nacho's voice from the front door, "Hello...could use a little help here."

They put down their sandwiches and headed toward the front. Nacho was on crutches just inside the open door.

"Little brother, your dad is having a little difficulty getting Ron out of the truck and into his wheelchair."

The two men rushed down the porch steps and out to the truck. Gunter was leaning on his cane. He pointed to the wheel chair in the truck bed. "Sometime today, boys."

Mike lowered the tailgate and Dare pulled the chair out, unfolded it and rolled it over to the open rear door. They assisted Ron out of the truck.

He was wearing a T shirt and a baggy pair of drawstring shorts that just covered the thick white bandages around his thigh—his right arm in a hospital sling.

"Damn, Ron, thought you'd be joggin' by now...been almost twenty hours," Mike quipped.

"Bite me, Big Eagle."

"He's gonna bunk in my room with me in the other bed. Gonna need a little TLC for a while," Gunter remarked.

"Ya'll hungry? We were just having lunch," Jill offered.

"Damn straight...tried to stop at Taco Mucho in town, but Nacho threatened to beat me with his crutch," Gunter replied.

"After hospital food, I couldn't stomach the thought of eating imitation Mexican food…Don't know how they stay in business," Nacho stated from the porch.

"I am so ready for some good ranch chow," added Ron.

"Well, let's see what we can do about that." Mike grabbed the handles of Ron's chair and pushed it to the porch.

When they got to the steps, he and Dare lifted the chair and set it on the porch. Mike rolled him inside.

"We got some smoked turkey, sausage and barbecue brisket left from last night as well as a big bowl of German potato salad in the fridge," Mike offered.

Ron's face brightened. "That'll do for starters."

WARBIRD RESTORATION, INC.
NORTH TEXAS REGIONAL AIRPORT
DENISON, TEXAS

Kit Kitaen was putting the individual team reports together in his BEF office under the smaller hangar on the north side of the C-5M hangar.

Each team made their own operational reports, including recommendations for future changes to the FOPM. The team only had the modified Skycars for a little over a year.

All radio transmissions were transcribed—eight gigs of still photos were downloaded and stored permanently on the base mainframe. Another sixty gigs of real-time footage from *Manta* were similarly archived—including the LADAR, infrared and visual spectrum images.

Kit glanced at his watch. *Almost 1800 hours. Got another hour's worth of work before I can transmit the report to Dare for his review.*

Several things had received special attention. First, the DoD and State Departments were particularly interested in the taped conversations between the Mexican Army Huey pilot and Major De Lopez. Second were the numbers of active duty Mexican troops involved in the attack—four squads with two APCs and Stingers would never sell as just a rogue officer trying to make some bucks on the side. Last was the CIA's strange response when the DoD disseminated the identification of the known Mexican and Guatemalan victims of the massacre.

The folks at Langley went downright ballistic on two names that were on the victim list. They demanded to have a accounting of all personnel who had access to the information and wanted to know who generated it. The CIA also wanted a confirmation of the level five reliability of the report. They did not offer any information in return and stonewalled the BEF when queried—something about the need-to-know.

This wasn't Kit's first rodeo—by a long shot. That CIA response set off his inner alarm bells and he made special note of his thoughts in the report preface for Dare's eyes only. He picked up the phone and gave Partsman a call.

Up in the big central hangar, Meadows was signing off on routine repairs and maintenance done to the *Galaxy*. The radio telephone on his waist vibrated.

He jumped and unclipped it from his belt. "Damn, thought a snake got me."

"Forgot you left it on vibrate?…How's it coming?"

"Fine, the aluminum overcast is all back together after the 100 hour check. Just a couple MCO's and we should have them done in the morning…Had to overnight a backup copilot's pitot heater…Nothing major. Mama Bird is fueled and ready to load."

"What's the status on the Eagles?"

"Three took three hits on the bottom of the fuselage with 7.62s…no penetration. Just gotta get the slugs out of the Dragonskin and patch the exo-skin…two hours tops. Two took a round in the nose and through the seat pan as well as the one that hit the right nacelle forward engine.

"We've already plugged the fifty cal hole in the nose and replaced the seat pan…Just checking the install on the engine as we speak. We'll re-Teflon the patches in twenty-four hours…after they dry."

"Have the next shift load three 600s and one 200 in Mama Bird with standard armament…I have a feeling we're going to be launching in the near future."

"You got a little mole in the SecDef's office there, Kit?"

"Nah, just a feeling in my gut…just a feeling in my gut."

EAGLE NEST RANCH

Dare watched as the last of three army two and one-half ton trucks rolled past the road to the airstrip with its somber load of green body bags. It would take them until midnight to get back to Fort Sam Houston and the refrigerated lockers.

What a waste, he mused. *So many lives lost and for what? At least they weren't US soldiers this time.* He climbed back into the Humvee, started the engine and headed back toward the ranch house. It was going to be dark in an hour and he wanted to see how the heavy machinery was doing in the vehicle cleanup.

Halfway there, he met a long flatbed olive-drab tractor trailer rig. Dare pulled to the side of the narrow ranch road to give way to the heavily-laden truck. Chained to the bed were the shot-up and burned hulks of the two Mexican Army deuce and a half trucks. The tires were reduced to blackened coils of reinforcing steel wire. Every square foot of sheet metal bore silent witness to the fury of the *Black Eagle* mini-gun pass. Neither was readily identifiable as to whom it had belonged, were it not for the manufacturer Identaplates on the frame rails.

The familiar stench of burned bodies was still present, even though the cadavers had been bagged and tagged earlier. As the truck passed only three feet from Dare's windowless Hummer, the cloud of white caliche dust and the sights, smells and sounds brought back strong memories of similar hot dusty days in Iraq.

He glanced down at the bloody seat and broken bits of glass on the floorboard and, for a moment, he was there. *Fallujah all over again.* He reached for his M-4 carbine—it was not on the seat. Dare turned and looked at the truck as it rolled out of sight. His breathing was rapid—as was his pulse. He took in a deep breath and squeezed his eyes for a moment. "Damn."

He had thought they were gone. It had been months since the last one. Iron Horse guessed that the intensity of the events of the last two days were just too close to keep the flashbacks at bay. He dropped the vehicle back in gear…

***

CHAPTER ELEVEN

EAGLE NEST RANCH HOUSE

Nacho walked on crutches into the kitchen and grabbed a bottle of water from the fridge. The pain meds the doctor gave him that morning were wearing off and he needed two more capsules to get through dinner and the night—he hadn't slept well in the hospital—he had been too concerned about Ron.

He wasn't really all that hungry and besides, the stitches in his chin and his teeth hurt when he ate, but Blaze had insisted. There were two ways to argue with her—neither one worked.

Mike had laughed and told him earlier that he would teach him how to roll when he got shot at, so he wouldn't look so funny with that silly bandage on his chin. Nacho never would understand Marine humor.

Jill and Mike finished the aircraft systems portion of the M600/A and were halfway through the Avionics and Weapons

Fire Control portions of the checkout course. She had earned a 4.0 GPA in college with a nose-to-the-grindstone discipline some of her classmates lacked.

It came as no surprise that Mike was an honor student, but she found it odd that he played football and never studied. Mike's ability to speed-read with high retention was amazing. When she hooked up the joystick, he was like a kid with an old familiar video game.

She marveled as he went through all the simulated missile firing scenarios and looked at the sixty inch flat screen in awe. "You have got to be kidding me!"

"What?…What am I doing wrong?" He never took his eyes from the screen.

Dare entered the room and whispered, "How's it going?"

A slightly frustrated, clearly impressed and perhaps a little envious, Jill simply pointed at the monitor.

Mike engaged a moving T-72 tank target with a PAASM missile and a hostile Russian Hind Mi-24 helicopter with a Stinger three seconds later. Both targets were destroyed.

"I'm out of missiles."

"We'll buy more," came the surprise reply from Dare.

Mike pressed the F12 button on the keyboard and the words *Situation Freeze* appeared on the big screen. "Hey, boss…didn't hear you come in."

"Looks like you're starting to get the hang of it."

"Ya'll are good teachers." Mike placed the joystick on the arm of the recliner and got to his feet. "Anybody else gettin' hungry?…Nearly supper time."

EAGLE NEST RANCH
BLAZE'S ELECTRONICS LAB

Blaze studied her twenty-five inch monitor displaying the schematics on the Gatling Gun. The engineers working at Dillon Aero in Arizona had done some nice updates to the older General Electric version.

Feeding glitches were less common and the design was robust. It first appeared that the biggest problem in converting the GAU to a coil gun was going to be in the receiver. *Wonderful*, she thought.

She pondered the idea of lengthening the receiver and maybe shortening the barrels a bit—maybe increasing the coil coverage to allow for the larger diameter of the projectile.

The 7.62 mm bullet was almost three times wider than the sixteen penny nail.

She had thought of several different ways to try to address the problems of supplying power and triggering the firing of the rapidly spinning barrel and coil assemblies. The precise electrical connections to those subassemblies would be a nightmare to machine and maintain clean contact points in a combat environment—plus the high voltages involved would possibly lead to arcing across adjoining contacts.

The mental gymnastics of the project were giving her a headache. Blaze closed her eyes and pressed her index fingers firmly against her temples. She focused on her breathing and cleared her head in a Zen-like state.

Thirty seconds later, she released the pressure. The pain was gone and she smiled. *Silly girl. You're not dealing with a conventional cartridge weapon.* Her eyes lit up after that basic fact came to the forefront of her engineer's brain. *Stop trying to apply yesterday's solutions to tomorrow's problems.* The words of her favorite professor at Rice came to her like a bolt from the blue.

Dr. Roman Ortowski, was as much a friend and philosopher as a cutting edge Professor of Physics at Rice University. Although she majored in Electrical Engineering, his courses in physics and thermodynamics had fascinated her to the point where she graduated with two degrees in her undergraduate studies as she did in her doctoral programs.

She particularly loved his lecture on Thinking Outside the Box. He taught her that there was no box—unless you build one for yourself. That little gem served her well in this project.

Why did the GAU have six barrels? The need for heat dissipation was one primary reason. You can't fire 6,000 rounds per minute of any conventional ammunition through a single steel barrel without destroying it.

Even the addition of a stellite lining in the bore would not allow the barrel to take that kind of abuse. Six barrels to share the workload dropped the individual cyclic rate to 500 RPM. That was significantly less than the old Army standard, the M-60, at 800 RPM or the new M-240 at 950 RPM. *No! Wait a minute. Bore heat is not a limiting design factor in my coil gun.*

Multiple barrels increased the overall rate of fire by slightly over 300 percent in comparison to single barrel weapons. *Why is that a factor?* Okay, multiple small arms hits were more lethal than a single hit. *But, why had all the AC-130 Spectre Gunships gone to larger caliber weapons including a 40mm rapid fire cannon and a 105 Howitzer?*

The answer was simple—increased terminal effectiveness of each round on target and increased standoff range, improved the *Spectre's* survivability against ground fire and gave it the chance to deploy countermeasures against missiles.

Once her mind reached clarity on what she needed to achieve, Blaze realized she was falling into the trap Professor Ortowski warned against. It became crystal clear that she had been trying to make an improved Gatling gun. What she needed to make was a *multi-barreled coil gun.*

Gone were the sixteen penny nails—she designed a new forged 7mm diameter projectile three inches long. It had a fourteen ogive finely tapered point on each end, like a long skinny football. The bullet would have a ballistic coefficient of approximately 1.58. Even better, they would have a greater penetration than the nails—if she and Gears could get the velocity close to the 12,000 feet per second achieved by the coyote gun.

Blaze glanced over at a 1845 Walker Colt mounted in a shadow box above her work bench. *That's it!*

She eliminated the revolving barrels and instead, had the feeder mechanism revolve. That simple change eliminated the need for complex mechanical devices required to rotate the barrels and maintain power to the coils. The only moving parts were in the revolving loader assembly and the projectile plunger.

Blaze had envisioned a titanium/beryllium cylinder with six grooves machined into the sides. Each groove would correspond to one of the six chambers in the fixed barrel assembly.

In each cycle, ferrous 7mm projectiles would be fed into the cylinder as it made one turn to a preset stop. A plunger with six specially machined titanium rods would be attached to an electronically controlled solenoid. When it forced the plunger forward, the projectiles were driven into the six barrels and the weapon was ready to fire.

Now all she needed was the GAU-17/A Dare promised for her test bed—her phone rang.

"Hello?"

"Hey, Sis, you coming home?"

"What time is…?"

"Dinner time," Mike cut in.

"On my way." She hung up the phone.

Blaze saved the information on her CAD program and unplugged the laptop—closed the screen and slipped it under her arm.

EAGLE NEST RANCH HOUSE

Jill had the dining table set and had the vegetables sautéed for the Hunan stir fry. She was waiting for Blaze before she finished the shrimp in the pungent spicy sauce. Mike had shown her how the kitchen was laid out and the big freezer—where the Hermann's kept the frozen meats.

Living as far from town as they did, the family usually power-shopped once or twice a month and had a lady who worked at the commercial smokehouse bring fresh fruits and vegetables twice a week. Melinda was glad to have the extra cash for the service and the Hermann's appreciated not driving forty miles to a decent sized grocery.

Blaze entered the front door and was met by the aroma of dinner. "Oh, that smells wonderful…Hey, girlfriend, need any help?"

"Got it covered," Jill replied from the kitchen. "Give the guys a call. Be ready in two shakes."

Blaze smiled when she noticed that Jill was wearing her apron. *Gonna make some man a good wife*, she thought.

Mike came in from the downstairs bathroom wearing Gunter's apron—he grinned. "Glad you could join us, Professor."

Blaze was quite aware her brother only called her that when she got carried away with a lab project. It was his shorthand for *Absent Minded Professor.* "Well, smart ass, you're gonna like what I'm working up."

"Do I get a hint?"

"Nope…Uh, you're not actually cooking anything are you?" she asked with a hint of suspicion.

"Just steamed the brown rice…No steaks tonight."

That made sense, because the only things she had ever seen him cook were steaks, pizza and breakfast. In her eyes, he was house broken—but only barely.

She walked to the stove and took a peek at the vegetables in the large sauté pan and sniffed. "Yum…Hunan or Szechwan?"

"Hunan," said Jill.

Blaze gave her a thumbs-up and went to wash her hands. *Yep, she's gonna fit right in.*

MANSION DE LA CRUZ
MEXICO CITY

Juan was very angry at the text message he received from Paloma Cantu in Washington. One of his plants in Homeland Security had intercepted a message to the Chief of Operations in ICE headquarters with a list of known dead Mexican nationals in some major battle along the border in Texas.

She did not know the exact location where the deaths occurred, but the names were to be released to the Mexican Embassy the next day. Nothing was in the US or Mexican press. Two of the names matched the operatives Juan had sent to Texas and both were missing—things did not look good. "Chuy, get me Javier again."

Juan's most trusted assistant, Chuy Murrieta left to get the phone. He had already talked to Javier's man twice that morning. He had told Ronaldo to call when he found anything concrete and no call had come—*perhaps they were not back from Nuevo Laredo.*

He could only make conjectures. One thing for certain, Javier had better come up with something solid pretty soon or Juan would take matters in his own hands. *And that would not be pretty.*

After getting a good signal indication from the transceiver, Chuy punched the ten digit number for Javier. In seven seconds the Iridium phone in Javier's office rang.

A lower level hireling in Javier's employ was the first to reach the unattended phone. "*Bueno*," said Ramon Vasquez.

"Let me speak to Ronaldo," Chuy demanded.

"*Señor* DeSantis is not available. You will have to call back later." Ramon started to hang up. The screaming on the other end changed his mind.

"Make him available! Now! Don't give me that shit!"

People involved with Javier could be deadly when crossed. "*Señor*, a thousand pardons. What I meant to say was Ronaldo has not returned from his trip to Nuevo Laredo. Can I connect you to anyone else here on the island?"

"Get me Javier," the voice said coldly.

"And who should I tell him is calling?"

"Juan de la Cruz wants to talk to him…Personally!"

The ashen-faced Ramon swallowed hard. Two of the richest men in Mexico were going to talk together—and both of them were going to be mad. He only hoped they would not be mad at him. "*Si señor*, I'll get him right away!" Ramon hurried up the stainless-steel spiral staircase to the massive carved wooden doors leading to the bedroom chamber.

The doors were closed and he could hear the sound of a woman moaning on the other side. *Oh God!* The boss was having sex with one of his harem and he knew the standing orders not to disturb him. He got a sick feeling and leaned against the door as sweat poured from his face. *Why the hell did I have to pick up the damned phone?* He held his head hard against the door and tried to catch his breath—it opened unexpectedly and he fell backwards into the boss' infamous lair.

Vivian and Nicki Masterson, a redhead from California, looked down at the young bean counter and laughed. They were wearing see-through black negligees over well-tanned and oiled bodies and nothing else—not even shoes. They scampered down the hall toward their apartments as he got back to his feet.

He turned toward the huge custom round bed. Javier was still mounted on another blonde who lay face down facing the foot of the bed. "What the hell do you want?"

Ramon could hardly speak. "Uh…Sorry, sir, phone call from *Señor* Juan de la Cruz…He sounds upset."

Javier slid out of the blonde and slapped her playfully on her bare butt. He held his hand out as the statuesque model crawled off the bed, grabbed her nightie and walked out with her head held high—just as she had done on so many fashion runways.

Ramon averted his eyes and placed the phone in Javier's outstretched hand.

"Get out," he said in a measured tone as took the phone. "Juan…Javier, how nice of you to call."

DEPUTY NATIONAL SECURITY ADVISOR'S OFFICE, WHITE HOUSE

Deputy National Security Advisor, Clarence Ogilsvey was still fuming over the inability of ICE to terminate the BEF contract.

He picked up his phone and dialed Ronald Diggers' personal number.

He answered after two rings, "Diggers."

"Ronald...Clarence. Question...Who do you know in the Cabinet who isn't in favor of the BEF?

"Well, besides you and me, there's Admiral Samson Valenti, Chairman of the Joint Chiefs and I've heard that the VP Jonathan Cobb is on the fence.

"Arrange a lunch meeting with the Admiral and Cobb at Refugio's...ASAP."

"I'll see what I can do."

Refugio's was an Italian restaurant near the Hart Senate office building that was very popular with members of Congress and staffers. Just as many, if not more, bills were negotiated there over a good Italian lunch and a few martini's as were on the floor of the Senate and House.

OFFICE OF MARTINE AGUILAR

Ronaldo DeSantis was between a rock and a very hard place. He and his four shooters had spent all afternoon trying to locate *El Toro* and nobody was talking.

To the locals, the guys in floral shirts were just a bunch of out-of-towners, people nobody knew—and nobody trusted. Hell, they could be working for the DEA of the Estados Unidos for all they knew. The decision to pay the bookkeeper a visit was a no-brainer. Luis Torrejon had always kept close tabs on his money, but for some reason, Martine was not answering his cell phone either. *Time to pay the puto a little visit*, thought Ronaldo.

It was after eight-thirty in the evening when he and his crew arrived on the quiet brick street on the east side of downtown. Ronaldo checked the plates on the orange Volkswagen parked a few feet west of the entrance to the plain looking two story building. "Hermano, is that his car?"

Alejandro DeSantis looked at the printout provided by a cooperative, but corrupt young man at the Mexican DMV. "That's a match, brother."

"Let's go."

The five men stepped out of the white rental Chevy Tahoe.

As they neared the front door, Ronaldo told one to stay and watch. Bernardo nodded and took up a position with his back to the brick wall.

Alejandro cautiously opened it. Ronaldo looked both ways and entered the doorway, followed shortly by the other three. Inside and to the right, a worn painted concrete stairway led upstairs to the office of Martine Aguilar. They pulled their weapons and eased silently up the stairs.

Outside, an attractive young couple walked arm-in-arm around the street corner, talking and laughing as they approached where Bernardo stood guard. The woman wore a short black leather miniskirt which showed off her shapely legs and dark stockings. Her white blouse contrasted well with the black skirt and was unbuttoned enough to show ample cleavage.

Her twenty-two year old boyfriend wore a traditional white Mexican wedding shirt outside of his black slacks.

Fifteen feet from Bernardo, they stopped while the young man attempted to light the cigarette hanging from her bright red painted lips. He had trouble with his BIC until he finally threw it to the sidewalk in disgust.

"What's wrong, Baby, you can't light my fire tonight?" she teased.

Obviously frustrated, he grabbed her by the arm and walked her over to Bernardo. "Excuse me, *señor*, can you give my lady friend here a light?"

Bernardo smiled his best crooked teeth smile as he fished out his prized stainless steel Zippo and produced a flame. She drew in on the cigarette and then slid her tongue seductively over her gleaming white teeth as she exhaled slowly into Bernardo's face.

He was captivated by her tanned cleavage and finely sculptured face. He never saw her boyfriend slip the suppressed Walther PPK out of the back of his slacks. Bernardo was still holding his Zippo in his outstretched right hand when the first hollow point tore into his side. It was followed by one more to the ribs and one to the head. Bernardo's Kevlar body armor and trauma plate covered only his chest.

One shot was all that was necessary—his heart stopped beating almost immediately. He slumped unceremoniously against the building—the couple turned and scurried away.

Several seconds after they disappeared around the corner, seven armed men wearing jeans and T-shirts—red bandanas around their faces—ran to the front of the accountant's building and entered the front door.

One stayed downstairs as the other six silently crept up the steps. Two men in the back carried TEC-9 machine pistols. The man leading the procession carried an UZI and was followed by two armed with MAC-10s.

They reached the top without being seen and slowly edged their way closer to Martine's office. They could hear raised voices coming from the partially open door.

Tio Morales stood guard just inside. He couldn't help but be distracted by the argument raging behind him—Ronaldo and his brother were bent out of shape by the empty safe. The reason that Martine had not answered the phone was obvious—he skipped out with the money.

"The chicken-shit *pendejo* ran like a yellow dog!" Alejandro protested.

Tio turned back to the doorway and leaned out for a look. The sight of six gangbangers with weapons caught him off guard. He raised his MP-5, but the *Tres Locos* gunman shot first, hitting him in the head. Tio dropped like a bad habit, hitting the floor with a thud.

The mood inside the room changed instantly as the three men went into a murderous rage. One after another they charged blindly into the hallway, firing their fully automatic machine guns and carbines pointblank into the line of tattooed thugs.

Bullets flew like lead rain as the three armored men took and returned fire from the *Tres Locos*. In an instant, the carnage was complete and all the masked men lay dead on the floor.

241

Blood splattered the walls, ceiling and the floor of the dimly lit hallway. One of the three men in floral shirts staggered and fell.

"Alejandro…Hermano!" Ronaldo screamed.

Blood streamed from a wound in the trapezious muscle above his brother's Kevlar vest as well as from a ragged hole in his left triceps.

All three had taken numerous hits to the bulletproof vests underneath their brightly colored tropical attire and were bruised, but otherwise unharmed. Ronaldo knelt down by his brother—he pointed to the other man and tossed him the keys. "Check downstairs, Chico…Get the car."

Chico took off down the hall.

"Baby brother, you hit anywhere else?"

"Don't think so. It hurts like hell to get shot."

"No shit, Sherlock. But if you hurt, it means you're not dead…So get your ass up."

"We gotta get outta here."

"Now you're starting to think." Ronaldo helped him to his feet.

A short burst of fire came from the stairwell.

"That sounded like Chico," Alejandro said as he picked up Tio's weapon lying beside his body. "What do you want to do with him?"

Ronaldo looked at the bullet hole just above Tio's left eye. "Nothing…Get his vest off…Leave him for the locals."

Ronaldo walked down the hallway to the body of one of the thugs. He bent down, jerked the red bandana off—there was a distinctive tattoo on the side of his neck. "Just as I thought…*Tres Locos*. Must have thought we were trying to rip them off…Probably heard we were asking a lot of questions."

Alejandro called to Ronaldo, "Hermano, need some help here getting Tio's shirt off. I can't turn him over with one arm."

"You need to start working out more."

"Eat dog shit and die, puto."

***

CHAPTER TWELVE

NUEVO LAREDO, MEXICO

Chico kept looking over his shoulder as he drove along Avenida Monterrey toward the airport. Ronaldo was applying pressure to the wounds in his brother's arm and upper torso as they raced through the streets.

"Slow down a little! You're either gonna get us in wreck or have the cops on our ass!" Ronaldo yelled.

Chico slowed to fifteen kilometers over the limit as they turned right on Calle Anzures—only three miles from the private aviation ramp at the airport.

"Artemis, get the Gulfstream ready! And break out the first-aid kit. My little brother is hurt," Ronaldo shouted into his cell phone.

"Yes, sir! I'll be ready...Tomas, move your ass! The guys are on the way...Alejandro is hurt," he said to his young copilot. "Pull the chocks and make sure the fire cart is clear...We're going to take off with or without a clearance."

After making the last right turn onto Avenida Aeropuerto, Ronaldo looked back and noticed three sets of headlights coming up fast. "Got company! Hit it!"

The Tahoe surged forward as he slammed the pedal to the floor. The white rental Chevy blew past the passenger terminal. Chico braked hard and made a left hand turn and gunned it toward the cargo and FBO area. The Tahoe skidded as he yanked the wheel back to the right and raced up to the awaiting Gulfstream.

Chico slid to a stop, jumped out and yanked opened the left rear passenger door. The wounded shooter moaned loudly as he was grabbed by his injured arm and jerked out. Ronaldo slid across the blood-soaked white leather bench seat clutching three weapons by their slings.

"Help us!" Chico yelled to the copilot.

Tomas crossed the forty feet between them quickly and wrapped his arm around the staggering Alejandro's waist– they hustled the younger DeSantis to the plane.

Ronaldo dropped the two carbines as he brought an H&K MP-5 to his shoulder. The first vehicle, a dark blue sedan, made the turn through the open gate in the chain link fence. He opened fire.

Bullets crazed the windshield as a dozen 9mm rounds punched tiny holes in the laminated glass. The car careened toward the hangar and crashed into a parked fuel truck. Ronaldo fired another two bursts into the front and rear passenger doors to discourage any one from exiting—the dead men had no intention of ever leaving.

Across the ramp, cargo loading crews servicing a DHL MD-11 dove for cover. They could not see the Gulfstream in the shadows, but the gunfire spoke louder than words. Living in Nuevo Laredo had made them well aware of gang turf wars.

Artemis engaged the starter on engine number one—it spun up rapidly and he placed the fuel lever to *Run*. Tomas and Chico struggled with Alejandro on the narrow steps, pulling and pushing him into the cabin.

Tomas' heart was racing. He had heard stories from Artemis about his adventures and had dismissed them as the delusions of a foolish old man. Nobody would want a job like that. He suddenly realized his own life was on the line and was scared like never before.

Gunfire from the passenger side of the second *Tres Locos* vehicle erupted even before their gray Ford Taurus passed the chain link fence. Some of the rounds hit the fence and sparked off the galvanized steel in a miniature fireworks display.

The ricochets spun wildly into the air past the security vehicle parked near the MD-11. The lone guard slid down in his seat when a stray bullet broke the back window inches behind his head.

Ronaldo slapped another mag in the MP-5 and led the Taurus as it roared through the gate onto the ramp. His disciplined fire shredded the driver and his cohort in the front seat as well as the back seat shooter firing the TEC-9.

The characteristic red bandana of the *Tres Locos* did him little good as two rounds permanently wiped the smile off his face. His limp hand dropped his smoking pistol—it skittered and sparked across the concrete apron.

The Taurus continued out onto the taxiway and crossed runway 14/32. The driverless car bounced though the ditch on the west side of the airport and finally stopped when it became entangled in a barbed wire perimeter fence.

"Come on!" Chico yelled at Ronaldo.

Ronaldo took one look at the white Ford pickup that had braked to a hard stop just outside the fence. He fired a short burst and the passenger window shattered. The driver slammed into reverse—the rear tires belched smoke as it backed erratically toward the main road.

Ronaldo reached down and picked up the other two H&Ks. The plane had already begun to roll forward as he sprinted toward it. Tossing the two rifles into the open portal, he took the steps up into the moving craft in two bounds. "Go, Go! Get the hell outta here!"

The aircraft surged forward as Artemis slammed the throttles forward to their stops. DeSantis was caught off-guard and fell into the bulkhead.

He regained his balance, stood up and hit the *Entry Door Close* button in the panel beside the door. The aircraft was moving at 45 MPH when the pilot braked hard to make the turn onto the parallel taxiway. He was thrown off his feet once again and landed on the floor almost inside the cockpit.

"Sit down!" Artemis yelled.

Ronaldo scrambled back to the cabin seat, strapped in and looked out the window on the left side. The Ford truck had driven back onto the apron and was accelerating. *Son of a bitch! This is gonna be close!*

The controller in the tower was going crazy. "Dispatch! I say again! Full blown gang warfare has broken out on the tarmac. Send backup!"

The policeman in the vehicle parked in front of the terminal would not answer his radio.

The controller dropped the handset and grabbed the radio mic. "Aircraft on the high speed taxiway...hold your position! I say again, hold your position!"

The plane had not been given clearance and now there was another vehicle on the airport tarmac without tower permission—driving on the parallel taxiway.

"Flaps twenty!" Artemis yelled.

Tomas moved the flap lever and confirmed as the position indicator started to move. "Flaps coming to twenty!" he nervously replied. "Oh shit!"

He was sure he would lose his pilot's license. They were taxiing without permission and had disregarded the controller's order to stop. *He can't be serious about taking off on runway 14! We only have half the runway to use!*

Inside the stolen Ford pickup, the shooter with the wounded right arm handed his M-16 to the man in the middle of the bench seat. He aimed out the shattered passenger window across the other man at the rapidly accelerating Gulfstream as the truck screamed down the parallel taxiway. "Faster, they're getting away!"

The driver already had the gas pedal floored and the speedometer passed one hundred-ten miles per hour.

Sixty yards to the southwest, the Gulfstream's nose wheel was lifting off the ground when the gunman fired a long burst—it did not take long for the twenty-round magazine to run dry. The three *Tres Locos* watched in frustration as the jet became airborne and the gear retracted.

Somebody should have been paying attention ahead of the speeding truck. Somebody should have seen that the taxiway ended at the south end of the terminal. Somebody should have seen the phalanx of police cars converging on the airport with their blue lights flashing—but nobody did.

The truck left the pavement, entered the barren area where a ditch had eroded over time. It plunged into the four foot deep ravine, hit the far side and exploded in a ball of fire.

"Aeromexico 432, landing clearance canceled. Go around! Go around!" The controller's voice was frantic.

The pilot responded, "Say again for Aeromexico 432?"

"Aeromexico 432…"

The Gulfstream flashed through the bright beam of the landing lights as it passed only fifteen feet beneath the nose wheel of the MD-80.

"Caramba!" The silver-haired captain pulled back hard on the yoke and initiated a go-around.

"Nuevo Laredo tower, what the hell are you trying to do? Kill us?" the copilot screamed.

"Aeromexico 432, climb and maintain two thousand-five hundred for vector back to approach runway 32."

Inside the Gulfstream, the indicated airspeed climbed through three hundred knots. Tomas looked at the ashen-faced pilot. "Are you gonna climb, Artemis?"

"Set flight level two-five-zero." He pointed to the altimeter selection box on the glare shield and toggled the auto pilot switch to *On.*

The nose rose and the vertical velocity indicator climbed toward four thousand feet per minute. "Damn. That was close," he said weakly.

"When we get back to Isla Gukumatz, I'm turning in my resignation…You guys don't pay me enough for this shit."

Artemis nodded. "Tell me about it."

Unknown to the crew, the rounds from the M-16 fired at the craft did not all miss. One of two bullets pierced the heavy rubber tread cap around the left nose wheel, but did no damage.

The other, however, had entered the forward electrical equipment bay, clipped the valve on the crew and passenger emergency oxygen bottle just below the copilot's feet. The shiny copper valve immediately began spewing high pressure pure oxygen into the cabin.

In the second row of seats, Ronaldo applied bandages to Alejandro—Chico had already removed the bloody shirt and Kevlar vest. DeSantis finished the triage and put his arm in a white cotton sling.

"Am I gonna be okay, big brother?"

"Sure, I got shot worse than that lots of times."

"Can I have a smoke?"

"Can't do any harm, you've earned it." Ronaldo pulled out a pack of Marlboro's from his shirt pocket and shook a cigarette out and placed it between Alejandro's parched lips.

He reached in his pocket and retrieved out his gold plated, engraved Zippo—a gift from Javier. He smiled as he flipped the lid open and thumbed the hardened steel wheel against the flint.

The lighter instantly produced a fourteen-inch yellow flame like a blow torch. DeSantis instinctively dropped the burning lighter into the sling.

In the high oxygen content atmosphere in the confined cabin space, the cotton erupted into a massive, uncontrolled conflagration...

EAGLE NEST RANCH HOUSE

Nacho sat on the swing under the big wrap-around porch sipping on a bottle of Shiner Bock. He looked up at the sky just in time to see what appeared to be a shooting star. "Star light, star bright...first star I see tonight. I wish I may, I wi...What the...?"

He was confused by the smoke trail from the falling star. It blocked out the stars behind it and was readily visible in the moonlight.

The bright light gradually arced toward the horizon and disappeared in the vicinity of Falcon Reservoir.

"Strangest meteor I ever saw." Nacho took another sip of his beer.

ISLA GUKUMATZ
COJONE COMPOUND

Javier had spent almost twenty minutes on the phone consoling the upset Juan de la Cruz. He had told him how his personal envoy had identified the culprits responsible for the shipping problems and had them dismissed from the Nuevo Laredo shipper. "My friend, I can assure you this will never will be arriving within two weeks. I will personally call when we have taken possession of the special delivery."

"Madre Dios! What the hell else can go wrong this week?" Javier yelled out when he disconnected from his satellite call from Chico not an hour after he got off the phone with Juan.

Cojone had lied in his best mega-salesman fashion to act as if he had a clue about what had gone down along the border. None of his contacts had any information about Luis Torrejon's whereabouts.

Ronaldo's mission to Nuevo Laredo met with disaster. Tio and Bernardo were dead, Alejandro was wounded. Then, all he had heard at the end of Chico's airborne call was two, maybe three men, screaming for a couple of seconds before the call disconnected. Javier had tried calling back—but to no avail.

He set the phone down on the night stand, got up, pulled on his cotton robe, slipped into his lambskin slippers, walked to the elevator and pressed the down button.

He emerged three stories lower on the ninth floor men's apartment level. Javier walked three doors down, knocked twice and entered as a man's voice responded, "Come in."

Roberto "Bobo" Vicente was in bed reading a Spanish language version of the British magazine, *The Economist*. He sat up as his boss entered with a look of deep concern. Javier had never been in his room before.

"Something wrong, Mister Cojone?"

"I need you to make some calls. I think something happened to my Gulfstream tonight...There was big trouble up in Nuevo Laredo...we lost Tio and Bernardo."

"Jesus...What happened, boss?"

"Ambush, gang turf war...who the hell knows? The important thing is to find out under the radar...Say our plane was hijacked in Nuevo Laredo, stolen...whatever."

"You can count on me, boss."

"If Ronaldo and Chico don't make it back tonight...you are my new number one...Don't disappoint me."

"No, sir."

Bobo rose to get dressed after Javier left. He pulled on his khaki pants and aqua-blue polo shirt, walked to the faux marble sink and splashed cold water on his face. He looked into the mirror and smiled broadly. *Mother of God! My CIA handler is gonna shit a brick when I tell I just got promoted to numero uno*

253

in the Cojone organization. This asshole's house of cards is coming down.

Javier stepped off the elevator and walked to his bed. He picked up the interphone on his night stand and punched a number.

Vivian picked up. "Yes, my love. What is your pleasure?"

"I want you, that blonde girl, Crystal, and a bottle of Patrón."

"We'll be there in two minutes…Anything else?"

"No, you're always better than an Ambien."

"I do my best, my love," she purred seductively.

Fifty minutes later, the three lay naked in the large bed. The tequila was gone. Javier and Vivian were entangled in a lover's embrace and passed out.

Crystal was still awake as she had only sipped her tequila. Having seen the satellite phone on the night stand, she was determined to contact the outside world. *If I'm caught…I won't live to see the morning…but I've got to try.*

She slid her left arm off the naked couple, slowly and ever so gently rolled to the edge of the bed, picked up her negligee—but did not put it on. Crystal slipped silently around to the night stand. Her hand trembled as she reached for the Iridium phone.

Javier rolled to his left—she froze. His mouth moved as if to say something, but he was only swallowing in his sleep. She never took her eyes off him until she felt the hard form of the phone under her fingers. She flicked her eyes at it, slowly lifted it up and rolled it into the negligee.

Silently, she walked to the master bathroom, opened the exquisitely carved mahogany door, stepped inside and closed it. She took extreme care not to have the latch click.

Using only the night light, she fumbled with the unfamiliar device until it turned on. *God, I hope mama hasn't moved or changed phone numbers since I was kidnapped three years ago.*

She had only made one international phone call in her life—that was to tell her mom she made it safely to Barbados and to thank her again for the best graduation gift ever. She punched the number...

In an upper middle-class neighborhood in Tuscaloosa, Alabama, a phone rang beside the bed of a pretty forty-one year old blonde divorcee. It was two in the morning. Angie Coopersmith looked at her alarm clock, *Who in the hell could be calling in the middle of the night?* She picked it up and mumbled, "Hello."

"Mama?"

EAGLE NEST RANCH AIRSTRIP
The Following Day, June 30

It was almost sunset when Gunter drove up to the. He parked next to the hangar—he, Mike, Dare, Blaze and Jill all got out.

Dare looked around. "Guys, with the C-5 coming in here on a regular basis, we're going to need a wider turnaround at each end of the runway. We'll also need about fifty thousand gallons of storage for jet fuel…If you hadn't noticed, Mike, the Eagles can use jet fuel as well as av-gas."

"Yeah, I was amazed at that. Those rotary engines are something else."

"No problem on the turnarounds, I can have the area paved in about two days…Have the pit dug for the tank at the same time. Can get that started while ya'll are gone up to Denison…Just takes a phone call to order the tank…Where do you want me to bury it?" asked Gunter.

"Actually, we have engineers, crew and suppliers available through the DoD that will come down and take care of all that. We can design the facilities that will be needed here while we're at base…the additional hangar space, offices, dorm, underground weapons bunker and maybe some field training space for our Raptors…We have room in our budget."

"Whatever you say, Iron Horse." Gunter nodded and grinned.

Mike unlocked the hangar side door, turned on the lights and pressed the switch to open the big overlapping front doors. Jill walked in while they were still moving and started to preflight the *Eagle*.

He came over as she was checking the right forward nacelle inlet. "How 'bout I preflight and you check me?"

She stared at him for a second. "Why didn't I think of that?"

"'Cause two heads are better than one," Mike deadpanned.

Jill was confused for a second. "Marine humor?"

"Just a guy thing."

Jill shook her head and watched as he continued the preflight. Three seconds passed when she realized what he had meant. She slung her helmet bag at his backside.

Mike chuckled. "Grandma's slow...but she's old."

She swatted him again. "Men."

Blaze approached her father and Dare. "You gonna be okay for two days while Mike and I are up north?"

Gunter placed his left arm around the tall drink of water.

"Baby girl, I know you have difficulty believing this, but I knew how to cook before I met your sweet mama...And just who do you think put the family name on all those smoked meats we sell all over the country while you two were kids? Huh?"

"But, Dad!...."

"But nothing! You children think anybody over fifty is primed for the rocking chair. Keep it up young lady...not too dinged up to take you over my knee one more time."

Everybody chuckled at the mental image of Blaze getting a spanking.

She leaned over and gave him a sweet peck on the cheek. "I love you, Dad."

"Love you, too, Baby...Now, ya'll need any help getting that Eagle out?"

"Think we got it covered," Dare replied.

"I'll just supervise, then." Gunter leaned on his cane.

Shortly after sundown, he watched as they lifted off with a STOL departure.

Jill followed Mike on the controls, but once they had retracted the gear and accelerated to two hundred knots she took her hands off.

The small black craft quietly disappeared into the increasing darkness. Gunter thought about all the changes brought about since the incident started. *Wonder what tomorrow will bring?*

He drove to the ranch house, stopped to watch as the last reddish purple streaks of light disappeared in the western sky—and slowly made his way inside.

WARBIRD RESTORATION, INC.
NORTH TEXAS REGIONAL AIRPORT
DENISON, TEXAS

It was after 2300 when the M600/A approached the facility from the southwest. Jill took control of the bird as the VTOL was considerably more demanding than STOL. Plus, they didn't exactly like to advertise the position of the BEF home base.

She brought the craft low over the west end of the airport and set down on the darkened ramp just a short distance from the central hangar doors. They opened approximately thirty feet, Jill folded the rear nacelle wing struts into the upright position and taxied the craft into the dark structure.

The tower regularly closed at 2200 due to low traffic volume late at night, but the airport was still open for uncontrolled civilian traffic.

Once the hangar doors closed behind her, she removed her night vision goggles and the lights flooded the interior.

"Nice job, Jill," Mike said.

"Thanks...You'll get a chance at it tomorrow night after you get a few hours in the sim."

They ran through the short *Engine Shutdown* checklist and *Remaining Overnight* checklist, insuring all weapons systems were safe, their oxygen masks stowed, parking brake set and battery switches turned off. All four left the *Eagle* as the big aircraft elevator reached the bottom floor.

"This is what the aircraft carriers use to raise and lower their planes to the flight deck?" Blaze asked Dare.

"It is indeed...In fact, this particular one came from USS *Oriskany*. The *Mighty O* earned a total of seven battle stars for service in the Korean War and Vietnam. We got it after they decommissioned her and sold her for scrap...The old girl was sent to the bottom in 2006 and is now the world's largest artificial reef."

"Impressive," she commented.

Two BEF crewmen met the craft after the elevator was flush with the bottom floor and placed red *DO NOT FLY* streamers and *safe pins* on all the weapons while another drove a tug up, hooked on to the nose gear and towed her away to the maintenance bay for a full check-over in the morning.

"I'll show you to your quarters in a few minutes. We have areas here where we stay when we are on call," Jill said to Mike and Blaze.

Dare gave them a brief wave. "See ya'll in the morning. I've gotta check on any last minute items which could have landed on my desk."

Jill took the new members of the team by the duty desk and made brief introductions to the various night shift team members in the maintenance, communications and supervisory command positions.

"It never occurred to me that this was a 24-7 operation," Blaze said.

"Some place you got here," Mike added.

"We can be tasked at any time, so there is always a full crew on duty...No rest for the wicked," Jill joked. "We'll get your security clearance and ID process underway in the morning...Run a tight ship here."

Jill showed Blaze her room first. It was a moderate-sized twelve-by-fourteen with a wide-screen TV, satellite cable reception, a queen-size bed, table and chair.

A door led to a small toilet with a washbasin. No shower or bath facilities were incorporated as all members had access to their sex appropriate locker room and shower. Each room had a night stand and reading light as well as wall-mounted lights for working at the desk.

All rooms also had a different 36x60 framed color picture of a tropical beach or alpine landscape picture over the bed. A wall-mounted clothes rod and folding luggage rack completed the utilitarian, but comfortable furnishings.

After Jill got Blaze situated and briefed the breakfast schedule in the facility mess hall—she took Mike to his room. He thanked her for the tour and shook her hand. They held the contact a few extra seconds.

Jill stepped back. "I'm two doors down in room twenty-two if you need anything…see you at breakfast…got a big day ahead of us."

Mike didn't really want to see her go, but she was right. Five or six hours in the simulator would be a more than a full day. They never knew when the next mission was going to be assigned—he wanted to be ready for it…

BLACK EAGLE FORCE
UNDERGROUND FACILITY
1 July - O600 Hours

Mike had been too excited to sleep very well. When the white light above the door started flashing, he literally leapt out of bed, grabbed a fresh white towel and headed down to the men's locker room.

After a quick shower and shave, he walked back into his room and found a set of black BDUs laid out on his bed with a pair of black zippered flying boots— in his size twelve. *Damn, better service than a hotel.*

He slipped the gray T shirt on and then the BDUs—a perfect fit. *How did they do this?*

There was a knock on the door. He opened it and found Jill standing there in her own clean set of black BDUs. Her blonde hair was freshly washed and pulled back in her usual pony tail—she had her hands on her hips. "You gonna take all day, rookie?"

"Waitin' on you, boss lady…Thought you might be sleeping in like you did at the ranch."

261

"Yeah, right…Been up for over an hour, developing a sim program that's going to kick your ass…Hungry?"

"I could eat the side boards off a gut wagon."

"Eeww." She grimaced. "I take that as a yes?"

"Close enough."

"This way to the mess hall…student."

They stepped out into the hallway just as Blaze approached. "I assume you guys are headed to the cafeteria?" she asked.

Jill motioned with her hand. "Yeah, but we call it the mess hall…follow me."

SIMULATOR ROOM

Inside the large room were three sets of advanced computerized simulators. Each had an exact mockup of the inside of the M600/A cockpit. Where the windscreens would normally be were four large flat-screen high definition monitors.

Both daylight and nighttime scenarios could be programmed with airports, cities, villages and a half-dozen types of varied terrain. The look outside was impressive. Even the left and right forward nacelles could be seen in the outboard monitors and SFX computers duplicated the sounds of electrical pumps, starter motors and engines.

Jill and Mike had been at it for three hours. She put him through the wringer, with back-to-back systems problems, engine failures, fires, oil leaks, hydraulic and electrical failures.

He was getting mentally tired and starting to make small errors. *Time to take a break.* Jill selected a suitable landing spot in the terrain and pointed at it. "Set us down over there next to those trees."

"Yes, ma'am."

As the craft hovered to within 10 feet of the ground, the computer generated landing gear aural warning spoke through the helmet speakers in a woman's voice, "Landing Gear Unsafe."

"Damn…not again," Mike moaned.

Jill reached over and dropped the gear handle to its down position and the gear extended and locked. The red *Gear Unsafe* caution light extinguished and Mike set the bird down smoothly with only the slightest hint of left drift.

She engaged the *Situation Freeze* button on the instructor's panel and the artificial sounds of the eight engines running stopped. "Okay, Cowboy…time for a break."

They stood up, removed their helmets, dropped them back into their respective pilot seat and stepped back through the narrow space between the seats.

A slightly dejected Mike glumly analyzed his performance. "I suck."

"Really? A little hard on yourself, I think."

"Come on…I tried to land gear-up three different times. If it weren't for Bitchin' Betty, I would have sucked up a lot of FOD, and trashed the engines…That sucks."

"Gotta agree with you there…But let me ask you something."

"Shoot."

"How long does it take to retract or extend the gear on your Cessna?"

"The gear are fixed on the 180."

"Do you ever think about the gear on the 180 before you land?"

"No. Of course not, they don't re…"

"Right. Habit patterns…You have a habit pattern based on a fixed gear plane. Time to replace it with a different one." Jill had a slight smile.

"You mean I don't suck?"

"Didn't say that." She turned and walked toward the mess hall, chuckling.

Mike fell in behind her like a puppy following its master.

Dare walked in and filled his huge old Marine Corps mug with fresh coffee. Emblazoned on one side was the unit insignia of his last command and the words *Iron Horse* on the other. He took a sip of the still steaming brew and approached Jill and Mike sipping soft drinks and reviewing the morning's simulator period.

"How's the training going guys?"

Mike shrugged and deferred to Jill.

"He's coming along great for someone on his first sim…All I have to do is teach him to extend the gear before he bends one of our birds on landing."

"I knew he could do it. The boy's got good hands for a ground poundin' jarhead." Dare grinned.

"Whatcha got going on, boss?"

"You'll probably get a kick out of this, Cowboy…Been called up to Washington to meet with the President and the top cabinet members about the little fracas on Eagle Nest."

"Is that normal after a BEF ops?"

"No, not really." He sipped his coffee again. "I'm probably gonna get my butt reamed for telling the Deputy National Security Advisor to the President to perform an anatomically impossible sex act with himself."

Jill and Mike glanced at each other in disbelief.

"You didn't!" Jill exclaimed.

"Actually…I did. Told the Assistant Director of the Department of Homeland Security to tell Clarence Ogilsvey to do just that and that Iron Horse said so."

"Ogilsvey! That worthless bastard!"

"One and the same…I knew you would remember him."

"Remember? Sorry sack of shit was a disgrace to the uniform. Should've punched him out before I left the Corps."

"Would have gotten you thrown in the brig and made him look like a hero…Besides, I'm a big boy. I can take a dressing down…if it's called for."

"I've got a question…What did he do that set you off in the first place?"

"Oh…I forgot to mention that. He tried to cancel our mission shortly after we launched from Mama Bird."

"What?" Jill and Mike said simultaneously.

"I told 'em to pound sand in his ass and a couple other things I won't mention in mixed company."

"If you guys had canceled, none of us on the ranch would have made it," Mike said.

"Probably not" Dare turned to walk back to his office. He stopped and spun around holding up his left index finger.

"Oh...one other thing, Mike...Kinda weird. President Thompson asked that you and your dad come to the meeting. She directed your attendance...specifically. I just sent Killer down to pick him up in a Lear."

Jill and Mike were speechless as they looked at each other across the table...

***

CHAPTER THIRTEEN

WASHINGTON, DC
WHITE HOUSE, CABINET ROOM
3 July

Inside the room, adjacent to the Oval Office, Cabinet members, department heads and advisors were seated at the long conference table. Among them: Vice President Jonathan Cobb, Secretary of State Paden Osserman, Chairman Joint Chiefs of Staff Admiral Samson Valenti, FBI Director Marvin Huxley, Director of Central Intelligence William James Weber, Secretary Homeland Security Barbara Hoffner, DEA Director Weston McBride, Secretary of Defense Harold Baker and National Security Advisor Juan Montecan.

They all rose as the president and the Chief of Staff, Ralph Anderson, entered from the Oval Office.

"Please be seated." President Thompson sat down.

Annette Henry Thompson was a stately, trim and attractive woman in her late fifties with shoulder-length auburn hair showing a peppering of gray. She had been widowed during the campaign when her husband suffered a massive heart attack.

Her chair was on the east side of the table, in the center—the back, two inches taller than the others. Each had the names of the cabinet positions on brass plates attached to the back, her's was just engraved with—*THE PRESIDENT*.

She nodded to an aide standing by the door to the hallway. "Please show Mister Phillips and the Hermanns in."

He spoke to another aide just outside.

In a moment, Dare, Mike and Gunter were admitted into the Cabinet Room.

"Hello, Hermie, how are you?"

"Hermie?" Dare whispered as he turned to Gunter.

Mike glanced quizzically at his father.

"Hi, Annie...I suppose I should say Madam President."

"For you, Hermie...it'll always be Annie."

She looked around the room at the stunned individuals. "But, no one else...is that clear?"

Annie got to her feet, walked around the table to Gunter and gave him a big hug. "It's so good to see you again. It's been far too long."

"That it has, Annie, that it has...May I present my son, Michael."

"I've heard a great deal about you, young man. It's a pleasure to meet you. You look so much like your father when he was your age." She hugged him as well.

The rest of the room, including Dare and Mike, were in an absolute state of shock.

"Not that we owe anyone here an explanation, but I was Hermie's girl friend in college." She glanced at Gunter. "Matter of fact we were voted Mister and Miss Bobcat at Southwest Texas State College back in the day. He was captain of the football team and I was head cheerleader.

"Now enough of that...I thought I would fill you all in before your tongues started wagging like magpies...Hermie, would you, Michael and Dare please step over in front of our flag."

A still stunned Dare nodded as he, a grinning Mike and Gunter stood in front of the Stars and Stripes, facing the table of high-ranking government officials.

The president nodded to another aide who extended the boxes toward her. She opened one and took out a gold-rimmed white star attached to a blue and white ribbon and draped it around Mike's neck. "For an especially meritorious contribution to the security and national interests of the United States of America...I award you, Michael Otto Hermann, the Presidential Medal of Freedom."

She kissed Mike on the cheek and gave him another hug.

The president repeated the same ceremony with Gunter, whispering in his ear while she hugged him, "We can visit in my study after this little shindig is over."

She took the last box from the aide, removed another Medal of Freedom and hung it around Dare's neck.

"Thank you, Madam President, but I think the majority of the credit belongs to the entire Hermann family. They held off the Mexican forces until we could get on station. It took us an hour to get there…I've asked both Mike and his sister Carla to join the BEF."

"You were on station within an hour from notification?…Amazing," remarked Vice President Cobb.

"Their motto is *Semper Paro Bellum*, Always Ready for War," added Secretary of Defense Baker. "They get in and get out…the bad guys never know who or what hit them."

The dignitaries at the table were all, for once, speechless as the president indicated to Dare, Mike and Gunter to take seats at the table across from her.

"In the folders in front of you, provided by Secretary of Defense Baker, you will find the complete report of the BEF activities in Webb County…more specifically on Eagle Nest Ranch belonging to the Hermann family.

"Secretary Osserman and Secretary Hoffner, I would direct you to the section involving the incursion of Mexican Federal troops and equipment on United States soil. I would expect that you will have a meeting with the Mexican ambassador…I want your report no later than day after tomorrow."

"Madam President, this is hard to believe, but the photographs and other evidence is convincing. The Mexican ambassador is not going to be happy," replied Secretary of State Osserman.

"What's more important, Paden…I'm not happy. If it weren't for the BEF, the Hermanns wouldn't be here today."

Chairman of the Joint Chiefs of Staff Admiral Valenti spoke up, "Madam President, if we had known of this incursion, we could have sent in a MEU, rather than a group of contract cowboys that…"

"And been three days too late, Admiral. I suggest you hold your tongue. The entire reason President Reagan set up the Black Eagle Force was for ultra-quick strike and response purposes.

"Some things are much easier without government bureaucracy involvement. Check their records back to inception…which you'll find in the flash drives also in front of you…And I shouldn't have to remind you that all of this information is still TOP SECRET NOFORN.

"Their missions have all been exemplary. I didn't even know they existed until SecDef Baker brought me their files…I just wish we could recognize the BEF for all their contributions to this country, but I suppose that would defeat the purpose of clandestine, wouldn't it?…Now, please show Mister Ogilsvey in," President Thompson added.

Admiral Valenti and Vice President Cobb exchanged worried glances as Clarence Ogilsvey was ushered into the room. He stood with an air of arrogance in front of the President, not noticing Mike, Gunter and Dare behind the high-backed chairs in front of him.

"Mister Ogilsvey, I noted in your recommendation to the National Security Advisor, you believe the Black Eagle Force should be disbanded."

"Yes, Madam President. It's my considered opinion that the BEF is a very dangerous paramilitary organization. Without proper oversight, their actions could result in severe

271

international complications…In addition to being a sizable drain on the black ops budget in the DoD."

"Since when does the National Security Advisor's office concern itself with the DoD budget? I note in your own budget that you personally spent over a quarter of a million dollars in redecorating your office…Mister Ogilsvey," offered SecDef Baker.

"Mister Secretary, it's my job to assist in advising the President on matters of National Security…"

"I see in your personnel records, Mister Ogilsvey, that you had an altercation with a Marine Captain Michael Hermann when you were stationed in Afghanistan," the President interrupted.

"Uh…yes, Ma'am, it was a matter of insubordination. I was going to have Hermann court-martialed, but he resigned before I could bring charges."

"I would like to introduce Mister Michael Hermann and along with his father, Gunter…the latest recipients of the Presidential Medal of Freedom," the President said.

Gunter and Mike turned around in their high-backed chairs and glared at him.

"I know all about you, Ogilsvey…If it was up to me, I'd put you on your ass like Mike wanted to, but I don't want to spoil the President's carpet," Gunter said bluntly.

"See here, I…"

"No…You see here, Mister Ogilsvey. You exceeded your authority in trying to cancel the Black Eagle Force operation. And worst of all, you allowed your personal considerations to cloud your judgment. Had the BEF stood down as you ordered, a dozen innocent United States citizens could have died.

"My administration has no place for personal vendettas. I won't tolerate it...I want your resignation on my desk by noon," President Thompson stated.

"And I want your resignation of your reserve commission in the United States Marine Corps on my desk also by noon...You, sir, are no Marine.

"Your attempt to sucker me into your nefarious scheme proves that. You're damned lucky I don't throw a Bad Conduct Discharge at you," fumed Admiral Valenti.

The color drained from his face. "You'll regret this, Madam President."

"Is that a threat, Mister Ogilsvey? I'm sure the Secret Service will take note." President Thompson leaned forward. "That will be all, show this person to the door," she said to one of her Secret Service agents, Mickey Williams.

The well-built agent took a slightly resistive Clarence Ogilsvey firmly by the arm and forcefully escorted him to the hallway.

"You haven't heard the last of me," Ogilsvey shouted over his shoulder before the agent closed the door in his face.

"There goes the greatest danger in appointing major campaign contributors to a government post," the President said. "I apologize for my error in judgment."

There was a knock at the Cabinet Room door. Williams opened it slightly and spoke briefly to someone outside. He closed it and turned back to the president. "Madam President, there is an FBI Special Agent Winston Hanley outside with an urgent communiqué for Director Huxley.

"Show him in, Mickey."

Special Agent Hanley entered with a red folder, handed it to the FBI Director and whispered in his ear.

Huxley nodded. "What's the level of reliability?"

"Level five, sir."

"Thank you, Special Agent Hanley."

He nodded and left the room.

The director opened the folder and scanned the first page. "Jesus H. Christ! When it rains, it pours." He looked up. "I'm sure you all remember that high school girl, Crystal Coopersmith, that disappeared three years ago while vacationing in Barbados...The case remains an ongoing investigation of the FBI."

There were nods around the room.

"As you may or may not know, we have monitored her mother's phone line since the incident and last night..." He glanced at the assemblage. "...she received a call from Crystal.

"Her daughter had somehow gained access to a satellite phone...Now the kicker. That number is one and the same that was linked back to the Eagle Nest operation and to the recent gang war in Nuevo Laredo."

Baker leaned forward. "Who does it belong to?"

"...Javier Cojone." He paused. "The call came from his private island, Isla Gukumatz, in the Gulf of Mexico."

CIA Director Weber broke into a smile. "Hell, this is getting better all the time. We've had a deep cover operative with

Cojone for over three years who just got moved up to his number one man. Cojone's former number one died when his Gulfstream IV blew up south of Nuevo Laredo, in an action we believe was related to the Eagle Nest affair."

"Cojone has been on our most wanted list for ten years. He won't leave that island for any place where we have extradition," stated DEA Director Weston McBride.

Weber continued, "We know Cojone has been getting restricted US weapons...just haven't found his source yet...We also suspect he may have secured two Russian RA-115 suitcase nukes from a contact in Syria...There have been coded messages between Cojone and Juan de la Cruz, head of the ultra-nationalist Veintiuno de Abril Negro in Mexico City for delivery of two cases of Mediterranean candles within two weeks. Our analysts believe that to be code words for the suitcase nukes."

President Thompson made an executive decision and her announcement was forthright. "Gentlemen, I've heard enough...I hereby task the Black Eagle Force to lead a joint operation of the BEF, CIA, DoD, DEA, NSA, FBI and DHS to secure the suitcase nuclear devices, rescue any hostages, and sanction...with extreme prejudice...Javier Cojone and any in his employ within ten days.

"Mister Phillips, are you ready to accept operational responsibility of this mission at this time?"

Dare studied the roomful of faces. He understood the full weight of the task being given to his small band of elite warriors. He looked at his watch. It was 10:05AM Eastern Daylight Saving time.

"Madam President, as CEO of the Black Eagle Force, I hereby accept operational responsibility, Standard Protocol, at 1405 Zulu."

"BEF accepts operational responsibility, Standard Protocol, 1405 Zulu. DoD designates this Joint Strike operation as *Operation Viper*," SecDef Baker concurred.

Dare looked at President Thompson. "The BEF will need some help from the other branches, especially the Navy...Can we count on their support?"

"I can assure you, Dare, that all assets of the United States government will cooperate fully with the BEF with whatever you need," the President said with a stern demeanor as she looked at each person sitting at the long table.

"I don't want to see any interagency rivalries of any sort...I hold each of you personally responsible. Any problems in this area and your resignation will be expected forthwith...Do I make myself clear?"

All nodded.

"Admiral, can we get carrier or other support in the Gulf?"

"Well, Ma'am, we have a Wasp class amphibious assault ship, USS *Iwo Jima*...homeported at Norfolk. She carries a mix of thirty helicopters, including four MV-22 Ospreys, six to eight Harrier IIs and the 26th Marine Expeditionary Unit.

"The Iwo can be underway in two days, putting her on station in the Gulf in a total of eight days with any additional assets that the BEF deems necessary...Even if it seems an improbable operation," Admiral Valenti replied.

"The improbable we do immediately, Admiral, the impossible takes a little longer." Dare grinned.

"Fine. You people have work to do...Hermie, why don't we move into my study and visit...We've some catching up to do." President got up from her chair and led Gunter toward the study...

ISLA GUKUMATZ
COJONE COMPOUND
3 July

Javier had taken the news about the loss of the Gulfstream with all souls on board in stride. *Part of the cost of doing business.* One thing he noticed about Bobo—he was fast and very thorough. He now saw why Ronaldo had hired him.

"Javier, I have contacted the Gulfstream factory in South Carolina...here are photos of an aircraft for your consideration. The G IV has been replaced by the 450...Similar paint scheme to your last one with matching interior.

"It was acceptance flight flown two weeks ago and is available now...It has full IFR and INS capabilities...plus new onboard satellite phone, as well as Internet and fax capability." Bobo slid the portfolio over the desk to Javier.

"How about pilots? The ones we lost were the only two I had for the Gulfstream...I don't want the float plane guys to spend a month learning how to fly the jet."

"I took that into consideration, sir. Your helo pilots have had very little fixed-wing experience either…and they have next to no IFR experience. Here are pictures and resumes of three top candidates I would suggest for your consideration…All are current in the G450, single, as you require, and this one, Cabrillo, I have known personally for several years.

"He too is from Costa Rica and has worked throughout Mexico, North and South America and the Caribbean."

"I want these three run through the background checks…just like Ronaldo showed you. Make it quick. I'll choose two when I have your reports.

"There is a very special shipment coming in from Syria that we have to deliver directly to Mexico City."

"What about the plane, sir?"

"Buy it. Wire transfer from the Cayman bank…No, on second thought, use the Swiss bank and the Libyan dummy oil company for registration…Let me know as soon as the three pilot prospects are checked out."

"Yes, sir." Bobo turned and headed for the elevator. He had some work to do, and fast. It had taken his CIA handler and eleven assistants almost twenty-four hours to set up three detailed, bulletproof backgrounds for pilots working for an undisclosed contract company. These guys were so secret the agency would not even tell Bobo who they really worked for. *They must be some serious operators.*

***

CHAPTER FOURTEEN

BEF COMMAND CENTER
Machine Shop
July 5

Gears turned off the CNC machine and waited thirty seconds for the coolant mist to dissipate before opening the sliding gray cabinet doors. Blaze stood by anxiously awaiting the results of their third iteration of the feed mechanism.

A more positive projectile feeder pressure, coupled with a seven degree change in the mating angle of the feeder to the rotating charging cylinder should get them the results they desired.

Samuel Colt had come up with the idea of a percussion revolving cylinder handgun in 1832. He was granted a US patent for the first successful model in March 1836—the same month and year that Santa Anna rampaged across the Eagle Nest en route to his victory over the brave defenders at the Alamo. Blaze thought it serendipitous that the two events were somehow connected in time, and here she was today, designing one of the most modern and deadly weapons ever conceived, using a modification of Samuel Colt's claim to fame—the gun that won the west.

Gears opened the doors, unlocked the machine clamp blocks holding the work, and produced the slightly oily silver-gray titanium cylinder, complete with six parallel grooves running lengthwise along its sides.

One octagonal recess for a locking nut was machined at the end of the cylinder around the centrally located shaft hole through which the mounting bolt would be installed.

"Beautiful," Blaze remarked as Gears passed the piece to her for her inspection.

Let's go mount it to the drive and feeder assemblies…and give her a whirl."

They made their way into Gear's lab and wasted no time in getting the test bed assembled. Donning their ear and eye protection, they stepped behind the acrylic safety shield.

He handed her the control unit. "Your baby…You take the honors."

"Let's press it together."

"On three."

As Gear's count hit three, they pressed the button. The electric motor spun and fifty-eight steel projectiles cycled through the six stubby steel test barrels in 1.997 seconds. They looked at the elapsed time on the digital display. He turned to the red-haired beauty and said in a mock British accent, "By jingo, I think we've got it."

Blaze laughed. "An Alabama redneck doing an English accent...I've heard it all." She threw her arms around the smiling engineer and gave him a big hug. "Let's check out the high-speed camera and make sure!"

They watched the flat screen monitor as the ultra-slow-motion video confirmed the feeding mechanism very functional. The next challenge was to fabricate the nanotube impulse coils for the real barrels and see if Gear's idea for multiplexed charging was a possibility. The projectile feeding was based on his computer projections of a .245 millisecond recharge rate per barrel.

She had achieved slightly better than one second per recharge on her single-barrel coil rifle, but they would have to hit his theoretical projections to make the fire rate capable of her feeder rate.

If all things worked, the new weapon would fire at a rate of 1440 rounds per minute with a impact equal to or better than the 30mm multi-barreled cannon on the *Warthog*. The *Black Eagle* would indeed be transformed into a very serious force to be reckoned with.

Gears had not let much grass grow beneath his feet on his version of Blaze's Coyote Gun. His application of three aluminum ion batteries into the test rifle showed a real improvement on the original design. He had made up four of them in anticipation.

He was not able to replicate her flexible carbon fiber nanotubes in his lab and therefore had chosen to wait until they both returned to Eagle Nest for that fabrication. Gears noticed she was distracted for a second. "You Okay?"

"Sure…Tell me, what type of power is available from the 600's electrical system?"

"Standard aviation mil-spec twenty-eight volts DC, and through an inverter, 400 cycle, 115 volt AC, plus or minus fifteen volts…Why?"

"Sorry to interrupt your demonstration, but I think I just solved the problem of recharging our capacitors on the six-barrel coil gun."

"How?"

"We have been so busy trying to get the feed and chambering mechanism perfect, I left my brain back at the ranch."

"Dang, girl, don't think I'm followin' you."

"I've been stuck thinking about the batteries needed to charge the coil capacitors that I blocked out the fact we have massive amounts of excess electrons being produced by the engine-driven generators on the 600…Almost a limitless supply as long as we have fuel to run the engines."

"My God, that's right!…We could have four coils per barrel if we used the system you already have designed. The capacitors will boost the twenty-eight volts to twenty thousand every .235 milliseconds to mesh with the multiplexed sequenced signal generator for the coil discharge relays and a wiring harness to deliver it."

"Can't believe I didn't think of it earlier." Blaze shook her head.

Gears held up his hand in a high-five. She slapped it and smiled.

"Let's get busy."

DARE'S OFFICE

Kit sat in Dare's office as the two reviewed the tasking memorandum. He had never seen anything like it in all the years he had been involved with the BEF. A joint tasking from the DoD, NSA, CIA, DEA, FBI and DHS?

Of course he had worked with all five agencies individually, but this was different. Just two days earlier, three specific BEF pilots had been requested to be available on a moment's notice for an undisclosed assignment of undisclosed duration. The only information the CIA had released was for them to be current on the Gulfstream 450—it raised some serious questions...

"Boss, is this related to the Castillo, Mendes and Sosa tasking from Monday?"

"My gut tells me, yes, Kit...Those Langley guys are still trying to play it close to the vest. They indicated the company has a man on the inside that has been in deep cover for three years...They don't want any leaks to blow their operation."

"That's all well and good for them, but those Ivy League desk jocks need to remember one thing...It's our butts on the line here.

"This is the largest operation we've ever had...and by far the most dangerous. Russian RA-115 suitcase nukes?...I read an intel report from Switzerland that they lost an entire team trying to recover one that a former Soviet agent had reported was stashed there. Something about a lightning booby trap trigger to set it off if it's moved without a special code...If we screw this up..."

Dare nodded. There was no sugar coating this mission. The possibility of losing the team had crossed his mind—he knew that going in. "We have our work cut out for us...Got ten days to plan, prep and get into position...At least we got Admiral Valenti on board...USS Iwo Jima can be on station in eight days out of Norfolk...plus the 26th MEU will have four Ospreys in addition to their regular compliment."

"Damn swabbie brass pukes can be such a pain in the ass...If they don't get to play, they want to cancel the whole ball game...Especially when they occupy the chair of the Joint Chiefs...They're just God damned politicians by the time they get that far up the chain."

"Look, Kit, I don't like intra-service rivalries and Pentagon politics any more than you, but look at the bright side...The SecDef and the President are both behind us and the BEF itself has gotten over most of that bullshit...It's one of our biggest strengths."

"You're right, as usual...I get bent out of shape sometimes...What's new from the DIA?"

"Yeah, glad you reminded me. They tagged the cell phones used during the raid on Eagle Nest and tracked them to six different accounts...One belonged to the head of the Tres Locos gang which was the primary organization behind the delivery of the illegals...The CIA accessed his phone records and tied him to the Mexican Army colonel arrested in Nuevo Laredo...It also tied him to a satellite phone number believed to be used by our new target…Javier Cojone."

"You are kidding, right?"

"Kid you not…The DIA set up a special unit to monitor that phone frequency and record all transmissions. One of the calls was by the little blonde American cheerleader, Crystal Coopersmith, who disappeared from Barbados three years ago."

Kit pushed back his chair and exhaled slowly. He had a daughter by his ex-wife who was the same age. That story had always had such an effect on him—he nodded slowly as he digested the information. "So that's where the FBI fits in this puzzle…Some of the sex slaves being held are American."

Dare looked at his COO and knew what he was thinking. "Now you see why we need the Navy. According to Crystal, there are between eighteen and twenty-five girls being held on Isla Gukumatz at any one time…We need the MEU's Ospreys to get them off the island in a rapid manner.

"The Mexican government won't be happy when they find out we put one of their billionaires out of commission…Permanently."

"Fuck the Mexican government…They've allowed this asshole to operate under their protection for too damn long…Who are the buyers of these sex slaves anyway?"

Dare glance at him. "I asked the Director of the CIA that very question after our meeting with the President. Best information we have is the former Minister of Defense for Venezuela is the prime mover and shaker in white slaves in this hemisphere…They bring big dollars from drug dealers and rich people in the orient and middle east."

"Why don't we ever hear of one of them escaping and blowing the whistle?"

"The oil-rich shaykhs use them until they tire of the girls and pass them to their sons, who do the same thing…Eventually they're too old and worn out to be desirable and end up in shallow graves in the desert…Not a pretty picture."

Kit sat quietly for a moment. His eyes met Dare's. "After our business is finished on the island…think I might make a little trip down to Venezuela…No charge."

"If you need a copilot, I know someone…Looks a lot like me." Dare flipped through the folder. "Now, back to business. We can send Mama Bird to NAS Jax and drop off four 600s and our new 200…They can fly out to the Iwo on her way by…That will give us nine craft on station."

SIMULATOR ROOM

Jill had set up Mike for the one simulator scenario she knew he could not pass—no one had, not even her. It involved a multiple emergencies in which the ship's battery was shorted out by a thermal runaway internal fault. The Ni-Cad batteries would fail, causing a massive short and spiking the electrical system with amperage the wiring could not handle.

The solution was to isolate the battery electrical bus and kill the battery switch. In that configuration, the battery switch could not be turned back on as it was no longer powered via a safety relay intended to protect the aircraft from electrical fire.

The compound problem she planned was to introduce a fuel contamination issue resulting in all eight engines being starved for fuel. When the engines quit turning, the unpowered craft would plummet to the earth like bowling ball dropped from a skyscraper.

Mike would pull the emergency parachute handle. Jill wanted to see his reaction to the failure of the solenoid to fire the cartridge deploying the parachute. She had been looking forward to this as he was acing the checkout program—it was time to give him a little lesson in humility.

Mike was at the controls at 4,000 feet setting up for a missile attack on a bridge when the *Master Battery Caution* light illuminated. He discontinued the attack and rolled out in a slightly climbing right turn. He noticed the battery voltage display at forty-six volts and climbing as he directed his pilot in command, "Master battery switch *OFF*."

"Master battery switch is *OFF*," Jill confirmed.

"DC Battery bus *ISOLATED*, confirm."

"DC battery bus is *ISOLATED*. All DC systems operating normally." She confirmed the engine driven generators were powering all other system busses.

Now came the part Jill was waiting for. Her job as instructor entailed that she play all support and control contacts over the radios in the simulator. "Eagle Two, Mama Bird."

"Mama Bird, Eagle Two, go."

"Eagle Two, One and Three report suspected fuel contamination. Maintenance reports rags found in damaged pump assembly. Recover immediately to rendezvous point X-ray."

"Eagle Two, roger." Mike looked over at her. *What is she up to?*

Jill pressed the *Enter* button on the instructor's control panel behind her throttle quadrant left of her seat. *Fuel Pressure Low* amber caution lights illuminated in short order on all eight engines followed by *Engine Failure* master caution red lights.

All eight lights illuminated for a short period, then the cockpit lights failed as the last engine-driven generator went off line.

The M600/A dropped like a stone with no power available.

Mike reached for the emergency parachute deploy *T* handle and pulled it firmly—nothing happened. He pulled it again to its mechanical stop with the same result. Jill grinned as he got up and stepped back between the two seats.

"I would pull the snaps off the fabric panel behind the Raptor seats...Reach back about thirty inches to the green manual safety *T* handle lock on the parachute deployment solenoid, pull it down, and then release it...If it didn't fire, I'd hit it with the butt of my survival knife to try and fire the cartridge."

Jill hit the *Situation Freeze*. The plummeting craft stopped at 1,500 AGL. "I'll be damned!...That just might work!"

Her mind raced as she went over the systems in her head. She had seen a schematic of the parachute system in the reference manual, but didn't know it could be reached from behind the fabric panel. She stood up. "Okay, what would you do if that didn't work?

He slipped his left hand around the back of her neck and his right arm around her waist. He kissed her sweetly—she responded with passion. As he broke away from her gently, she looked confused.

"Why did you do that?"

"Because if I thought I was going to die, I'd have to know what kissing you was like." He turned to walk out.

Jill stood there for a full ten seconds as she tried to comprehend what just happened. *How the hell did he do that? All the other pilots had died in the simulator when faced with the same no-win situation, including me.*

That kiss had really upset her homeostasis. She was the instructor. She was in charge—or was she?

Jill jogged down the hall and caught sight of him as he made the turn into the mess hall. She caught up with him at the beverage dispenser. "Cowboy!…How did you know? Nobody ever gets out of that scenario…Gears made it up before I got here."

"Iced tea or Dr. Pepper?" He turned to her and grinned.

"Tea, please…that carbonated stuff will kill you."

Mike poured the two drinks and walked her over to an empty table. "Tell me something, gorgeous…Have you ever read the complete maintenance manual on the M600/A?"

"Nope, I just fly them. I let the other guys fix 'em…Why?"

"Just a personal habit I got into on the ranch…See, we live so far out, it takes hours, sometimes days, for a dealer or factory mechanic to get out to fix our farm equipment. Tractors, balers, frontend loaders, backhoes…you name it. Dad and I got into the habit of always ordering a maintenance manual as well as an operators manual for everything we owned."

"And just when did you have time to read the maintenance manual?" She looked at him with a slight hint of distrust.

"Well, last night after we got back from DC…Couldn't sleep, so I went up the hangar deck and watched the night shift change out the air conditioner on one and gear door latch on another. They were real excited to see a pilot interested in what they did and loaned me a laptop with their manual."

"And you read all that last night?"

"All but the chapter about nacelle vane removal…That was pretty straight forward and it was almost 0200."

She could only stare in a mixture of amazement and admiration. *What a kisser!*

***

CHAPTER FIFTEEN

EAGLE NEST RANCH
Blaze's Electronics Lab
6 July

Gears and Blaze worked all morning getting the flexible carbon-fiber nanotubes filled with liquid mercury. Her sealed vacuum chamber fascinated Gears. "Wondered how you got the mercury into those little eight micron-wide tubes."

"You can't touch it, of course...the stuff will destroy two-thirds of your brain cells." She smiled.

"Not to mention kill you...so they say...When I was a kid, we used to play with mercury from thermometers. Made pennies shine like dimes." Gears chuckled.

"My dad told me that, too...I'm amazed your generation lived long enough to grow up."

"I know...we even used to drink raw milk and go to the swimming hole all by ourselves...Let's go out to the range and see what this bad boy will do." He picked up the last of the six barrels they had modified.

They took forty minutes to attach the last barrel to the mounting assembly and connect the wire from the capacitor complex to the sequenced superconducting projection coils.

Blaze attached the heavy cable clamps to two twelve-volt truck batteries wired in series. Twenty-four volts would be less than the twenty-eight volts provided by the 600, but was close enough to make a test bed functional.

They spooled out fifty feet of control wire connected to the start/stop button and donned their ear and eye protection.

"Let her rip, kid." Gears gave her a thumbs-up.

She pressed the button and they heard the familiar rapid metallic buzz of the clacking titanium loader lightly through the ear protection.

They checked the gun for visible damage. Gears counted out six of the custom 7mm projectiles and loaded them in the temporary feed box attached to the receiver/feed cylinder.

Blaze rechecked the barrel alignment with the target 200 hundred yards distant using a laser boresighter. The beam reflected brightly off the twelve inch stainless-steel disc attached to a plywood sheet bolted to metal poles in the ground.

Gears checked the high-speed camera and the chronograph—they were ready. They walked to the end of the control cable, turned to face the gun as she picked up the box and held it out.

"Ladies first," Gears insisted.

"Here goes nothin'."

The test was over in less than a quarter of a second. A faint blue line flashed between the gun and the target. It made a odd sound like a tattoo gun crossed with a hissing snake.

Blaze lifted her binoculars and studied the target. There were six holes the size of a half-dollar in the three-eighths inch stainless-steel plate—the pattern was identical to the displacement of the six barrels. She handed the glasses to Gears. "And what do you think, Professor?"

He looked at the target and smiled. "Bless your heart, Missy, you are a genius."

"Likewise, I am sure." She curtsied.

They laughed as they disconnected the power source, and then strolled triumphantly to the target. The chronograph had shown 13,115 feet per second—over a thousand more than the original coil gun.

As they approached, Blaze bent over to see the impact points more closely. The smile vanished from her face. "My God in heaven." She stood back up.

"What's wrong, little lady?"

She pointed at the holes as she dropped to her knees.

Gears could not see the problem and knelt down beside her and peered through the holes—there was blue sky visible through the berm.

They stepped behind the plywood backstop and stared with disbelief at a four-inch diameter hole burned completely through the thirty-five foot thick limestone hill.

"Think we're gonna need a bigger hill." The tall redhead shrugged as the speechless Gears nodded.

BEF CONTROL CENTER
Dare's Office
6 July

Dare, Cabrillo, Sosa, and Mendes listened intently as Kit reviewed the only technical data available about the RA-115 suitcase nukes.

He was the most knowledgeable in the BEF about the top secret devices. "As the GRU defector Colonel Stanislav Lunev indicated, some of these devices have been recovered in Switzerland where the KGB operatives had placed them back during the cold war. At least one Swiss recovery team was killed attempting to move it...That is a fact, gentlemen.

"Lunev indicated that there was something called a Lightning booby trap installed on the units...triggered by unauthorized movement...Don't know the exact nature of the switch...mercury contact, accelerometer, etc. There could be other types...He didn't say and none of us are trained as bomb disposal experts anyway."

Dare noticed the general look of unease as the three pilots absorbed the information and took the opportunity to exert some leadership. "Gentlemen, I appreciate your concerns...Let me make a couple of points here. The technical data on these devices showed a battery life of only two months. Back in the 1980's batteries were not very advanced...There is a strong possibility that these bombs are, in fact, inert. The original batteries for the timing and firing mechanisms are long dead…However, we cannot safely make that assumption. All we want you to do, if you are hired as Cojone's pilots, is to ascertain there is fissionable material in the boxes."

Miguel Cabrillo spoke up, "Fine, boss, how do we accomplish that little task without opening them?…Pretty sure we won't be carrying Geiger counters with us."

"Actually, you will."

The three looked at each other as if to say, this guy is going to get me killed.

Dare turned to Kit. "Show the men their toys…compliments of our new friends in the spook shop over at the CIA."

Kit took three boxes out of his briefcase. He tossed one to each—they opened them and took out different versions of pilot watches with stopwatch second hands.

They stared in disbelief.

"Hey, boss, this one is used," Miguel observed.

"So is the one it's replacing," Kit pointed out.

"Press the top button once for a sweep second timer. Again to stop. Press once more to reset…Same for the bottom switch and the other sweep second dial…Now the good part.

"Press and hold the top button for two seconds. If the watch has been exposed to significant plutonium radiation, the bottom sweep hand will spin. Release and it will stop…Any questions?" Dare looked at each man.

Roberto Mendes glanced at the watch. "Did you say plutonium?…Isn't that Pu-239?"

"You get the gold star, Bobby…Any questions on your back stories or employment histories?…Now is the time to ask. This is some deep cover you are going into…We can't afford mistakes." Kit didn't smile.

No one said anything.

Dare stood up. He shook each man's hand in a solemn show of his best wishes for their safe return—Kit followed in turn.

"That's it guys, make sure you don't have any conflicting ID or credit cards in any of your personal items, shaving kits, checked bags and so forth. Hammer will be positioning you this afternoon to your departure flight points for Cancun…Good Luck."

Dare watched as they silently streamed out of his office. The deployment of *Operation Viper* had begun…

DARE'S OFFICE LATER

Gears knocked on the frame. "Boss, you got a minute?"

He and Blaze entered.

Dare looked up from his paperwork. "Sure guys, just going over the satellite images of the island. Can't see an airstrip there for the Gulfstream that the CIA claims he owns. Other than the helipad and a oceanfront ramp for the Grumman Goose…I can't make one out."

Blaze looked over his shoulder at the pictures. "Have you looked at the infrared spectrum?…Might be camouflaged."

"He couldn't hide a jet runway with netting."

"Maybe not, but Sherlock Holmes said that if you eliminate all possible solutions, then the impossible, no matter how improbable, is the answer," Gears added.

"Thanks, I'll remember that if I'm ever up against Professor Moriarty...Sorry, what was it ya'll wanted to see me about?"

"We finished the gun modification for the first 600 and wanted to see what you think."

Dare was somewhat confused. He remembered talking about Blaze looking into the possibility of doing so, but had been so tied up with intelligence gathering he had forgotten what they were working on. "You mean you've got a mock-up ready? In only seven days?...That was fast."

Blaze and Gears looked at each other and shrugged.

"Uh, no, Boss, we have actually completed the modification of the first line bird...It tested great. The penetration on granite and basalt measured thirty-two and limestone forty-one," Gears said.

Dare held his hands about three feet apart. "Wow, over three feet. Lot better than the 7.62 round...Good job guys."

Blaze and Gears glanced at each other again. They shook their heads.

Dare remained confused. "Oh, millimeters! Sorry guys, I just had my mind on the mission...Still, not bad."

Both shook their heads again.

"What? Centimeters?"

Gears grinned like a Cheshire cat. "Uh...feet, boss...We're talking feet of penetration...Thought you knew."

Dare sat stunned for a long moment, and then stood. "No shit? Hell, this I gotta see."

In the underground hangar, Gears pointed out their handiwork. Since the six Gatling barrels no longer rotated, they had replaced the solid central axle with a hollow hardened tube containing an ultra-powerful targeting laser.

Blaze laid her hand on the nose gun and smiled. "We have the option to choose visible or infrared lasers depending upon flight and target conditions...with a range of over twenty miles in clear air. It's also capable of literally burning through a moderate cloud cover...And we can even tie the Hellfire and PAASM guidance system to the IR laser identifier on the HUD."

"And you did all this in one week?"

"No, no. Blaze took weeks developing the original coyote gun. We just adapted the technology to our needs...Oh, by the way we built six functional coyote guns that are ready for this mission...Already got Raptor Team Four trying them out...We get 100 rounds per battery now with the improvements."

"How long will it take to build a second multibarrel unit?...Be nice if we had two."

"Well, Dare...the machine shop should be finishing the feed mechanisms for the other nine tonight. We built all the superconducting projection impulse coils we needed, plus spares, down at my shop on Eagle Nest.

"Assembly takes an hour each and about that for pulling the old units...Magazine capacity is now three thousand rounds…since we don't have to have a catch drum for the brass or worry so much about weight.

"We can have the fleet converted by tomorrow night without running maintenance into the ground," Blaze added.

Gears chimed in, "I can have the HUD fire control pippers recalibrated for the increased range and the 13,000 feet-per-second muzzle velocity by tomorrow morning…It's just a software rewrite."

Dare grinned and shook his head as he turned to head back to his office. "You know where I'll be if you need anything…By the way, remind me to give you guys a bonus…I gotta go take an aspirin."

When Dare got to his office, he buzzed Kit. "Need you to come down, please."

"On my way."

In a few minutes he walked in. "What's up, boss?"

"You are not going to believe this…I'd tell you, but you gotta go see what Blaze and Gears have come up with…Suffice to say, it's hot.

"They're modifying our entire squadron of Eagles plus the 200 with the new multibarrel coil guns and will have the pippers recalibrated by in the morning…How about we call the guns, Blaze G2s.

"Team Four is already familiarizing themselves with their G1 coil rifles. We need to load up four 600s and the 200 on Mama Bird and get them to NAS Jax as soon as they're done with the mods…Assign Jill to the 200…The Iwo is underway from Norfolk and we should be able to coordinate transfer off the Florida coast."

"I'm on it."

BEF COMMAND CENTER

Duty rosters and assignments for the upcoming Operation *Viper* mission were posted on the Ops Team bulletin board. Several members gathered around to see where they were being assigned. Jill was assigned the pilot slot as *Eagle* Five, the M200.

It was the logical assignment as she had the most training as a pure fighter pilot and the ten-engine, two-seater M200 had been designed as such. Faster and more nimble than the attack aircraft, it could top five hundred knots and pull seven G's. She was set to deploy the next day, July 7th—as soon as the upgraded six-barreled coil guns were installed on all the Black Eagles.

Mike was somewhat surprised to see his name on the list as pilot in command of *Eagle* Four. "Hey, Jill, is this a misprint?"

"No, big boy…Don't be so modest. I taught you every thing I know about the 600…and you even taught me a thing or two. Dare says you're ready and I agree."

He could sense a hint of sadness in her voice and placed his hand on her shoulder as she turned to face him. "What's wrong, Baby? It's not like we're never gonna see each other again."

"I know…It's just…well…I've kinda enjoyed the last week together."

"Me, too," Mike sighed as the realization hit that she was deploying the next day. "How about I buy you dinner?"

Jill thought for a second, and then smiled. "Got a better idea...Be right back."

She headed down the hall to Dare's office and knocked twice before she entered. "Hey, Boss. Need to ask a favor."

He looked up. "Go ahead. Make it quick...kinda busy."

"Any chance Mike and I could take off for a while? I'd like to make him dinner at my place."

Dare smiled, *A few hours out of the building could do them both good.* "Sure. Be back by ten hundred...Have fun."

Mike was still looking at the personnel pairings on the board when Jill skipped back up to him. "Cowboy...put on your boots and jeans...We're eating at my place tonight."

He was waiting outside his room when Jill stepped out of hers. Gone were her BEF utilities and flight boots—in their place, a light blue summer-weight dress that flowed across the contours of her body. She wore her hair down and sported a pair of four-inch strapless open-toed heels.

"Wow!"

JILL'S CONDO
LAKE TEXOMA

"Once again, that was wonderful...Sugar, you are one fine cook. That was the best chicken marsalla I've ever eaten."

"Thank you, kind sir." She curtsied. "Guess we better put these things in the dishwasher."

Jill dried her hands on the apricot-colored hand towel and tossed it over the whimsical terra cotta rabbit's head mounted above the back splash. She turned to him. "Got room for dessert?"

"Take a rain check?"

"Not likely." She started unbuttoning his shirt…

The sun was streaming through the shear curtains on the upstairs bedroom. It danced on the long golden strands of blonde hair cascading across Mike's chest. She stirred slightly—a slight moan escaped her lips. He held her gently and brushed her hair with his hand.

He'd been awake for twenty minutes, but wanted to savor every minute of his time with her. He thought back about every other woman he had ever known and cared about, and none had ignited the feelings he had for Jill. *This one is so very special.*

The alarm clock on his side of the bed made a rude buzzing and he reached out to silence it. Her lids fluttered open and the intense blue of her gorgeous eyes said hello even before her lips whispered, "Morning, Cowboy."

"Morning, Pretty." He kissed her tenderly. *I could get used to this…*

BEF HEADQUARTERS
7 July, 1000 hours

Mama Bird was backed into the big central hangar, her rear ramp down at the edge of the big elevator. Loadmasters were loading the new M200 as Jill, Mike and Kit watched.

"So that's the new fast fighter? Just nose gun, right?" asked Jill.

"Yep, supposed to do over five hundred knots with that fifth nacelle...And with the new coil gun, it'll be like having both cannon and a multiple shot laser-guided LAW with twenty times the penetration power...It's one bad dude," said Kit.

"Guess I'll get to practice flying that little puppy while we're on the Iwo."

"You guess right...And you'll be in command of the Iwo unit," added Kit.

"Do my best."

"I know you will."

Mike and Jill embraced.

"Watch your six, girl."

"I've done this before, Cowboy...you watch yours."

The loadmasters loaded the four newly modified M600/As back into the massive cargo bay of the C-5M and then closed the ramp.

"Looks like you need to get your team aboard...See you at the rendezvous point." Kit shook her hand.

AL KUZIYAH, IRAQ
7 July

A beat-up 1998 Mercedes stake-side diesel truck with a canvas top, loaded with boxes of fresh melons and fruit pulled up to the crumbling remains of a mud-colored abandoned house and parked. The derelict one-story house stood alone one-half mile east of a sleepy little village located just south of the Euphrates River—100 miles west of Tikrit.

No one saw the truck pull behind the house and park. Three men got out, walked around to the front and through the opening where a door had once stood. Two of the men began to break down the rear wall of the small bedroom with sledgehammers as the third held a powerful flashlight.

The plaster and mud-brick wall gave way begrudgingly and an opening approximately three feet by six feet appeared.

Hamani Al Hussein shined the light on two medium-sized wooden crates. "That's them. Load them in the truck and cover them with boxes of melons."

The two helpers did as they were told, and then all three climbed back into the truck. After twelve miles of driving on the dirt road, the truck made the right turn onto highway 3. It was another twenty-five miles to the Syrian border and the Iraqi checkpoint just east of Abu Kamal.

Hamani did not expect any problems at the border as many produce trucks exactly like this one rolled all night to deliver to the markets of Damascus. His papers were in order and he had plenty of American $20 bills to help grease the palms of anyone who might be too interested in his cargo.

He had no idea what was in the crates, except that they were some type of weapon. But the ten thousand American dollars he was to be paid upon delivery entirely eliminated his curiosity.

Hamani had hidden the two crates in January of 2002 at the direction of his late cousin, Saddam Hussein. He figured since Saddam had been captured and hung, he no longer had any use for them.

Dawn broke over the bustling city of Damascus as Hamani and his cargo rolled up to a warehouse on a deserted back street. He stepped down from the truck while the driver and helper waited, knocked four times on the metal roll-up door.

A slim Arab man in light blue warm-up pants and a matching stood in the opening as it rattled to the top.

Mahmoud, the driver, could not make out what they said, but Hamani motioned for him to drive the truck inside—the metal door closed behind it and the street was quiet again.

Umair Hassen watched as Hamani's men unloaded the two wooden crates. One of them had a slight rash on his right forearm and hand. *Must be the heat*, he thought. Much of the produce covering the crates had turned black. "It is a pity you took so long to get here, the melons have all gone bad."

"A thousand pardons. It was the wretched heat…we made good time."

Umair counted out ten packages of one hundred dollar bills and handed them to Hamani.

He recounted them and bowed slightly. "May Allah be with you."

"And with you."

As Hamani straightened up and turned to go to his truck, a slight trickle of blood began to flow from his nose. He quickly whipped out a filthy, formerly white handkerchief and wiped it. "Is nothing. The dryness of the desert still follows me."

Umair merely grunted and turned to raise the door to allow the Iraqi to leave with his rotten cargo.

Mahmoud drove back out the door, the Arab closed it once again, opened his cell phone.

Roberto Vicente answered, "Bobo here. I was expecting your call."

"Your Mediterranean candles have arrived. I will bring them to the airport personally, when the Gulfstream arrives in Damascus."

"The wire transfer of your funds will occur as soon as the merchandise is loaded."

***

CHAPTER SIXTEEN

CANCUN INTERNATIONAL AIRPORT
8 July

Miguel Cabrillo passed through customs and security with his bag. A slightly built Hispanic held up a small hand-lettered cardboard sign with his name on it. Miguel raised his index finger and nodded to the smaller man.

"Hi, I'm Miguel Cabrillo."

"Hey, Miguel, pleased to meet you. Ignacio Diaz...Captain on the Grumman Goose. You're the last candidate to arrive...Got the other two guys outside. Any other bags?"

"Just the one...If I get the job, I'll send for my stuff."

They walked outside to a rented SUV cab and Miguel tossed his bag in the back with the two other rollaboards. Scores of sunburned tourists made their way into the terminal as they headed home while a sea of pale-skinned new arrivals moved outside en masse and tried to find their resort shuttles.

"Looks like shift change," Miguel observed.

"Like that almost every day down here...Big business," Ignacio confirmed.

They took their seats in the bright yellow Ford. The driver drove four hundred yards down the paved road and turned right into the Fixed Base of Operations.

Out on the ramp, a shiny 1938 Grumman G-21 *Goose* sat parked. The blue and white aircraft looked much as it did the day it was launched.

The SUV pulled up next to the wingtip. The four men got out and the three prospective pilots retrieved their bags—Ignacio paid the cab driver.

"Miguel, this is Julio Sosa and this is Bobby Mendes. Guys...Miguel Cabrillo." Ignacio showed the way into the small hatch on the side of the *Goose*.

The three men shook hands and cautiously regarded each other as potential competitors for the two job positions—they didn't let on they had been working together for years.

Inside the old aircraft, only three passenger seats were installed. Normally, there were none as this normally was an airborne grocery delivery vehicle.

At least three days a week, it flew to Merida or Cancun for supplies for the remote island fortress. They strapped in as Ignacio climbed into the left seat. The copilot had already started the first of two Pratt and Whitney radial engines. The noise was considerable as the unairconditioned plane had both sliding cockpit windows open until the amphibious craft reached the hold short point on the taxiway.

"Grumman X-ray Whiskey November One-Four-Eight, Cancun tower, you are cleared for takeoff runway two-niner," came the clearance from the controller.

"X-ray Whiskey November, roger. Cleared for take off," the copilot replied.

Captain Diaz reached overhead to the twin throttles mounted on the overhead panel between the two pilots and smoothly slid them forward. The antique marvel started down the runway as the captain fed in rudder to maintain directional control.

The three passengers tried to look calm, but inside, each had a small knot in the pit of his stomach—it was game time and the stakes were high.

They couldn't see much out of the tiny porthole windows except the warm clear waters of the southern Gulf. The surface appeared closer as Ignacio ordered the landing flaps set. The aircraft pitched slightly nose down when the copilot moved the flap lever down.

As the aircraft slowed even more, Ignacio trimmed the nose up and pulled the power back until the *Goose* seemed suspended on a string just inches above the blue water. One last rearward movement of the throttles brought the boat-shaped hull gently into contact with the surface—the water split evenly on either side of the prow.

"Gear down," said Ignacio after they had slowed.

The guys in the back heard the command, then the whine of the updated hydraulic system as the gear extended into the water. Each smiled at the apparent backwardness of the sequence. None were seaplane rated and the idea of landing, then extending the gear was foreign—even if correct.

The experienced captain added power and the amphibious bird crawled up the inclined concrete ramp. He taxied a short distance to a paved turnaround and pressing the left brake, spun around and pointed back at the water. He shut the engines off and as the props stopped turning, climbed out of the seat and made his way to the rear hatch.

The three pilots briefly glanced at one another and followed Diaz out the door. A impressive looking Hispanic man in a jade-green polo shirt and khaki slacks stood outside. Beside him were two stone-faced smaller men in black T-shirts and black cotton cargo pants. Each wore combat boots and carried a H&K MP-5 and looked as if they knew how to use them.

"Gentleman, welcome to Isla Gukumatz. I'm Roberto Vicente…the man who invited you here…My friends call me Bobo."

BEF CONTROL CENTER
July 10

Julio Sosa sat at the large conference table being debriefed by Dare, Kit, Gears and Raptor Four leader, Leroy Poole. Julio had been the odd man out for the two pilot positions at Isla Gukumatz.

"They didn't give us a tour, but I had the opportunity to talk briefly with Bobo in private. I've prepared a sketch of the island with the defenses marked in red. They have two Zeus 23-4 AAA units…one at each end of the island and a SA-15 Gauntlet

310

missile battery west of the pyramid outside the perimeter wall."

Sosa slid over a chart he had created along with a 3-D drawing of the pyramid. "This is as close as I could get on the basic floor plan for the pyramid. I was only on the eighth floor, but noticed that the elevator went from B3 to twelve...Apparently there are three floors underground."

"What about radar?" asked Gears.

"The Zeus and the SAM have their own stand-alone radar and there's a fourth radar unit at the north side of the helipad on top of the building."

"How many kidnapped women did you see?" Dare inquired.

"Didn't see any, but Bobo told me there were twenty-one in the pyramid...They have their own master quarters on the tenth floor...except when they're keeping Javier company."

"What about the airstrip?" Kit asked.

"Nada...no sign at all. That damn island is all jungle, except for the compound. There was a concrete ramp and turnaround for the Goose...but that was it."

"Gotta be one someplace," Dare offered.

"Bobo said there was, but we had to cut our conversation short when a guard came to take me back to the Goose."

"Dare, has anybody done a infrared satellite scan of the island?" asked Gears.

"Not to my knowledge...but we can check with the SecDef and get access to the DoD's schedule for the Gulf...Blaze mentioned it the other day and I just forgot...Kit, you want to take care of that?"

"Can do, boss."

"Gears, get with DoD also and confirm the frequencies that the AAA and mobile SAM sites are known to use."

"Boss, don't you think I already keep up with that crap?" Gears grumbled.

"My bad…Guys, we gotta lot of lives riding on this…Apologize if I'm being redundant…Just can't overlook anything."

"What else can you remember, Julio?" asked Leroy.

"Well, that perimeter wall is solid cut-coral limestone, four feet thick and ten feet tall with two guard towers…Also counted upwards of twenty foot soldiers, all with MP-5s…Except a couple of guards at the main gate had SAWs.

"Pretty sure the main weapons bunker is underground. There was a road that crossed the one we took from the ramp to the compound…It went north and disappeared into the jungle."

Kit pulled up the satellite photo of the island and pointed to the road. "Here it is. It just stops about a half-mile from the crossing…Five'll get you ten, there's the bunker…Far enough away from the compound to be safe and close enough to the dock for transport."

"All right people, you've got what intel we have, put together your ops plans for a night incursion…We launch in two days." The interoffice phone buzzed. "Dare."

"Mister Phillips, I've got a Mister Weber with the CIA on two."

"Thank you, Kaye." He punched the flashing button. "Director Weber, how are you today?"

"Fine, Dare…Got some good news for you. We managed to get an operative into the Gulfstream plant under the guise of an FAA inspector. He planted a GPS unit on Cojone's new 450. They're picking it up today…I'm sending you the code…via secure email."

"Great news. That will help immensely…We're putting together our ops plans now and keeping an eye on tropical storm Ellen east of Honduras. The National Hurricane Center is forecasting her to be upgraded to hurricane status tomorrow and may impact our operation on the twelfth…We'll keep you advised."

GULFSTREAM 450 OVER THE ATLANTIC
12 July

"Santa Maria, Santa Maria, Gulfstream X-ray India Tango two-two-three position," copilot Mendes broadcast on the HF radio.

The interior of the G-450 smelled like a new car to Miguel and Bobby—only better. Several million dollars better. Three hundred miles west of their Lajes Azores refueling stop, the sleek executive jet cruised at FL 360 on a custom flight plan well south of tracks flown by most commercial flights from Europe to the United States.

The fourteen hour travel day from Damascus to Isla Gukumatz was a long duty-day—but the deadly cargo was on-time to arrive before sunset.

Cabrillo had downloaded the special navigation update given him by Bobo before he and Bobby were flown to Cancun for the commercial flight to South Carolina. He was still not exactly sure what Bobo had meant by his statement: "Fly the GPS approach to Runway 36 on autopilot and let the aircraft auto-land...Do not believe what your eyes tell you."

That had hit him as very strange, but he was prepared to follow instructions. He figured that Bobo would not put a thirty-eight million dollar airplane plus the valuable cargo at risk.

USS IWO JIMA
Gulf of Mexico
100 Miles Northeast of Isla Gukumatz

Jill had landed VTOL on the flight deck after a short hop to gain aircraft familiarity and testing the new multibarreled coil gun. The flight deck seemed almost full of sailors and Marines mesmerized with both the M200 and the pilot.

She stepped out of the cockpit, Systems Officer and copilot, Carl Reynolds, climbed out shortly thereafter.

"Holy cow! Did you see the hole in the ocean that gun made? Looked like we dropped a Mk82 500 pounder!"

Jill had a broad smile on her face. "Think we got that dangerous fifty-five gal drum alright...This little bird is hot. Got more moves than Lady Gaga."

"I'll pull the gun camera memory stick and we can see the first hit."

"Have maintenance top off and rearm her...We launch tonight at 2200."

"Yes, Ma'am."

The crowd parted as the Officer of the Deck, approached Jill.

"Miss McElhaney, I'm Commander Willis, I have the deck today. The Captain has informed me that Hurricane Ellen has been upgraded to a category three and he's moving the ship to a location north and west of the island. Ellen is forecast to make a turn more due north...We'll be safer on the northwest quadrant...We have advised the SecNav."

"I understand, Commander. I'll inform my crews...Any chance I can look at a real-time view of the storm?"

"Yes ma'am. If you will follow me to the CIC." He led the way to the bridge on the starboard side of the flight deck.

AIRSPACE NORTH OF CUBA

Miguel Cabrillo had begun the descent one hundred and twenty-three miles from Isla Gukamatz. The 450 continued westward at .80 Mach as he watched the bands of thunderstorms off to the southwest on his long range weather radar. "We should beat the storm to the island...Hope Javier lets us take the airplane someplace like Miami or Matamoros before it hits...It looks like a bad motor scooter."

"Roger that," Bobby agreed.

One of the two men sent to keep an eye on the new pilots came forward. He had a rash on his wrists and looked unwell. "Hey, Captain Miguel, Jesus is not feeling well back there. Can you call ahead and let the doctor know?"

"Sure, Manny...glad to help...You don't look too good yourself."

"Musta been something in those box lunches we got in the Azores...Tasted fine, but you know, I do feel a little sick."

"Go sit down, we'll be on the ground in twenty-five minutes.

Miguel looked at Bobby and whispered, "Radiation...My watch jumped off the scale when we loaded those crates...Damn things are leaking like a mother." He pointed to the radio and nodded.

Bobby switched the transmitter to the 121.5 Guard Frequency they monitored on the secondary radio when over water. "Miguel, it's gettin' hot in here." He held back on the VHF radio rocker switch on the copilot's yoke.

He turned the air conditioning rheostat a couple degrees colder, just in case one of their two watchers had been paying attention. Bobby switched the transmit switch back to the Cojone headquarters' frequency on the secondary radio...

USS *IWO JIMA*
Gulf of Mexico

The radio operator handed a slip of paper to an E3 to deliver to the OOD. The coded message sent in plain text over the guard frequency had been received:

Nuclear weapons on board the Gulfstream.

AIRSPACE WEST OF CUBA

Descending through FL 220, Miguel Cabrillo listened to the ATIS information at Cancun International. He received the latest weather forecast for the Yucatan. Cozumel was closed with gale force winds. *The hurricane has not reached there yet, but was only a matter of a half hour,* he figured.

BEF COMMAND CENTER

Tom Tallman was manning the operations desk when the call came from the Pentagon—he pressed button one. "BEF, Tallman here."

"Mister Tallman, Admiral Samson Valenti, Chairman of the Joint Chiefs."

"Yes, sir."

"I have been advised by the captain of the Iwo that the confirmation signal has been received. Positive ID on the nuclear devices on board the Gulfstream. Please advise Mister Phillips."

"Yes, sir, right away sir," Tom said just before the secure line went dead.

He turned in his chair and looked up at Dare. The silver-haired warrior was dressed once again in his BEF flight suit and had been studying the hurricane progress on the seventy-two inch screen above Tom's station.

"Cabrillo's signal confirmed weapons on board, boss."

"Open the hangar doors...Mama Bird's about to fly," Dare said resolutely, then turned and headed for the elevator...

ISLA GUKUMATZ
Cojone Compound

Inside the small office, an elderly man watched the radar screen. He also had an automated weather station which provided all the information a pilot would need for an approach and landing at the single runway. "Whitebird, current weather eight thousand overcast, visibility two-zero, wind one-one-zero at eight gusting one-five. Altimeter two-niner-one-five. Cleared to land runway one-eight."

"Roger, cleared to land on one-eight, altimeter two-niner-one-five," Bobby Mendes responded.

Cabrillo set up the autopilot for the GPS approach to one-eight and set autobrakes to medium. He had flown Category III approaches many times where the aircraft had to autoland due to poor visibility. *The clouds are blocking the sun. Going to get dark early tonight*, he thought.

The Gulfstream rolled out heading south eight miles from the runway—he slowed to approach speed—Bobby configured the aircraft as Miguel called for flaps and gear. The aircraft descended below 200 feet—the island still appeared mostly jungle.

One hundred feet to go—Miguel and Bobby could feel their own hearts beating wildly. *Do not believe what your eyes tell you*. The words Bobo had said were haunting him as he started to hit the go-around paddles on the throttles.

"Miguel!"

The sight of trees and vines filled the windshield. Trees towered over them on both the right and left sides of the plane.

He hit the go-around paddles just as the tires chirped on the realistic jungle mural painted on the asphalt. Miguel instantly punched the autopilot off, pulled the two throttles to idle and up into reverse. He smoothly braked as he kept the aircraft centered on the runway, using the jungle on each side as guide—they could finally breathe normally again.

"Fuckin' Bobo could have mentioned the runway was painted like a God damned jungle mural," Miguel said bitterly.

"Bastard scared me outta three year's growth…think he did it on purpose." Bobby nodded in agreement.

Toward the south end of the runway, a man with lighted orange wands walked out in front of a huge building completely covered with the same mural. Hangar doors opened making the bright lighted interior visible. Miguel followed the hand signals of the marshaller until he was given a stop signal, followed by a cut engines signal when they were inside.

"We made it, pardner. " He managed a weak smile.

"Yeah…my ass is draggin."

The smile faded from his partner's face and was replaced with a look Bobby couldn't quite decipher. "What?"

Miguel pointed at the view through the copilot's sliding window. Bobby turned and looked past the Grumman *Goose* at an armed Bell *Jet Ranger*—and a shiny, fully armed Russian MiG 29 *Fulcrum* A…

***

319

CHAPTER SEVENTEEN

USS *IWO JIMA*
Gulf of Mexico
2040 Hours

Jill listened to the change of plans as Dare described them on the comm center radio.

"The heavy cloud cover precludes the use of Manta plus winds in the target area have risen to unsafe levels for Team Four to make a HALO drop. We need a eight-man Marine Force Recon squad from *Iwo*."

No other operation had ever required any active duty personnel to go in harm's way with the BEF, but this was unlike other missions. Americans were being held hostage and the obvious threat of portable nuclear devices in the hands of American-hating Mexican ultra-nationalists more than justified the actions being taken.

Jill left the comm center and headed into the CIC. "Commander Willis, I urgently need to speak with the Captain."

"Follow me."

At a window in the bridge, overlooking the flight deck, they approached a stocky, black, five foot nine Navy captain.

"Captain Lowry, Miss McElheney would like a word with you."

He turned around and looked up at the blonde pilot. "McElheney. McElheney...Your dad an Air Force pilot?"

"Yes, sir..."

"Thought you might be related...big tall linebacker from the Air Force Academy...Broke one of my front teeth in the Air Force/Navy game...'79...Knocked me cold as a wedge. He felt real bad...later."

She shrugged. "Sorry about that, sir...They did a good job on the implants."

"Yeah, sometimes I don't even know they aren't mine...What can I do for you?"

"I need eight Marines in full battle rattle to fast-line onto the island to support Operation *Viper*."

"How soon do you need them?"

"Twenty minutes, sir...if that's possible?"

Lowry turned to Willis. "OOD, you heard the lady. Make it happen."

"Aye-aye, sir."

"Thanks, Captain, we appreciate it."

Lowry shook her hand and smiled broadly. "Those jarheads get bored riding around in this boat. Better to let them blow off a little steam before they start killing one another...Tell your dad Cannonball Lowry said hi."

321

"Will do, sir." She matched his grin.

C-5M AIRSPACE OVER THE GULF
75 miles Northwest of Isla Gukumatz
2100 Hours

The cargo ramp opened on the giant bird as the last of the *Black Eagles* made ready to launch. Mike Hermann sat at the controls of *Eagle* Four on his first actual launch and tried to maintain an air of confidence.

Weapons Systems Operator Glenn "Bug" Haug had just returned from sick leave and was still a little sore from his run-in with the APC. He smiled as he heard Mike's breathing rate start to increase when they eased out of the cargo bay. "Easy son. It's just like the simulator…except if you screw the pooch…we die," Glenn said dryly.

"Try to keep that in mind."

"Okay, here we go."

As the bird floated off the ramp into *Mama Bird's* turbulence, Mike couldn't help yelling, "Holy shit!"

The ride smoothed out as he pushed the nose over and descended below the huge black craft.

"See, told you…Just like the sim." Bug chuckled.

Mike rolled right and joined up on the other three *Eagles* of Dare's team, in tight echelon formation. They accelerated to four hundred knots and quickly disappeared into the clouds below.

The ramp and the clamshell doors on the C-5M closed as the dark craft began a climb to 28,000 feet.

Twelve thousand feet below the descending *Eagles*, Jill and her team of five from *Iwo Jima* were already hugging the wave tops as they raced toward the island fortress…

ISLA GUKUMATZ
2110 Hours

Pepe Hernandez stood watch on the south wall of the fortress. The wind was blowing at thirty-five miles per hour, gusting to forty-five. He looked with apprehension at the wall of dark clouds approaching from the south.

Lightning flashes from the innumerable thunderstorms lit up the southern sky from horizon to horizon and cast macabre shadows on his face—torrential rain would be coming.

The guard house was only four by twelve with solid rock walls extending four feet high all around. They would provide great protection from normal small arms fire if the island ever came under attack. A stacked limestone stairway led down to the manicured lawn of the compound.

Inside the two Russian *Zeus* weapons systems—deployed on the north and south ends of the island—former Cuban Army soldiers sat cursing the same weather. Normal duty on the island was a boring bliss—lots of sun, endless fishing and an occasional glimpse of a naked beauty atop the pyramid.

The lightly armored, radar-guided, self-propelled AAA units sat idling only when the main radar on top of the pyramid was down for maintenance. Most of the time, they were shut down with the hatches open.

Thirty other guards inside the pyramid remained in their dormitories on the second floor watching videos. One man watched the primary radar paint a curved band of thunderstorms closing in from the south. There was no other traffic visible on the sixty mile scope—he couldn't see the nine stealthy *Eagles* approaching from the north.

Three miles out, Jill's 200, flashed above the churning green and white-capped waters at 505 knots. She streaked ahead of the slower 600s to make a last minute recon of the six mile long island.

Jill pulled back firmly on the stick and left the salt spray below her and her copilot, Pete Reynolds. She leveled at 3,500 feet and overflew the entire island in less than eight seconds.

Pete operated the thermal scanner in the reconnaissance system and took fifteen high resolution shots of the island.

Jill rolled left and pulled the throttles back as she initiated a turn. She stopped her descent at 150 feet above the stormy waters and came to a hover one mile east.

"What've we got, Pete?" She cross-checked her flight instruments through the green glow of her night vision goggles.

He studied the enhanced displays on the copilot side of the cockpit—rolled a cursor over the images and clicked a yellow button on the side of his joystick. "Three in the top Zeus...Four in the SAM and three in the south...Engines are cold. They must be waiting for a call from the primary radar to power up."

"Bodies moving outside the compound?"

"Negatory."

"Mama Bird, any other targets detected on your review of the images?" Jill radioed.

"We have the two guards on the main east gate, two on the west gate and one in each tower. Defensive systems as Pete analyzed," Lanie responded.

"Eagle Five copies. Initiating phase two."

ISLA GUKUMATZ BEACH
2115 Hours

All eight of the M600s moved into position along the eastern shore. The pilots had a hard time maintaining a steady hover, even with their system computers, as the winds were strengthening to thirty-five miles per hour and gusting to fifty.

One by one, their entrance doors opened hydraulically and Raptor Team Four members fast-lined the twenty-five feet from *Eagles* One though Four to the sixty foot wide beach. Marines followed from *Eagles* Six through Nine.

In four minutes, all sixteen men were deployed and checked in on their headset radios. Overhead, the *Eagles* buttoned up and moved away from the beach like shadows in the night sky.

Master Gunnery Sergeant Jamal Washington led his other seven Recon Marines clad in standard night black and gray digital BDUs up to Leroy Poole who had his seven Raptors in a defensive semicircle. "Second Marine Force Recon at your service."

"Master Gunns, happy to have you...Leroy Poole, friends call me Bad."

"Don't need to ask how you got that handle…Say, what kind of weapons are those men carryin'?" He pointed to the coil rifles.

"Electromagnetic coil guns. We call them Blaze G1s…Bad news."

"Any chance the Marines getting hold of some?"

"You'll have to talk to our boss, Dare Phillips."

"Iron Horse Phillips?"

"One and the same." He noticed two of the Marines carried suppressed M-14s. "Master Gunns, I want these two with me and Davy. We'll take the guards at the front gate. Use secure comm…we'll have Mama Bird block all others.

"Break into groups of four and introduce yourselves. Make it quick. Jamal…send one of your teams to the dead-end road. We think the weapons bunker is there…You'll have two of our guys with their G1s…Maybe you'll get to see 'em in action…Alright, on your toes gentlemen…Hell is about to happen."

The two Marine snipers, "Rock" and "Ten Ring", joined with Poole and William "Davy" Crockett and the first four-man team moved out in overlapping short sprints up the road leading to the compound.

Two would provide cover while the others moved swiftly at the edge of the encroaching jungle. Time was running out as the front wall of rain bands moved steadily closer to the island. The rest of the teams disappeared into the jungle like wraiths.

COJONE COMPOUND
Pilot's Quarters
2115 Hours

Miguel and Bobby lay fully dressed on their beds in their fourth floor room as they watched movies from the DVD library. They had been fed a nice dinner with the other staff members, but had seen Javier only briefly.

Both were unsure if the room had any listening devices planted. They had accomplished their part of the mission, but felt like they should be doing something else.

Kit had briefed them not to try anything heroic or stupid—they got the part about not blowing their cover. However, as warriors, it was difficult to sit and wait—perhaps the planned raid was called off due to the impending storm.

Javier had never worried about the weather. The pyramid design had thwarted hurricanes for fifteen hundred years in the Yucatan and would continue to do so. The island's proximity to the north side of the peninsula helped protect it from massive wave damage.

There was not enough open water to the south to allow the waves to build close to thirty feet high. Sea walls and topography of the island prevented flooding. Javier had laughed at Cabrillo's suggestion to evacuate the Gulfstream.

He had assured the customer in Mexico City that the devices had arrived safely and were fully operational—with new batteries. His men would deliver them the afternoon of the 14th after the storm had passed.

ISLA GUKUMATZ
Road to the Compound
2118 Hours

Gale force winds whipped the tops of the trees and vines ninety feet above the heads of the advancing invasion force—it was almost pitch black with the cloud cover at five thousand feet.

The BEF operatives and the Marines could see each other as greenish-gray figures as they moved along the edges of the jungle with their sophisticated NVGs.

Seventy yards of clearing separated the jungle from the cut-coral wall surrounding the compound.

Marine sniper Rock and Leroy Poole worked the left side of the road and moved into position for taking out the guards at the gate.

Ten Ring and Davy took the right side and readied themselves for their assigned targets. Closed-circuit television cameras were mounted on opposite sides of the gate facing the approaches. Their wide-angle lens provided broad area coverage for the guard in the second floor security office.

COJONE COMPOUND
Second Floor Security Office
2118 Hours

Felix Almador watched as the trees in the background of the video feed from the front gate were shaking from the incessant winds. "Those poor bastards out there are in for a rough night," he mumbled. He opened the pages of a *Girls of Ixtapa* magazine and whistled softly as he checked out the bronzed hard bodies and rearranged his genitalia.

COJONE COMPOUND
Main Gate
2120 Hours

"Eagle One, Raptor Four in position," Leroy said into his headset as he placed the red dot on the seated guard inside the bulletproof glass of the small guardhouse on the left side of the massive wrought-iron gate.

AIRSPACE ABOVE ISLA GUKAMATZ
2120 Hours

"Eagle One, Eagle Five in position," radioed Jill as she hovered 150 feet above the pounding surf at the east end of the island.

"Roger that." Dare studied the disposition of his forces. He calculated they had fifteen to twenty minutes till the first wall of thunderstorms hit. "All units, Eagle One. Cleared to engage."

Jill centered her IR targeting laser on the rotating radar transmitter atop the pyramid. It showed up as a large basketball sized spotlight in her NVGs—from 3,500 feet away it was a chip shot. She pulled the red trigger on the pistol grip on her stick.

A faint blue streak of light from the plasma field surrounding the 7mm projectiles flashed on then off as she released the trigger. Eighteen rounds impacted the target in less than a third of a second.

The first destroyed the electric drive motor before the last of the three-quarter second burst was fired. Sparks flew from the transmission line as it was severed and the major revolving assembly was cut in two.

The white eight by three foot transceiver toppled over and the wind pushed it off the roof where it clattered down the side of stone pyramid. It came to rest on the verdant lawn—but no one inside witnessed its fate.

"Target destroyed," confirmed Pete as he looked through his *FLIR LANTERN* System.

"Copy that," Jill said calmly as she climbed to three thousand feet.

"Mama Bird confirms radar neutralized," Lanie transmitted.

COJONE COMPOUND
Main Gate
2122 Hours

"Three, two, one," came the call over the tactical radio from Poole.

Four shots were fired simultaneously, but the constant roar of wind masked the two *pfutts* and the two *ponks*. Inside the twin bulletproof guard posts, the bodies of Javier's men exploded from the G1s.

The walls were covered with a mixture of blood and tiny former body parts as the ferromagnetic rounds zipped through the glass like a hot knife through butter.

The two TV cameras shattered when the 7.62 rounds from the M-14s hit the glass lens and took the electronic CCDs out of the cylindrical frames. Ten Ring looked at Davy with shock and wonder as he pointed at the Blaze G1 he held. "I need me one of those."

"Get in line if…"

"Move out," Leroy called over the radio.

COJONE COMPOUND
South Wall
2122 Hours

Several hundred yards to the south, Pepe Hernandez was having trouble lighting his cigarette. The winds were so strong, that his lighter would not maintain a flame. Disgusted, he stuck the Camel back in the soft pack, replaced it in the thigh pouch of his cargo pants along with the BIC.

It wasn't cold, but the sixty-five mile per hour steady winds tore at his skin. He looked out toward the mobile antiaircraft site. *Huh! Looks like lightning.*

A pale blue flash from the southern sky streaked down right at the Zeus as he watched. The lightly armored vehicle sent shards of metal into the sky as it exploded in a huge yellow and black fireball. Burning pieces of debris arced up and away from the unrecognizable piece of scrap iron that lay where three friends had been just seconds before.

Pepe stood transfixed for a second. The blast was scarcely heard as the wind at his back blew the noise out to sea—he picked up the VHF transceiver.

He tried to transmit—no response, too much static. Pepe saw an ominous thunderstorm only fifteen miles out to sea. He watched in fascination as a multi-pronged lightning bolt struck the water.

The light show illuminated a black shape five hundred yards away near the beach. The strange craft did not move. It just sat there at an odd angle tilted into the gale force wind. "*Madre Dios!*" were the last words he would ever utter.

A faint blue light appeared between the craft and the guard house. Pepe disappeared as the four columns holding the stone roof instantly turned to dust.

"Target destroyed," Bug announced over the interphone.

"Jesus!…That's a hell of an understatement," said Mike.

Hammer Gibbs in *Eagle* Six lined up on the *Gauntlet* Mobile SAM launcher.

The three men inside had started the diesel APU generator when the radar signal from the main unit was lost.

In another 30 seconds they would have the K band pulse Doppler radar unit up and running.

The green world in the NVGs left an slightly destabilizing feeling in both Hammer and WSO Bull Gaspar. Both were used to the sensation, but it did take muscle memory to reach and touch the correct controls on the various panels.

The *Gauntlet's* generator glowed with a light greenish-gray signature as she squeezed the trigger. Gusty conditions made it extremely difficult to keep the pipper centered, even on a stationary target. Hammer held down for a full second and a half as the pipper walked the length and width of the deadly SAM system. With two full containers of missiles per side, it would only take only one well-placed hit to knock it out of commission.

The one and a half second burst of hypersonic steel projectiles from her G2 stuck one, and then another magazine. Each missile had a large solid propellant rocket motor and a fifteen pound HE/Frag warhead. The first detonated when the steel and plasma field sliced through it like a scythe cutting through ripe wheat.

The chain reaction blasts from the missiles exploding on their launchers would be heard and felt even inside the massive pyramid—it had been only eight hundred yards west of the Mayan edifice.

A huge yellow and black cloud of burning debris from the shattered system mushroomed into the night sky before the raging winds of Hurricane Ellen tore it asunder.

Hammer and Bull were temporarily blinded by the white flare in the NVG's. The units had a self-protection circuit to prevent injury to the user or the electronics. She still flipped up the goggles to try to regain her night vision as she banked away from the west side of the island.

"Glad we made the shot from 3,500 feet. Any closer and we could have taken hits from the exploding warheads."

"Think I figured out how you got the nickname Hammer," Bull deadpanned as he replaced his NVGs.

To the north, Kit Kitaen watched the explosion and adjusted his aim on the remaining Zeus. A one second squeeze on the trigger and it too, was history.

So far, the plan had gone like clockwork. The weather was worse than expected and extraction might have to be delayed until the storm passed.

"Target destroyed," confirmed WSO Dave Garner.

"Roger." Kit added power, climbed to 4,000 feet and selected *Altitude Hold*.

COJONE COMPOUND
Javier's Bedroom
2122 Hours

Javier was watching a porn flick with two of his girls when ghosts and pixilations on the wide screen TV flickered intermittently, *Must be a bad DVD.* He tried to stop the play and realized the controller did not work.

The TV remote didn't function either. He ran through his knowledge of electronics and could not put the problem to the approaching storm. "Hand me that phone." He became visibly agitated.

Vivian complied with a smile. He took the Iridium phone and hit the speed dial number six. As he pulled it to his ear, all he could hear was a loud static.

He walked to his clothes tree and pulled his pants off the mahogany hanger. "Caramba!" He grabbed the shirt as he slipped into his slippers. When Javier strode to the TV and hit the *Off* button, the room became silent, except for the howling of the winds around the cut-stone exterior of the massive ancient design he called home.

The explosion of the SA-15 unit brought his confusion to a swift end. He—a merchant of death—knew exactly what had transpired outside. The brief flash before the sound and tremors hit the building was something he could get his head around.

His island was under attack. Javier looked outside at the guard tower on the south side of the compound. As he watched, it sparkled and turned to dust—he rubbed his eyes and looked again. Perhaps it was the tequila—but no, the stone tower had just vanished...

COJONE COMPOUND
Second Floor Security Office
2124 Hours

Night shift security supervisor Almador was going crazy. The storm had knocked out the radar on the top of the building and now the main gate video feed was out. None of the guard posts responded to the radio—all he got was static. "Manny!...Manuel Vargas! Get your useless ass in here!"

The man walked in from the next room. His black T-shirt stained from eating Cheetos while he watched a recording of a World Cup soccer match on a laptop computer. He was obviously not in a good mood. "What in hell do you want? I'm right in the middle of the second overtime and Brazil has the next penalty shot. Can't you wait until I finish the damned game?"

"No, dammit! You lazy pendejo. The radar is off-line and the radios are out. Boss is gonna be seriously jacked-up if you don't get them back pronto!"

"Bullshit! He's probably gettin' laid right now. All he cares about is his dick...Besides, that damned hurricane is almost on top of us. I can't go out..."

The feel of a steel barrel on the back of his neck stopped him cold. His eyes grew wide as he glanced back and saw who was wielding the Sig 226.

"Better stop worrying about my body parts and start worrying about your own. You can go out...You will go out. Now...or I'll kill you where you stand." Javier pushed the muzzle harder into Manny's neck.

"You got it, boss...I was just joking with Felix here. I'm going, I'm going," he stammered as he stumbled to get his tool kit, flashlight and rain gear.

Felix felt as if his life flashed before him. He looked at the icy stare of the billionaire and felt a chill run down his spine.

"Sir, radios are out and the radar is too. I can't raise any guards. I was just getting ready to call you."

"We are under attack, you idiot. Deploy all reserve units and launch the MiG...They must be using helicopters." Javier calmly turned and walked back the way he came.

Felix pressed the red button tied to the compound alarm system. A loud klaxon sounded three long blasts through the hardwired intercom. Red rotating beacons flashed in every room on the second floor. Three dozen men rolled out of lounge chairs or beds and snatched up their weapons. Those inside their rooms grabbed rain gear—those outside headed back in a semi-panic.

Javier stopped a big man in the crowded hallway. "Enrique! Take two men and see that Vasilli launches the MiG. Screw the weather. If he won't fly…shoot him."

"Yes, sir!" Enrique spat back. He grabbed two guards milling around and started dragging them by the arm. "Downstairs! Move it!"

They raced two floors down the stairwell to the well-lit tunnel. Fifteen hundred feet away was the concrete and steel hangar and the alert quarters for the former Russian fighter pilot, Vasilli Yukovich.

Enrique yanked the power cord from the four-seat electric golf cart. He jumped in the driver's seat as the two black-clad guards piled in. Silently they pulled away and sped down the corridor.

COJONE COMPOUND
Outside Lawn
2129 Hours

Leroy and the eleven other members of the assault teams had made their way across the mostly open two hundred yards between the main gate and the pyramid. Rock and Ten Ring had knocked out every flood light and CCTV camera attached to the trunks of the palm trees bending to the winds.

When they were within 100 yards of the building, Leroy redeployed Ten Ring and Davy to go with Master Gunns and three others to the north side of the structure. He and his team took the south entrance.

Overhead, the dense band of clouds momentarily broke as Hurricane Ellen bore down on the island. Thunder crashed incessantly from the nearest cell only eight miles away. The moon would reach its zenith in two and one half hours—the waxing silver orb was over ninety percent full.

The green world through their NVGs looked like day with the intermittent moonlight streaming across the image intensifiers. The extra light meant that those in the building could see them better as well.

"Damn!" Leroy muttered.

The other squad members looked at him. He pointed to two men to his right and held up two fingers, then pointed at the doorway. They nodded and moved toward the right side of the south doorway in a tactical run. He made a similar signal to two on his left, sending them forward as he and Rock covered the doorway eighty yards away.

One of Javier's men led fifteen others through the south entrance yelling and screaming into the wind. Only the right door could be opened because of the pressure. As it banged hard against the stop, the leader rushed out directly into the sights of Rock and his suppressed M-14. He crumpled as the silent round hit him cleanly in the chest.

The next man through the doorway bent down to help, thinking he had tripped, and Rock's second shot went high. A prone Raptor with a G1, lying only ten yards east of the door, took him out. The single round of the super high-velocity weapon virtually disintegrated him.

On the north side, thirteen black-clad guards swarmed out like ants. The wind was fierce as it changed direction to flow up and over the building. Several times the men were knocked off their feet and had to struggle to regain their footing.

Jamal reached the northeast corner first. He took a knee to look around the building—a seventy mile per hour gust blew him down and around the edge. He rolled over twice and looked up to see a surprised guard only fifteen yards away. They exchanged bursts simultaneously—both died instantly.

Ten Ring dropped prone and fast-crawled to the corner, slapped a full twenty round magazine in the M-14 and rose to a kneeling position. He swung the muzzle quickly around the stonework corner and dropped the closest three guards with three rapid shots.

The remaining nine defenders made a tactical retreat, intermittently firing their 9mm subguns at the corner.

Ten Ring sat with his back to the stonework to catch his breath. He swallowed hard and waved the rest of the team toward him.

UNDERGROUND WEAPONS BUNKER
2130 Hours

Marine Staff Sergeant Keller and three others of his team reconnoitered the end of the road. It did indeed end at an underground bunker. He could see two guards just inside the entrance.

One was trying to make contact with the island security office on his radio. "Enrique, are you there?" All he got was static. "Caramba…storm is screwing with the radio."

Keller hand-signaled two of his men to bracket the entrance. He and Corporal Harrell lay prone fifteen feet apart in the edge of the jungle bordering the road. He held up three fingers and closed them in sequence—they simultaneously dropped the two guards when the third disappeared.

Lance Corporal Conway and Corporal Amos moved from their positions on either side of the entrance. As they entered, Amos took a round to the chest from deep inside and went down.

Conway quickly ducked back behind the protecting corner, took a flash-bang grenade from his combat vest, pulled the pin and threw it deep into the tunnel. There was a loud roar and a blinding flash of white light. The corporal quickly ducked inside and sprayed the length of the tunnel with his M-4.

Keller and Harrell sprinted to the entrance and covered Conway as he eased down the tunnel through the smoke.

"Two more tangos down," Conway radioed from the end of the tunnel. He glanced quickly around. "Clear."

Keller moved to the downed corporal. Amos groaned, rolled over and propped up on one elbow.

"Damn, that hurts…Thank God for Kevlar."

"Better hurt than dead."

"Heard that." Amos slowly got to his feet.

From down the tunnel Conway called to Keller, "Damn, Sarge, there're enough weapons down here to start WW III."

"Copy," said Keller. "Eagle One, Marine Team Three. We're at the weapons bunker at the end of the dead-end road. Beau coup arms and munitions here. Guards neutralized."

"Roger that, Marine Team Three. Much obliged. Get the hell away from there. It's fixing to become a big hole in the ground."

"Marine Three moving to compound."

"Copy move, report to Team Four leader. Eagle One out."

HANGAR ON THE AIRSTRIP
2134 Hours

The machinegun toting thug had given Vasilli Yukovich an ultimatum he could not refuse. Ernique and his two gunmen would kill him if he defied Javier's order to launch.

Vasilli pulled on the bulky Russian helmet as he sat in the cockpit and glared down at the man. The power cart was on-line, the avionics were up to speed as the maintenance technicians pulled the ground safety pins from his air-to-air missiles and removed the chocks.

I'm a dead man either way. There is probably a helicopter gunship waiting outside to shoot as soon as I taxi out. If that doesn't kill me, the seventy knot crosswinds on takeoff will, he figured. Enrique had told him the main radar was out at the compound. *Starting a fight in the middle of a hurricane without radar GCI support was suicide. If I get airborne, I'm heading for Miami or New Orleans to seek asylum. The American CIA will pay big dollars to have another Russian line fighter.* That was Vasilli's plan. "Open hangar doors. I'm ready to start."

The technician pressed the large button on the hangar wall—the electric motors whined as the huge rack-and-pinion system groaned against the extra drag created by the wind. The doors slowly opened as Vasilli began the start sequence.

One minute later, both engines were at idle and he signaled the crew to disconnect the power cable. He lowered the canopy, saluted the crew chief and pushed the throttles up to taxi.

Outside, the sky was clear and the stars were bright, even if only for a few minutes. The jungle cut the crosswind down more than he had anticipated and his hopes were elevated.

As he set flaps and stabilizer trim, the thought that he might actually survive the takeoff brought a smile to his pursed lips. He added power to military as he sat on the mural coated runway. The landing lights barely reflected off the darkened surface.

Former Hero of the Soviet Union, Vasilli Yukovich released the brakes and punched the throttles into full afterburner. With a familiar slam backward into the ejection seat, he rocketed down the painted asphalt toward his fate...

***

CHAPTER EIGHTEEN

COJONE COMPOUND
Outside Lawn
2134 Hours

Five dead guards littered the green grass outside the south door—the moonlight illuminated the grotesque shapes where they had fallen.

One of Leroy's men had taken a 9mm round in the upper arm. Two of the bodies outside were killed by a single shot from his G1. The force of their demise knocked down two others who had scrambled back into the pyramid under heavy fire.

Those wounded men had taken refuge behind a heavy oaken door which could not be opened. Leroy's second shot through the wood coated the hallway with their blood. The surviving nine guards on the south side abandoned the idea of fighting in the open, retreated into the first floor and dispersed. The strong odor of blood and offal permeated the air.

Bad made his way to the right of the doorway and pressed his back against the stone wall. He could hear the distinct roar of a jet fighter in afterburner over the howling winds. Back to the east, he could see the twin cones of white fire trailing the fighter as it lifted above the trees. "Eagle One, Raptor Four Leader."

"Raptor Four Leader, Eagle One, go," Dare responded as he hovered four thousand feet above the island.

"Tell me that fighter is one of ours."

Dare looked down as the craft departed the north end of the runway—the afterburners winked out.

"Negative. Unknown rider…Presume hostile."

AIRSPACE OVER WEAPONS BUNKER
2135 Hours

Dare in *Eagle* One and Mike in *Eagle* Four descended and targeted the underground weapons bunker from a slant range of 3,500 feet. They bracketed the location and each fired a three second burst from their G2 coil guns.

One hundred and forty-four of the plasma generating steel rounds penetrated over thirty-five feet into the hardened steel and concrete bunker, breaching the inside—leaving ragged two foot holes in the top.

Immediately upon releasing the firing button for their multi-barreled G2s, each *Eagle* WSO simultaneously fired a *PAASM* missile using the same IR laser target.

They instantly rolled their crafts away and climbed to 5,000 feet. The two *PAASM* missiles screamed toward the holes in the bunker leaving a momentary V-shaped trail of smoke. A tremendous explosion lifted the ground—a ball of fire and tons of debris shot skyward.

Eagles One and Four rocked momentarily from the concussion, and then stabilized.

"Damn!…Good thing we got far enough away. That shock wave could have knocked us down," Mike exclaimed.

"Yeah, buddy." WSO Haug grinned.

AIRSPACE ABOVE ISLA GUKAMATZ
2135 Hours

Jill, in *Eagle* Five, called visual contact with the departing MiG-29. "Eagle Five, tally ho. I'm on him."

She lowered the nose as she slammed the throttles to the limit and all ten Rotopower engines responded instantly. The stealthy black fighter accelerated quickly—the speed increased to over four hundred knots by the time she descended through three thousand feet. She was still higher than the MiG as Vasilli rolled out of his turn headed west.

The MiG pilot checked his search radar and saw nothing. The tiny *Eagles* with their radar deflecting coating would not paint—even at close range. He glanced over his left shoulder and saw the towering thunderstorm crossing the east side of the island.

Barely made it off. His missile alert caution light flashed red as an aural warning went off in his helmet. "What the hell? Who could be shooting at me?"

The *Stinger* was off the lower right front rail of Hammer's *Eagle* Six as she and Bull locked up the MiG on their IR scanner.

"Eagle Six, fox two," she announced on the frequency.

The range was so close that the missile had not reached full velocity as it closed on the MiG.

Vasilli had a visual on the white smoke trail in the moonlight as it bore down on him. His G-suit inflated to maximum as he yanked the stick into his lap for a 9G pull-up. He slammed the throttles to max afterburner hoping it would be enough.

The small fins on the AIM 92 Stinger could not match the angle and turn radius necessary for a frontal attack. Its proximity fuse fired, but the fragmentation pattern of the blast was well below the rapidly climbing fighter leaving the MiG unscathed.

Once the missile exploded below and behind him, Vasilli realized the shot had missed. He released back pressure and cleared his six o'clock position as he rolled south. He could see a strange shape silhouetted against the moon above him. It had two stubby wings with engines on pods close to the fuselage like an A-10.

The strange craft was trying to pull lead on him for a gun shot. He dumped the nose, pulled the throttles well back below military, kicked in full left rudder, inverted and pulled hard into the attacker.

The two aircraft missed each other by less than 100 feet, with the MiG's belly passing underneath the bottom of the M200 on the nose-to-nose pass.

"Jesus! This guy is good!" Jill broke into a level left turn to try and reacquire the elusive MiG.

"Holy crap, I lost him," exclaimed Pete.

"Give me a *PAASM*," Mike instructed Glenn.

"Cowboy, the *PAASM* is an air-to-surface missile."

"I know...it also has a Tri-Mode active radar homing...Make it work."

"Whatever it takes." Bug launched the missile.

"Eagle Four, fox one."

The missile roared off the right rear rail like a white-hot meteor in pursuit. Mike watched in amazement as the MiG-29 lit both afterburners and cut south directly into the towering nimbocumulous cloud discharging bolt after bolt of lighting onto Isla Gukumatz. The *PAASM* followed it into a pilot's worst nightmare.

Inside the thunderstorm, torrential rain and severe turbulence buffeted the aging Russian fighter. Yukovich had taken a calculated risk. He knew something the young American pilot who just shot a missile at him did not. He clicked the black button on his stick to deliver three bundles of chaff into the bowels of the violent thunderstorm.

Highly charged positive electrons gathered on the swirling masses of aluminum foil and attracted the negatively charged ions in the air. When the *PAASM* followed through the charged trail left by the fleeting MiG, a massive discharge of electrons occurred. A huge bolt of lightning struck the chaff, exploding the missile three hundred yards behind the MiG.

"Anyone have eyes on the MiG?" asked Dare.

The silence was not encouraging. Radar could not differentiate the rain and wet hail in the thunderstorm from the MiG.

Lanie could offer no help from *Mama Bird,*. The outer band of Hurricane Ellen was passing directly over the Cojone compound and the ability of the *Black Eagles* to offer assistance to the ground team was about to come to a temporary halt.

Dare looked at the options available. His aircraft could not provide close air support to the ground forces while they were inside the building with the hostages.

The MiG was no present threat to the ground forces. Either it was shot down or had bugged out. The orbiting Ospreys assigned to hostage rescue and ground team extraction, would maintain their orbits northwest of the island until the weather improved.

"All Eagle Aircraft, Eagle One…Execute recall plan alpha. I say again, execute recall plan alpha. Fly heading 360."

COJONE COMPOUND
2136 Hours

Bad glanced to the east at the huge fireball from the weapons bunker. If the squads stayed out in the open, they would be at risk of air strikes. The hostages were reportedly on the tenth floor above. A numerically superior force of armed men waited inside for the Raptors and Marines—he chose to attack. "Master Gunns, what's your status?" he asked over the radio.

"Master Gunns is down. Ten Ring in command. Standing by to breach the north doors."

"Frag grenades in ten. We'll hit 'em from both sides…On my mark."

Ten Ring and his six men bracketed the north doorway that had one door blown open by the wind. Three men removed grenades from their vest pouches and pulled the pins in anticipation of the coming command.

"Mark!"

Seven grenades were tossed down the polished granite floors. Javier's men were waiting with their H&K sub-guns raised. Several broke and tried to run, but the ensuing maelstrom of metal from the frags cut them down like wheat before a scythe.

Two seconds later, well-trained operatives flooded in from both sides. Shots rang out from all directions as bullets flew and grown men screamed.

On the tenth floor, frightened women huddled together in their dormitories. The sounds of the storm mixed with that of gunfire and explosions had most of them crying. They were all looking around and asking what was happening—all but one.

A beautiful blonde girl from Alabama was strangely calm. She knelt beside her bed and whispered a prayer of thanks.

On the twelfth floor, Javier watched from the windows as the unknown soldiers fought their way into his private domain. He had seen the MiG take off and expected him to knock the enemy helicopters out of the sky. He had no plans, however, to stay and watch it personally after having just witnessed the giant fireball from his weapons bunker. "Son of a bitch!"

He grabbed Vivian by the arm and led her to the elevator. She was obviously nervous and more than a little scared. "Where are we going, my love?" She tried her very best to fake a smile.

"I have a special little hideaway where no one can ever find us." Javier escorted her into the elevator.

He swiped a master control card against the security mechanism and pressed B-3. The doors closed—he wrapped his arms around her and smiled broadly. "Everything will be just fine, my dear."

COJONE COMPLEX
2138 Hours

Davy was pinned down by three of Javier's gunmen. One of the Marine corporals had taken a round to the neck—Crockett had stabilized the man's wound and pulled him into an alcove near the center of the building.

The whole first floor was little more than a museum to the Mayan heritage—priceless works of art and original carvings were incorporated into the structure.

In contrast to a real Mayan pyramid, this one was open inside and had a modern steel structure to support the tons of cut stone on the exterior.

Two of the shooters Davy faced were behind a huge carved jade jaguar. The third hid behind an Olmec stone head that measured five feet across and weighed tons. He couldn't get a clear shot and was out of grenades. Davy looked at the G1 rifle and wished he had an M-4, *This G1 is great for sniping but I need firepower*. He tried to remember what Gears had said about penetration and wished he had paid more attention—rather than looking at the redhead who designed the weapon.

Hell, worth a shot. He aimed at the two thousand year old Olmec head and placed the red dot between its sad eyes—he squeezed the trigger.

Ponk.

Blap.

The guard on the other side simply disintegrated. A quarter-sized hole appeared in the stone head as smoke lightly curled out of the glazed surface.

"Good Godamighty!" He swung the rifle thirty degrees left and tried a shot at the heart of the jaguar.

Ponk.

Blap.

A scream unlike any thing he had ever heard emanated from behind the statue. A second man in black dropped his submachine gun and ran screaming from behind the stone art.

Davy instinctively fired as he cleared cover. The terrified man was coated in the other man's blood and tissue and for a half-second, he almost felt remorse for shooting him.

The young guard disappeared in a mist of red—there was nothing he, nor any one else could have done to save him.

"Jesus H. Christ." Crockett sat stunned for a full minute—he realized that only a short time earlier he had been the one on defense. He listened for twenty seconds. Nothing. No shots, no yelling—only silence.

"Raptor Four leader…Sitrep," Poole called over the headset.

"Davy ops ready, with one wounded Marine."

"Williams ops ready."

"Chopper ops ready."

"Rogers ops ready."

"Travis ambulatory."

"Hessian ops ready."

"Marine Team Three ops ready," responded Staff Sergeant Keller as his team arrived from the weapons bunker.

Several seconds passed with no other transmissions.

"Charley, check in," Leroy directed.

Silence did nothing to ease the men's feeling of unease.

"Anybody have eyes on Charley?" asked Bad. "Anybody with contact with tangos?"

All seven men looked about and could not make out any movement in the building.

"Ten Ring, how copy Team Four Leader?"

"Five by five. Negative contact with tangos. We have one dead, two wounded and one unaccounted for."

"I've got Corporal Simpson with a neck wound…He'll make it," said Davy.

"Marines all accounted for," Ten Ring announced.

"Travis, get to Davy and watch over the wounded man. Ten Ring, move toward the stairwell. Time to clear the upper floors."

"Ten Ring copies."

AIRSPACE OVER GULF OF MEXICO
2143 Hours

Sensor and weapons operator, Lanie Hayes, watched her master screen as the loose formation of *Black Eagles* neared the turn point to the carrier. USS *Iwo Jima* lay thirty miles west and was in heavy seas.

Blaze looked over Lanie's shoulder. Gears had tried to dissuade her from coming aboard as she wasn't qualified on any crew position. She had countered that today was as good as any to get some on-the-job training.

The two *Ospreys* were in a holding pattern thirty miles northwest of the island that was completely out of view under the band of thunderstorms.

Blaze watched the situation develop when a small blip appeared out of the heavy band of precipitation southwest of the island. The next update on the information moved the blip north.

"What's that?" She leaned in and pointed at the screen.

Lanie moved the cursor over the target and hit the *identify* button on her keyboard. An icon appeared, *M-29*. "Dammit! The MiG!" She keyed the button on her radio. "All Eagles, be advised MiG is now bearing 240 at thirty miles, level angels seven."

AIRSPACE OVER THE GULF
2144 Hours

Jill immediately broke left from the formation and started a descent from ten thousand to eight thousand. She pushed the throttles to the limit as the little bird accelerated from three hundred fifty knots toward the five hundred knot top speed.

Vasilli turned his search radar back on, was immediately picked up by the *Mama Bird* ELINT system and subsequently jammed by the powerful ECM transmitters on the *Galaxy*.

He selected *missile arm* on his touch screen display and all four missiles indicated self-test okay. The Russian made version of the American *AMRAAM* missiles were called the AA 12 *Adder* by NATO forces. He had no way of knowing the exact distance to the aircraft, but the missiles he carried could operate in a home-on-jam mode. They had a max range of forty-three nautical miles and were ready to launch.

"Viper One and Two be advised you have a MiG 29 bearing 160 at twenty miles angels seven," Lanie transmitted.

Both sets of MV-22 pilots looked at each other. *What the hell? Nobody mentioned any MiGs in the brief. Is it Cuban?*

Vasilli pushed the power up to military and the big fighter stabilized at 600 knots. He pulled the nose up forty degrees and fired two missiles—one off each wing. The two missiles blasted upward as they accelerated to Mach 4.5 and disappeared into the cirrus cloud deck at twenty thousand feet.

AIRSPACE OVER GULF OF MEXICO
2145 Hours

"Missile launch," the automated warning system aboard *Mama Bird* announced in a sedate woman's voice.

Gears turned the big bird into the threat to reduce radar cross section.

"Kill the jam! Kill the radar!" Blaze shouted.

"That's not procedure! The Eagles will be blind!" Lanie protested.

"Just do it! I'll explain later!"

"Gears?" Lanie shouted.

"Do what she says…Now!" Gears replied via interphone.

He wasn't sure what she had in mind, but he knew how Blaze thought. Lanie selected *Off* on the ECM and primary aircraft search radar.

"Launch decoys bearing 180 angels thirty," Blaze directed.

Lanie shook her head and complied. *The woman isn't even a member of the crew and she's telling the AC what to do?*

The pair of decoys launched from special pylons under the wing of *Mama Bird* mimicked the radar signatures of F-16 *Falcons*. The small solid-fuel rocket motors accelerated the little decoys to 600 knots as they climbed to the programmed altitude.

AIRSPACE OVER GULF OF MEXICO
2146 Hours

Vasilli was pleased when the radar jamming stopped. He picked up the radar returns of the two *Ospreys* and started a slow roll to intercept. He was about to fire when the radar returns of two F-16 *Falcons* approaching fast from the north triggered warning messages on his HUD.

He banked hard right, engaged the afterburner, and then started a climb. He clicked on the data link to his *Adder* missiles and updated the radar to the F-16s. He selected IR mode on one missile, acquired a lock on the left *Falcon* and a radar lock on the right.

Jill could see the afterburner glow climbing through her altitude at two miles. She had fought the MiG 29 dozens of times at Tonapah and in the simulator. But that was when she was flying the *Raptor*. The 200 *Black Eagle* was no *Raptor*. It had stealth, and a wicked gun—but no missiles.

"Gotta dance with the one that brung ya."

"Say what?" asked Pete.

She pulled back hard on the stick and the tiny *Eagle* responded quickly. With an 1,100 mile per hour closure rate, it took just seconds to merge. Jill put her pipper on the MiG and pulled the trigger.

The swarm of lethal steel bees flew beneath the right wing of the MiG. She moved the pipper above the fighter and pulled the trigger again. This time, the 7mm projectiles blasted several fist-sized holes in the right wing root and two just missed the canopy. Jill was losing airspeed rapidly. She rolled inverted and pulled hard on the stick.

Vasilli cursed loudly when the holes appeared in his right wing. He had been concentrating on the airborne radar display and his HUD and had not seen the craft come from below. Nothing had shown on his radar.

The small fighter that flashed past was silhouetted against the cloud deck beneath him. It was the same type he had avoided earlier.

He broke off the attack on the F-16s and looked back at his five o'clock low to track the descending 200. He pulled the throttles out of afterburner and made a slicing right descending turn to keep it in sight in the bright moonlight.

Jill leveled out of the dive and rolled quickly into a sixty degree left turn. Her airspeed was over four hundred indicated as Pete called out the contact.

"He's breaking right! Nine o'clock level!" He grunted against the G force.

She saw a brief glint of moonlight off his shiny wings. The aircraft were three miles apart and turning toward each other in a deadly game of chicken.

Vasilli flipped the arming selector to *Gun*. He was highly confident in his Izhmash Gsh 30-1 30mm cannon. One hit from the massive round destroyed a British *Tornado* fighter during Desert Storm. The Allies claimed it was ground fire, but Vasilli had his gun camera footage to prove it. The water cooled, gas-operated weapon fired at a rate of 1,500 rounds per minute, but the MiG 29 only carried 100 rounds. He would line up the pesky little gnat in his laser range-finder and blow it out of the sky.

Jill had Pete call out range to target based on the restored radar from *Mama Bird*.

"Only going to get one shot now that he knows we're here."

"Roger that…the *Ospreys* are no match for the MiG and *Mama Bird* won't be safe if he catches a visual…Two miles."

Jill rolled out directly at the MiG. Her hand clenched the throttle as it remained at the forward stop.

"Bogey twelve o'clock," warned Lanie on the C5.

Vasilli looked at the tiny black craft he could barely see through his helmet mounted display. *This crap is useless,* he thought as he transitioned to the IR eyeball mounted on the aircraft nose.

It showed a faint target. Laser range was rapidly decreasing. When the range finder hit 1,700 meters, he fired a one second burst. The big aircraft shook as the 30mm cannon in the left wing root opened up.

Jill pulled the trigger as she tried to keep the aircraft steady in the swirling winds. The lethal steel that flew out in a short burst closed the distance between them in less than a half-second.

Vasilli was shocked as the rounds impacted his aircraft. He felt he was well out of range of the American 20mm gun—he was correct. The 7mm coil gun rounds tore into his port engine—another penetrated the high-mounted bubble canopy and left a one inch hole in the front and back.

It missed his head by two inches. He broke hard right reacting to the hit. He glanced down and saw that his port engine gages confirmed that it was destroyed.

Eagle Five took three hits. One impacted the starboard forward nacelle taking out both engines. A second struck the starboard aft engines. The third ricocheted off the slanted Kevlar armor in front of the glare shield and tore into the cockpit, killing Pete Reynolds instantly. It continued the path of destruction aft to the center nacelle on top of the fuselage.

The mortally wounded M200 yawed hard to the right before the craft's flight computer could pull the power back on the good engines. The twin vertical stabilizers snapped off as the aircraft slid sideways and started to roll, uncontrolled.

Vasilli turned back left as he pulled the left throttle to idle. The automatic fire detection system vented Halon gas into the destroyed combustion section. The fire was extinguished, but smoke continued to trail behind.

He watched with a small satisfaction as the gnat he had swatted tumbled toward the angry seas below. *Okay, maybe not a gnat, a wasp*, he thought as he considered the damage done to his prized MiG. He pulled the remaining throttle back and entered a steep descending turn to watch his mortally wounded adversary fall.

A large white parachute deployed from the top of the little craft in the moonlit sky.

Vasilli checked his ammunition status. The shell counter showed sixty-eight rounds remaining. *No enemy pilot had ever lived to tell about a one on one encounter with Vasilli Yukovich.*

He rolled out of the turn and pressed forward on the starboard throttle. He added a little right rudder to compensate for the offset thrust and extended out three miles. He made the 180 degree turn back and lined up for his kill shot...

***

CHAPTER NINETEEN

COJONE COMPOUND
Fifth Floor
2147 Hours

Bobo stepped off the elevator on the fifth floor. He had just searched the twelfth and eleventh floors and could not locate Javier. He presumed the man had gone into hiding and he certainly did not know all his secrets.

He walked down the deserted hallway to the pilot's quarters and stood beside the doorway as he reached carefully out and tapped three times on the door.

The two BEF undercover pilots looked at each other apprehensively.

"Come in," Miguel said.

Bobo opened the door cautiously and saw them laying fully clothed on their beds watching a DVD. They were propped up against the headboards—hands clasped behind their heads.

He took one last look down the hall, stepped in and closed the door—he held a Mac computer under his arm. "How you guys doin?"

"Fine...considering it sounds like World War fucking III down there," Mendes replied.

"Yeah, I think the visitors are kicking the home team's ass." Bobo grinned.

"We didn't know if Javier was going to come down here and put a bullet in our heads...or what," Miguel added.

"Think he's hiding somewhere below. Even I don't have access to the bottom floors...They're blowing the hell out of everything else," Bobo stated.

"Yeah, we heard the weapons bunker go," said Cabrillo.

"Ya'll got anything to write with?"

Bobby shook his head. "Nothing but a can of shoe polish."

"Pitch it."

Mendes opened his dopp kit, took out a flat tin and pitched it to Bobo. He opened the door, rubbed his index and middle fingers over the black wax and printed on the front in large letters: *BEF*.

"When your boys get to this floor, it's best they know we're on their side before they kick it in and start spraying."

"Ya think?" said Miguel.

Bobby held up a finger. "Hey, we've got to get word to Dare that the nukes are leaking...Hot as a fresh fucked fox in a forest fire...The techs are gonna have to be protected...We left the crates on the plane."

"The muscle that Javier sent along to handle them and watch us were sick as dogs when we landed," Cabrillo added.

"What's with the computer?" asked Bobby.

Bobo held it up. "Cojone's personal computer...Once our geeks break the password and codes, we may find some useful info about his operation."

They could hear the gunshots from the floor below.

"Sounds like the boys are getting close," said Miguel.

Bobo pointed. "I suggest we all go over to the beds...They're gonna be all hyped up when they bust in...Guarandamntee it."

He lay down. "So...how's the movie?"

COJONE COMPOUND
Second Floor
2148 Hours

Ten Ring led half the combined Raptor and Marine force as they methodically searched the guard dormitory—all the living quarters were empty.

In the primary security office, Felix Almador fired two shots at pointblank range into Hessian's chest—he and Charley double teamed him with simultaneous bursts from their M-4s.

"You ok?" asked Charley.

Hessian looked at the holes in his BDU blouse directly over his heart. Both nine millimeter rounds would have been fatal, had it not been for the Dragonskin. "Don't leave home without it." Hessian as he tapped the body armor.

"Got that right."

COJONE COMPOUND
Fifth Floor
2149 Hours

The search teams cleared the third and forth floors, taking two dozen service workers, mostly gardeners, cleaning staff and cooks, into custody. Two team members escorted them downstairs past the Marines guarding the stairwell.

Leroy stepped out into the south hallway on the fifth floor and motioned to his Raptors to follow him as the Marines under Ten Ring split and took the other three hallways.

Each higher floor of the pyramid was progressively smaller and the searches would go faster if no further resistance was met—one by one, the doors were kicked open.

Leroy stood before the door with BEF scrawled on it. *What the hell?* He knew there was a CIA man on the inside, but the sign confused him. A size twelve boot burst the door open. He had traded his G1 to the wounded Travis for his M-4. "Freeze!"

The three men on the beds didn't flinch.

Leroy immediately recognized Miguel and Bobby and swung the muzzle away. "What the hell are you guys doing here?"

Cabrillo grinned as he slipped off the bed. "Waitin' for you…asshole…What took you so long?"

He and Leroy embraced as Bobby and Bobo got to their feet. Mendes slapped Bad on the back and shook his hand vigorously.

Poole looked at the two men. "Damn, can't believe they didn't tell me you were here."

Bobo extended his hand. "My fault...Roberto Vincente, CIA...friends call me Bobo...Told Sosa not to mention these guys in the debrief...Only four people in the BEF knew where they were...Sorry."

"Leroy Poole...most call me Bad...Hell, guess you boys can keep a secret when you have to." He chuckled as he shook Bobo's hand. "Where'd you leave the nukes?"

"They're in the hangar, still in the Gulfstream...But, they're hotter than a two dollar pistol, leaking like a muthafucker," Miguel responded as Bobby nodded.

Leroy opened a vest pouch and removed his CSEL radio. "Mama Bird, Raptor Four leader."

"Raptor Four, Mama Bird, go ahead," Lanie replied.

"Recovered Cabrillo, Mendes and the CIA man. Am advised the suitcase nukes are in the hangar still inside the Gulfstream. Repeat, the nukes are in the Gulfstream...Be advised Cabrillo states the packages are very hot. Advise recovery teams, over."

"Roger, Raptor Four, copy all. Be advised the Eagles are in process of recall."

"Copy recall for Eagle birds."

"Weather forecast indicates Hurricane Ellen will turn to track north northeast toward Mobile. Eye projected to drift over your location in four-zero minutes. Expect extraction at that time, over."

"Team Four copies all. Will require an additional Osprey for prisoners. Will advise. Team Four out." He switched off the radio. "You heard the lady."

Bobby pointed at Leroy's M-4. "Got any more of those?"

"No, but there's a shit-pot full of H&Ks on the first floor. I'll call and let the guys know you're coming...Can use all the help we can get."

AIRSPACE OVER GULF
2148 Hours

Vasilli had a good laser bore sight on the crippled black craft swaying under the sixty foot wide white parachute. His radar range indicated 1,200 meters. *I will close to 1,000 meters and make an easy kill.*

Inside the 200, a bruised and battered Jill McElheney looked over her left shoulder at the MiG leveling off at her altitude. The thick trail of gray smoke from the port engine left a ragged line pointing at the seasoned pilot who had bested her.

At least I got a piece of him, she thought as she tried to console herself. She prayed aloud, "Our Father, who art in Heaven..."

Vasilli prepared to squeeze the trigger as the range finder passed 1,000 meters. The pistol grip on top of the stick exploded in his hand as a 7mm steel projectile ripped through his aircraft. He howled in pain as his fingers disappeared.

The MiG disintegrated under the two streams of devastating fire from *Eagles* One and Four. One round set off the remaining missile on his port wing—sending the flaming wreckage of the MiG down in a rapidly spinning fireball trailing dense black smoke all the way into the churning gulf below.

"Splash one MiG," Dare announced.

Cheers went up inside *Mama Bird* and the two *Eagles* awaiting landing clearance aboard *Iwo Jima.*

A cacophony of sounds echoed throughout *Iwo Jima's* CIC. Jill and Pete had saved countless lives in their losing battle with the MiG.

Mike pulled back hard and drew the throttle to idle—*Eagle* Four performed a rapid deceleration maneuver known as a *Cobra* as she came to halt with the nose almost vertical.

Bug's eyes were big as saucers. "Whoa!…Where the hell did you learn that?"

"From her."

He smoothly added power and rolled toward *Eagle* Five, closing the six hundred yards to the damaged bird drifting toward the surface. "Eagle Five, you okay?" He glanced at Bug with a grin when a female voice came back.

"I'm okay…Pete didn't make it," she said weakly.

"We'll get you out. Be ready to swim…that bird won't float very long in these seas."

"I'll be ready."

Overhead, Dare in *Eagle* One considered the situation. The thirty foot seas and sixty knot winds would make a rescue operation hazardous for a single aircraft. *The waves are going to be the biggest danger.*

He continued his descent and moved into a loose formation with Mike. "Cowboy, I'm going to light the water upwind of Jill after she exits the bird. Stay clear of the chute and watch your ass."

Mike looked over to see that Dare had turned on the powerful halogen landing lights under the forward nacelle struts. He had not thought of that, while using the NVG's—he quickly removed them.

"Jill, I want you to jettison the canopy now. Do not wait until you hit the water," Dare ordered.

They looked on as Jill hit the emergency canopy jettison switch. It blew upward and then tumbled into the whitecaps below.

"You are at 300 feet. When you hit the water, release your shoulder harness and roll out upwind. The chute will drag the bird downwind. Copy?" Dare said in a calm voice.

"Roger that." Jill's confidence started to return.

"Lose your helmet and disconnect your oxygen and comm cord now."

As Jill complied, Bug unbuckled and climbed back between the seats in *Eagle* Four. He checked the heavy green braided nylon fast-line still attached to the silver metal D-ring above the entrance door. He quickly made a four foot loop at the end of the rope and tied it off in a bowline.

"Jesus!…Look at that water," Mike remarked nervously to Glenn as the twin halogen lights illuminated the raging sea.

Jill's 200 clipped the top of one wave and was pulled off by the billowing chute only to slam into the next.

As the craft was being dragged up the face of the thirty foot menacing green mass of water, her lithe form rolled out of the cockpit and sank beneath the surface. A second later, it reappeared when her LPU deployed under each armpit. The flashing white strobe on her survival vest activated and pinpointed her location as she rose and fell with the water. The damaged craft quickly filled with water and sank, pulling the parachute down with it.

Bug hooked a safety line to a D ring on his survival vest, opened the side door and tossed the rope down. Noise from the wind and two hovering *Eagles* made conversation impossible without the headsets. He stuck the auxiliary comm cord to the connection at his waist.

"Left thirty feet," Dare directed Mike.

Mike complied.

"Forward ten."

Bug leaned out and saw Jill waving. "Down ten, Cowboy."

Mike concentrated for all he was worth, easing the bird down as Jill rose and sank with the mountainous waves.

"Left three."

Mike nudged the stick ever so slightly.

"Hold it there."

Jill reached for the loop and just touched it when the wave crested—she dropped thirty feet.

"Down five…She had her hand on it!"

Mike watched the waves for several seconds as the next crest brought Jill up to the loop, he followed the wave down. She grabbed it, slipped it over her head and under her arms, just like she had been taught in Air Force Water Survival School.

Mike kept his eyes on the oncoming green giant that appeared higher than his bird.

"Pull up, Cowboy!" Dare shouted.

Mike heard Bug's call first. "Got her!"

He added power and smoothly lifted her up and out of the water. Glenn tried to pull her up. Her weight, with all the water-soaked gear, and a wet rope made it almost impossible for the fifty year old. His hands weakened and the rope slowly slipped through his fingers.

"I can't hold her!"

Mike climbed to one hundred feet above the maelstrom, unbuckled his harness, engaged *Altitude Hold* and stepped back between the pilot seats.

Dare and Bull looked on and started to say something—words would not come. They watched as the two men pulled a grateful Jill up into *Eagle* Four and closed the hatch. They glanced at each other, bumped fists and grinned. Mike cradled Jill in his arms, looked over at the exhausted Bug. "Take us home."

"You got it." He climbed in his seat, strapped in, clicked off the autopilot and radioed Dare. "Eagle One...All chicks accounted for."

"See you at the boat...Eagle One out."

USS *IWO JIMA*
Gulf OF Mexico
2155 Hours

At the request of the BEF, a standby MV-22 had taken off and was following *Vipers* One and Two through the middle bands of thunderstorms comprising Hurricane Ellen. *Viper* One used his weather radar to pick a path between rain shafts as they worked their way through at 2,000 feet above the gulf.

The technique was tricky, but the deadly down drafts from the outflow of the mighty storms could usually be avoided. The ride was rough and crews kept their radar pointed upward eight degrees to try to pick up any incipient hail or rain.

In the back of *Viper* One, Gunnery Sergeant Homer Tompkins filled up his second barf bag. He was the most senior bomb disposal technician on *Iwo Jima*, but never had the stomach to go along with his nerves of steel.

Lance Corporal Reggie Jefferson, second in command, refused to cut him slack. "Yo, Gunny, you want some of this bean and onion burrito I had Cookie make up for me?...Got hot sauce just like you like, my man."

Homer turned a little greener as the noisy *Osprey* bounced hard again. Reggie grinned as he rocked and rolled with the turbulence.

"Just like Six Flags, but they pay me to be here!" Reggie egged him on.

COJONE COMPOUND
Tenth Floor
2157

Bobo entered the girl's dormitory followed closely behind by Ten Ring, Leroy and Miguel. Two men bracketed the first closed door. The other two covered the room across the hall.

Ten Ring pounded on the locked door. "United States Marines...Open Up!"

Up and down the X shaped hallway, doors opened and twenty beautiful women stepped out wearing only negligees or thong bathing suits. Ten Ring stood with his mouth agape. One young blonde girl ran up to him, jumped up, wrapped her legs around him and began kissing him all over his camouflaged face.

"I knew ya'll would come when I told my mama where I was!" she cried with an unmistakable Alabama accent.

The others ran down the hall toward the four men. One of the girls stopped in her tracks and pointed at Bobo. "He's one of them!"

"No ma'am, he's with us. He's been undercover here. You have to trust me on that," Leroy said with authority.

"Ya'll got any more clothes you can wear?" asked Miguel.

All the girls shook their heads.

"What are ya'll gonna do with us?" asked a redhead.

Miguel smiled at the apprehensive girl. "We're gonna take you home."

ISLA GUKUMATZ
2220 Hours

Viper One settled down in the darkness on the painted mural runway outside the expansive camouflaged hangar. Two of the Marine detachment from inside the pyramid had made their way down the underground corridor and were standing guard inside.

Four Russian ground crew and mechanics for the MiG 29 were face down on the hangar floor. The bodies of three former Cojone guards lay nearby. The hangar doors were open and light spilled out onto the ramp.

COJONE COMPOUND
2221 Hours

Overhead, *Eagles* Two, Three and Six provided air cover for the evacuations going on below. *Vipers* Two and Three were parked on the lush green lawn adjacent to the massive pyramid. Their rotors were shut down as the line of former Cojone staff were hustled quickly aboard.

The kidnapped girls were brought out next. Cabrillo and Poole had managed to liberate some men's clothing and a limited amount of women's from the staff dormitories. The mix-matched garb looked atrocious, but no one cared. Footwear was another story.

All the girls had to wear were high heels—there were not enough sandals and athletic shoes to go around.

With all the excited girls aboard, Kit ordered the two loaded *Ospreys* to depart. "Viper One, reposition to the pyramid."

The lead MV-22 lifted off from the hangar as the two bomb disposal technicians removed the second suitcase nuke from the sleek Gulfstream.

"Guys, you have twenty-five minutes max at these radiation levels," Navy corpsman Jim Turner advised.

All three were wearing special HAZMAT radiation gear and the bomb techs had even more gear on. The tropical heat and humidity was beginning to really make them sweat inside the suits.

Reggie opened the toolbox, handed the dikes to Homer, who quickly cut the metal straps holding the top on the first crate.

"Those were new bands," he noted.

They didn't match the overall condition of the wooden crate that they estimated at least twenty-five years. Homer tugged at the top, but it wouldn't budge. He held out his hand and Reg placed a yellow twelve inch pry bar in it. He pried the top until the it became loose. They lifted the lid and placed it to the side. Inside was a green painted metal case with Cyrillic markings.

"It's a RA115S, Soviet design, from back in the early eighties…I'd guess. They showed us in school what they thought the device looked like," Homer said calmly.

"When was that?" Reggie asked.

"Nineteen ninety-eight."

COJONE COMPOUND
2228 Hours

Viper One was shut down on the lawn, as the four MiG crew detainees were loaded aboard followed by the olive drab body bag containing of Master Gunnery Sergeant Jamal Washington.

Three of his team carried him aboard while the other Marines of his command and the Raptors stood at attention and saluted as he passed by.

"Viper one, Eagle Two, what's your status?" called Kit.

"Eagle Two, Viper One, standby, I'll check with load."

The AC sent the copilot back to inquire.

ISLA GUKUMATZ
Hangar
2228 Hours

Jim Tuner looked at his watch. His Geiger counter was clicking like a popcorn popper. "Eighteen minutes guys and that is a no bullshit time…Copy?"

"Yeah, Yeah, we got it, Jimmy Neutron," Reggie responded.

"What's the safe distance if this thing goes off?" Jim asked nervously.

"San Antonio?…Hell, I don't know, man…Ask the professor here, but not now, we be kinda busy," Reg said as the two disposal techs gingerly sat the metal suitcase onto the concrete floor.

Corpsman Jim started backing away slowly—as if it would do any good.

COJONE COMPOUND
2229 Hours

Viper One copilot passed the report on to the AC.

"Eagle Two, Viper One," Marine Captain John Rogers stated.

"Eagle Two, go."

"Load advises all personnel aboard except the two bomb techs and the corpsman."

"Roger that. Get the rotors turning. I want you out of there as soon as they are ready."

"Can do, sir." Rogers spun his right index finger.

The turbines began to wind up and in less than a minute, both the rotors were turning.

In the back, fifteen worn-out warriors looked at each other across the noisy cargo bay. They had shared a day of terror and exhilaration and mourned the loss of a brave Marine who lay on the deck between them. *There but for the grace of God...*

"Viper One we have a problem."

"Say again for Viper One, who is calling?" Captain Rogers looked at his copilot who just shrugged.

"Sorry, Captain, Gunnery Sergeant Tomkins...Bomb disposal technician."

"Go ahead Gunny, what kind of problem?"

"Sir, the Russians had a tamper switch on the bomb body. When I lifted the device, it started a timer...We got less than 15 minutes."

"Gunny, Eagle Two, can you shut it down?"

"Negative, sir, it's built into the device body."

"Viper One, Eagle Two. Lift off and get the hell out of Dodge. We'll pick up the guys at the hangar."

Captain Rogers didn't need any more encouragement. The power was transferred to the rotors and the lightly loaded *Osprey* lifted off, climbed over the north wall of the compound and disappeared.

ISLA GUKUMATZ
Hangar
2231 Hours

Eagle Two swooped out of the dark skies and looked like a UFO descending when it turned on the halogen landing lights. *Eagles* Three and Six were seconds behind him. The two techs and the corpsman ran as fast as they could in the cumbersome HAZMAT gear and literally dove into the waiting ship. As the doors were closing, the agile craft lifted off, and then sped northward at max speed...

USS *IWO JIMA*
Gulf of Mexico
2244 Hours

The three *Eagles* had flown ahead of the slower *Ospreys* and recovered on *Iwo* first. *Viper* Three was on the elevator being lowered to the hangar deck.

Inside, twenty nervous and very thankful women were extremely glad to be aboard.

AIRSPACE OVER GULF OF MEXICO
2244 Hours

Viper One was still eighteen miles out and traveling northwest at three hundred and twenty miles per hour. Hurricane Ellen provided a tailwind that increased separation from the impending nuclear detonation.

The copilot glanced at his watch. "Thirty seconds."

"Roger that." Rogers turned the interior cockpit lights up on the *Osprey*, clicked off and raised his NVGs.

The copilot did the same. They knew that all the aircraft systems were shielded against EMP. Neither could remember if the NVGs were likewise protected, therefore, they had reached the decision to turn off all nonessential electronics prior to the blast. They hoped the *Osprey* would stand the shock wave at sixty miles—they didn't know exactly how powerful the two devices were.

Johnny held the controls with his left hand as he extended his right to his copilot. "Steve, it has been an honor serving with you."

Steve took his hand and grasped it strongly. "And with you, Johnny. Semper Fi, brother."

Both men looked back at the flight instruments and awaited their fate…

Climbing through FL 350, the crew on *Mama Bird* was as prepared as could be. They were heading 290 degrees directly away from the island and had a separation distance of 137 miles.

Lanie, Sparky, Gears, Blaze, the two loadmasters and eight reserve members of Team Four were confident they would weather the blast, but they all had concerns for their teammates and the crew aboard *Iwo Jima*—most were praying.

ISLA GUKUMATZ
Inside the Hangar
2245 Hours

The red digital numbers on the timer clicked down one by one. The south wall of the hurricane eye was six miles north and the full fury of the category three storm was ripping tops out of tall trees in the jungle.

The pounding rain blasted the blood from the bodies of the three dead guards on the hangar floor as the howling winds swirled and were drawn into the cavernous building.

When the timer hit **0:00**—the triggering mechanism fired the blasting caps in the Semtex explosive, driving three kilos of Plutonium into the awaiting five kilo cup-shaped receiver. The supercritical mass initiated a fusion reaction equivalent to five kilotons of TNT.

That reaction detonated the other device, creating a combined seven point nine kiloton explosion. A brilliant light—many times brighter than the sun—emanated as the center third of the island instantly vaporized. The intense heat and shock wave cleared all vegetation leaving only two crescent-shaped atolls where the island had once been.

A mile wide fireball rose from the blast, carrying tons of molten sand and glassy remnants of Isla Gukumatz forty thousand feet into the thunderstorm overhead. The nuclear explosion created an eighty foot wave which tried to propagate outward, but was broken up by the existing wave patterns from Hurricane Ellen.

Energy from the detonation inside the wall of the category three hurricane had an immediate effect. The thunderstorms for five miles around were superheated and the clouds literally vaporized.

The tremendous shock wave blew the downstream circulation out of its pattern. To the west, the thunderstorms moving toward the center were stopped. Barometric pressure increased rapidly in the eye of the storm as Ellen ceased to generate rotation.

NOAA, NESDIS
Suitland, Maryland
2247 Hours

At the Satellite and Information Center of the National Environmental Satellite Data and Information Service, a lone meteorologist assigned to the late night shift returned to his desk with a fresh cup of coffee. He sat down and looked at the radar feed from the Atlantic geostationary satellite.

"What the...?" He looked at the ragged center of the dissipating storm.

He tapped several strokes on his keyboard activating the zoom feature of the satellite infrared control and in seconds, the heat signature of the blast was visible. "That can't be right." He returned to the radar image as he picked up the phone and pressed number eight on the pad.

"Maintenance," came the reply.

"Sorry to bother you, Archie, but Atlantic One is on the fritz. Can you run a diagnostic?"

"You bet."

USS *IWO JIMA*
2248 Hours

Dare was waiting as Kit stepped out of *Eagle* Two. They turned and watched the glow on the horizon fade away.

"Got the girls and I would say that Javier and his nukes are history," Kit said.

"Roger that," said Dare as they bumped fists.

Captain Rogers set *Viper* One down firmly on the pitching deck. The winds had died to sixty knots, but landing on a carrier was always tricky at night. The shock wave from the blast wasn't as bad as the weather related turbulence they had encountered.

Captain Lowry read the latest sea and weather conditions and made the decision to head toward the former Naval Station Ingleside at Corpus Christi. Sea conditions were better to the west—the wounded and hostages could be airlifted to Fort Sam Houston and Lackland Air Force Medical Facilities in San Antonio from the port.

President Thompson had directed the State department to assist the foreign captive women in returning home or grant political asylum, if requested.

Dare made the decision to recover *Mama Bird* and the *Eagles* at Eagle Nest Ranch. The crews could rest during the day and fly back to BEF headquarters the night of the thirteenth. He called Gears and passed the word.

Down on the mess deck, anxious sailors took turns having their pictures taken with the grateful rescued girls. The Russian detainees sat glumly in the brig while the overflow crowd of Javier's staff were checked for gunshot residue and watched by grim faced MP's.

In the comm center, Crystal Coopersmith was on a satellite link to her mother, Angie, in Tuscaloosa.

"Mama…I'm comin' home," she said through her tears.

"Oh, my God, my baby, my baby! God has answered my prayers." Angie's tears flowed down her cheeks as well.

"Mine too…Mama, mine too."

EAGLE NEST AIRSTRIP
0300 Hours

Mama Bird gently touched down on the newly widened Eagle Nest runway. Gunter was waiting at the hangar, without his cane as the crews deplaned from the *Eagles* and C5-M.

Blaze beat everyone over to Gunter and gave him a big hug and a kiss. She stepped back. "Dad, where's your cane?"

"Figured I was depending on it too much…Walking without it is making my leg stronger. Still limp a bit, but it's less each day."

"You're just hardheaded, that's all."

Gunter grinned. "That too."

Dare and Mike walked up.

"Can't believe you got the strip widened and the turnarounds put in just two weeks," said Iron Horse.

"No hill for a stepper…Got the fueling facilities installed, the underground offices and dorm, too, and we're almost done with the hangar. You weren't kidding when you said those contractors for BEF were fast. The steel side wall frame for the hangar is already up awaiting delivery of the roof trusses."

The last of the 600s were put to bed—the crews shuttled to the main house and bunkhouse for a meal and well-deserved rest.

EAGLE NEST RANCH
Main House
0345 Hours

Dare listened intently as Gears related how Blaze had made the critical right decisions about defeating the MiG 29 missiles. Her actions had possibly saved the *Galaxy* and crew.

He turned to the suddenly shy redhead. "How did you know about the home-on-jam capability?"

"I subscribe to the Defense Industry News magazine and there was an in-depth article about the Russian missile designs back in 2007."

"Unbelievable...How did you know about the ELINT systems and integrate all that knowledge into a defensive plan?...It was your first flight."

"Gears let me read the manual two days ago. He said he didn't think you would mind...Do you?"

He laughed. "No, no, no...Anything you want to read, you go right ahead...Are you one of those people with a photographic memory?"

Blaze blushed and nodded. Beer spurted out of Mike's nose as he took a swig of Shiner Bock.

"Sorry." He chuckled as he wiped his nose with the back of his hand. "Told you you'd like her, Iron Horse."

"She is something else." Dare looked at her with more than heartfelt admiration.

Jill stretched and winced noticeably.

"You okay?" asked Mike.

"Nothing a little time and a hot tub won't cure."

"Well, Punkin, we just happen to have one of those out on the west side of the house."

***

EPILOGUE

EAGLE NEST RANCH
15 July

Air Force One turned around on Eagle Nest Ranch's strip and taxied to a parking space parallel to the C-5M. A dozen Secret Service agents moved into position as the special air stairs were rolled into place.

The presidential security detail escorted her and the Secretary of Defense down the stairs to the greeting committee. President Thompson was dressed smartly in a blue pinstriped business suit. Secretary of Defense Baker was attired in a conservative dark gray suit and dark red tie.

Dare Phillips and Kit Kitaen stood next to Gunter, flanked on the right by Mike and Blaze. Following brief handshakes, the entire group was escorted to a line of black Chevrolet Suburbans and whisked to the large white open-sided tent adjacent to the ranch house for the presentation ceremony.

A brief memorial service was held for BEF aviator Peter Reynolds Jr. lost in the air battle against the MiG. His parents, Peter and Andrea Reynolds had been flown in from their home in Lansing, Michigan and were presented with Pete's Medal of Freedom.

President Annette Thompson also presented the same award to Jill McElheney for her actions defending the other aircraft and USS *Iwo Jima*.

The president spoke with pride and a hint of sadness as she related the events of a similar ceremony held just two hours before at the Corpus Christi Naval Air Station. The crews of *Iwo Jima* and her Marine detachment were cited in a closed ceremony.

The widow of Master Gunnery Sergeant Jamal Washington was deeply touched that the president had come all the way to Texas to pay tribute to her late husband.

As she had done at the Air Station, President Thompson shook hands and offered her country's and her own personal thanks to each member of the Black Eagle Force.

Following the ceremony in the tent, President Thompson approached Gunter. "Hermie, I'd love to see the Hermann ranch house. Never got to see it when we were in college."

"Of course, Annie, I'd be proud to show you our family home...It has a lot of history."

Blaze dug her elbow into her brother's ribs and whispered, "Hermie? Annie?"

"Told ya." Mike grinned.

The tour of the house and the view of the Rio Grande took only thirty minutes. After she and her entourage exited the front door, she turned to Dare. "Mister Phillips, any chance I could get a look at the aircraft your team used on the mission?"

"Of course, Madam President. We have four of them on alert status here."

Inside the hangar, President Thompson was fascinated by the sleek, deadly craft and asked a dozen questions. The last one drove the Secret Service detail into a near panic. "How about a little demonstration ride?"

Dare knew that he had her hooked. "I'll have one of my best pilots take you up for your dollar ride."

He turned and grinned at Jill. She was still a little sore from her tumbling flight in the 200. *Her confidence could use a boost*, he figured. *Got to get back on the horse that threw you...as the saying goes.*

"Sir, I think there are a lot..."

"Miss McElheney will do just fine," the president agreed.

The only concession she would begrudgingly make to the Secret Service was to allow the lead agent to join them in one of the Raptor seats in the back. "Mickey, you can ride with us...if it makes you feel better."

"Yes, ma'am," he replied reluctantly.

After a short STOL roll, the M600 lifted off effortlessly and accelerated down the paved airstrip to three hundred knots. She did a couple of easy turns to the left and right, and then climbed to four thousand feet where she turned back toward the airstrip and dove to two thousand at max speed.

The nose came up to vertical and the little bird appeared to brake hard and come to a stop in midair as she performed her *Cobra* maneuver.

Dare looked nervously at Mike—he shrugged and grinned.

The nose of the *Eagle* returned to a level attitude and accelerated quickly as it dove and turned toward the river. It disappeared behind the trees and Dare could hear the Secret Service agents talking lowly into the microphones on their wrists. They didn't seem to be too nervous, but he was.

After a few minutes, the craft screamed overhead at her full speed of over 400 knots, barely fifty feet above the heads of the assembled crowd—causing some to duck in response. It pitched up in a steep climb, made four rapid aileron rolls and performed a Split S maneuver to come back to the field.

"Jesus, Jill," Dare muttered.

Mike chuckled, shook his head and kept smiling.

The craft flared to a stop, hovered briefly, set down fifty feet from the crowd and the engines spooled off.

Agents quickly surrounded the plane as the left side door opened. An ashen-faced Mickey Williams deplaned from the back seat and almost falling as he stepped to the tarmac. He was visibly sickened, but somehow managed not to throw up. The president stepped out next, frowning as she pushed the helping hands of the agents away.

"Damn, we're in trouble now," Iron Horse mumbled. *How could she have been so thoughtless?*

Jill stepped out, ducked under the low door, and then straightened up her six foot frame.

Dare walked to her and whispered, "Jill…What were you think…"

"Wasn't me! Madam President had the conn." She pointed at the beaming woman.

The president turned and broke into the widest smile any of the agents had ever seen. "Now that's what I call a ride!" She gave Jill a high-five.

A stunned Dare was shocked back to his senses when the president clasped his hand with both of hers.

"Thank you, thank you, thank you! I haven't had that much fun since my first solo!…Got a winner there, Iron Horse…I see now why you chose it!"

"Uh, yes, Madam President. Uh…I'm glad you enjoyed your ride. Come back any time. It would be our pleasure."

"I just might take you up on that, sir…Now, as much as I hate to leave, I do have a country to run." She walked over to hug Gunter and say her personal good byes.

An aide came down the stairs from Air Force One with a package of Top Secret documents just received over secure satellite fax. He walked to the SecDef and whispered something in his ear. Baker scanned the documents and motioned Dare to join him.

"Well, Dare, it appears your vacation time here is going to be cut short." He handed him the file.

"Rebels from the Abu Sayyaf radical Islamic faction in the Philippines have taken eleven American tourists for ransom on Mindanao. Three Americans were killed in the raid…We want the hostages back and the threat eliminated."

"Sounds like just the mission for the Black Eagle Force," Dare said.

RIO DE JANEIRO, BRAZIL
RELAIS & CHATEAUX
(SANTA TERESA HOTEL)
15 August

Clarence Ogilsvey sat on his spacious balcony overlooking Guanabara Bay in the shadow of Sugarloaf Mountain. To the southwest, he had a view of one of the New Seven Wonders of the World, the Cristo de la Concordia—the giant statue of Christ the Redeemer.

Dressed in a flowered shirt, brushed white cotton duck pants and deck shoes, he was drinking a large Caipirinha cocktail over cracked ice. A beautiful topless Brazilian woman with a jade-green sari wrapped around her hips, walked onto the balcony with a plate of Biscoitos de Maizena, Brazilian cookies.

"Thank you, Gabriela." He took one from the plate. "How's your drink, Javier?"

"Marvelous, Clarence…Do you need a refresher, my dear?" Javier asked Vivian.

"Yes, I love it, what's it called again?" she asked Ogilsvey.

"Caipirianha. It's made with cachaça, the spirit of choice in Brazil, distilled from sugar cane and stored in oak casks for twelve years. Mixed with lime and sugar...It will get your attention."

"I can believe that." Vivian took a cookie from Gabriela's plate and had another sip.

"So, tell me, Javier, how did you escape your island when those idiots tripped the booby trap on my little nukes?"

Javier handed a pair of binoculars to Ogilsvey. "Take a look at that Russian freighter down at the docks. They're unloading my secret as we speak."

Clarence focused on the Russian freighter with a large deck crane unloading a silver sixty foot cigarette boat into the waters of Guanabara Bay.

"Check out the name on the stern," added Javier.

Ogilsvey moved the binoculars and with a little more focusing, he saw in black and gold lettering—*BACK DOOR.*

"Always have a back door, my friend...always have a back door...I kept my little toy in a sea cave with a secret tunnel connected to the compound. It was a simple matter to get to the mainland...even in the storm."

Clarence nodded. "You know, I still have over four hundred million in US military hardware...and two more nukes...Have you selected a new location for your operation?"

Javier smiled cryptically and sipped his drink. "I think I've found something suitable."

****

TIMBER CREEK PRESS

BLACK EAGLE FORCE

Sacred Mountain

CHAPTER ONE

SOUTHERN NEW MEXICO

Morning sun was breaking over the Alamo Hueco Mountains to the east and casting deep blue shadows on the foothills as the convoy of vehicles made their way south through the ruggedly beautiful desert land of southern New Mexico. Two state motorcycle police led the procession down a lightly traveled two lane road, followed by two black Suburbans, an armored black Lincoln limousine, two more SUVs and bringing up the rear, two more motorcycle police.

Overhead, an olive-drab Army AH-64 *Longbow Apache* attack helicopter, fitted for combat, kept pace with the convoy. The group of government vehicles and escorts headed south on

New Mexico State Highway 81 for a rendezvous with Border Patrol officials. Antelope Wells lay between the Animas Mountains and the Alamo Hueco Mountains in the boot heel of New Mexico.

This barren desert landscape was well-known as a major entry point for illegal aliens and drug smugglers. The Treaty of La Mesilla—also called the Gadsden Purchase—completed the acquisition of the area in 1853 from Mexico. It still had a predominately Mexican population as did much of southern New Mexico, Arizona and Texas.

Inside the limo, Mickey Williams, a muscular Secret Service agent in a dark nondescript suit, spoke to an attractive, stately woman with flashing antique-gold eyes. Her gray-flecked auburn hair was shoulder length and she wore a smartly tailored dark blue pinstripe pantsuit.

President Annette Henry Thompson was the first woman president of the United States, as well as, the first person of Native American descent to hold the highest office in the country. Her maternal grandparents were full-blood Mescalero Apache. She had been widowed two years earlier when her husband suffered a massive heart attack during the campaign.

"Madam President, I still don't think this is a good idea for you to be taking a personal tour of the border area."

"Nonsense, Mickey...You've got sixteen of your crack Secret Service team, New Mexico State Police escorts and an Apache gunship overhead."

"I think I have to agree with Mickey, Madam President. Even with all this protection...this is outlaw country. With over

1,900 miles of border with Mexico, we just don't have the manpower to adequately cover the area," said the Director of Homeland Security, Barbara Hoffner, a stocky, middle-aged masculine-featured woman with short-cropped brown hair.

"Well, I think that's why we're here...isn't it Barbara? To see if we can come up with a solution to the problem."

"But why do you personally have to be here, Madam President?" asked Mickey.

"You should know by now that I'm a hands-on president...unlike my predecessors. If they had gotten their butts out of that office and put their feet on the ground more, we might not be looking at this situation now...Besides, my ancestors roamed this part of our country...Speaking of which, I've got to call my baby brother at the Mescalero Reservation. He'll have my hide if he finds out I was in the area and didn't let him know."

"He's the President of the Tribal Council, isn't he?" asked Hoffner.

"Yes...we both grew up on the reservation, I went off to college at Southwest Texas State and he went to New Mexico Highlands University...He couldn't stand to leave our people. That's one reason they elected him as President of the Council."

"Being a leader must run in the family." Mickey grinned.

"One has to do what one has to do."

"Yes, Ma'am."

"Call 505-888-5956 extension 2 on the sat phone for me, will you? It's Mark's private number."

"Yes, Ma'am."

He removed the phone from the cradle in the console and punched in the number. The secure encryption tones took almost five seconds—Mark picked up on the second ring.

"Mark Henry, that you Sis?"

Mickey handed the phone to her.

"Hey baby brother, nice weather we're having here in the Land of Enchantment, isn't it?"

"You come all the way out here and all I get is a stinkin' phone call? That's almost as bad as the T-shirt you brought me from Moscow…Thanks a lot."

"I know, I know…I'll make it up to you…Wish things were different sometimes. Miss you…What've you been up to?"

"Miss you too, Sis…it's tough being the leader of the free world and all…As for me, been busy with the tribal council. Still working on the definitive novel about our people's migration from southern Chihuahua…Need to make another field trip down there to that area where great-grandfather said Pancho Villa's hideout was."

"Pancho Villa? I thought you were talking about the Tsebekinéndé, our clan of the Mescalero?"

"I'm still convinced that Villa was descended from the Chichimeca, the parent group of the Tsebekinéndé, the Rock People of the southern Sierra Madres.

"Right…Good luck with that…Listen, gotta run, call you back after we have our meeting…Love you."

"Love you, too. Don't give Mickey too hard a time, big sister. You know how spoiled you are…Tell him I said hello."

"Yeah, yeah. All hat, no cattle. Later bye."

She handed the unit back to Mickey.

"Mark says hey…What's our ETA to Antelope Wells?"

He checked his watch. "We are due there in twenty…"

The President's limo was rocked by multiple explosions both in front and behind.

"Mickey! What…"

"IED's! Get down!" Mickey physically shoved her lower, and then keyed his radio. "Lilac under attack, repeat, Lilac under attack!"

The *Apache* quickly gained altitude to get into an offensive posture in response to the radio alert.

"Jesus H. Christ! Six IED's…both sides of the road! Took out all the support vehicles bracketing Lilac's limo!" exclaimed Captain Gleason.

"Missile launch, missile launch, five o'clock!" shouted WSO Bison from the back seat.

"Chaff and flares! Get me a target!" commanded Gleason as he banked toward the missile to reduce his heat signature.

WSO Bison launched two bundles of chaff and two magnesium flares as the chopper continued to gain altitude in the bank. "Missile! Eight o'clock!"

"Damn!" was all Captain Gleason was able to say before the second shoulder-fired *Stinger* missile went into his port exhaust.

The gunship exploded into a white and yellow fireball and spun flaming to the ground below.

Desert camouflaged tangos rose up from under their well-concealed spider holes on either side of the road flanking the burning wreckage of the convoy. One leveled an RPG-7 at the president's armored limo as its driver attempted to maneuver around what remained of a burning Suburban.

The yard-long rocket closed the forty yards in less than a second and impacted the black Lincoln on the left side of the grill—it easily defeated the light armor. The warhead blew the hood several yards into the air as it destroyed the big V-8 engine—along with any chance for the president to escape.

Airbags deployed inside the limo and filled the driver and passenger compartments with a smoky brown haze. The agent in the front passenger seat was stunned from the explosion, but instinctively struggled to get the hot air bag off, unbuckle his seat belt and draw his weapon.

Mickey drew his Sig and moved to a position covering the president with his body as the vehicle slowly rolled to a stop. "Are you hurt, Madam President?"

"I don't think so."

Seven surviving members of the Secret Service detail staggered from their destroyed SUVs only to be quickly gunned down by the terrorists with their automatic weapons. One of them climbed on top of the limo and emptied a magazine from his AK-47 through the lightly armored roof into the front seat, killing the Secret Service driver and the agent riding shotgun.

The vehicle was quickly surrounded by gun-wielding desert camo-clad Mexican terrorists.

"All right, you inside, you're surrounded. Your support detail is all dead. Come out now…hands in the air!"

commanded Arturo Jimenez, leader of the attack force. "I said, now! I am not in the habit of repeating myself!"

President Thompson looked at Mickey. "How could they know?"

"There had to be a leak, Madam President. White House staff or the military."

Homeland Security Director, Barbara Hoffner sobbed hysterically.

"Oh, shut up, Barbara...show some spunk," President Thompson admonished.

"They're going to kill us all!" Hoffner wailed through her tears.

"No, they're not...We're being kidnapped."

Mickey looked at the president and keyed his satellite radio inside his coat pocket to open mic. He unlocked the side door, threw his Sig 220 out and followed with his hands in the air.

"Now you...Madam President...and that other slut with you," Arturo said sarcastically.

The president exited followed by the still crying Hoffner. They joined Mickey outside with their hands in the air also.

An Arab man also clad in desert camo approached. "Well done, Arturo," said Abbas Al Hakim. "The emir will be pleased."

"Al Qaeda has been most helpful, Abbas. The infidel dogs of the great Satan will know our power and resolve now that we have taken their whore leader."

President Thompson and Mickey exchanged confused glances as Hoffner increased her blubbering. Mickey looked up when he heard the familiar whump-whump-whump of a helicopter coming over the nearby ridge. As the chopper grew nearer, he was able to determine that it was a dark green Bell Jet Ranger.

The helicopter settled down fifty yards from the highway, parallel to the president's limo, stirring up a large cloud of red dirt and sand until its rotors spooled down.

"Our chariot has arrived." Abbas smiled and motioned President Thompson toward the chopper.

"That Jet Ranger only seats five," she said.

"So it does…Pity." Arturo turned, drew his Beretta M9 and shot both Mickey and Director Hoffner once each in the chest—they dropped where they stood. "Now we have room…I was tired of that wench's wailing anyway."

"You murdering bastards," hissed President Thompson through her clenched teeth, her antique-gold eyes snapping. "You'll pay for this."

"Shut up, woman! It is you and your country that will pay," Arturo replied.

"Where are you taking me?" She knelt beside Mickey's body and gently caressed his face—tears streamed down her cheeks.

"To our base in the Sierra Madres where the great Mexican Revolutionary general, José Doroteo Arango Arámbula hid out…the place your General Black Jack Pershing could never find in 1917."

Abbas Al Hakim nodded at Arturo. "Its beauty reminds me of the mountainous border country between Afghanistan and Pakistan. I think it is why our exalted leader Osama bin Mohammed bin Awad bin Laden chose it for our new command center six months ago."

AIRSPACE OVER EAGLE NEST RANCH
SOUTH TEXAS

Ten thousand feet above the Eagle Nest Ranch remote base for the Black Eagle Force, Jill "Lucky" McElheney with her WSO, Glenn "Bug" Haug, Mike "Cowboy" Hermann and his WSO, Maria "Double D" Sanchez, were putting their stealthy M600 *Black Eagles* through a mock dogfight.

Maria, a five foot six beautiful Hispanic with long silky black hair, was the newest WSO/Pilot to join the Black Eagle Force. A former captain in the Marine Corps, she was a crack F/A-18 *Super Hornet* pilot.

The M600—a four nacelle VTOL manufactured by Moller International, had been modified extensively starting with ultra high-tech avionics and a stealth coating of multiple layers of a radar absorbing type of Teflon like the F-117 *Nighthawk*.

The coating had a major difference—its final layer was a new transparent, color spectrum frequency modulating adaptive coating containing chromatophores developed by BEF's resident electronic genius design gurus, Carla "Blaze" Hermann and Frank "Gears" Formby.

The photovoltaic coating could, when electronically activated, adapt almost instantly to match its surroundings like a chameleon. When inert, the *Eagle* was a flat dark gray, but upon activation, would become a light sky blue when viewed on a clear day; a dull gray in cloud cover; a dark blackish gray at night or even multicolored digital camo if under 500 feet or on the ground.

The sensors covering the entire skin area of the craft detected the ambient light spectrum and controlled the chromatophores on the opposite side—giving the illusion that the aircraft was transparent. The BEF named this new technology, *LIZARD* in reference to the chameleon that inspired Blaze and Gears to mimic with their electronic wizardry.

Lightweight Dragonskin armor, composed of silicon carbide ceramic matrices, Graphene sheeting and titanium laminates, was installed inside the aircraft's skin under critical cockpit, avionics and engine nacelle areas.

The unique craft was twenty-six feet long, fourteen feet wide with the rear nacelles folded up and twenty-two feet wide with the rear nacelles extended. It had a gross weight of 3,800 pounds with eight 1500 cc rotary engines for the four nacelles, developing 170 hp each.

A G2 7.62mm six-barrel, laser-targeted, electromagnetic coil gun was mounted in center of the aerodynamic nose. Six *Griffin* LRX 415s missiles on two triple-launch pylons flanked by two *PAASM* or *Hellfire* missiles, pylon mounted on top of the rear wing nacelle struts and four AIM 92 *Stinger* heat-seeking air-to-air missiles were mounted under the front struts.

The *Black Eagle* had a top speed of over 400 mph with a ceiling of 36,000 feet and four person capability—plus weapons. The fuel cells were self-sealing inert foam-filled bladders under the passenger compartment, giving the craft a range of over 700 miles—it could be in-flight refueled.

As briefed, Jill and Mike closed on each other from a three mile distance at an altitude of eight thousand feet over the Texas brush country just north of the Rio Grande. With a closure rate of eight hundred knots, they would just barely be able to pick each other up visually as they came together with a hundred feet of planned vertical separation.

"I've got 'em," Mike announced.

"Contact," Maria noted as the relayed radar image from the *Manta* URF or Unmanned Reconnaissance Fighter circling high above them appeared on the weapons systems display screen.

The radar signature of the stealthy craft was less than that of a mocking bird. Without a flight information transponder in *ON* status, neither would have shown up on the most advanced fighter radar and was visually almost undetectable.

Maria called out the range, "Eight hundred yards and…"

Her update was cut off as Jill transmitted over the secure BEF frequency. "Fight's on!"

Jill pulled back hard on the stick as the two diminutive craft crossed paths in opposite directions. She rolled right and climbed steeply. Both she and Bug strained against the four and one-half G acceleration that pressed them hard against the black Recarro leather-covered custom bucket seats—the 600s did not have anti-G suit capability like larger active duty fighters.

Both fliers tightened their abdominal muscles and performed the visceral *grunt* maneuver like fighter pilots in World War II had learned.

Mike broke into a hard level right turn as he and Maria were straining to see where Jill's *Eagle* One had gone. When he finally picked her up, she had turned inside his radius and was inverted, pulling down toward his six o'clock for a high angle-off shot.

Damn, she's good! He pulled the power back to eighty percent and rolled out of the turn while sharply increasing back pressure to force the nose higher. G forces increased to a full five Gs as airspeed fell off quickly.

"Two fifty! Two hundred!" grunted Maria.

Jill set up for a simulated *Stinger* shot—concentrated on the HUD display and watched as *Eagle* Two appeared to rotate almost 90 degrees in a small space on the top of her canopy. Her airspeed hovered around 300 knots and was to climbing rapidly when Bug dryly announced.

"No tone."

She didn't respond verbally to the call out, but released back pressure and allowed the small craft to accelerate under zero G conditions as she rolled wings level. Her chance at a missile shot was gone and she only had two or three seconds to put some much needed distance between her and the deadly coil gun in *Eagle* Two. "Flare, flare."

Bug toggled the inert switch twice. If the combat conditions had been real, two silver cylinders would have been ejected from the top of the fuselage to decoy any heat-seeking missile.

Each contained a chemical compound that, when activated, oxidized at a temperature of 1100 degrees Celsius. It was well within normal fighter afterburner range, but without the telltale magnesium visual flare to give away the aircraft's position.

Mike pulled the pipper for his coil gun toward the nose of the rapidly disappearing *Eagle* One. He watched in his HUD as the tiny target jinked up and down to keep him one step behind. Suddenly, *Eagle* One disappeared. "Damn, she went LIZARD on us!"

"That's not fair!" Maria exclaimed.

Glancing at his HUD, Mike realized his eighty knots of indicated airspeed was allowing his adversary to rapidly increased the separation. *What a moron!* he thought as he slammed the throttle forward to engage in a fruitless tail chase. In two minutes she and Bug would reach the exercise airspace boundary and call for another merge.

"Attention Eagle Aircraft. Attention Eagle Aircraft. All training is canceled. Execute emergency recall plan Beta."

Jill glanced at Bug with a slightly confused look. She recognized the voice on the radio as belonging to the Black

Eagle Force CEO Dare Phillips. Glenn hit the *Acknowledge* button on the Flight Management System display.

"What's going on? We've never done this since I've been here," asked Jill.

"Not since the Colombian cartel attacked the government in Bogota back in the 90's," Bug replied. "That was long before your time."

She toggled the transmit button on her throttle as she turned back toward the center of the airspace over the three thousand acre ranch. "Cowboy, knock it off and rejoin right side, angels twelve." She turned off the *Lizard* function.

"Cowboy copies," Mike responded.

The latitude and longitude of the rendezvous location with their modified C-5M mother ship, nicknamed *Mama Bird*, was streamed to each fighter via secure text. None of the four fliers recognized the location.

Glenn pasted the lat/long into the ground map display—a location thirty miles west of Big Spring, Texas appeared. *That can't be right.*

He rechecked the coordinates and checked again when another line of text appeared. *Angels 12, 250 kts for recovery.* He was stunned for a second. *Airborne recovery aboard the C-5M?* The pilots had practiced it in the simulator, but no one was actually certain it would work—*What the hell is going on?*

Bug selected the range display on the FMS and saw the green arc extended almost to Riudoso, New Mexico. Fuel would be no problem for a standard rejoin. If necessary, the two *Eagles* could aerial refuel from the airborne carrier platform. However, the fact that these two aircraft had been defanged for the day's training flight made them incapable of offensive operations.

Jill looked at the message as Glenn pointed at the FMS display. Mike pulled into a tight echelon formation on *Eagle One*'s right side as she initiated the turning climb toward Big Spring.

She differed to the older member of the team. "What's the rush, Bug? This recovery technique has never been done under actual flight conditions."

Bug Haug, a graduate of United States Naval Academy in Annapolis—class of '78—was the elder statesman aviator of the group with over twelve years service with the BEF. His last duty before retiring from the Marine Corps was test flying the AH-1Z *Viper* variant of the *Super Cobra*.

"Won't hurt to ask." He typed in a short query into the FMS. *"What's up?"*

A few seconds passed before a message came back across the *MILSATCOM* link—*LILAC IS MISSING.*

***

TIMBER CREEK PRESS

www.ingramcontent.com/pod-product-compliance
Lightning Source LLC
Chambersburg PA
CBHW051543250626
47157CB00001B/163